FAMILY

ROBERT F BARKER

Paperback Version first published in 2018

Copyright@Robert F Barker 2018

All Rights Reserved. No part of this book
may be reproduced in any form other than that in
which it was purchased, and without the
written permission of the author.
Your support of authors' rights is appreciated.

All characters in this book are fictitious.
Any resemblance to actual persons,
living or dead is purely coincidental.

By Robert F Barker

The DCI Jamie Carver Series

Last Gasp (Worshipper Trilogy Book # 1)
Final Breath (Worshipper Trilogy Book #2)
Out Of Air (Worshipper Trilogy Book # 3)

Family Reunion

Other Titles

Midnight's Door (Northern Noir#1)

FREE DOWNLOAD

Get the inside story on what started it all...

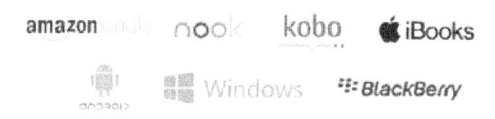

amazon   nook   kobo   iBooks

Windows   BlackBerry

Get a free copy of, *THE CARVER PAPERS,* - The inside story of the hunt for a Serial Killer, - as featured in LAST GASP

Visit the link below to find out more and get started
http://robertfbarker.co.uk/

To my wonderfully supportive family and friends who are so generous with feedback, help, advice and encouragement. I hope this does it all justice.

CHAPTER 1

Armenia, close to the border with Azerbaijan

A second after the high-pitched whistling stopped, the shell hit with a heavy, double 'WHUU-UMP."

The other side of the field, beyond the Institute's perimeter wall, a clump of olive trees rose into the air, seeming to hang there a split-second before exploding into a maelstrom of soil, rock and splinters. As the thunderous boom reverberated, the deadly cloud rushed towards the concrete building that now stood alone in the middle of the bleak landscape. But even as it spilled over the wall, through the pitted railings topping the brickwork, its momentum slowed, sharply, its lethal cargo discharging back to earth in a clattering hail of debris and charred timber.

Even before the dust settled, manic whoops of fear-tinged glee erupted from the building's third-floor windows. Covered only by chicken-wire - the glass had gone long ago – the yells and cat-calls echoed over the once fertile river valley that day by day was turning into a war-zone.

'Fuck ME, Melkon, did you see that?' Antranig Koloyan's cry mingled with the others as he turned to address his friend. But Melkon was down on his haunches, cowering against the wall, hands pressed to his ears.

Apart from The Monster himself, young Melkon was the only other inmate Antranig ever bothered with. Though his behaviour could be erratic, sometimes even as disturbed as the other shaven-headed residents of Ward G19 - particularly when he started with the howling - there were periods when he could pass for being as sane as Antranig himself, almost.

'Now THAT was CLOSE. Come see, Melkon.'

But rather than accept the wild-eyed Armenian's invitation, Melkon simply wrapped his arms even more tightly about his body and rocked back and forth on his heels. At the same time, a half-strangled wail – not quite the wolf thing - escaped him. When he looked up, his young face was full of fear.

'Come away from the window, Antranig,' he croaked, barely able to make himself heard over the clamour that had reigned since the shelling started up again. 'You'll get yourself killed.'

Intent on proclaiming his defiance, Antranig turned back to what was happening beyond the boundaries of what was the nearest thing to home most of them had ever known.

'I don't CARE. Come ON you bastards. I'm WAITING. Blow me up, you *FUCKERS*.' As if in answer to his prayer, another blast, closer this time, rocked the building.

Antranig threw himself to the side as a hail of dirt and debris hurtled through the windows, bouncing off the ceiling and walls to shower down over beds already covered in dust and ceiling plaster.

Not quite as ready to welcome death as he was

making out, Antranig decided a few moments respite were called for. He back-slid down the wall to squat next to his friend.

'What do you think Melkon? Is this what we've been waiting for? The divine retribution that will cleanse us of our sins?' His eyes rolled as he laughed and he threw his head back to reveal a mouthful of stained ivory.

'Don't say that,' Melkon lamented. 'Someone will come. They wouldn't just leave us.'

The older man gave Melkon a pitying look. 'Of course they would you crazy bastard. Where do you think the orderlies are? Do you see them?'

Melkon turned to look towards the barred gate that separated the ward from the corridor leading to the stark offices and barely-equipped treatment rooms. There was no one in sight.

'I tell you,' Antranig continued. 'The cowardly bastards have legged it. That's fucking Kurds for you.'

'But what if we escaped?' Melkon grasped at another straw. 'What if, *He* escaped?'

As if reminded to check there was no immediate prospect of such an unthinkable event happening, they both turned to look down the other end of the ward. The gate to the purpose-built cell in the far corner was still locked, its single inmate clearly visible through the bars.

Vahrig Danelian, known to them all as simply, 'The Monster', was sitting on the floor, his back against the wall, head down, sunken eyes closed. His grey-flannel covered legs were stretched out in front, arms loose at his sides. To all intents and purposes he was sleeping. But even from here, Antranig could see the thin smile he recognised as marking the man's 'meditations'.

For a couple of seconds, the smile Antranig had

stitched to his own face when the explosions resumed, flickered and almost died. But he forced himself not to dwell on the potential dilemma Melkon's question had raised. What did it matter? Even if *He,* or even any of them, did manage to get out, chances were they wouldn't last five minutes. The Azerbaijanis roaming the countryside didn't care who they killed. And a mad Armenian was still an Armenian.

So much for promises, Antranig thought.

'What do *they* care?' he said, dismissing his friend's hope. 'The only thing on their mind is staying alive. They don't give a shit what happens to the likes of us, certainly not Him.'

'But I don't want to escape,' Melkon pleaded. 'I just want the noise to stop. Make it stop Antranig, please make it stop.' With that he curled himself into a ball and started to let out a long wail that Antranig knew heralded the wolf-howls that always reminded him of the mountain forests outside Odzun where he had grown up.

For a moment, the haunting sound rose above the cacophony of yelling and yowling and everyone stopped. But when they realised it was only young Melkon, they all returned to what they had been doing, responding to the situation in their different ways, praying, crying or simply shouting obscene defiance at the yet-to-be-seen Azerbaijanis. Some had already retreated into themselves in the way they did when the world around became too much to bear, crawling back into their cots and wrapping themselves in the thin, grey blankets that years of washing had made transparent.

'That's it, Melkon,' Antranig said, grinning down at his friend. 'Howl like the devil. That will stop them.'

But as he looked up, his gaze fell again on the cell at the far end of the room. A chill ran through him and his mood changed.

Though The Monster's head was still bowed, the black eyes Antranig was sure were the devil's own were staring right at him in a way he had seen only twice before.

The first was just before that time he went for the new orderly. It was the young man's first day on the ward and no one had taken the trouble to warn him properly. Or so they all thought at the time. It was only later that someone said that the man's mother was half-Azerbaijani. They never saw him again. Word was, he never recovered. The second time was the day they were visited by some Government Inspectors. Unusually, one was a woman. She looked good for her age and smelled nice in her neat grey suit and black shoes. As she stood outside the Monster's cell with the other inspectors, the man they had made an excuse to come and gawp at, came up to the bars, pressed his face between them and stared at her, fixedly, as he was now doing to Antranig. Without him even saying anything, the woman fainted away and had to be carried out. She didn't return either.

Over recent weeks, as rumours of trouble outside had grown, Antranig had finally succeeded, much to his surprise, in engaging The Monster in what could almost have passed for conversation. As far as he knew he was the only person in the place to have done so, save perhaps for Doctor Kahramanyan. But despite the dark matters they discussed, the gravity of undertakings given, Antranig now found the Monster's gaze as unsettling, terrifying even, as anything he had ever seen.

He was sure it contained a message, one that right now, he didn't care to think about. It stirred him to action.

Jumping to his feet, he left Melkon to his howling and ran across to the entrance gate, remembering to keep his head low as he passed the windows. Grasping the cold iron in both hands he shook it as hard as he could so that it rattled, loudly, on its frame. At the same time he yelled down the corridor.

'SOMEONE GET US THE FUCK OUT OF HERE.'

CHAPTER 2

The hills of North Wales, above Colwyn Bay

The metallic clunk brought Carver awake with a start. For a split second, he wondered what in God's name was happening. But as the familiar low rumble kicked in and he recognised the sound he had already come to hate with a vengeance, he let out a long, low groan. Within seconds the noise changed, settling into a sequence of harsh growls interspersed with nerve-cringing grating noises. A dark-haired forearm stretched out from under the duvet to grab at the alarm, turning it towards the bed.

'Six-a-bloody-clock? I don't believe this.'

Driven by the annoyance surging through him, he swung his legs out of bed, got up and padded over to the window. As he went he trod carefully to avoid splinters, which was another thing. How long does it take to decide on flooring for Christ's sake?

The last few nights had been unusually warm for spring and he had discarded his usual cotton shorts after noticing they seemed more snug round his waist than previously. It had made him think again about getting back to the weekly badminton sessions that used to help counter Rosanna's cooking – as well as being a diversion from other things. Much as he enjoyed the succulent meat dishes and hearty soups that are the mainstays of Portuguese cuisine, he had long ago learned the truth of the phrase, 'too much of a good thing.'

Not bothering to cover himself, he pulled back the curtains. Dawn's early light flooded the room.

As he gazed down on the building site they hoped may one day be a garden, Alun Cetwin-Owen, Master Builder - or Odd Job Man, depending on who you spoke to - lobbed another spadeful of gravel into the mixer. About to stoop for another, the Welshman stopped and looked up, as if some Celtic sixth sense had alerted him to the fact he was being watched. Seeing the naked man at the window, he lifted an arm and mouthed what Carver knew would be, had be been able to hear it over the machine's incessant gloppetter-gloppetter - an excruciatingly cheery, 'Morning Mr Carver.'

'YOU WELSH BASTARD,' Carver mouthed back through the glass. The older man smiled and waved.

Carver was certain now that Alun's 'other project', the one he'd hinted about working on during the afternoon - hence the early starts - was a fiction. A few days before, he had mentioned it to Gwynn Williams at the farm where they got their eggs. Carver had gone to ask if Gwynn was interested in the hay-making opportunity the overgrown field at the back of the house presented. Carver had never suffered with hay-fever in his life but the past few weeks his sinuses had become increasingly irritated. During his last weekend off, his eyes had turned painfully red. When Gwynn asked how the building work was going, Carver had lamented over how Alun's other commitments were hampering progress.

'Work?' Gwynn had said. 'In the afternoon? Alun? Noohhhh. It's just he doesn't sleep, see? And if he's not in The Three Dragons by two o'clock, then something's wrong isn't it?'

At first Carver had wondered how it was that his supposed 'Wizarding Abilities' hadn't caused him to spot the lie. Then he realised. When Alun spoke of having, 'other things to do in the afternoons,' he hadn't actually mentioned building work. And whilst it would have been obvious to Alun that Carver assumed he was talking about another project, maintaining the illusion required nothing more of him than he keep his mouth shut.

Shaking his head, Carver thought on his options. If it wasn't for the fact that builders in that part of Wales were scarcer than the country's legendary gold mines, he'd have sent Alun packing long ago. They were already three weeks behind the 'rough schedule' he had let the man talk him into when they discussed the job. And just that weekend he had spoken of having to, 'Revise the original estimates.'

Then there were the rest breaks.

To begin with, Carver thought Rosanna was joking when she told him the boxes of tea bags he came across whilst rooting for his coffee one morning were just one week's supply.

'I didn' realise these *Wales-,*' – she still had difficulty with 'Welsh,' - 'These Wales drin' more tea than you Engleesh,' she had said, shaking her head.

That said, Alun's bricking was as good as any Carver had ever seen, and he was regular as clockwork.

A bit too regular, he thought.

But even as the thought came that it may be time for him and Alun to sit down and thrash some things out, maybe over a pint in The Three Dragons, he felt the urge arriving that standing at the chill window had brought on. But as he turned from the window, the duvet over the still-occupied half of the bed stirred and he stopped. A face, bleary-eyed but beautiful enough under the gauze of flame-red hair stuck to it to remind him of what he stood to lose, poked itself out.

'No' again,' she said. It was followed by the string of expletives Carver had heard many times but was yet to discover their true meaning.

In that moment, the incongruity of her tirade, her natural beauty, their still-new environment and the awareness of what he, they, had been through the past couple of years, conspired to bring on a rush of emotion that stopped him in his tracks. Caught out, he gulped air to get over the catch that was suddenly in his throat. Still not strong enough to throw off the clawing memories, he looked back over his shoulder.

Away across the valley, through the morning mist and filling the gap between two mountains, he could just make out the stretch of the lake - Llyn Geirionydd, according to the map - that every now and then pulled his thoughts in the direction of another body of water. This one, also inland, was many miles away, mainland Europe, in fact. And as always happened when his thoughts turned in that direction, the image of a woman's body, hanging in the dark depths came to him. But even as his pulse started to quicken, Rosanna's tirade continued. For once, he was grateful.

'You mus' tell heem, Jamie. This is getting ridiculous.' As always first thing in the morning, her accent was thicker than it would be later.

'You wanted it finished,' he said, as he crossed to the still doorless en-suite.

Having come round a little, he was beginning to feel more forgiving about their early wake-up call. Besides, he'd set the alarm for six-twenty anyway, to give him time for one last run through the paper he would be putting before the Crime Committee later that morning. *Times past it would have been an Operational Briefing. And* he'd decided to call at Sarah's on his way in. His elder sister hadn't sounded good the previous evening. Despite her insistence that she was, 'alright,' he wanted to see for himself. But, turning the cold tap off, he forgot to do it slowly. As water-hammer triggered the juddering that echoed around the bare pipework and unfinished walls, his lighter mood evaporated.

'Shit,' he said, turning the tap back on. He waited for the jarring noises to stop before turning it off again, more slowly this time. Not for the first time, he wondered if maybe they hadn't bitten off more than they could chew.

At the time of course it had made good sense. At least it did to him. Given the associations parts of the North West still had with events he hoped to one day forget but suspected he never would, an abandoned barn conversion in the North Wales hills above Colwyn Bay seemed ideal. It was close enough for work – barring accidents the A55 and M56 were good roads and most mornings he made Salford well before half-seven. But, crucially, it was far enough away so he didn't have to live surrounded by reminders of what lay beneath the surface of a city that liked to talk up its cultural and 'cosmopolitan' aspects, and a county - Cheshire - that revelled in its reputation for 'poshness'. Given the problems they'd been having around that time, he also thought it would be good to have something they could pour their energies into as a couple. Something that might finally expunge both the memories *and* Rosanna's doubts about moving away from the cottage they'd both once loved, but was now contaminated by nightmarish memories neither would ever forget.

As he often did when he thought about such things, he recognised the never far away knot of regret that he'd had to abandon the places where he'd grown up; the areas where he'd honed his skills. Not for the first time, he wondered where else might end up so blighted before his career ended.

Of course the novelty of living in someone else's half-completed project had worn off long ago. Well-dodgy plumbing – the cash-strapped previous owner had done it himself – and an intermittent power supply soon saw to that. And while he wasn't entirely sure about Rosanna – she never talked about it – he knew that somewhere in his mind's deepest recesses, the doubts and fears still lingered.

'Besides,' he said, returning to the bedroom and picking up on the subject of Alun's early starts. 'You know the only person he ever listens to is you. Now why is that I wonder?'

A pillow hit him in the face.

'Policemen. You are useless at everything apart from catching the criminals who are so stupid they leave their DNA everywhere.' Then she remembered. 'And hounding-dog *motoristas*.'

Two weeks before, she had picked up her second three points on one of the coast road's many cameras, adding fuel to what he feared was a growing disillusionment with *his* - not *their* he always noted - choice of home. Knowing better than to rise to the bait, he sought a diversion.

'What time is this thing tonight?' Looking round for his shorts, he spotted them at the side of the bed. As he bent to step into them, her silence signalled a warning and he turned. She was propped on an elbow, glaring at him. Chiding himself, he made a mental note to not refer again to the Royal Northern College of Music's Mediterranean Folk Festival as 'thing'.

'Half-pas' seven,' she said, pointedly. 'I tol' you las' night.'

'Just checking.'

'*Please* don' be late.' The eyes became those of a little girl, a technique she could deploy to devastating effect. 'I am second on the programme. If you are late, you will miss me.'

He threw himself down beside her so that she bounced and her luscious tresses flew around her head before settling back about her shoulders.

'Would I miss you?' He reached for her, but she slapped his hand away, not willing to play until she had the commitment she was looking for.

'You missed me at Liverpool.'

He waved it away. 'That was a simple mistake. The doorman said. People always confuse the Empire with the Philharmonic.'

'If you had listened, instead of thinking always of your work you would have known.'

Recognising a loser when he saw one, he decided another change of subject was called for. 'How's the throat?'

She sniffed, gave a little cough, then reached for the water bottle beside the bed. After a couple of sips, she hit and held a long, soft, 'Aaaaaaahhhhhhh.' She drank some more, then tried a couple of scales. 'Ah-ah-ah-ah-ah-ah-aaahh.'

'Sounds good,' he said, hoping to be sufficiently encouraging.

The ploy worked. Forgetting the cajoling, she got out of bed. Unwinding her sinuous body she stood straight, taking a long, deep breath. Her arms lifted into the pose she usually adopted at the start of a performance, and she sang.

Way too small, enclosed and echoey, the bedroom was hardly the best place to appreciate the seductive rhythms and subtle cadences of Fado, the mountain folk-music that is to the Portuguese what the Tango is to Argentina. Nonetheless, as Carver listened, relieved to hear the cold had cleared, the hairs on the back of his neck stood up, as they always did whenever he witnessed her transform from mere beauty, to angel.

But as he stood there, entranced, the words that still invaded his dreams from time to time returned. '*..and that other bitch. You're both dead…*' A shudder ran through him. With an effort, he willed the memory away. Pray God they would always remain just that. Words.

The singing stopped and she rounded on him - 'How was that?' - jolting him out of the morbid reverie threatening to take him.

'Wonderful.'

In that moment Carver decided. He didn't want to lose her, and would do whatever it took to make sure he never did, even if that meant staying away from the sort of cases that had ensnared him in the past. Which, unfortunately, would also mean delaying his return to CID beyond the eighteen months he had originally planned.

'An' you promise you won' be late?'

He crossed to her, took her face in his hands and placed his lips on those his father had once likened to the old Italian actress, Gina Lollobrigida. 'I promise.' But as they parted, he saw the green eyes narrow, the disbelief within them. Before she could say anything, he placed a finger to her lips, sealing them shut. 'I'll be there.'

Then, not wanting to risk going over the issues that seemed to raise themselves more often these days and knowing what she could be like in the morning, he decided it was time to answer the craving for caffeine that always grew rapidly once he was awake.

As he made his way down the stairs he remembered not to reach for the non-existent banister rail. He'd made that potentially debilitating - and painful - mistake once already, and didn't intend to repeat it.

CHAPTER 3

One floor below Antranig Koloyan's vain attempts to attract attention, Doctor Mikayel Kahramanyan was doing his best to stay calm as he spoke into the telephone. He was also trying to ignore the pain from his upper-left pre-molar. Two weeks before it had shed a filling, but there had been no time to seek out a dentist, even if there was one within twenty miles of the Institute, which he doubted.

'I understand that Colonel. But I still have over forty patients here. You promised me the rest of the trucks would be here the day before yesterday.'

'But that was before the rebels crossed the border at Damnah.' The voice was that of someone resigned to the inevitable. 'You must understand Doctor, I am fighting on three fronts and right now I need every transport available. Our Gorshki Division is on its way from Aliverdi and should be here tomorrow. You will get your trucks then.'

'TOMORROW WILL BE TOO LATE,' Kahramanyan yelled, frustration finally spilling over. *Did the man not realise what was happening? Did he not care?*

Across the room, the nurse with soft brown hair that

seemed to be turning greyer each day carried on pretending not to listen. She did not want to further burden the man for whom she worked by letting him see how alarmed she was, especially when his, to her. transparent anxiety signalled well enough the seriousness of their situation.

Gadara Nalbantian had worked with Mikayel now for five years, ever since she accepted the post no one else wanted so she could be close to her ailing mother in nearby Martuni. And though her mother had died within the year, Gadara never thought to seek another position. By then she was happy working for a man who, unlike many of his peers, abhorred the ignorance through which their charges were classified as either 'demented' or 'evil'- save perhaps in one exceptional case.

During those five years, Gadara had never seen Mikayel lose his temper, not even during the laborious negotiations he had to suffer each month with the Health Ministry just to secure enough supplies to cover their basic requirements. But over the past few days, a change had come over the man she admired above all others. Gone was the caring clinician who had worked long enough within the country's rudimentary Health Service to both understand its limitations, *and* remain philosophical about what he could ever achieve as Head of Psychiatry and Assessment for the institution housing the country's *Forgotten*. In his place was a man increasingly desperate, worn down by The Ministry's prevarications over moving them somewhere safe. She knew, without having to ask, he hadn't slept well in weeks.

Of course, neither she nor Mikayel ever referred aloud to the desperate souls in their charge by the term in common use throughout the Ministry, *The Forgotten*. Whenever they heard it, they were quick to denounce the inference. To emphasise that the care given out to the one hundred and twelve inmates – the maximum number of cots available – was the best they could manage under their impoverished circumstances. In reality they both knew the truth. That as far as the Ministry was concerned, the rudimentary fragments of humanity housed within the Armenian State Psychiatric Institute and Correction Facility could disappear off the face of the earth tomorrow, and no-one would give a damn. Why else locate an asylum for the criminally insane so close to a disputed border which, even before the place was built, was prone to Azerbaijani incursions into the lands they still regard as their own?

As Gadara listened to Mikayel's tortured pleadings, at the same time continuing to pack the medicines and supplies they would need if the trucks ever came, her conviction that her efforts would prove wasted grew stronger.

'So, what do you suggest, Colonel?' Mikayel said. 'You are the sole authority in the region now. You tell me what to do with forty-odd men the authorities think are too disturbed for prison, but not enough, apparently, to merit proper psychiatric care.'

A weary sigh preceded the military man's answer. 'Leave them.'

A crackle on the line gave Mikayel hope he had misheard. 'I am sorry, Colonel, I didn't catch that. For a moment it sounded like you said, 'leave them'.'

Another sigh. 'I did.'

For long seconds, Mikayel stared at Gadara's back as

she rooted over her boxes. But the sudden silence made her turn and as he saw the alarm flood into her face, he knew she had been listening.

'Y- You cannot mean that, Colonel,' Mikayel said, knowing in his heart he did.

'You have no choice Doctor. Even if I wanted to, and believe me I do, there is nothing I can do for you from here. According to intelligence the rebels will overrun that area within the next few hours. You know what will happen if you are still there when they arrive.'

Conscious of a growing feeling of dread, Mikayel persevered. 'But I can't just leave them for the Azerbaijanis. It would be as good as sentencing them to death.'

The casual tone in the Colonel's reply made clear that at that moment, the psychiatrist's problems were well down his order of priorities. 'Then set them free.'

'WHAT?'

'Either that, or leave them for the rebels. It is your decision.'

Mikayel's drawn face grew red and his voice rose. 'What you are suggesting, Colonel, is outrageous, and not worthy of your profession. It would be tantamount to a war crime.'

The Colonel's voice rose to match his. 'Face reality Doctor. This *is* a war. Or the nearest thing to it. In such circumstances we all have to take difficult decisions. I am sorry I cannot help you further.'

'But what about… Him?' the psychiatrist said, referring back to the problem they had considered when they first discussed the so-called evacuation plan. 'How can I set Him free? If by some miracle he avoided the rebels….'

The Colonel became abrupt. 'Then deal with him yourself.' He had more pressing problems to attend to.

'Wh- what do you mean… *deal* with him?'

'The box on your wall, doctor. We spoke about it during my assessment visit.'

As he pondered the little good that had come of it, Mikayel turned to the red wall-cabinet behind the door. He remembered now the interest the military man had shown in it. *Had he known all along it would come to this*? The psychiatrist's blood turned cold and his stomach lurched at the thought of what the Colonel was suggesting.

'But I- I am a doctor.' His breath started to come in gasps. 'I could not contemplate….' As he sucked air, pain erupted again in his broken tooth and he winced.

'In that case you must live with the consequences. I am sorry doctor. I cannot waste any more time on-.'

His words were lost as a thunderclap rent the air and the building rocked with the shock-wave of another explosion. But this time the noise was so loud, the shaking so violent, Mikayel's first thought was they had suffered a direct hit. He held onto the desk to stay on his feet while across the room Gadara pressed herself between two metal cabinets. Chunks of plaster rained down from a rent that suddenly appeared in the ceiling. After several seconds, as the shaking subsided and the leakage from above trickled to dust, an eerie silence descended. Mikayel waited long enough to be satisfied that the ceiling wasn't about to cave in, then returned to his conversation.

'Did you hear that Colonel? That was-. Colonel? COLONEL?' But the line was dead, and as he saw the blanked-out computer screen on Gadara's desk – it was usually connected to the creaking Health Service Network – he knew that their communications were gone. He imagined a large crater in the ground at the side of the building, where the service ducts were buried.

For long seconds he stared at the phone, stupidly, before placing it back on its cradle. He looked across at Gadara. Her face was a picture of fear.

'Wh-What did he say?' she said. As she spoke he saw her eyes slide in the direction of the cabinet. She had seen him look at it, probably guessed what was being suggested.

Mikayel swallowed. 'He said they are not coming. And that I must… deal with him.'

For long seconds neither spoke as the desperateness of their plight finally struck home.

Then Mikayel moved, quickly, like he had made a decision and needed to act on it before he changed his mind. He started opening desk drawers, rummaging through them, urgently.

'Where is it, Gadara? I remember I had it once.'

'What Mikayel? What are you looking for?'

'The key. It must be here somewhere.'

She joined him to help look. Eventually she found it, in the match box Mikayel had stuffed at the back of one of the drawers, certain he would never need it but keeping it safe in case some paper-wielding Government Inspector demanded he produce it. Taking it out, he crossed to the cabinet, unlocked it. As he pulled the doors open, he thought again how ridiculously large it was for its meagre contents.

A cardboard box, about three inches deep, rested on the upper shelf; another, smaller but more squarely proportioned, on the one below. Taking one in each hand – they were both heavier than they looked - he carried them back to his desk. Gadara appeared at his side.

The larger box was emblazoned with the logo of the American gun manufacturers, Smith and Wesson, a faded pen picture of a revolver, just like ones he'd seen in western films, beneath it. Mikayel lifted the lid. The gun was folded in stained oil-paper. As he took it from its nest and unwrapped it, a bitter, metallic smell caught the back of his throat. Though it must have been thirty years old or more, it seemed as new. Unused by the look of it. Its black metal was covered in a thin film of oil. As he weighed it, he noted at once how strange it felt. He was used to wielding instruments that in their various ways were designed for use on the human body, but not in the way this was intended. Another shudder ran through him. He turned the weapon in his hand, peering into the chambers. They appeared empty. He lifted the lid off the other box. Neatly arranged rows of bullets stared up at him, the rounded lead tips in their brass casings pointing up, six to a row. He took one out, but as he raised it to the gun he suddenly realised. Never having handled such a weapon in his life, he hadn't the faintest idea how to load it. He was wondering how the bullet fitted into the chamber when Gadara's hands appeared.

'Let me,' she said, taking the weapon from him.

He looked at her in surprise.

'My father was militia during the soviet. He used to let us shoot mouflon on the slopes behind our farm.'

As he watched her confident handling of the instrument, Mikayel suddenly realised, with regret, he knew almost nothing about her life before the Institute.

'Like this.' She pushed a catch and the revolver's cylinder flipped out to the side. She took a round and pushed it into one of the empty chambers.

'Okay,' he said, taking it back from her as she was about to reach for more bullets. 'It is my responsibility. I will do it.'

She stepped aside as one by one, his shaking fingers loaded five more rounds. When he was finished he pushed the barrel back into its housing. It locked in place with a loud, 'click'. Then he stood there, looking at her, the gun dangling at his side. In the distance, more explosions went off.

'You must go, Gadara. Catch up with David.' An hour earlier Mikayel had ordered the young American-Armenian who had recently come to work with them to leave.

But she shook her head and, to his surprise, smiled. At first he thought she was simply trying to convey her understanding of what he had to do. But then he thought he saw something more than just sympathy in her eyes.

'When we leave, we will leave together, Mikayel Kahramanyan.'

'But this is…. I would rather you-.'

'Hush.' She pressed a finger to his lips. 'I will go when you go.'

He looked down at her. There was a moment's awkward hesitation, then he put his arms round her and drew her to him.

'Pray God will forgive me,' he whispered in her ear.

In that moment, Gadara Nalbantian was almost tempted to surrender to the feelings she had held in check for so long. But then she remembered the gun in his untrained hand, and twisted in his arms so she could keep her eye on it.

CHAPTER 4

Antranig Koloyan pulled at Melkon's sleeve, urging him through the gate that the institute's Head of Psychiatry was holding open.

'Come ON, Melkon. We must GO.'

At the doctor's side, the good-looking nurse Antranig had always hoped – in vain – would one day visit the ward alone, stood watching. He was starting to think that there might still be time when another explosion, much nearer, rocked the building again. It lent renewed impetus to his new-found desire to stay alive. But Melkon was standing directly in front of the psychiatrist as if he had taken root. His arms were hanging loose at his sides and he seemed to be staring at something Kahramanyan was trying to keep hidden, behind him.

'MELKON,' Antranig shouted again.

Alerted by the Armenian's cry, Mikayel Kahramanyan turned from watching the other inmates disappear down the corridor in time to see the hopeless look on young Melkon's face.

'Hurry Melkon,' Mikayel said, doing his best to not sound too alarmed. 'There is no time to stand around. You must go. Now.'

Melkon looked about to burst into tears. 'But where will I go Doctor? Who will look after me?'

Feelings of guilt and inadequacy swept through Mikayel. If only he had been more demanding in his dealings with the Ministry. 'Head for Vardenis. The soldiers there will help you. But you must go quickly.' He turned to where he had last seen Antranig, and a feeling of revulsion ran through him when he saw he was staring at Gadara in a way that sent shivers up and down his spine. For the first time the psychiatrist was glad of the gun in his hand.

During his time at the institute, Mikayel had always tried to find room for compassion for the desperate souls the state's less-than-consistent justice system sent their way. After all, most were there due only to a want of proper care in their early years. Not so Antranig Koloyan. A man whose crimes were almost as shocking as those of The Monster himself, Koloyan was one of the few Mikayel had never turned his back on.

'ANTRANIG.'

Mikayel's cry jarred the mountain man out of whatever lurid fantasy was vying with his urge to escape. Reluctantly it seemed, he turned his gaze away from Gadara.

'Get Melkon out of here,' Mikayel commanded.

Giving Gadara one last, lustful look, Antranig took a hold of Melkon's sleeve and pulled him along as he scurried away down the corridor.

'Goodbye doctor,' he called over his shoulder. 'And you, Nurse Nalbantian. Maybe we'll meet on the outside some time.' As he rounded the corner out of sight and his cackle died away, Mikayel saw the shudder of revulsion that rippled through her.

'Forget him, Gadara. You will never see him again.'

'I hope not,' she said, and shivered again.

Unable to think of anything that may allay the images he suspected were playing through Gadara's mind – she knew Koloyan's case-history as well as he did – Mikayel turned his attention back to their task.

As the last of the ward's occupants ran, skipped or loped away down the corridor, he tried again. 'You don't have to-.'

'Let us do it,' she said. 'Then we can leave this awful place.' As they passed through the gate and into the now silent ward, Mikayel felt her fingers entwine themselves in his.

He had last visited G19 less than eight hours before, soon after the shelling started. He could barely believe how it had changed in that time. Though it had then been in its usual state of run-down semi-dilapidation, the beds and furniture were in their proper places. As always, the early-shift orderlies had done their inadequate best to ensure that in appearance if nothing else, G19 bore some resemblance to the Special Treatment Centre it was supposed to be. But as they passed down the ward, Mikayel saw that now, every bed was either upended or stacked on top of cabinets and cupboards to form a rudimentary shelter. The stench of shit, piss and vomit hung in the air.

As he witnessed the chaos, he wondered if the place would ever re-open now that its primary purpose – somewhere to house The Forgotten until something happened to make them go away – had been fulfilled.

As they approached the cell at the end of the ward, Mikayel realised he was disappointed to see it still standing secure. Had it been otherwise he might have been spared the grim task to come.

The institute's most infamous inmate was sitting on

his bunk, smiling broadly as he observed the doctor's approach.

'Hello, Doctor,' Vahrig Danelian said. 'I didn't expect to see you again.' Then, seeing Gadara he stood up. 'And Nurse Nalbantian?' He gave Mikayel a disapproving look. 'She shouldn't be here Doctor. You should have made her leave with the others. What is that in your hand?'

Before leaving his office, Mikayel had decided he wasn't going to let The Monster lure him into conversation. He dare not. If he started trying to justify what he had to do, to explain why he had no other choice, to apologise even, he would never do it. The Monster's quick wits and sly tongue would work their magic and Mikayel's already reluctant intentions would quickly unravel. He stopped a few feet from the bars, willing himself not to listen to the words coming from the smiling lips, nor to the voices in his head - the ones telling him he was a doctor and could not do such a thing. Another voice – reason - railed against them.

Do not think about it. Just do it. Hesitate and you are lost.

As the man in the cell stared at the object dangling from the psychiatrist's hand, mouthing something Mikayel strained not to hear, the psychiatrist lifted his arm and pointed it at him. But to Mikayel's consternation, The Monster's only reaction was to smile more widely than ever. So unnerved was he, Mikayel's barely-formed defences shattered, letting the words through.

'So, Doctor. They have sent you to do what they did not have the will to do all those years ago. How foolish of them. Clearly, they do not know you as I.'

As other voices rang in his ears – *are they real or is it my imagination?* - Mikayel suddenly felt a piercing stab of pain and tasted blood in his mouth. His tongue traced the jagged remains of his broken premolar. It had split open from the pressure between his tightly-clamped jaws. Doing his best to ignore it, he felt for the trigger, feeling its coldness come snug against the first joint of his right index finger. He wondered how much force he would need to pull it back.

But at that moment, to Mikayel's further dismay, rather than retreating to the back of the cell as he had hoped, his intended victim stepped forward, presenting an easier target for the revolver now pointed squarely at him.

That Mikayel Kahramanyan was not just nervous, but also terrified was plain to see. As Vahrig Danelian came forward he stepped back, even though he was a good eight or so feet from the bars and there was not the slightest danger the man could reach him. First Mikayel's hand, then his whole arm, started to tremble, violently.

'Come come, Doctor. You must get a grip on your nerves,' the inmate sneered. 'A man such as you, someone dedicated to doing good in the world must see the necessity of what must be done. You know in your heart it is only right.'

Mikayel's tongue flicked across his upper lip, tasting salty sweat. *One small movement. That is all that is needed.*

'Doctor?'

Gadara's voice drifted in from his left and he did not need to look to know her expression was fraught. She needed reassurance he was alright. That he could go through with it.

'Mikayel? Are you alright?'

His hand shook more, the tip of the gun barrel describing an erratic circle as he fought to keep it pointing straight. He knew what he had to do. But his finger wouldn't move.

'Do it Mikayel,' Gadara said. 'You must.'

'Yes, Mikayel,' the Monster echoed. 'Nurse Nalbantian is right. You *must* do it. There is no more time. KILL ME.' But even as the echo of his words died away he dipped his head, lowered his voice and regarded the doctor through half-closed eyes. 'For if you do not, I will surely kill you both.'

Despite the man in the cell being completely at Mikayel's mercy, such was his confidence that a wave of panic washed over the psychiatrist. For a moment he wondered if he was missing something. Was the door not locked after all? Had he managed to somehow remove one of the bars? As Mikayel's blood ran colder than ever and rivulets of sweat streamed down his face, he struggled to force himself to do what he had feared all along he would be unable to do the very first moment the Colonel suggested it.

If only the trucks had come when he asked for them, none of them would be in this situation.

Glancing to his left, he saw the terrified look on Gadara's beautiful face. *She thinks I cannot do it. That she will have to do it after all*. He must not let that happen. He was in charge. It was his responsibility.

'Mikayel,' she said softly, taking a step towards him. 'Give me the gun.'

He moved away from her.

'Don't listen to her Mikayel,' the monster's voice

roared in his ears. 'You are in charge. It is your responsibility.'

Is he reading my thoughts now? 'No Gadara,' Mikayel said, his gaze wavering between her and the man still thrusting his chest against the bars. As her hand reached towards the gun, he took another couple of steps away 'I can do it. I MUST do it.'

'YES Doctor,' The Monster shouted, almost hysterical now. 'YOU MUST.'

'Mikayel,' Gadara pleaded, her voice full of urgency. 'You cannot do what is not in your nature. I told you. I can handle it.'

'No.' Mikayel moved back further. 'I cannot allow it, I will-.'

Several things happened at once.

Gadara screamed, 'WATCH OUT MIKAYEL.'

There was a blur of movement from Mikayel's right and, too late, he realised. Intent on keeping the gun out of Gadara's reach he had strayed too close to the cell. A sinewy arm snaked out, grabbed the collar of his jacket and hauled him backwards.

But even as Mikayel felt himself flying through the air and a victorious grin spread across the Monster's maniacal features, Gadara launched herself forward, reaching for the gun that was spiralling, uselessly, in the air.

Though Mikayel would not know it until long after, the image of her in that split second, flying through the air towards him, her face twisted in horror, would remain with him for the rest of his life. For in that moment there was a thunderous roar, far worse than anything that had gone before, accompanied by a blinding flash of light. Mikayel felt a stunning blow to his whole body, like being hit by a bus, then he was falling, but slowly it seemed, into a bottomless black void.

He saw no more.

CHAPTER 5

Standing before the plain front door, Carver was uncomfortably conscious how shabby it looked compared to the others along the street.

One of those where narrow, low-walled gardens front the Victorian terraced houses, the past decades had seen Arthur Street's fortunes see-saw between genteel propriety and run-down decrepitude. Carver could still remember from his police probationer days – not that long ago in the overall scheme of things – how it had then generated more than its fair share of police calls; house burglary, electricity meter theft, domestics. Not any more. Nowadays its residents were more likely to be young solicitors, marketing people and sales executives. The sort who, in the nineties, would have drawn secret delight at being labelled 'sloanes'.

The street's re-acquired position of social respectability was reflected in the care the new generation of owners took to ensure that the small part of their properties fronting the street – the houses were narrow but long - were scrupulously maintained, recently painted, and clean.

Sarah Carver's house was the notable exception.

The dull, green paint on the featureless front door – supposedly temporary she'd said, while she waited for a 'friend' to get her a new one – was faded and, in places, peeling. The first-generation aluminium-framed double-glazed windows were pitted by weathering. The greying net curtains behind the glass added to the house's downbeat look. As Carver waited – he was never sure if the doorbell worked – he began to experience the same feelings of regret and anger that often accompanied his visits.

Without any warning, the door opened and she was standing there in her terry-towelling dressing gown, cigarette in hand. The shoulder-length blond hair through which dark roots showed looked like it hadn't been brushed and the make up around her bleary eyes was smudged. She didn't say anything but flicked her head back – a greeting of sorts - before turning and padding back down the hallway in her slippers.

'Not working this morning?' he said to her back as he closed the door behind him.

'No.'

The finality in her voice worried him. *Not again….*

He followed her into the room she and the kids called the parlour but which he always thought would make a very presentable dining room. The television was showing some CGI cartoon. Patsy and Jack perched on the sofa, still in their jammies. As their mother went through into the kitchen and threw the switch on the kettle, they saw him and their faces lit up. 'Hi Uncle Jamie,' they said together. The fact they weren't dressed yet added to his concerns, but he returned their smiles.

'Hi kids.' He tried not to ask, but couldn't keep the question in. 'No school today?' *Jesus. Thirty seconds and you're already playing bloody social worker.*

It was Patsy, the talker, who answered, though as she

spoke she looked through into the kitchen, wary of saying the wrong thing. 'Mum says that 'cos its half-term next week anyway, we don't have to go in today.'

'Is that right?' Carver said, keeping the smile going. 'Well aren't you the lucky ones?'

As he turned to where his sister was waiting for the kettle to boil, she must have caught his look. Flicking ash off her cigarette into the sink, she said, 'Don't start. I'm not in the mood.'

He just caught Patsy's otherwise hilarious, 'Oops,' face, before she returned to whatever it was the Disney Channel was showing at eight o'clock in the morning. Throwing his only niece and nephew a reassuring smile, he left them to it and stepped down into the kitchen, pushing the door shut as far as he thought wouldn't make things too obvious. The night before she had sounded more down than usual, and the look in her face confirmed it. Whatever it was, he was glad he'd decided to call on his way to work, like he did sometimes when he thought something may be wrong. Or when she was going through one of her crises.

'What's happened?'

She stubbed her cigarette out in the sink – a habit he loathed – and took a deep breath. 'They let me go.' He waited, saying nothing. 'They're cutting down on staff. I was one of the last in so I'm first out.' She shrugged again, as if relying on benefits when you've got a mortgage and two children to bring up was no big deal. But as he looked into her face, he saw that alongside the self-pity he was used to seeing, there was also defiance. Ready to come back at him if he said anything.

Though Carver's attempts to try to understand his sister's problems - those not of her making as well as the ones that were – were never meant as criticism, he knew she saw it otherwise. For that reason he chose not to question her story, even though as far as he knew Tesco was crying out for check-out staff everywhere. She had started with them before Christmas. Four months or so was about average. She hadn't done too badly this time.

He watched as she went through the motions of looking for coffee-makings, opening cupboards and drawers, banging them shut, all the time avoiding his gaze. He could tell she was close. But he had to at least try. For the children's sake.

'You shouldn't keep the kids off school. It'll only bring problems.' It brought the inevitable reaction.

Banging the tea spoon she had taken from the drawer down on the counter top, she leaned forward on both hands, head down over the sink, like she was about to throw up, or burst into tears. He checked back in the parlour. The children were still engrossed. He pushed the door shut a couple more inches, moving to stand behind her. He raised his hands, uncertainly, to the level of her shoulders. The Carver family had never been big on hugging, though Jess had started getting him into it when they worked together.

Eventually, he placed his hands on her upper arms. Their meagre boniness prompted the thought as to whether she was eating. But before he could say anything she turned. Her eyes were brimful with tears. To his surprise, she buried her head in his chest.

'What am I going to do, Jamie?' Her shoulders shook as the sob broke and after a moment's hesitation, he pulled her into him.

'Hey-hey. It'll be alright. I'm here.'

But even as she began to let it all out and he tightened his grip on her, shoving the door with his foot to shut it further, he was already remembering, painfully, the beautiful, laughing girl he had grown up with.

Carver had two sisters, both older than him though Sarah, the younger, was the one he related to most as he was growing up. Constantly in awe of her in his youth – she had always seemed so *grown-up* - he was never so proud as when his pubescent friends used to come round to pretend to listen to music so they could drool over her, tongues hanging out as she came and went from their Salford semi - the family had moved out of Liverpool by then - teasing them all with her disdainful smiles and tosses of her long, dark hair. The day she went off to Uni, – the only Carver ever to do so - he thought there was nothing the bright, confident young student wasn't capable of achieving. He was certain that one day, she would be somebody, famous even.

He only ever saw that Sarah once again. It was the night she arrived home for her first Christmas break, and then only for half an hour. She was in and out in a flash leaving him and their parents gasping in her wake as she dumped her things, gobbled a sandwich and disappeared out the front door, eager to catch up with the former High School friends she hadn't seen for a whole term.

It was a cold, wet, Manchester night and the girl who returned to the family home several weeks later was not the one who had skipped out the front door after ribbing him about the, 'bum-fluff,' on his chin he had waited several weeks to show her. It took them all – particularly their mother - a long time to come to terms with the fact she was gone, probably forever.

Now, as he held onto the sobbing shell he had only recently come to realise had so influenced the course of his career, his thoughts turned to the papers now sitting in his bottom desk drawer. The ones he had finally managed to recover, after much haggling, from the force's archive. He had already concluded that if his instincts were right, a spot of legwork and some discreet enquiries – given the SIO's current position they would have to be *very* discreet – may prove productive, even after all this time. But his musings also brought on a resurgence of the anger he'd felt the first time he read through the file. If things had been done right to begin with, if the victims, not just Sarah but the others as well had been allowed some sort of closure, then perhaps things might have turned out different. She might even have-. He stopped. It was too soon for all that, and he was always careful about falling into the 'if only' trap. Things weren't certain, and nor could he prove anything. Yet.

But as he drew his sister closer to him, Carver knew he shouldn't leave things too long. Despite his words of brotherly reassurance, things were clearly a long way from being, '*alright.*'

CHAPTER 6

Pain, like skewers being driven into his spine, lanced through Mikayel Kahramanyan's back and legs. Stifling a scream – for all he knew the rebels could still be nearby, picking over the remains - he stopped trying to shift his weight off the concrete block digging into his ribs. His medical background meant he was only too aware of the horrific possibilities of such a fall. Forcing himself to ignore the aching afflicting the whole of his body, he took stock of his condition. But that he hurt so much, and could feel it in his legs especially, was a good sign – provided his backbone wasn't fractured in a way that would sever his spinal-cord as soon as he tried to move.

For the first time since managing to stay conscious more than a few seconds – several times he had come half-to, but each time the blackness returned swiftly - he tried opening his eyes. Blurred images of chaos and destruction filtered through the dust cloud that still shrouded the demolished building and he breathed a sigh of relief. That he could feel pain *and* still see was exceptional luck. His right hand was sticking up through the rubble in front of his face and he tried wiggling his fingers. They moved. Ignoring the pain it brought on, he tried his toes. He felt them shifting around inside his shoes. So far so good.

For the next few minutes he checked out the rest of his battered body. By the time he was finished, and to his amazement, he deduced that his worst single injury was probably the one to his left arm and shoulder; either broken or dislocated. It didn't matter. He was alive.

But having come to that conclusion his thoughts turned to Gadara. The last he had seen was her flying towards him, reaching for the gun. And as the image came to him, another part of his brain fixed on the man who was the main cause of his being here in the first place. But like himself, he was either alive or dead in the rubble and right now Mikayel Kahramanyan didn't give a damn.

'Gadara,' he called, weakly. He gathered his strength. 'GADARA.' The effort brought on a coughing fit which made everything hurt even more, but as it subsided the silence returned, his call unanswered. Desperation took over.

Steeling himself, he rolled onto his side, hoping to shed some of the debris he could feel pressing on his back. The sky came into view and he realised again how lucky he was. He was lying almost on top of what had once been the Armenian State Special Psychiatric Institute and Correction Facility - now a heap of smoking rubble. Bit by bit, wincing in agony every time he moved his arm – not dislocated, but almost certainly broken - he pulled himself from the remains and rose slowly, first to his knees, then, shakily, his feet. Looking around, he saw that, with the exception of the south east corner where the remains of two adjoining walls still stood, the whole facility had been flattened. A direct hit. How in God's name had he survived?

'GADARA,' he called again, hoping to hear some small cry to indicate that she, like him, had escaped with her life. He called several times without any answer before deciding he had no choice but to start searching, which would mean digging, broken arm or no.

He looked down to check his footing before trying to move over what he knew was probably a dangerously unstable surface, which was when he saw her. She was half-buried, a foot or so beneath him. He had been lying almost on top of her all this time, her head and shoulders less than a metre from his. But the cold stare emanating from the now faded blue eyes confirmed what his instincts were already telling him. For one person to survive the blast that brought the building down was against the odds; two would have been miraculous. He reached down through the lumps of concrete and plaster to touch her face. There was residual warmth there, but not as much as there should be, and the lack of skin-tone gave final confirmation to his fear.

'Oh Gadara,' he cried. 'I am sorry. I'm so sorry.'

He dropped to his knees, and wept.

How long he stayed like that he never knew. He didn't try to reach her. She was jammed under too many layers of concrete and rubble for him to even think of digging her out, especially with only one arm. It would need lifting gear. But as the light started to fade and his reserve of tears emptied, his thoughts turned, inevitably, to *Him*; the man who Mikayel's concern for public safety had told him must be prevented from escaping at all costs. Well the costs had turned out to be more terrible than he could ever have imagined. He cursed himself, over and over, for not insisting she leave when he had the chance. And right there, he determined that if nothing else, he would make sure her death wasn't in vain.

Doing his best to ignore the searing pain that every movement in his back and shoulders brought on – every so often he had to freeze, like a statue, until it receded - he rooted through the rubble. When darkness descended he carried on searching by the light of a flash-lamp he found in the remains of a store-cupboard. All the while, no-one came and he saw not a living soul. The shelling had already stopped when he regained consciousness and though he paused in his work several times, straining to listen, there were no sounds of the incursion in the distance, just a foreboding silence.

It was nearing midnight when he came across it, on its side, half-buried in the remains of what presumably was once Ward G19, and covered by ceiling boards – which was why it took him so long to find it.

Manufactured to be assembled on site, the cell was basically a box comprising six pre-formed sheets; four – of steel bars - that were the walls, and two reinforced concrete slabs for the ceiling and floor, both finished with metal sheets as added protection against an occupant digging their way out. A sturdy, solid construction, it was designed to withstand any possible escape attempt by its resourceful inhabitant. As such it had almost, but not quite, withstood the stresses imposed on it when it fell with the rest of the building.

The walls were still locked together, the bars dented and twisted in places, but still intact and secure enough to stop anyone within getting out: even the door looked like it was still locked. But while the seals between floor and walls were unbroken, there was a hole in a corner of the ceiling, where something heavy had landed on it. The impact had ripped the covering steel plate away from the bolts that secured it to the walls, bending it inwards. It wasn't a big gap, only half a metre or so. But it was enough for a man with a slim frame to squeeze through, and the Institute's kitchen hadn't been famed for its wholesome food.

As he stood looking down into the cell's dark emptiness, shining the flashlight around in the hope he was mistaken and that in some dark corner he would spy a body, Mikayel read the evidence.

Protected within what was in effect a very adequate safety cage, the Monster would have survived the building's collapse with relative ease. Bruised and battered like himself no doubt, but nonetheless alive. And the smears of blood on the metal ceiling sheet, near to the corner, showed where, cut and bleeding, he had worked to widen the opening until he had managed to squeeze through.

But despite the indications before him, Mikayel searched the surrounding rubble for another hour, until fatigue and despair sapped what little strength was left in him and the flashlight finally gave out. As it flickered one last time and died, he sank down on top of the rubble, exhausted.

After finding the cell empty, Mikayel had clung to the desperate hope that even if he had got away, the Azerbaijanis would find him and, in their eagerness to kill any hated occupier of 'their' land, would carry out the sentence that the court should have imposed in the first place. But then Mikayel realised. In the hours he had been searching, he had neither seen nor heard anything that hinted of Azerbaijan. They had gone, focusing their efforts elsewhere perhaps, maybe even driven away by the Colonel's gallant counter-attack. Either way, the result was the same. There was no one within ten, fifty miles maybe, capable of posing a threat to the man who would even now be putting as much distance as possible between himself and the place that had held him these past twelve years.

As the dire truth sank in, Doctor Mikayel Kahramanyan shook his head. Vahrig Danelian was gone, freed by the same hellish chain of events that had taken Gadara and, very nearly, himself. The Monster of Yerevan was abroad again in the world from which he had been taken and where he could now return to the perverted missionary work that defined him as the monster he was.

Mikayel gave out one last cry of despair before collapsing onto his back to lie on top of the ruins, utterly spent. There was no one around to hear his lamenting cry but it echoed and re-echoed round the valley of death for what seemed an age.

'GOD HELP US ALL.'

CHAPTER 7

Deputy Chief Constable Geoffrey Able QPM, Chairman of the National Police Chiefs Council Crime Committee referred to his agenda.

'Umm… National Crime Agency? European Protocol on Cross-Border Homicide?' He glanced down the right hand side of the table to where Carver was sitting alongside his boss, Nigel Broom. 'DCI Carver. This is you I believe?'

Taking his cue, the detective whose exploits were known to most of those round the table, and not just thanks to the Sunday Times Magazine articles, cleared his throat and gathered his papers. He hated these policy forums and, after staying longer than he'd intended at Sarah's and busting a gut to make it in time for his ten-thirty slot, intended to be brief. Especially seeing as he'd had to wait the best part of another hour while the twelve-strong committee tied itself in knots debating some obscure point contained within a paper headed *'Investigation of Crime Within The Asylum-Seeker Community.'*

Carver had attended such NPCC committees before, several times in fact. He knew what to expect. Nevertheless it alway irked him to witness such a high-powered gathering wasting its time on what usually turned out to be little more than semantics. He hoped the paper he was about to deliver wasn't set to get similarly bogged down. From what he'd been hearing, they needed to get things moving.

Carver opened his mouth to begin when, having introduced him, the Chairman spoke again.

'Most of us will have already read your paper Mr Carver,' DCC Able said. 'But there are a couple of *in-locum* members with us today. For their benefit, would you mind summarising the main points again?'

'Just what I was about to do, sir.' *What did he think? I was going to read through all eleven pages*?

It took Carver less than two minutes to cover the issues he had been discussing for months with former colleagues at the National Crime and Operations Faculty and a dozen or so detective contacts on the continent - ever since the De-Mesa debacle in fact. Given the freedom of travel within the European Union, and ignoring Britain's now unique position in this respect, it was clear that the incidence of Trans-National Homicide – once comparatively rare – was growing year on year. Already, and despite the structures that existed through which UK police forces shared crime intelligence, worrying numbers of murders and sex crimes, later found to be connected, were still managing to slip the net – hence the Government's continuing obsession with police force amalgamations. But where crimes transgressed national boundaries, the chances of linking them in the vital early stages were slim indeed, which was why Carver and his colleagues were lobbying for the 'Interim Special Measures' outlined in the paper he was presenting.

The key proposal - temporary until a more formal

framework could be put in place - was simple. The Investigators were asking that a Euro-Intelligence Forum, essentially a Serious Crime 'Swap-Shop', be established. But unlike Interpol which, contrary to most people's understanding is a mainly administrative body, Carver's forum would comprise Operational Detectives. Meeting regularly – every two-to-three months seemed about right – they would share information on cases of murder and sex-crime where it wasn't yet certain that the offender was 'local'. They weren't suggesting databases or anything yet, nevertheless Carver was confident that provided the right people got involved, it would greatly reduce the chances of another Luigi De-Mesa-type cock-up.

The enquiry into how the itinerant Spaniard had managed to travel freely around Europe for fifteen years, kidnapping, raping and, in nine cases at least, murdering teenage girls, was still on-going. But from what they'd learnt already, Carver and his colleagues were agreed. Had such a forum as the one proposed been operating, De-Mesa's depraved pattern of offending would have been picked up much sooner. Some of the girls would, undoubtedly, still be alive.

But as he came to the end of his summation, Carver was surprised by the subdued response around the table. Given that there was nothing particularly controversial in it, he had been expecting a fairly positive reception. But as the eyes of those opposite swivelled to his left, in the direction of the one member of the committee Carver had met in an operational setting, a warning bell began to ring.

Within his home force, Nicholas Whitely, Deputy Chief Constable of Thames Valley Police, was regarded as capable, fair-minded and less prone than many senior officers who lacked physical stature to, 'go off like a bottle of pop.' It was unfortunate then that the circumstances under which they first met, were such as to give Whitely what he would probably consider good reason to harbour a grudge. Carver wondered if something had been said before he arrived. Certainly everyone seemed to be waiting for Whitely to speak. As if on cue, the DCC leaned forward, squaring the papers in front of him, like a television newsreader wary about relying too much on the auto-cue.

'Chief Inspector.' He looked up to see Carver waiting, and smiled. 'Nice to see you again, Mr Carver.'

Though Carver recognised the assassin's smile for what it was, he acknowledged the man's greeting with a courteous nod. But as he saw the look in the man's eyes, the bell rang louder.

'I just have a couple of questions concerning your proposal. If I may?'

'Of course, sir.'

The smile widened. Whitely was obviously at ease in an environment where there was no danger of encountering something that might test his Operational Command Skills - unlike the scene of the Right Honourable Alistair Kenworthy, MP's murder.

Carver could still remember the look on Whitely's face when he arrested the dead Government Minister's English rose wife for the crime - one of several she commissioned to preserve the inheritance she stood to lose if her puritanical father ever learnt of the sordid activities she and her husband had once engaged in. Whitely almost fainted on the spot. Only moments before, he had been promising her that he would do, 'everything humanly possible to find your husband's killer.'

At the time, Whitely was already struggling over a member of the Government being found murdered on his patch, trying but failing to give the impression he was in control of things, as his Chief expected him to be. But never having worked CID long enough to learn much, Whitely had little experience of major crime. Instead of leaving things to Carver, which would have made sense, he panicked and started issuing orders - mostly nonsensical - to the detectives and Scene Managers beginning to gather, as if he knew what he was doing. And when Carver suddenly exposed Anne Kenworthy's conspiring, Whitley was left floundering.

Whitely didn't make anything of it at the time, but it would have been clear to those present that he had been caught out of his depth, lacking the operational experience needed to deal with such a sensitive yet serious situation. It was a good thing that Carver's old boss, The Duke, was on hand or the whole situation could have degenerated into farce, particularly when Whitely tried to insist that Carver should brief a local DCI to there and then take over the investigation Carver had been running for several weeks. Carver had never intended to humiliate the man, but he doubted Whitely would ever see it that way. And such things weren't easily forgotten.

'This…,' Whitely checked Carver's paper again, as if having trouble remembering the phrase. '*Euro-Intelligence Forum* you propose. I assume someone would have to take a co-ordinating role?'

Carver thought he could see where Whitely was going. He had discussed any possible 'resource implications' with his colleagues, several times.

'That's correct sir, but the feeling is, it wouldn't involve too much work. I've discussed it with Mr Broom.' He turned to his Director who nodded in confirmation. 'And he supports the view that if, for example, I as the UK rep were to take on that role but using a cascade system through my opposite numbers in other countries, it shouldn't interfere with my present duties. I know my colleagues abroad think the same.'

'I've no problem with that, Chief Inspector.'

Whitely's casual dismissal of the point caught Carver by surprise. If he wasn't out to undermine the proposal on cost grounds, then where was he headed?

Whitely drew himself up in his chair as far as someone can who only comes up to most police officers' shoulders.

'Please don't take this the wrong way Chief Inspector, but I think most people around this table will be aware of your, aah, rather singular case history?' Carver caught some of the confirming nods in his peripheral vision.. 'And I think it's fair to say we've all been quite entertained by the coverage given to some of your more... interesting exploits.' Carver felt his stomach muscles clench and steeled himself, wondering where Whitely's deceptively light-hearted delivery might be leading. 'Now I may be entirely mistaken on this, but I am aware that the same thought has occurred to some of my colleagues....'

Carver looked round. Whoever they were, they were keeping shtum.

'You see, it strikes me that this *coordinating* role you foresee yourself playing-.'

'I didn't say it would be me, sir. In fact, I-.'

'But there seems to be a strong inference in the paper that it may well be.'

'No, sir. What I-.'

Whitely's hand came up. 'Please Chief Inspector. Let me finish.'

Carver stopped. He hoped his tendency to colour whenever his past threatened to cast a shadow over the present wasn't starting to become apparent.

'*Whoever* coordinates this group is going to find themselves in a fairly high-profile position, wouldn't you say?'

'Umm… maybe, but that-.' The hand again.

'And given the way certain sections of the media like to obsess over anything to do with-,' he paused for effect, '*Serial Killing*, it strikes me that a group charged with looking at the subject on a multi-national level may well attract considerable media interest. Particularly whoever is responsible for coordinating the activities of such a unit?'

'WHAT?' Carver felt the colour starting to rise in his face. The intimation behind Whitely's comment would be clear to everyone. About to voice his feelings, Carver felt a hand on his arm. He looked round to see Broom's almost imperceptible shake of his head.

Confirmed in post as NCA's new Operations Director only three weeks earlier, the former Chief Constable and one-time of Director of NCA's precursor, NCIS, was a veteran when it came to the politicking that is an integral part of NPCC gatherings. Usually happy enough to fight his own corner, for once Carver was glad Broom was present. He couldn't think of a better ally to help him refute Whitely's slur. Broom turned to Whitely.

'That's rather unfair, Nick,' he said, calmly. 'As Mr Carver's Head of Service I am familiar with both his background *and* the thinking behind this proposal. I have never found anything to suggest that Jamie courts media attention. Just the opposite in fact. He even-.'

'Maybe so, Nigel,' Whitley broke in, determined. 'But in that case I wonder if DCI Carver would mind explaining how it is then, that a researcher from a Channel 4-sponsored, TV production company has already contacted the NPCC Secretariat enquiring about, the "Euro-Serial-Killer Cops"?'

Around the table the gasps and sharp intakes of breath were clearly audible. Even Broome looked stunned. Carver felt the grip on his arm again and turned to meet his Director's intimidating gaze.

'Do you know anything about this, Jamie?'

Carver felt himself redden. Only this time he knew it would be obvious to everyone.

CHAPTER 8

It was late in the afternoon when Carver finally caught up with the man most referred to as simply, 'The Duke' - his former boss, Detective Chief Superintendent John Morrison. On the way he had to detour to drop off a batch of the latest 'Grapevine's at the NCA's Longsight offices. The newsletter was the Agency's official organ for keeping staff appraised on internal matters. The past few months there had been only one, real topic of interest - the ongoing renegotiations concerning the official status of former police staff, in particular those that had a bearing on future pay scales, pension entitlements, and 'posting rights' when 'Agents', as they were now known, returned to their home forces.

A couple of days before, a Daily Telegraph reporter had contacted the NCA Press Office, asking for comment on a piece they were writing drawing attention to the 'Crisis in Britain's FBI'. The article purported to highlight the 'shabby' way agency staff around the country were being treated as the latest round of reorganisations progressed. Someone in the Agency's Human Resource section at its Vauxhall Bridge HQ had decided it would be a good idea to pre-empt the inevitable internal fall-out by running off a special edition of Grapevine, handily pointing out that such reports were based upon, 'rumour, lies and deliberate misinterpretations.'

Carver wondered what planet they were living on and where they thought the Telegraph got its story from in the first place?

Despite all the pre-discussion and supposed, 'consultation', former police officers - as opposed to direct entrants to the NCA - were still waiting to learn how their pension entitlements might change under the new structure. The prevailing view was that the lack of urgency being given to resolving the matter reflected the level of importance those orchestrating the changes – Home Office and HM Inspectorate Of Constabulary – attached to staff issues generally.

When he first heard about the Telegraph's enquiry, Carver got his contact at the paper's Trafford Park printers to E-mail him a draft. Having read the response in Grapevine, he knew whose version he thought was closer to the truth, and suspected that by the time people read the newsletter's pronouncements about the problems being, 'exaggerated out of all proportion,' the NCA's personnel department would have succeeded only in making things ten times worse. 'They'd have been better keeping their mouths shut,' he observed when the batches of newsletters arrived via special courier the previous day.

By the time Carver came away from Longsight, having done his best to answer the questions from those not out on operations, the sounds of discord were ringing in his ears.

Neil Booth, an old DCI colleague pulled him to one side as he was leaving. His take on it all was typical.

'I don't know how you see things from where you

are Jamie, and I know you're just the messenger. But take my word for it. They're shitting on us. Look at this.' He produced a letter from inside his jacket. It was from the NCA's Human Resources Section, addressed to his home and dated a few days before. Carver started to read it, but Neil couldn't wait.

'It gives notice that as, technically, I'm no longer a serving police officer, I could be posted anywhere in the country once the Staffing Review is complete. Dianne threw a fit when she read it. We've only just moved to the catchment area for the school where we want to send our Amy.' He picked up a copy of the newsletter and waved it in the air. 'If you know who's putting this crap out, tell 'em to stick it up their arse.' He balled the paper and lobbed it into the nearest waste bin.

Carver hadn't argued. He'd been hearing such complaints with worrying regularity.

Now, after shelving the organisational problems afflicting the agency to which he remained seconded, Carver awaited The Duke's reaction to his account of the abortive NPCC meeting that morning.

The big man across the table stopped his pint inches from his lips. 'You do know Whitely set you up.' It was a statement, not a question. His eyes locked onto Carver's as he let the glass complete its journey, taking a good third of its contents in one long sup.

Carver watched the amber liquid disappear before taking some of his own, but didn't attempt to match the other's quaff-rate. The Duke's ability to down pints was like many other things about him - legendary.

From the corner table where he'd found his former boss waiting on his arrival, Carver surveyed the rest of the bar's clientele. It was an instinctive, though redundant precaution.

The Great English Pride, in the heart of Manchester, was once infamous as the place where elements within the old Manchester CID used to rub shoulders with the villains they stalked. No more. Nowadays its clientele consists mostly of sharply-dressed, management consultant whiz-kids - many still fresh from university – who flock there to groom their would-be clients with expense-account lunches in a place with a bit more atmosphere than the ubiquitous city-centre bistros. But at least the change meant that Carver and his former boss could meet within reasonable distance of the Manchester Force's Chester House HQ, without having to worry about someone starting a rumour.

When he'd first sat down, Carver had asked after Cathy. But after a vague, 'We're dealing with it,' it became quickly clear that Morrison preferred to talk of things other than his wife's recently-diagnosed cancer. Carver brought him up to date with his ill-fated presentation of that morning.

'My first thought was any leak must have come from the Faculty. But they're just as keen to get a forum up and running as we are.'

The Duke nodded into his pint as if he'd already come to the same conclusion. Having worked there, Carver was on excellent terms with the Faculty's cadre of geeky analysts and 'liason' officers. Given the difficulties they faced on an almost daily basis, the last thing they'd do would be to scupper the forum's chances.

Carver continued. 'Then I remembered. Whitely missed out on the Northumbria Chief's job a few months back. Broom knows someone in the Crime

Commissioner's office up there. Apparently Whitely didn't respond too well when the Kenworthy case came up during his interview. He's been heard citing it as the reason he didn't get the job.'

'So you think the leak may have been engineered by Whitely himself, to embarrass you?'

Carver stared into his pint before looking up to meet the other man's gaze. 'Let's put it this way. I wouldn't put it past him.'

The Duke nodded, slowly, as if considering it. 'What did the rest of them think?'

Carver shrugged. 'Difficult to say. I like to think most believe it was nothing to do with me. But there's no way they'd admit one of their own would do something like that out of spite.'

The Duke harrumphed, loudly, shaking his large head. 'Bloody Chief Officers. Sometimes they can be naive as hell.'

Carver let a lift of an eyebrow signal his agreement. He'd already gone over the possibilities during his lively discussion with Broom after the meeting. Eventually Broom had accepted that the leak to the TV company was nothing to do with Carver. But he was understandably angry, not to mention embarrassed, that a NCA-sponsored proposal had come to grief so spectacularly. His advice to Carver as he left to catch the train for Newcastle – the next leg of his provincial tour – had been uncompromising.

'Everyone knows your investigative record Jamie. That's why I welcomed your secondment. Your credentials can help us navigate our way through all this re-organisation bullshit. But if the baggage you carry round with you becomes a problem, I won't hesitate to bounce you.' At this point he leaned forward to make sure his next words weren't misunderstood. 'From now on, forget operations. Keep your head down, *and for God's sake keep your name out of the papers.*'

It wasn't exactly a bollocking, but it felt like one.

'Is that all he mentioned?' The Duke sounded like he sensed there might be more.

Carver gave a wan smile. 'He did say something about it being time I moved up. That a Super's job would take me away from the, how did he put it, '*source of my problems'?*'

'Well fancy that.'

The knowingness in The Duke's voice was unmistakable. He'd expressed similar views, many times, as, indeed, had Carver's retired Chief Constable father. Carver had always responded that he was more suited to investigating, than command. His view hadn't changed. Carver continued.

'He also asked me if I was seeing much of you.'

The Duke spluttered into his pint so he had to put it down. A hand like a bear's paw wiped across his mouth. 'And what did you say?'

'I said I'd only visited SMIU once, to talk about the Forum, which is the truth.'

'Hmmm.' The Duke cocked an eyebrow. For several seconds, unvoiced thoughts and understandings passed between the two detectives who had been through so much together.

As soon as it was announced that the newly created, national Special Murder Investigation Unit was going to be set up in the adjoining half of the complex that already housed the NCA's North West arm – a nondescript set of offices tucked away at the back of a

Salford trading estate – Nigel Broom was on the phone to The Duke. Ostensibly it was to offer his congratulations on his appointment as head of the new unit whose brief was to take on the investigation of murder cases which, by their nature, didn't lend themselves to traditional methods of investigation. In reality that meant those that fell within either the, 'Too Hard To Do' or 'We've Tried And Got Nowhere' categories. But when Broom referred, casually, to the coincidence of Carver working next door and the pair's shared history, the message was clear. '*Carver is NCA. Don't involve him in SMIU affairs.*'

Carver almost broke a smile when The Duke rang to report the conversation, having already turned down his former boss's several offers to use his pull with the powers-that-be to get him re-posted. 'SMIU's tailor-made for someone with your background,' The Duke had argued.

Not that Carver wasn't tempted. His most recent experiences could almost have been designed to equip him for the sort of work that would come to the unit that was the service's response to the Rawcliffe Report's scathing criticism of its record on investigating cross-border homicide - amongst other things. But his promises to Rosanna, and himself, had to stand. Thankfully, The Duke understood. He knew what they'd been through.

'I respect your decision, Jamie,' he said when Carver rang to tell him. 'But the offer stands. Any time you are ready.'

Carver never even mentioned it to Rosanna.

Now, as The Duke rose, glasses in hand, he winked. 'Just as well Nigel Broom doesn't get in here much then, isn't it?'

Carver watched as the six-foot-four former rugby forward headed towards the bar, broad back and shoulders rolling in the John Wayne-swagger that, along with the old movie star's real surname, had long ago given rise to his nickname - 'The Duke'. Not for the first time Carver regretted they were no longer working together. He even wondered if it wasn't some sort of weird destiny that had brought them together again, almost. Okay, he wasn't actually part of SMIU. But being next door, there should be plenty of opportunities to…. He stopped.

There you go again, he thought. Giving in to it. He let out a sigh. *When will you get it through your thick skull? You're not operational anymore. And if Nigel Broom catches so much as a whiff of you taking an interest in SMIU, you'll end up Uniform Ops Manager on some out-of-the way divisional posting.*

He was still musing on how he was going to manage to resist the temptations he could already see arising, when The Duke returned with their pints of Smooth Flow. Squeezing back into his seat, he returned to the subject they'd been discussing.

'Whoever was behind the leak, it's a bloody shame. Your little set-up would have complemented SMIU nicely.' Despite the downbeat observation, Carver had to stifle a smile. The Duke's West Country lilt made his new unit's acronym sound like a cross between a cat and a cow; 'Smeee-ooo.' But though he agreed wholeheartedly, Carver had dwelt enough on the morning's events.

'Speaking of which, how is it coming along? Got the rest of your staff in place yet?'

To his surprise, Carver just caught a hint of a smile as The Duke picked up his glass, took another long swig then banged it down. He nodded at Carver's pint.

'Drink that up,' he said, a glint suddenly showing in his eyes. 'Then I've something to show you.'

CHAPTER 9

Temel Ozalan picked his way across the field he'd ploughed only that morning, bobbing and weaving to keep the tray he was carrying evenly-balanced. On it were the pitcher of aryan his thoughtful wife had ordered he take to their new hand, along with a beaker and jug of water.

Somewhere near the half-way point, the shadow of something passing overhead drew him to look up. The distinctive outline of a golden eagle, one of the pair nesting in the cliff across the valley, soared overhead. But he was only able to follow its progress across the cloudless sky for a couple of seconds before he had to look away. Now approaching midday, the sun's glare was too much for even his mountain-born eyes. Evening was the best time for eagle-watching, when the sun was setting beyond Turkey's Taurus Mountains, behind the hill farm where Temel had lived and worked his fifty-two years. But it was nice to know they were still there. He hadn't seen them for a few days and was beginning to worry that hunters may have taken them.

He carried on across the rough-hewn soil towards the woodshed from behind which the sounds of the new man, hard at work, had continued all morning. Since the stranger's arrival a week or so before, the man had hardly stopped, happy it seemed to work long hours without rest. It was almost as if outdoor work was something he had been deprived of, which judging by the pallor that was only now beginning to disappear, Temel thought could well be the case.

But in this heat a man needed refreshment, hence the aryan that Sisi had made fresh that morning. Along with a jug of crystal-clear mountain water, the diluted-yoghurt that was a staple amongst the hill-farmers in the Konya region was enough to slake any man's thirst.

Temel rounded the corner of the shed, just as the axe split the half-round of timber in two. The two quarters fell away from each other to join the steadily growing piles either side of the block. As Temel cast about for a flat surface where he could put the tray, he kicked some logs out of the way.

The axe-man span around.

Had Temel given it any thought, he may have wondered why the man wielded the axe across his chest as if making ready to defend himself. But his attention was diverted by the sight of Versile, trying to slide away, unseen, from her seat on the fence-post next to the shed door from where she had been watching the man at work.

'Why are you here, Versile?' Temel called. 'You should be helping your mother.'

The conflicted look in Temel's youngest daughter's face spoke of the clash between abashment at having been caught out, and the independence of spirit that was ever more a part of her these days.

'I was just going, Papa. I was simply being polite to our guest. Did you know he has English blood in him?'

Despite the curiosity her words aroused, Temel's first

reaction was to register his displeasure at her back-talk. He threw her an admonishing glare, but didn't say anything. Such words as her skiving merited were not for the ears of strangers. And it would fall to her mother to lecture her on the subject of the disgrace it would bring on the family if one of the neighbours had happened along and seen her, alone, in the company of a bare-chested man who wasn't even family. Nevertheless, her snippet of intelligence intrigued him, a reminder that they still knew little about the man who had wandered onto the farm looking for temporary work the week before.

'A man's family is not for others to ask after unless he chooses to share it,' he reminded his daughter. 'A well brought-up young woman should know that.' He glanced over at the man now stacking logs against the side of the woodshed. If he was aware of the father-daughter tension his presence had triggered, it didn't show. *Probably comes from a family of boys*, Temel thought.

'Attend to your chores Versile. Your mother will speak with you later.'

The set of her beautiful young face betrayed her annoyance at being treated like a child in front of their new hand.

'Hmmph.'

Gathering her skirts, she stomped back up towards the house. She didn't look back.

The man set another log on the block and picked up the axe. About to swing it, Temel thrust the pitcher of aryan in front of him.

'Take a drink, Hersek. It is hot work.'

The man who went by the name Hersek looked at the

clay vessel in Temel's hand as if it were a big decision. Then he put the axe down and took it. About to drink, he seemed to remember something.

'Thank you.'

Temel nodded, and watched as the man slurped the thick buttermilk down, following it up with a long swig from the water jug. There had been a couple of times when Temel thought there was something about the man's appearance that didn't wholly fit with the eastern origins to which he had alluded. Now, thinking about what Versile had said, Temel could see it. The features, particularly the eyes, and nose perhaps, did have something of the west about them. An unusual combination, even for these times.

'So,' Temel said, studying the man's face as he poured himself more aryan. 'You are not full Kurd then?'

Hersek wiped the back of his hand across his mouth, and took another drink. His unusually dark eyes - Temel thought that if they were blue, they were the darkest he had ever seen – bore into Temel's, as if deciding how much to say.

'My mother was half-English.'

Temel nodded again. *Interesting.* 'Is she still alive?'

Normally, he would have shown more respect for a man's privacy, but his trip into the village that morning had given him cause to delve more deeply than he had done thus far. In any case, he always found anything to do with the English fascinating. Even in school, all those years ago, his teacher had rebuked him for showing more interest in the English Sea Lord, Nelson, and the famous Battle of The Nile, than in the great victories of their own Kemal Re'is. To his surprise

Hersek shrugged, as if it was of little consequence.

'I do not know if she still lives. I am on my way to find out.'

'She is here? In Turkey?' Again to Temel's surprise, the man laughed and shook his head, as if it were a stupid question.

'Not quite.' Turning, he looked south, over the mountains towards where the Mediterranean Sea lay. Temel followed his gaze, wondering. The only other land in that direction – apart from Egypt and Africa - was the island of Kypru. But Hersek didn't elaborate.

'You must tell us about her sometime,' Temel said. 'Sisi will be interested. She went to England once.'

'Your wife has been to England?' A note of interest that Temel had not heard before sounded in Hersek's voice.

'Her uncle's funeral. He moved there from Kypru. After the Greeks kicked him off his land.' They both spat in the dirt, as convention required.

They stood there for a while as Hersek finished the aryan and Temel reflected on the longest conversation he had had with the Easterner since he'd arrived. English eh? Who would have thought it?

He picked up the empty pitchers and the tray, and was about to return to the house when he remembered the other reason he had taken the tray off Sisi, telling her that today, he would take Hersek his morning refreshment.

'By the way. I was in Hadim earlier. It seems that the Prefect of Police is visiting farms around, asking to see workers' papers. Something to do with some border alert.' He gave a weary sigh. 'Bloody police, always finding reason to poke their noses in people's business.

Anyway, I remember you said you have papers, so I take it, this is not a problem for you, yes?' The day Hersek arrived, Temel had glimpsed one of his satchels, stuffed full with bundles of papers.

Though the man was staring at him, he didn't answer straight away. Eventually he said, 'Yes. I have papers.' He looked south again and, just for a moment, a strange blankness came into his face. Then he reached for the axe leaning against the block.

'Good,' Temel said. 'Then I will leave you to your work.' As he turned away, Temel saw the way the man hefted the axe in his hands, making ready to hoist it above his head. It made him wonder if he had ever worked in forestry. He would ask during their next conversation, whenever that might be.

'Thank you again, Temel,' he heard the man say, though Temel thought there was something strange about the way he said it. Then he heard the swish of the the axe as it cut through the air and the man from the East whose mother was English executed as clean a cleave-stroke as any he had made that morning.

CHAPTER 10

A long corridor divided the NCA side of the building, from the suite of offices to be used by the Special Murder Investigation Unit. Access was through a single door at the far end. Carver waited as The Duke punched in the door-code. As far as Carver knew, he was the only person outside SMIU who had it. As the door clicked open, The Duke turned to him and actually winked. If Carver hadn't seen it, he wouldn't have believed it. The man whose responses to the most unexpected developments during major enquiries rarely rose above a restrained, 'That's interesting,' seemed to be having difficulty containing himself.

As he'd driven back from the pub, pondering on what it was The Duke was so eager to show him – and reminding himself that whatever it was, he mustn't be late for Rosanna's performance - the germ of an idea came to him. But he'd dismissed it. *Too obvious.* Now, seeing his former boss as animated as he'd seen him since Cathy's cancer had been diagnosed, the idea bounced back. Right or wrong, he was about to find out.

Carver's first thought as he came through into the open-plan suite was that it didn't look any more organised than the last time he'd visited. Stacks of case-file boxes, some of which he recognised from Chain-

Link, dotted the floor. Half-assembled desks amongst those already occupied indicated that decisions were yet to be made about seating arrangements and office allocations.

A couple of the DS's he'd met before – he from the Met, she, West Yorkshire he remembered - were unpacking cardboard boxes containing the detritus of their previous lives. He nodded a greeting. As they nodded back and he took in their lost looks, he remembered how he'd felt the first time he was uprooted from an operational environment and dropped into one where, on the face of it, nothing seemed to be happening.

The Duke turned to him. The self-satisfied look on his face now almost bordered on comical. To Carver's surprise he simply said, 'I'll, umm, be in my office.'

Leaving Carver guessing, he headed down the room towards the set of offices at the far end. The offices were of glass, with horizontal blinds affording privacy. He paused at the door to the one Carver knew was his, to lean across to the one next door.

'Visitor,' Carver heard him say to whoever was there, before retreating back into his and shutting the door.

It was then Carver knew his suspicions were confirmed. A strange feeling came into his stomach. Something between trepidation, and nervy excitement. For a moment unsure of himself, he turned to where the two detectives were looking at him wearing expressions that read, '*So what brings you over this side this tlme?*'

Carver was yet to move beyond nodding terms with those of the Duke's new team he had met so far, but he was aware they had all been selected for the new venture on the basis of their experience and proven investigation skills. He wondered what their take on him was. 'How's it going?' he said.

'Great,' the older, Met man answered. 'We've no frigging filing cabinets. The computers aren't working and no one has a bastard clue what we're supposed to be doing.'

Carver held back on any smart retorts. Much the same in the NCA offices of late, it was no joking matter. Thankfully the operational staff – in the main former Crime Squad officers – were carrying on with their surveillance and evidence gathering activities more or less as before. They weren't the sort to let unanswered concerns around future working conditions interfere with their work, which was as well. But for the desk people, the analysts, support staff and administrators, being able to find their way round the rapidly changing organisation actually mattered. Even the E-mail system was beginning to throw up weird anomalies of late.

As if sensing Carver's hesitation, the Yorky swivelled in her chair to look down towards the offices. Seeing no sign of anyone, she turned back, and in a voice rich with her native dialect, said, 'Aah believe you used to work with her?'

Carver nodded.

'In that case, we'll have to take thee for a pint sometime and have a chat.'

She winked across at her colleague, causing Carver to wonder if the habit was catching. But he simply smiled, and said nothing. They'd find out soon enough.

Leaving the pair to their speculating, he followed The Duke's course down to the office from where sounds of things being moved around were emanating. As he went, he recognised some of the names on the box-files littering the floor. Stephanie Carter, The Durzlan Family, Dominic Wilkins, others.

As he arrived in the doorway, a tall woman with shiny, mid-length sandy hair had her back to him. She was arranging journals and files in a bookcase. The jacket of her grey suit was tossed, casually, over the back of her office chair and her cream-satin blouse shimmered in the early-evening sunlight streaming through the windows. One other thing he noticed. Her heels were higher than ever.

Without turning she said, 'Not pumping you by any chance are they?'

He gave a wan smile, and turned to look back down the office. The two DSs were trying not to look like they were interested.

'Don't worry,' he said, pushing the door closed enough so their words wouldn't carry. 'Your secret's safe with me.' Then he realised what he'd said. *Oops*.

Detective Inspector Jess Greylake turned slowly, the pencilled eyebrows above the perfectly made-up face already arching skywards. 'And what secret would that be, pray-tell?'

He winced inside. She didn't bother dodging round the subject these days, though when push came to shove, she never confirmed, nor denied anything concerning her personal interests. 'Enigmatic' was the word he thought best described how she handled enquiries into her private life.

'I was speaking rhetorically.'

'I'm sure.'

For several seconds they let their expressions substitute for the words of greeting neither felt it necessary to voice. It was Carver who broke the silence, as he had known it would be.

'Here we are again then.'

She grinned. 'So it appears. The Duke's spoilt my surprise.'

He nodded. 'Couldn't wait. I thought he'd won the lottery or something.'

'Typical man,' she said. 'No finesse. Coffee?' She motioned behind him and he turned. His old Russell-Hobbs was set up on a cabinet in the corner.

'Ahhh, I wondered what had happened to it. But I thought you don't drink coffee?'

'I thought you might be pining for it. And I couldn't leave it at Warrington. No one to look after it.'

He pulled a wry face. 'So I hear. When's the rest of the office coming?'

She gave a mischievous look. 'It's just me and Alec for now. But you never know.'

He just managed to control his shock. Alec Duncan as well? But then realised, he should have guessed. The Duke had always rated the wily Scottish DS, particularly his attention to detail - as he'd displayed, many times, during the drawn- out Worshipper Investigations.

'I'm guessing The Duke's never heard of nepotism?'

She pulled a wry face. 'He says he's too near retirement to worry about things like that.'

For the next few minutes, over his coffee and her mint tea, they caught up with each other's lives. Unsure, he danced around her present circumstances.

She feigned impatience. 'I'm not seeing anyone okay? Not regularly at any rate.'

He raised his hands, defensively. 'Just interested in your welfare.'

'Humph.'

She asked how things were with Rosanna. He wasn't sure whether she meant Rosanna herself, or their relationship. He played the straight bat.

'She's fine. In fact she's singing tonight, here in Manchester.'

'Good for her.' She seemed genuinely pleased. 'And the house in the hills? Last I heard it was shaping up to be a bit of a challenge?'

He gave her a progress report.

'How're you both coping?'

He blew out his cheeks. 'Choose another topic.'

She made a sympathetic face before moving back to safer ground. She told how things were back at Warrington, and brought him up to date with recent gossip. In response to her question, he described the state of things around the agency. She made the appropriate noises. Eventually he got up and wandered around the bare office she was yet to put her stamp on. Several cardboard boxes littered the floor. He wondered which one contained her Vettriano prints.

'So. Where are you all up to?'

Her face changed, a trace of exasperation showing through. 'Not where I expected we'd be. I thought it would be up and running by now.'

'Patience. Setting up a new unit always takes longer than people imagine. It was the same at Chain-link.'

'Speaking of which.' She pointed through the door. 'Aren't those some of your old files in there?'

He nodded. 'When are you going to start on them?'

'I've already begun.' She waved a thumb in the direction of a pile of boxes over in a corner he hadn't yet noticed.

About to ask which they were, he remembered his conversations with Broom and The Duke. She would ask if she needed anything. Forcing himself to resist, he nodded at the list of names she'd written on her white board.

'What's that?'

'The Duke's got me writing up the cases we've been sent so far. While we're waiting for live ones he wants me to allocate them out to the rest of the team to start summarising.'

'Good idea. It'll give them something else to think about.'

She threw him an uncertain look which he blanked, glad to know that the balance of power hadn't entirely shifted yet. Not sure if she had ever met The Duke's wife, he hesitated before asking if she'd heard about her illness. Her sad nod told him she had.

'I was so upset. The last time we met she seemed so well.'

Carver agreed. He still found it hard to believe that the days of the outgoing woman who was the only person he'd ever met able to overturn The Duke's moods, were numbered now in months.

'I believe she's going into a hospice?'

'The end of the week,' Carver said. 'It'll be hard for him. He wants to nurse her through to the end himself.'

Jess looked stunned. 'She's that far gone?'

Carver nodded. 'You may not see much of him after the next few weeks.'

'We'll manage.'

'I've no doubt you will.' But he couldn't stop himself adding, 'But you know where I am if you need anything.'

'Thanks.' She changed the subject. 'So when are you joining us?'

He gave a wry shake of the head. 'Don't you start. I've been told to keep my head down. And stay away from operational work.'

She looked dismissive. 'I seem to remember them telling you that once before.'

He nodded. He'd been under similar orders when Anne Kenworthy decided she ought to protect her inheritance by contracting a German hit-couple to get rid of potential threats.

She continued. 'And look what happened.'

He shrugged. 'Which is why I probably shouldn't even be in here.'

She pinned him with a look. 'Well I won't tell, if you won't.'

Uncertain as to her precise meaning, he checked her face, but she was giving nothing away. He let it go. As she turned back to her organising, he caught what looked like a sly, half-smile.

She seemed to remember something, turned back. 'How are… other things? Have you heard from that Lake Superintendent guy lately?'

The questions were typical Jess. Sensitive, but demanding answers. If she hadn't asked, he wouldn't have mentioned anything. *Let sleeping dogs…* Nevertheless, he was grateful. She could have been more direct.

Are you still suffering with the nightmares?

Are you still thinking she could have survived?

Are you still ringing the lake superintendent every couple of weeks, just in case a body has washed ashore and he's forgotten to ring you?

He remembered the last time he and Jess had spoken, months before. On that occasion, he had told her about the copy of the old Cheltenham Ladies College Student Record he'd turned up. It referred to the student-subject representing the college in county and regional level high diving competitions. He also mentioned the report from the lake superintendent concerning the rowing boat reported missing from its mooring sometime around the night in question, and which was eventually discovered beached across the other side of the lake, near the road. Jess was dismissive, telling him he was being ridiculous - *High-diving? Oh come on. She didn't 'high dive'. She fell. A hundred feet. And already half-dead.* - and accusing him of trawling for facts that could be made to fit within the scenario he was determined to weave.

This time, and given her previous responses, he thought non-committal was probably best.

'Yeah, they're good, and... Not recently.'

He didn't mention that just the day before, he'd decided to wait until Friday before ringing Monsieur Dupont again. Three and a half weeks wasn't bad. The longest he'd managed so far was nearly five.

She got the message, switched tack.

'So what about this morning? How did that go?'

He told her.

'They didn't go for it?' She was incredulous.

'Nicholas Whitely was there.'

'Oh.'

He showed his hands as if to say *And there you have it.*

'I thought you looked a bit down.'

'I'm not down.'

She pinned him with a look. 'Take it from me. You're down. I can tell.'

For several moments they stared at each other. Two detectives whose joint experience had forged a bond of which neither ever spoke. This time it was she who broke the silence.

'But if you say you're not, I believe you.'

Before they could get into further argument, Carver's mobile rang.

'Who?... Sarah?... Yes, she's my sister.... WHAT? Where?... How is she?...' He listened, then, 'I'll come straight there.' He hung up.

'What's happened?'Jess said.

He saw her concerned look. She knew about Sarah. Not all of it, but enough. 'Sarah's in Salford Royal. She stepped out in front of a bus.'

CHAPTER 11

It was long past two a.m. when the three young men - all Brits - finally found their way back to their budget apartment complex. As they approached the marble steps leading up to Reception, the tallest of the three, Mickey, shook off his companions' supporting embraces, making ready to attempt the climb unaided.

He managed the first step before catching his foot on the second and starting to keel over. As luck would have it, and despite the nine Keos and uncounted B-52s he had consumed that evening, there was vestige enough of his Sunday League Football training left in him that he managed an almost graceful mid-air twist so that he ended up in a sitting position on the third step, instead of face down on the marble.

'Jees-USS, Pikey,' Mickey slurred. 'I *must* be pissed.'

'Nahh,' the one called Pikey gave back. 'You're just rat-arsed,'

'PISSED *AND* RAT-ARSED,' the third of their number, Damon, called into the night, thus sharing the information with any holidaymakers who might still be awake at nearly three in the morning.

Their guffaws echoed around the complex.

'SSSSSHHHHHHHHH,' Mickey said, index finger

hovering over his lips and spraying spittle over his friends as they took his arms and lifted him again. 'We'll get another fuckin' bollocking from Georgey-boy, if we're not careful.'

'So what?' Damon said, brave for once. 'The Cypriot twat'll get a smack if he starts anything, right Pikey?' Being the youngest, he was also loudest.

'I'll give you a smack if you get us chucked out again,' Pikey answered. 'We had enough of that in Majorca.'

Chastened by their pack leader's reminder of their last holiday-in-the-sun disaster, Damon decided to contain himself as they staggered up the remaining steps. Eventually they spilled out into the semi-lit reception area.

George was waiting behind the desk.

'Georgey,' Pikey declared, as if delighted to see him. 'You've stayed up for us. Are you coming up for a drink? We've got some cans in the room.'

In his mid-fifties, George Opodopolis, had worked as the Limassol Almethia Garden's resident night-porter for fifteen years. He was well-used to dealing with drunken Brits. He smiled the patient smile he had learned to use in any number of ways as he regarded the trio.

'Thank you boys, but no. You need your rest before tomorrow. So you can start early for your last night in our beautiful Cyprus.'

Mickey's face fell. 'Las' night? Tomorrow?' He breathed the words out in a haze of alcohol before turning to Pikey. 'S'not our las' night, is it Pikey?' Pikey nodded. 'Aww, fuck.' Mickey meandered over to the desk. 'Giz the key then George. We better fuck off to bed so's we can recover.'

'Your friend has already taken it. You will have to knock him up.'

The three exchanged puzzled looks.

'What friend?' Pikey said. 'We're all here.'

'Yeah,' Damon confirmed. 'We ain't got no friends.'

Beginning to feel sick, Mickey collapsed into one of the vestibule's whicker chairs. 'Yeah….'

George frowned. 'You know. The other one. The one who has been with you all week.' He looked across at Pikey. 'The thin, bald one. I am thinking he is this one's brother.' He nodded towards Mickey, now slouching in the chair.

Stifling the belch that if he wasn't careful could become a hurl, Mickey managed to sit up. 'He might look a bit like me… *burp*… but he's not my brother. I haven't got a fuckin'… *urrch*… brother.'

George's frown deepened as Pikey stepped forward.

'He's just some local who mated up with us at the beginning of the week. He ain't one of us, George.'

'But he has been staying in your room. I am thinking he was with you?'

Guilty looks passed between the three. 'Errm… we've just been letting him crash with us, that's all. We just said he was with us so he wouldn't have to pay. We haven't seen him all night.'

George froze, his dark, Cypriot eyes sliding from one to the other, realisation dawning.

'Tch. You silly English sods.' He reached behind the desk for his passkey. 'Come on.'

George waited in the doorway as the three tried to work out what was missing. Given their condition it was a stop-start process.

'Me tablet's gone.'

'It's on the table, you wanker.'

'The bastard's had it away wiv me iPad.'

'Wot's that on the bed?'

'My spare fifty quid's missing.'

'So's mine.'

'Bastard.'

George raised his eyes to the ceiling and sighed. 'Passports?'

'What?'

'Where are your passports? You didn't hand them in to the hotel for safe-keeping. You must have them.'

Damon stood up, swayed, then went over to the chest of drawers. He opened one and started pulling out handfuls of shorts and socks, dropping them on the floor.

'S'alright. They're here.' He held the maroon booklets aloft.

'How many?' George said.

'Three.' Only then did he think he ought to check. 'Shit. Two.'

'Fuck,' Pikey said. 'Whose is missing?' The three huddled, looking for the pages with the pictures.

'This is….'

'…Mine.'

'And this one's…'

'Your's.'

They all turned to George, beginning to appreciate the fact he was sober.

'Bollocks,' Mickey said, his head clearing, rapidly. 'The bastard's nicked mine.'

CHAPTER 12

Carver cradled the phone between neck and shoulder so he could carry on typing. He had promised his Regional Director he'd let him have the assessment he'd asked for on Albanian involvement in High School drug-dealing around the North West the next day. But returning from his latest meeting with Neil Booth that afternoon, he'd decided to call in on Sarah again. Now he was way behind.

But at least Rosanna wasn't making an issue of him being late again, though he knew that the guilt-credit he'd earned when she ripped into him for missing her College of Music performance – before he managed to tell her about Sarah's 'accident' – would not stretch too much further.

'She's about the same,' he said in response to Rosanna's question. 'Still limping. But it's not her body that bothers me. It's her lack of interest in everything. It's as well Patsy's so capable otherwise I don't know where they'd be.'

'It is so sad,' Rosanna said. 'They are such lovely children…. To have a mother like that.'

Carver squirmed. Though not blind to his sister's failings, he still found it hard to acknowledge them to others, even Rosanna. 'If she could just get herself back to work, it would do her the world of good. I'm sure if someone gave her a break she would respond.'

Rosanna's silence spoke to her scepticism. 'What was the house like?'

Carver breathed deep. 'Not as bad as it has been. But I think that's mainly down to Patsy, and that neighbour of hers, Joyce. She's been great.'

'Perhaps you should send her something. As a thank you. Flowers perhaps?'

'Maybe,' though he knew he wouldn't. Joyce was a divorcee, and not bad looking when she put her mind to it. The couple of times they'd met at Sarah's, he'd seen the way she looked at him. Flowers - any gift for that matter - ran the risk of sending the wrong signals.

'Anyway,' Rosanna said, making an effort to sound brighter. 'What time will you be home? I am doing Espatadas.'

An image formed of the wine-soaked Kebab dish that was one of Carver's favourites, and he wondered again how to get the message across without hurting her. He much preferred to leave that sort of meal to his days off, when he could enjoy it properly. Now, as he had known he would, he regretted being tempted by the lunchtime steak-pie and chips that had been on offer in Longsight's cafeteria. He thought to try and put her off.

'Erm, not sure yet. Might not be until nine-ish.' *Too early.* 'Towards ten, more like.'

'S'okay,' she said. 'I will do it slow. It should be fine.'

Putting the phone down, he thought it was time he remembered. In Portugal, nine o'clock is considered early dining.

He focused on finishing his assessment, but his mind

kept wandering. The conversation with Rosanna had set it off, even more than his late-afternoon drop-in at Sarah's. After a few minutes he gave up, saved his work and closed down. He would come in early next morning and finish it. After all he would be up, Alun was still seeing to that.

Reaching down, he opened the desk bottom drawer. Two thick folders, one green, the other buff, sat side-by side, staring up at him. They were both bound with thick, white elastic bands, and as his gaze settled on them the illusion came, as it had done before, that they were in some way vying with each other to see which he dared lay hands on, which set off memories, regrets, doubts and fears he would choose to immerse himself in this day.

But even as he reached for the green one - in years gone by a green crime folder denoted 'Series Crime' - he felt the other tugging at him. But with nothing new to add to it - as there had not been for many months now - he managed to resist. The last time he had opened it, the best part of an afternoon disappeared in fruitless what-iffing. She may be dead - *keep telling yourself that* - but her ability to invade him remained undiminished.

He closed the drawer more firmly than was needed, placed the green folder square in front of him. As he did so, he felt the churning that always came in the moments before he opened it - just like the one still in the drawer.

He opened the cover and there she was again. The happy, smiling teenager who, knowing he was growing up behind her, used to take the rise out of him every opportunity she could get. He took a deep breath to purge the emotions that were a distraction, then started turning pages until he found what he was looking for, the sheet of paper headed simply, 'LIST OF EXHIBITS' Returning to the front of the folder, he picked up the list he'd compiled himself, the last time he read through all the depositions.

As he set about comparing the two, checking the reference numbers against the relevant witness statements in which they were referred to, he felt himself beginning to relax. It was the sort of work he was comfortable with - checking the evidence.

'Now then,' he muttered. 'Let's see where everything is.'

He was still there at half-past ten when Rosanna rang to tell him her Espetadas were ruined.

CHAPTER 13

Lucy Donovan checked her watch. It was nearly seven o'clock already. If she didn't catch the ten-past bus, the seven-thirty wouldn't stop if it was full. Swinging round the newel-post, she shouted up the stairs.

'What have you done with my black jacket, Mama?'

'I haven't seen it Lucine.' Her mother's plaintive cry echoed down to her. 'Is it under the stairs?'

'NO!'

Lucy scurried back down the hallway into the kitchen. Her mother's obsession with tidiness was becoming worse and Lucy was spending more of her time each day looking for things. A muffled shout came from above. Lucy shut the kitchen-cupboard door - there was no room for the jacket in there anyway - and poked her head out.

'What Mama? Did you say something?'

'I said will you check on Dadda before you go out? I don't think he's feeling well.'

'I'M LOOKING FOR MY BLOODY JACKET.'

She regretted the snap at once. The years seemed to be catching up with her mother faster than ever of late, and Lucy knew she found it hard during the day when she wasn't around to help. Of course she would check on him. She always did. He was still her father. That never changed.

Where's the damn jacket?

A minute later, having found it hanging in the utility room next to the kitchen, she pushed open the door to the downstairs front room and poked her head in. As always, she ignored the voices telling her she should leave him to stew in his own juices, *just once*.

The room was in semi darkness. Her mother had only drawn the curtains a few inches when she brought him his early morning darchin. He was sitting up in bed, waiting for her.

'What's wrong with you now?' she said.

He grunted, the way he usually did before speaking to his only daughter, so she would know how he begrudged having to rely on her. 'My stomach. It hurts. What was in that *goulash* you gave me last night?'

'Only what I usually put in it. Have you been to the toilet yet?'

'Paprika. You always use too much paprika. It does my stomach no good.'

You miserable, ungrateful old- 'Mama and I had it and we are fine. Go to the toilet.'

'Help me then.' He held his arms out. She checked her watch. Five-past already. Not enough time.

'OOHH!'

Coming round the bed, she lifted the seat on the commode, holding her breath so as to stifle the heave that always came despite her keeping it spotlessly clean. As she helped him swing his withered legs round, she saw that the sheets would need changing again. Mama would have to do it. She stood under him and let him use her shoulders and back to lever himself up, round and onto the chair. She pulled his pyjama bottoms off –

they needed cleaning as well – and left him to it.

She walked out, dropping his pants in the bin next to the door, then closed it behind her. She didn't expect to hear, 'Thank you.' She wasn't disappointed.

Leaning back against the door, she waited, letting her breathing calm. It was becoming harder to show patience with him these days, his surly demands more difficult to cope with. She wasn't sure whether it was him or her, but suspected it was due to seeing what the strain was doing to her mother. And the other thing of course. That never went away either.

It made her think again about what would happen when her mother could no longer look after him, which, the way things were going, might not be as far away as she had once imagined. She also wondered whether the ridiculous thoughts that came to her now and again as she lay in her bed were so ridiculous after all. The old conflict. Justice versus family.

Her mother's mottled legs appeared at the top of the stairs.

'Is he alright?'

'He's fine. He's on the loo. His bed needs changing. See you tonight.'

As she shut the front door behind her, she stopped on the step and breathed in deeply, letting the morning air flush away the old-person-in-care smell that pervaded the house and that not even fresh flowers and Lavender-Haze ever fully masked.

'Morning Lucy.'

She looked to her right. Mr Norris was next to his car on the hard-standing that had once been the small garden. He gave her his fatherly smile, the sort she wished she could have known when she was growing up, though she suspected that given half a chance, any attention Mr Norris might bestow on her would not be of the fatherly variety. She had noticed the way his bursts of enthusiasm for gardening always seemed to coincide with those odd occasions when she managed to find time to relax on their small patio at the back. What the hell, she thought. Nothing wrong in that. He was pleasant enough. She wondered how old he really was. Fifty? Well-past the 'mid-forties' he had once hinted at, that was for sure. Apart from the grey hair, the paunch that hung over his belt was the giveaway. Nevertheless, the thought that *someone* appreciated her - as a woman - made her feel better. She tossed her head back so her long, dark hair blew in the morning breeze as she returned his smile.

'Hello, Mr Norris.'

'How's your dad this morning?'

She managed to keep the smile going as she said, 'Okay thanks. Sorry, got to rush.' Giving a quick wave, she hurried off towards the main road.

She was still fifty yards away when the bus sailed passed, already slowing for the stop where she would have been if she hadn't had to see to him.

'Oh no.'

She started running, but knew she would never make it.

Barry Norris watched, admiringly, as Lucy sprinted for the bus. Since he'd started going to the gym regularly – he was almost averaging twice a week now - he was certain she had begun to look at him differently. And why not, he thought? He wasn't doing too bad for fifty three. It was just a damn shame her family circumstances meant there was never a chance to catch her on her own; it would have been nice to invite her in for a drink those weekends his wife was away at her mother's. Still, he thought, you never know; if that miserable father of hers ever pops his clogs….

About to get into his car he glanced across the road, and stopped. A man was there, looking off in the direction Lucy had just run. There was something about him Norris thought wasn't quite right. But he wasn't sure whether it was the pensive look in his face – as if he had just seen something he hadn't expected to see - or the fact that for the time of year he was overdressed in a long, dark coat; a bit like that weird bloke in those Matrix films. But before he could decide whether it was just his imagination or something he should do something about – the latest Neighbourhood Watch letter had mentioned a couple of burglaries in the area over the past month – the man seemed to sense he was being observed. He turned towards Norris and for the first time Lucy's neighbour realised he was ethnic. Definitely not white British, that's for sure. But which part of the world he, or his family hailed from, Norris could not even begin to guess.

The young man looked directly at him for several seconds in a way Norris found strangely unsettling, before he flashed a humourless smile, raised a hand in some sort of hello-goodbye gesture, and walked off down the street.

As he backed his car off his drive, the thought in Norris's mind was that maybe it was time he got round to fixing the window locks his wife had been nagging him about for weeks after all.

'Don't worry.'

Carver turned to see the man looking at him, knowingly, and guessed why. He must have witnessed the same reaction many times, probably even been waiting for it. His next words confirmed it.

'They take pressure readings every two months. The whole thing's as stable as the day they first started mining. Or so they tell me.' He turned back to the gate, rattling the large bunch of keys he had taken off his belt-loop. 'Let's get to it.'

As Carver watched his guide's ample frame huddle over the gate's locks, chains and electronic-keypads, he wondered what sort of policeman would apply for a job that required him to work deep underground, looking after the force's main Document and Property Archive.

A three years-retired Community PC, Dave Sawyer seemed normal enough and didn't appear yet to have turned into any sort of troglodyte. Nevertheless his little joke about the problem they'd been having with the worn winch-cable when the cage-lift suddenly lurched and juddered on their way down, evidenced a sense of humour that might be a little dark for some people's tastes. But he clearly took his job seriously. During the ten-minute-plus drive from the lift shaft to the storage areas – Carver couldn't work out how he found his way; he didn't see a single direction sign or marker – Sawyer spoke like an enthusiastic tour guide, giving chapter and verse not just on the facility itself, but on the mine's fascinating, two hundred-year history. By the time he finished, Carver didn't feel the need to take up Sawyer's offer to put his name down for one of the regular, VIP Guided Tours.

With a buzz, a click and a clank, the gate to the

compound swung open. They stepped inside.

Everything was stored in uniformly-sized boxes arranged on rows of shelves that ran away down the length of the vast compound. The racks were of black metal and Carver remembered Sawyer's words as they'd driven past an abandoned salt-digger. 'Metal doesn't oxidise down here. No water vapour in the air.'

Sawyer booted up the computer on the desk next to the gate and spent a few minutes checking the database against the details Carver had given him. 'Ah yes. I remember now. This way.'

He led Carver down the far right-hand aisle, deep into the store's bowels, switching on more lights as they went. After what Carver estimated must have been a hundred yards or more, Sawyer started checking shelf numbers and individual box bar-codes. Eventually he stopped, pointing at one of the shelves.

'This is where the file was. Right where it should be.' He read from the sheet of paper he had printed off from the computer. 'Now the exhibits should be….' He checked the shelf again. 'Here.' He indicated several boxes and between them they lifted them down onto one of the work tables that were spaced, intermittently, between the racks. As Sawyer brought the last one over he said, 'That's it. Check them out.'

Carver lifted the lid off the first. It was full of sealed plastic bags. He started pulling them out, checking their labels, examining their contents through the clear plastic and ticking them off on the list he'd brought with him. Satisfied, he moved onto the next box. Halfway down he came across a pair of shoes, in separate bags but clipped together. They were white, with straps inlaid with diamante, and high heels. Clubbing shoes. Even before he read the label the feelings of regret and bitterness started to rise. A sudden giddiness came over him and he had to grab the edge of the table to steady himself.

'You okay?' Sawyer said from a few yards away, concern in his voice. 'Just breath slow and deep. It happens like that sometimes. Creeps up on you without you realising it.' Carver didn't bother telling him his stall had little to do with depth-sickness.

As the feeling passed, he lifted the bag and examined its contents more closely. He had been right. They were the ones she'd bought from Manchester's Arndale Centre – Dorothy Perkins - that last Saturday afternoon they all went out together, a few weeks before the Manchester bombing. He could even remember her trying them on, pirouetting as she checked how they looked in the shoe-mirror, trying to embarrass him by asking him what he thought. Like a boy of fourteen would have an opinion on his sister's choice of footwear.

He put them to one side, along with the rest and carried on rummaging. But after finishing the second box and moving onto the third, a frown began to break across his face. It deepened as he moved quickly onto the next. 'Where's all the…?' By the time he finished checking the last box, the frown had become fixed. 'This can't be right.'

'Problem?' Sawyer said, appearing at his side, anxious in case the detective had unearthed a glitch in his carefully managed system.

'There's no under-clothing. Or swabs. The exhibit lists shows bras, knickers, that sort of thing, and swabs from all the victims but there's none here. This is all just outer clothing and random stuff recovered from the scenes and during the investigations.'

'Hang on.' Sawyer checked his papers then went and searched the shelves again. He returned, shaking his head. 'No. These are all the boxes listed.'

'Does your system show what should be here?'

Sawyer shook his head, regretful. 'All I have is a case file number and its relevant storage references. The packaging is all done by area staff. We just take the boxes and put them into the system.'

'Has any one else accessed any of this stuff?'

'No one's ever called for anything this old until you asked us to dig out the case-file a few weeks ago. I'd have remembered.'

'So if anything's gone missing it'll have happened before it came here?'

'Absolutely.'

'Damn.'

'Is this a complaint investigation?'

Carver thought a moment before replying. 'Not really. Just reviewing some old cases. Intelligence cross-checking, you know.'

'Never into that. I was a beat bobby.' He said it the way some men, out drinking and meeting other men, feel the need to stress their hetero-credentials. 'Anything else I can do?'

'You can let me know if anyone else asks about the file. Or me.'

'Will do.'

Carver was still musing on the significance of everything that might have contained trace DNA being missing as he stepped, squinting and blinking, into daylight. He handed his helmet and utility belt back to Sawyer.

'Thanks for your help.'

'No problem.'

As they shook hands Carver's mobile rang. It was Jess.

'Where've you been? I've been trying you for ages but all I could get was 'unobtainable'.'

'I've been undercover.'

'What?'

'Never mind. What's up?'

'I've had a call from someone who says he met us at that Staff College lecture you dragged me along to last year. The one you gave on repeat-homicide investigation? He wants to speak with you but wasn't sure where you are working these days. Says it's urgent.'

'Who is it?'

'A Doctor… Kahramanyan, I think he said his name is. He was ringing from Cyprus, but he's from Armenia apparently.'

Carver started. Cyprus? Armenia? Who the hell…? 'What does he want?'

'Wouldn't say, but he wants you to phone him back as soon as you can. Says it's a matter of life and death.'

CHAPTER 15

'Uh-huh…. Yes…. Right.'

Carver was slumped over his A4 pad, scribing furiously as he kept up the stream of monosyllabic grunts and acknowledgements that had been the pattern for the past ten minutes.

In a chair the other side of his desk, Jess was doing her best to follow his scribbles. Initially only mildly curious, her interest had risen as she saw the change in him once he finally got hold of the Armenian psychiatrist.

To begin with, he was politely cordial. 'Doctor Kahramanyan? Jamie Carver. You've been trying to get hold of me?' But once the initial pleasantries were out of the way – Carver professed to remember him, though Jess doubted it – his eyebrows began to knit together. Catching the laden glance he threw her as he reached over for his notepad, Jess came on full alert. When he started blowing his cheeks out and 'Good-God-ing' down the phone, she took a seat and concentrated on trying to pick out key words that might give her a clue. So far she had, 'asylum', 'escaped', 'butchered', 'Armenia' 'family' and 'Cyprus'.

Now she was trying to read his notes upside down, having provided him with another pen that worked in response to his urgent finger-clicking. Thereafter, his grave looks dwindled until they stopped. He hadn't glanced her way for several minutes now, concentrating on getting it all down. Eventually he finished scribing and sat up.

'Okay, I think I've got it all. That's one hell of a story, Doctor.' He stopped again as he listened. 'I will, you can count on it.' There was another lengthy pause, during which he slumped back into his chair. 'I'm not sure about that, but it rings some bells. I need to do some research this end. Yes I think you should. Let me know when you will be arriving.' The conversation was winding up. 'And thank you for contacting us…. I will, as soon as I can.' He hung up and sat staring at the phone.

Jess had seen it before and waited. After a minute's silence he came to and looked up at her. All he said was, 'Bloody hell.'

'What was the name again?' Jess called across the room.

Carver didn't slow in his searching. 'Durzlan. It was next to your Met guy's desk with a load of others.' As he spoke, Carver continued shifting plastic packing-cases containing box-files from one pile to another, double-checking the names-sheets against the contents, in case they had somehow missed it. Down the other end of the office Terry West, the Merseyside DCI Jess had said was beginning to show some regrettable traits and Alec Duncan muttered to each other as they searched through another stack. The Scotsman's distinctive burr drifted down the room.

'What was that, Alec?' Carver called, hopeful.

'I said the next time the lassie asks me if I want a job, I'm going to pass. I should'a known the only reason she got me here was so's she would'na hae to ruin her nails rummaging through boxes.'

'I'm looking as well, Mr Duncan,' Jess countered. 'In case you hadn't noticed.' She stood up so he would see the redness brought on by her exertions. About to resume her searching, she just caught Carver's disappearing wry smile. 'Something amusing?'

He threw her a glance. 'No.' Then added. 'I didn't realise you still did het-up.'

She turned to make sure the others weren't listening. 'Up yours, Chief Inspector. And this is hot, not het-up.'

'Ah.'

A triumphant shout forestalled any further point scoring. 'Got it,' West said.

A few minutes later they were gathered round Jess's desk, examining papers, studying photographs and checking lists of witness statements. The Duke had joined them. Carver was going through the report headed, 'Report of Investigating Officer', reminding himself of the gruesome facts.

'My God,' Jess said.

Carver looked up. She was holding a set of photographs in one hand, the other up to her mouth. The Duke stood next to her, looking grim. As the others gathered round to see what had drawn her reaction, similar expressions of shock emanated as they caught their first glimpse. Carver remained seated. He didn't need reminding. The images of the Durzlan murder-scene had been indelibly etched in his memory long ago.

It was getting on for five years since he'd last

perused the case-file that was among the first that came to him during his stint at Chain-Link, the National Crime and Operations Faculty's first attempt at linking undetected murders. But of the hundreds he reviewed during that period, the slaughter of the Manchester-Armenian family was the one that had stuck most in his memory as the most disturbing. Clearly the work of a seriously warped mind. Back then, the Durzlan case was destined to be classified as a one-off. Nothing else amongst all the cases Chain-Link reviewed ever hinted at a connection. Not that it would have needed analysts of any great profiling ability to spot one. The distasteful and, especially for those with families, distressing characteristic of the killer's MO, doesn't feature often in the annals of repeat homicide investigation, not in the way it did in the Durzlan Case at any rate. As a result it remained on the, 'Unlinked-but-Potential' list, one of several cases that had sufficient ticks against the relevant boxes to indicate that its pattern must, surely, show up again somewhere. But despite the analysts' expectations, no matches were ever found. Not, that is, until Doctor Mikayel Kahramanyan's phone call offered up the tantalising prospect of an explanation none of the so-called experts on Chain Link – Carver included – had ever considered.

Now, as he saw the look of horror on Jess's face, Carver stopped trying to work out the apparent problem with the dates – it was something for another time – and turned his attention to the matter in hand. But before he could start, Jess chimed up.

'Is this the same as what this Doctor Kahra-whatsisname is talking about?' Her eyes were glued to the photograph album as she leafed through.

Carver nodded. 'As soon as he described his MO, I remembered it. It's not the sort of thing you forget in a hurry.'

'I'll bet….'

But Carver wasn't the only one conscious of the apparent anomaly. Alec Duncan voiced his puzzlement.

'But why would he come all this way to kill one family, and then go back just in time to get himself arrested and banged away in some Asylum? And how for God's sake? It doesnae' make sense.'

Carver dropped the IO's report in front of him and leaned back in Jess's chair. About to put his feet up on the desk, he caught the look in her face, and changed his mind.

'That's *one* thing we need to think about, Alec.'

He saw Jess's eyes narrow, picking up on it. He didn't keep her waiting.

'The other will be finding out why he's coming here again, and who he's after.'

In the stunned silence that greeted his words, Carver drew meagre satisfaction from noting that temporarily desk-bound though he might be, he still knew about timing. Wary glances passed between them, before they all turned on him.

'WHAT?'

CHAPTER 16

Carver didn't need his detective skills to work out that the slight figure who rounded the screen into Manchester Airport Terminal 1 Arrivals Hall was the man he was there to meet. Most of the passengers were either returning holidaymakers pushing trolleys loaded with baggage, Cypriot students returning to their studies, or older Cypriots visiting family. Somehow, the man sporting circa-nineteen-seventies-NHS-style spectacles, a trilby and a jacket that was too heavy for even the early British summer, had 'Psychiatrist' stamped all over him. As Carver started to push his way through the waiting taxi-drivers and relatives, the man spotted him, raised a hand and headed over.

'Nice to see you again Doctor,' Carver said, as they shook hands. Close to, he thought he just about remembered him from their brief Staff College meeting.

Mikayel Kahramanyan's darting smile displaced some of the tiredness in his face. 'And you Chief Inspector. I'm only sorry we meet again under such circumstances.'

'Me too. Let me help with your bags. I'm parked just outside.'

As they left the airport complex, Carver decided he ought to check, just in case the long flight had changed his visitor's mind. 'Are you still okay to get straight on with it? The hotel's not far if you need to freshen up.'

Kahramanyan continued to stare straight ahead, the troubled look having returned. 'If your colleagues are waiting then I think I should meet with them at once. There may be little enough time as it is.'

Carver nodded but said nothing, already sensing the man's air of foreboding. *What are you bringing to us doctor?* he wondered.

Taking the M56 spur that would take them into Manchester, Carver checked left for traffic coming up on his inside. As he glimpsed his passenger's grim expression, he made a mental note to check with Jess later. When they first worked together they had quickly learned how their early impressions of people often matched. He would be interested to know if she also discerned an 'Angel of Death' quality in the Armenian's quiet demeanour.

They arrived at SMIU's offices to find platters of sandwiches and jugs of orange juice waiting. Kahramanyan's eyes lit up and the way he wasted no time tucking in made Carver wonder when he'd last eaten a decent meal.

The Duke had arranged for most of the team he had assembled so far – nine - to be present. As they ate, Carver introduced him to their visitor and the three spoke quietly together while Marcus, SMIU's young techie, set up the psychiatrist's presentation. After a couple of false starts, he materialised again at The Duke's elbow.

'Any time, guv'nor.' Not long out of college, the youngster had wasted no time slipping into the jargon.

As everyone took their seats, Carver settled himself

at the back of the room. It was a SMIU show and he intended - *needed* - to keep a low profile. Besides, he already knew most of what Kharamanyan was about to tell. There had been other phone calls after the first. Even so, he didn't intend to miss anything. And he was pleased to see that, like The Duke, the Armenian didn't waste time on preliminaries. Stepping up to the lectern, he nodded at Marcus who threw up the first photograph.

'This is Vahrig Danelian. The so-called Monster of Yerevan.'

The gaunt features of a shaven-headed man with what Carver thought were unusually dark pupils, though it could just have been the poor quality image, stared back at them. Had Carver not known the man was only twenty-four when the photograph was taken, he would have assumed they were looking at someone much older.

Kahramanyan paused long enough to let everyone take in the man's stark features. Apart from their colour, Carver thought there was something manic in the eyes. The longer he looked at them, the more he felt himself being drawn in, like two devouring whirlpools. The effect was almost hypnotic, not unlike someone else he'd known..

'And this is what he does,' Kahramanyan continued, nodding to Marcus. 'His first victim family.'

Carver heard the sounds of people sucking air through their teeth as Vahrig Danelian's face gave way to a scene that left everyone in no doubt they were facing something extraordinary in its depravity. Bloody Hell, he thought, talk about getting straight to the point.

The photograph showed a family of four, parents and two children, a boy and a girl, not yet teenagers by the look of it. Naked apart from the odd pair of knickers, they were arranged in the same circle-of-death sex-montage - father-daughter-son-mother - they had seen in the Durzlan photographs. What must have gone through their minds? thought Carver. And there was something about knowing they were looking at the start of it all that gave the image added impact. The silence was total as everyone stared at the screen, no doubt thinking the same thought.

What sort of mind comes up with such things?

CHAPTER 17

Having got everyone's attention, Kahramanyan began. He spoke in clear, precise English, keeping his voice even and not dramatising, as some might have done. Using more or less the same words as when he first spoke with Carver, he sketched in the background.

Vahrig Danelian had been detained in the Armenian State Psychiatric Institute and Correction Facility some twelve years before, having been declared too insane to be tried for the murder of the seven families he was deemed responsible for killing over a period of several years. Apart from the terrible evidence of his grandparents' bodies in their home where he was eventually arrested, there was nothing to indicate why he did what he did with his victims. The common assumption – that it had to be rooted in some family dysfunction of the most appalling kind - was never able to be investigated, as the rest of his family disappeared around the time of his arrest. One theory was that he killed them and hid their bodies. Another, that having realised the depth of their son's depravity, and unable to face up to, let alone live with the shame, they left to start a new life elsewhere. Either way, Vahrig decided he would do nothing that may shed any light on his motives.

Outwardly pretty normal, Vahrig Danelian had managed to go about life in the village where he grew up without attracting anything other than a reputation for being, 'mostly quiet, but given to being easily excited.' Once he was caught, however, it soon became clear that the 'Monster of Yerevan' - as he had by then been christened in the way mass murderers often are in Eastern Europe - had a deceptively complex personality. Unusually, he seemed able to maintain long periods of total silence, as well as abstinence, refusing food and all attempts at communication with no apparent signs of discomfort or ill effects. It also became clear, very quickly, that he was prone to unpredictable outbreaks of extreme violence, weeks, months even of seemingly peaceful contemplation being suddenly interrupted by bursts of violent anger directed at whoever happened to be around at the time. So seemingly out-of-character were these rages that those charged with looking after him had to be given special training to ensure they were not caught off guard. Even then there were lapses, incidents.... Eventually it was realised that the only way of ensuring the safety of his guardian-carers was to keep him isolated from fellow inmates and medical staff alike, any necessary contact with others – administering medication for example - being subject to the most stringent supervision.

Nor did he ever talk about what he had done; lapsing into one of his 'fugue states' if anyone tried to raise the subject. Time and again police interrogators and teams of psychologists came away empty-handed, having gained no insight whatsoever into the workings of the man's psyche, other than an impression he was harbouring secrets about which the authorities still had no inkling. And that despite his incarceration, he remained steadfast in his belief that, one day, something would happen that would enable him to return to his, 'Missionary Work'. The latter phrase, uttered during a session with Kahramanyan himself, was the only allusion he ever made, and then only once, to the horrors that had brought about his detention.

All this Kahramanyan recounted much as he had to Carver during their telephone conversations. But Alec Duncan was impatient.

'So what's his connection with the UK, Doctor? Does he know someone here?'

'I'm coming to that,' Kahramanyan said, glancing at The Duke, who nodded back. It was important they knew all of it. 'After his arrest the authorities were happy enough just to have stopped the killings. They weren't especially interested in trying to get to the bottom of why he did what he did, particularly in view of his lack of cooperation. They just wanted him put away somewhere where he could do no further harm. At one time they hoped to execute him, but it was around the time Eastern European states were trying to establish themselves as independent from the fragmenting Soviet Bloc. My country stopped executing people who were certified insane to demonstrate how civilised it was.'

'What does that say about Texas then?' Alec mused. It drew some ironic grunts.

Kahramanyan went on to describe his attempts, soon after taking over as the Institute's director, to get to the bottom of the mystery of the Monster of Yerevan. 'I suspect I was the first person to show any real interest in doing so,' he said.

As a first step, he visited the village where Vahrig grew up, spending time trying to get to know the locals. At first, they were so wary no one would speak to him, certainly not about the killer the community had spawned, or his family. But eventually, after repeated assurances he wasn't some government spy out to prove that they were in some way responsible for Vahrig's actions and therefore liable to share in any punishment, he managed to get some of them talking. Not much, but more than they had done up to that point. Through them he learned that most of the villagers didn't believe the theory about him killing the rest of his family. The Danelians were thought to have relatives in Cyprus, the Turkish-occupied sector in the north. Some said they fled there to avoid the attention of the authorities.

'Another thing I learned,' Kahramanyan said. 'Vahrig's mother was part-British. The daughter of an English soldier. Some Second-World-War liaison they believed.'

'The UK connection,' Jess said.

'That and the fact that England has the largest settled Armenian population in Europe. Split between London and, as it happens, here in Manchester.'

'But what makes you believe he's coming here?' Alec said, still focused on the point that had brought them together.

'After Vahrig escaped the blast that destroyed the Institute, I enquired with the police for information about any incidents that may indicate his handiwork. Eventually I heard a story that came from a border policeman. A Turkish hill-farming family had been found murdered. Supposedly, an itinerant migrant worker was responsible. I followed it up. It was the same as in the photograph behind me.'

The shuffles from his audience indicated their growing acceptance of the conclusion they had been led to anticipate, but needed to hear for themselves.

'This brings us to the Cyprus connection,' Kahramanyan continued. There is easy access from Turkey to Northern Cyprus and I wondered if that might be where he was headed. I went there and found another murder. Two weeks ago. A couple in their sixties this time. But like this again.' He half-turned to the image behind him before nodding to Marcus, who took it down. It had served its purpose.

'The police there are looking at the possibility they were related to the Danelians. We know they had connections with Armenia and the UK which makes me pretty sure they were. The thing was, the house was ransacked, which wasn't the case in Vahrig's other killings. It appears that as well as money, the killer also took all the family's photographs, documents, family records, that sort of thing. Presumably to stop anyone else picking up his trail.

'The border between North and South Cyprus is much more open than it used to be. Even without a proper passport, it's not difficult to get across if you are determined. If he did manage it, all he would have to do is steal a passport from a British holidaymaker who looks something like him then buy a ticket and put himself on a plane to the UK. He already speaks excellent English, learned from his mother. Like most countries these days, the Cypriot authorities are more interested in who is coming into the country than going out.'

'But he's still got to get through our own

immigration checks,' Jess said. 'We've tightened up a lot with all the terrorist alerts the last few years.'

Hearing the concurring murmurs, Carver decided a reality check was needed. 'That's the spin. But the NCA ran some tests through holiday-flight airports a few months back, at the Border Force's request. We found that once they've looked at a few hundred passports, most border staff tend to be on auto-pilot. They may be looking at your face while they scan your passport, but they're more likely thinking what they're going to be having for dinner. It's a big problem, and the reason they're looking to get facial recognition into all airports, not just the biggest. But I'd appreciate you keeping what I've just said to yourselves. Border Force are a bit sensitive about it.'

'So he could be here right now?' Jess said.

Kahramanyan nodded.

'Okay so the next question is, why? What is he after?'

Becoming pensive, the psychiatrist stepped from behind his lectern. He looked at the floor as he spoke. 'One of the few conclusions I came to when I was working with him, was that Vahrig hates his family, with a passion I never fully understood. He seems to blame them for what happened to him. My first thought was childhood abuse, but as I said, having lost the family we could never investigate it. Certainly he thinks they abandoned him to his fate when, as he believes, they should have stayed to help him. Not that they could have done anything.' He paused to look up at his audience as he spoke the words he had come to deliver. 'I don't think there is any doubt. Vahrig intends to find his family, then kill them.'

CHAPTER 18

Jess was first to find her voice.

'You think he wants to kill them.., the way he did the others?'

'I fear so,' Kahramanyan said.

Wary glances passed between the detectives as the realisation of what they were facing began to take shape. Jess twisted round to look at Carver. His face was a mask. She turned back to Kahramanyan.

'A question.' Kahramanyan waited. 'The Durzlan family. They were murdered a few months before Vahrig was arrested back in his home country. What are we supposed to make of that?'

The psychiatrist shook his head, regretful. 'I am sorry. It is not something I can explain. I have seen the photographs and I have no doubt it was him. But how he came to be here and why he killed them, I cannot say.'

For the first time since taking their seats The Duke spoke up, addressing his team. 'We'll be needing to establish if the Durzlan family knew the Danelians. There may be something in their background that will explain it.' Heads nodded.

A few minutes later, Kahramanyan concluded his presentation by taking questions from those wanting more detail about their quarry's personal history. Vahrig's original case notes had been destroyed in the blast that destroyed the Asylum, but Kahramanyan's staff had reproduced as many of the psychiatric assessments and police reports as they could get their hands on. He referred the detectives to them. 'For what they are worth,' he added, honestly.

After bringing proceedings to a close, The Duke thanked the psychiatrist for his presentation and called his team to order. 'We'll talk about where we go next after a comfort break. Marcus, we'll need plenty of copies of this bloke's photograph.'

'Right guv'nor.'

'Alec?'

The burly DS turned round, mug already, magically, in hand.

'We'll be needing to put out a PNC Broadcast when we've finished. You can start drafting it soon as you're ready.'

Alec growled his dismay. 'Och, isn't a man allowed to hae a cup o' tea?' The Duke ignored him, knowing the draft would be ready when he asked for it. While some continued to button-hole Kahramanyan, the man in charge of SMIU sidled over to where Carver was talking to Jess. Usually utterly forthright, on this occasion he was strangely reticent.

' Jamie, we, er-.' He stopped, took a deep breath and started again. 'Would you mind looking after the Doctor while we, er, do the necessary?'

Jess turned to her boss, puzzled. 'Won't we need Jamie here while we talk about setting up the enquiry?'

Carver stepped in quickly. 'It's okay, Jess, he's right. I'm supposed to be staying out of SMIU ops.'

'WHAT?'

As Jess turned on The Duke, Carver sensed his discomfort.

'But it was only through Jamie we even got to hear about this character. And he's reviewed the Durzlan case. That will be a key part of it. We ought to at least know how he approached it.'

'I know,' The Duke said. 'It's bollocks. But if Nigel Broom gets a whiff of Jamie getting involved, it's him that will suffer. Not me, or you.'

Seeing her about to try again, Carver threw her a warning look. 'It's alright, Jess. You don't need me for this. There's plenty of experience here and besides, there are other reasons why I ought to keep out of it.'

For a moment she looked blank, but then thought she saw where he was coming from. 'I'm sure Rosanna would-.' She stopped as she caught his glare. 'Okay. If that's what's you both think.'

A long look passed between Carver and The Duke. It ended with the two men nodding to each other.

'I need to catch Mikayel before he goes,' The Duke said, and moved away.

When he was out of hearing, Jess rounded on Carver, angry. 'What was all that crap about? Any other time he'd be telling Nigel Broom to piss off and mind his own business.'

Carver made a calming gesture. 'While I'm working for NCA, it is Broom's business. And right now The Duke's got other things on his mind. Have you ever heard him talk like that before?'

Jess looked across the room to where her boss towered over Kahramanyan's diminutive figure. 'Now that you mention it, no.' She turned back to Carver.

'Cathy?'

Carver nodded. 'He rang me this morning. She may not last as long as the doctors said she would. The last thing he needs now is an internal wrangle with the likes of Nigel Broom. For his sake I'm staying out of it.' Then he added, 'Officially.'

She seemed to take his meaning but still gave an exasperated shake of the head. 'Today's modern Police Service. Politics and bloody bullshit. Now we can't even let our best investigator get involved in helping to catch a homicidal maniac. Madness.' She spun on her heel, about to walk away.

' Jess.'

She stopped.

'Ring me later. Let me know what happens.' She nodded, then went to join the rest of her team.

Alec Duncan materialised at Carver's side. Carver could tell from the way the DS's eyes followed his departing DI, he had been following the conversation. Carver let out a long breath.

'Watch her back, Alec. And don't let her expose herself. I'm not sure yet about this lot.'

'Will do Boss.'

CHAPTER 19

It was lunchtime. The Starbucks on the corner of Oxford Road and Charles Street was as packed as it always is at that time. As Lucy picked up her tray, she spotted a man wearing a dark suit making ready to vacate one of the window stools. Weaving her way through the queues for orders, collections and milk, she slid onto the seat almost before he was out of it, prompting a huffy, 'In-my-grave-next?' look. She flashed what she hoped would pass for an apologetic smile before turning to her lunch and letting out a weary sigh.

It was coming on the end of term and the morning had been even more hectic than usual. Despite the crowded surroundings she welcomed the temporary respite from the lecturing staff's endless demands for reading notes, student assessments and the latest updates concerning next year's curriculum. When she'd applied for the role of 'College Administrative Assistant' her friend at her previous work told her the job would be fairly leisurely, that all she would have to do all day would be prepare the odd letter, write up timetables and make tea. *Wrong*.

But at least things weren't too bad at home at present. Her mother seemed to have rallied of late and didn't seem as tired as she had been. And it was over a week since her father last complained of some imaginary condition that required them to call out the night-locum GP. Their name must be mud at the surgery by now. Maybe it's the weather, she thought as she gazed out at the bustling crowds in their short sleeves and summer dresses. Eventually she remembered the time and came to. She had less than an hour for lunch and needed to get to Boots for her father's prescription.

She picked up her blueberry muffin and bit into it. But it was over-fresh and as the dough crumbled in her hand, half of it fell to the floor.

'How annoying.' A man's voice, right next to her. 'You should try the flapjack.'

Torn between looking down to see if any of it was worth saving or right to see who had spoken, right won. She looked round into eyes that were… strange, but fitted well with the nervous-seeming smile. At first glance she thought he was getting on a bit. But then she realised he wasn't as old as he looked; recovering from an illness maybe? His features were dark, not bad looking if a bit on the gaunt side, and with a vague hint of… where? Not English that was for sure. She was certain he hadn't been there when she sat down, she would have noticed. She tried to look annoyed at having lost half her lunch, but as she never managed a full muffin anyway, it wasn't easy.

He raised his plate, offering his flapjack for her inspection. 'They are very nice. And they do not fall apart.'

Definitely foreign, Lucy thought. The way he rolled his 'r's. But she was already beginning to panic, the swirling, fluttery feeling arriving right on cue.

Who was he? Had she seen him before somewhere? What was he after? *What should she do?*

She gave him a look intended to let him know she wasn't the sort of woman who talked to strange men. But as the initial reflex telling her she ought to get up and leave, *right now*, subsided a little, she had to admit. He wasn't *that* strange. Alright he had a bit of a wild look about him. And those eyes. But the smile seemed genuine, his clothes were clean enough – at least what she could see of them under his long coat - and though he wasn't crowding her too much, she was wary. She was always wary.

'Do I know you?'

'No, but I have seen you here before.' The smile again.

She mouthed an, 'Oh,' and went back to what was left of her lunch, staring intently out the window, pretending not to be conscious of his stare. She hoped she wasn't flushing the way she usually did.

But after a couple of minutes she could stand it no longer. *The best form of defence.* She turned to him.

'Do you want something?'

The smile melted at once, replaced by a look of hurt innocence. His hands came up, defensively. 'I am sorry. I am just being the… friendly. I didn't mean anything.' Suddenly he was like a little boy being railed at by his mother for dropping crumbs. And Lucy knew she had overreacted. *Again.*

'I- I'm sorry. It's been a bad morning.'

'It seems to be so.' He turned away from her, back to his flapjack. 'In that case I will not bother you further.'

Not too determined then.

As she studied his profile, her sense of guilt tempted

her to say something that would recover the situation. *Why? What good would it do? You know it would be a waste of time.* But just then he reached out for the magazine someone had left on the bar, and she knew it was, in any case, too late.

The familiar feeling of despondency washed over her. Biting her bottom lip, she turned around on her stool again. The last thing she had been expecting on such a bright, sunny day was a reminder of just how futile her life was at present. And just when she was thinking things may be improving.

Though she tried, she couldn't finish her coffee. After a few minutes she rose from her seat, making sure she kept her eyes downcast so she wouldn't have to look at him as she left, ashamed of the way she had reacted. *Is this how it will always be*?

But as she passed the window in front of where he was sitting, heading for Boots, she sensed his gaze upon her. For some reason she had the feeling he was smiling.

CHAPTER 20

The sun was disappearing behind the apartment blocks lining Salford Quays as Carver headed back to his office. A few minutes before he had dropped Kahramanyan off at his hotel to freshen up, before they met up again later to take him for something to eat. As they parted, the psychiatrist asked if anyone would be joining them.

'Your lady colleague, Jess, perhaps?'

Carver raised an eyebrow. *You not-so-old fox.* 'I'll ask her.'

But as he made his way through the evening rush hour, he had other things on his mind than livening up their guest's evening.

Though he'd talked it through with The Duke beforehand and had been at pains not to make an issue of it, having to walk out and leave the rest of the SMIU team to their planning had been a whole lot harder than he had imagined. Such investigation planning was his forte. And in all his service he hadn't felt as ineffective as he did right now. A detective unable to do what he does best.

Despite his slump, part of him, the analytical side maybe, was working hard to resist the unthinkable conclusion. That his CID career was over and that he was destined to remain stuck behind a desk until he gave in and put himself up for promotion. Since leaving Kahramanyan he'd been engaging in an internal dialogue, cross-examining himself like some schizophrenic barrister.

What's the matter with you? You know you're a good detective. So does everyone else.

He remembered Nicholas Whitely, at the abortive Crime Committee meeting the week before. *Okay, not quite everyone.*

But there's no reason to throw the towel in. Like Jess said, '*It's just politics and bullshit.*' You don't have to prove anything. You've been there. Done it. Lots of times. So you have to keep your head down for a while. So what? It'll do no harm. Probably a good thing. After all that's happened, it makes a lot of sense.

NO IT BLOODY DOESN'T, he came back at himself.

It only makes sense if you've given in to all this, 'Good for your career,' crap. Since when did you worry what's good for your career? Desmond Wilkins wasn't caught because you were thinking about your prospects. Nor Anne Kenworthy. And Edmund Hart certainly wouldn't have come if you'd been pussy-footing around, treading on eggshells.

Catching criminals. Rapists and killers. That's what drives you, Carver. Not worrying about what other people think. That wasn't why you became a detective. The case-file in your bottom drawer is why you do what you do. The people who do that sort of thing. *They're* why you chose CID over Traffic. So what if you end up back on Division? It's where you came from. *And* there's plenty of work there. Okay, not as interesting as

SMIU perhaps, but at least it's real policing - apart from all the performance and targets bollocks you have to deal with these days. But you can manage that. You've done it before. Better than being treated like a bloody liability.

He checked his watch. Jess still hadn't rung. Probably still at it.

He imagined them, sitting around, brain-storming lines of enquiry, Jess writing them up on a flip chart, like she had done with him, many times. And he thought of the ideas he had come up with as he'd driven Kahramanyan to the hotel, mainly in silence he'd realised after. No wonder the man hoped Jess might join them for some dinner. He probably thought Carver was a right miserable sod. He wondered how close the two lists – SMIU's and his own - may be. He suspected - arrogantly he knew, but what the heck - his would be longer.

He huddled over the wheel, animated by the ideas bouncing round his brain. He checked his watch again. There was probably still time. He could head back there right now and see how they are doing; pass on some of his thoughts. Tell them he couldn't give a flying fuck about Nigel Broom and his dire warnings, that he can help them with the Durzlans, and this Danelian character as well. He could already sense him, smell him almost. *If he comes anywhere near, I'll suss him. It's what I'm good at.* He thought about what he'd say to The Duke. *I'll tell him-*.

The Duke.

If Carver did get involved now, Broom wouldn't stop with him. Within twenty four hours – probably less – he would be making waves in NCA *and* with SMIU's Joint

Chiefs, complaining that The Duke had ignored his – entirely reasonable – request not to involve Carver. Waves like that had a habit of spreading rapidly in the police service. He'd seen it before, experienced it. And the way The Duke's life was right now, with Cathy, he could go under. It was the last thing Carver wanted on his conscience.

The enthusiasm that had suddenly come over him abated as quickly. He eased his grip on the steering wheel, settling back into his seat again. It was no good. Right now there was nothing he could do but bite the bullet.

On the passenger seat next to him, his mobile started ringing. It would be Jess. About to reach for it, he hesitated, unsure about receiving her update without being able to contribute something - assuming the items on his list weren't on hers. *There you go again. So bloody arrogant.*

He looked in the mirror and tried laughing at himself. But as he saw the haunted look reflected in his eyes, he realised. He was behaving like a sulking schoolboy. And Jess wouldn't hesitate to tell him so.

He checked the mirror again, this time to make sure the car behind wasn't fitted with roof lights before flipping the phone's cover back, and hitting 'accept' and the loudspeaker icon. At the same time he made ready to tell her how he'd wound himself up. She would think it amusing, hilarious even.

But in the same instant he accepted the call, his brain registered the fact that the name on the screen he'd barely glanced hadn't read 'Jess.'

'Je-Hello?'

'Jamie?'

'Rosanna. What's up?'

Silence. 'You said you would ring. To let me know what you are doing.' Noises in the background. Yelling and banging.

Oh, shit.

'I was just about to. I, er-.' *What the hell is that racket?*

'No you weren't. You thought I was Jess.'

'GIVE IT ME.' A child's yell. It didn't sound like Jack.

'She's supposed to be ringing with an update on something that's all. I was about to call you. Is that Patsy?'

'No. It's Jason.'

Jason? Oh God.

In that moment, all the dilemmas they were still struggling to reconcile around taking over Jason's custody from his maternal grandparents swooped back from whichever corner of his brain they had been lurking the past few days. And of the several issues he was juggling at present, he knew that his continuing inability to come up with a solution that the boy's grandmother, Sue, didn't regard as compromising on Jason's education and development needs was, right now, his biggest failure. Rosanna was speaking again.

'Sue dropped him off this afternoon. You didn't tell me we were having him as well.'

Carver rubbed his temple. With everything he'd had to do to get ready for Kahramanyan arriving, he'd forgotten he'd agreed to take Jason for the weekend while Sue and Paul took in some London show for their anniversary. When she'd first raised it at the beginning of the week, he'd thought he may manage a couple of hours off and get home early - one of the advantages of not being operational.

'I'm sorry. I forgot to tell you. I-.' He cringed, knowing how weak it would sound. 'I've been running round so much….'

She sighed into the phone. But before she could say anything, more screams in the background.

'JASON. DON'T. Now look, you've hurt Patsy.'

'I'll come now,' he said, guilt sweeping away other plans. If Jess was free he could call in a favour, ask her to look after Kahramanyan. He was sure he wouldn't mind. 'I'll be home….' he checked the time again. Rush hour was still at its height. '-In an hour.' *And pigs fly*.

But she had a point to make.

'How much longer Jamie? This is the third weekend we have looked after the children.'

'I-. We'll talk about it when I get home.'

More screaming.

'This isn't working.'

'It won't be much longer. I'll be home soon.'

'PATSY. DON'T.'

She hung up.

He let the phone fall back onto the passenger seat.

'Bollocks.'

CHAPTER 21

Jess shoved the top back on the marker pen before running her eyes down the list one last time. It was some while since she'd added to it, and now the well seemed to have dried. Which was annoying. She knew damned well that when she ran it past Jamie - assuming she got the chance to do so - it would take only minutes for him to come out with, 'What about…?' In the end, of course, it didn't matter. She could spend all night trying to come up with other things that would need doing. He would still find something. All she could hope was, it wouldn't be something too obvious, and therefore embarrassing. She liked to think she had learned *something* the past couple of years - apart from the obvious. Angling her chair towards the window - it was darkening outside - she leaned back, put her feet up on the desk and stared out, conscious it was something he used to do when he needed to let his thoughts drift.

Earlier, after the others had gone, The Duke had lingered, helping her pick at the couple of threads still to be tied off after their afternoon-long planning session. But even as he spoke about upping the priority on tracking down the Durzlan case-exhibits, Jess could see part of his mind was already elsewhere. 'I thought you're supposed to be seeing Cathy tonight?' she said.

His face said he was. 'You get off. I'll have the list on your desk by morning. We can go over it again then, fresh.' For once, he didn't argue. Now, she was conscious that after several hours of brainstorming, what-iffing, weighing options, and ringing round to see what manpower they could count on if a full scale manhunt became necessary, she was having difficulty focusing.

Over on the horizon, the lights of the Old Trafford stadium signalled that Manchester's most famous brand-name was playing at home that evening. It reminded her of her yet to materialise 'date'. The week she arrived, Dave Rigg, a DI and the only Manchester detective on the team, had slung her a line, boasting about how he could get tickets 'no problem' if she fancied going some time. Not having set foot in a sports stadium since her Uni days, and never having been to a Premier League game, she'd surprised herself by accepting, then added, 'But I'll pay for my own ticket.' Still finding her feet, she was wary about accepting favours, rightly as it turned out. She had heard since that Rigg was seeing a Fraud Squad DS. And when he told her what tickets went for these days, she wondered if she should have been a bit less hasty asserting her independence. Now, staring out, her thoughts drifted again to Jamie. They were doing so more and more of late.

It was clear now that he wasn't the same man who first drew her into CID work. The one she decided after just one week was as good a role-model as she was likely to get for the career she realised could be hers, provided she was willing to learn. But then again, how could he be? Given what he had been through the past couple of years, it would be more surprising, perhaps, if he still was. But she didn't let herself dwell long on the events that had shaped both their lives over that time, and certainly not on the decision that led them to engage the aid of someone who might point them towards the Worshipper Killer in the first place. She had done plenty of that over the past twelve months, and it had taken her precisely nowhere. Right now her concerns were with Jamie - which reminded her she was due to ring him.

She was certain now that his seemingly easy-going, 'I'm fine' assurances, were just a front. Before their meeting with Doctor Kahramanyan, he had spoken a couple of times about getting back to, 'proper investigation work', but seemed reluctant to put a time-frame on it. 'When I'm finished here,' was the best she got out of him. The past couple of weeks, she had sensed an underlying disquiet, mixed with over-interest in hearing about how the old team at Warrington were doing, what they were up to. The relaxed smile and easy banter *almost* convinced her she was mistaken, especially when he mentioned how things were better with Rosanna now they weren't suffering the sort of regular disruption CID brings. But his lack of real enthusiasm for getting back to operational work had set her thinking. It was similar to the sort of disillusionment she saw, now and then, in officers nearing retirement. Only Jamie was a long way off retirement age. And it was something she never, ever, expected she would see in him. It scared her.

The day he took Kahramanyan's call, then went and turned up the Durzlan case, he was as animated and focused as he'd ever been. The old Jamie Carver. But she had seen little of it since. Take that afternoon.

Presented with the ideal opportunity to get involved in something substantial - his previous involvement in the Durzlan case alone would have justified it - he passed, and more quickly than she would have expected. It was almost as if he could not wait to run Kahramanyan back to his hotel, like it was just the excuse he needed to duck out. It made her wonder what else might be going on with him she didn't know about.

The trouble was, there was little she could do. Apart from anything, Jamie had obviously been given clear advice – maybe even threatened - about not getting involved in SMIU affairs. She didn't want to risk tempting him into going against whatever he'd been told. That could only make matters worse. No, there was nothing for it but for her to stay alert and be ready to help him deal with whatever he was going through. Besides, it wasn't as if her life was entirely problem-free right now.

At that moment, an image of her mother loomed large. She was due to ring her as well, sometime. In fact she was supposed to have rung the previous week but never got round to it. Following her father's death, Jess had promised she would stay in regular contact with her mother. But she had always struggled to find the time to get down to the family home in Kent, and was now finding it equally hard to fit in phone calls. The trouble was, her mother's dull-as-dish-water accounts of the church meetings and WI gatherings that were now her life, didn't exactly fire her with enthusiasm for conversation. And then of course there was Howard Leather, and the fact she was yet to say anything to her mother about seeing him.

Based in London, Howard was one of her father's

former business associates. He and her mother still shared the same legal adviser, her avuncular Uncle Arthur. Jess knew that her mother often called in at Arthur's city offices during her regular shopping and theatre sojourns into the capital. 'Keeping in touch with your father's affairs,' she called it. But it meant there was a better-than-fair-chance that she would, eventually, bump into Howard. And Howard wasn't to know Jess had never told her mother about their occasional meetings when business brought him up North, despite them both agreeing that no one could read anything into him taking her out for dinner now and again. If he ever mentioned it to her mother, Jess could imagine her reaction.

Now in his mid fifties, Howard's reputation amongst her parents' former social circle had been tarnished by the disclosure that, throughout his thirty-year marriage to the universally loved and admired Amanda, daughter of one of Her Majesty The Queen Mother's Ladies-In-Waiting, he had availed himself, every Tuesday afternoon, of the services of a Mayfair-based dominatrix who traded under the name, Mistress 'Trixie' Timberlane. Now divorced, and with 'Trixie' having retired to marry a wealthy American client, Howard's oft-heard declarations that he had now come to his senses and turned over a new leaf, still drew sceptical looks from those who knew him best. When Jess first made contact with him - having seen his name on a, 'To be eliminated' list during the Worshipper Enquiry, she found the subsequent meeting and Elimination Interview embarrassing, to say the least. But she found his openness about his exploits, as well as his frank honesty about his marital shortcomings - 'What can I say? I loved Amanda and always will. But I had certain needs she could never satisfy,' disarmingly refreshing. He certainly must have charmed her enough that when he rang her a few weeks later to say he was visiting Manchester and would like to take her out to dinner, 'Just so that we may revive some memories of your dear, old Pa-pa,' - she accepted with good grace. She even managed to resist, during that first date at least, investigating his inferred claim that he no longer felt the needs to which 'Trixie' used to administer. And Jess was in no doubt that if and when her mother did get to hear of it, she would be straight onto her, pointing out how 'wholly inappropriate' such a relationship was; how Howard was old enough to be her father.

She was on the point of picking up the phone, Jamie first then mother, when it rang. It was Jamie. She listened as he explained his dilemma over Kahramanyan.

'Take him for something to eat?' She tried to make it sound like she might already have plans: in truth she didn't. In any case, she'd actually found the quietly-spoken psychiatrist charming in a 'Howard Leather-ish' sort of way. It wouldn't be too much of an ordeal. He explained further. After a couple more minutes she said, simply, 'You owe me.'

It prompted garbled words of gratitude, followed by a not overly-sincere sounding 'You're the best,' before he rang off.

Wow, she thought. He *must* be in trouble. She had been expecting he would fish for some indication as to how things had gone after he left, some acknowledgement at least that they had missed his input, his expertise in the area. But brief though the call was, it was also telling.

Jess knew all about Sarah. Carver had confided in her long ago about his troublesome sister's problems. But Jess couldn't ever remember him taking her kids weekends just to give her a break. And though he hadn't said much about what had happened, she got the impression that things were certainly no better in that department - worse, if anything. Jess had also been surprised to learn that Jason's situation remained unresolved. The last she'd heard - a couple of months after Paris - Jamie and his former girlfriend, Angie's, parents, were working towards some sort of permanent, shared custody arrangement. Which raised the question of what had happened to stall it? Not just the fact of his move to North Wales, surely? Okay, it's a bit of a way from Oldham for grand-parenting visits and such, but it's hardly the other side of the world. Then she remembered. Part of the problem previously had been the opposing views between Jamie and Jason's grandfather over the need - or not - for a paternal DNA test. Grandfather was for one, Carver against. 'I don't need a letter from a clinic to decide my responsibilities,' she remembered hearing him say one time. Which was when the thought came. What if he's taken the DNA test, and it's come back that he isn't the father. In which case…

Oh. My. God.

Jess never met Edmund Hart. He'd hanged himself in prison long before she started working on the Worshipper Enquiry. But she had seen the photographs - and some video. And as one possible explanation for Jamie's slump came to her, an image of Hart - bearded, sneering, horrific given what she now knew - displaced those of Jamie, Angie and Jason that had been swirling around her brain.

But even as the implications of her train of thought started to come thick and fast - not least for Jason himself - she took a mental step back, and stopped herself. Whatever pressures Jamie was operating under right now, they may be nothing to do with Jason. And her thinking about DNA tests and all that could be entirely wrong. She could be adding two and two and getting five - something she was always quick to criticise in others. Whatever was going on with Jamie, it was too soon to start making assumptions, certainly not without evidence to back them up.

Pleased for having stopped her imagination running amok, she reminded herself she needed to resist the impulses that caused her to want to pry into his private life. After all, he'd made a point of not prying into hers, several times.

About to call her mother, she realised the time. Kahramanyan would be expecting someone to pick him up in less than an hour, which meant she did not have time to drive home and freshen up. It didn't matter. She always kept a change of clothes in her office cupboard, though not the sort of thing she would choose for a dinner date. And for all the complaining amongst the NCA staff, the on-site shower and changing facilities were quite decent.

As she left her office, heading for the Ladies, hanger with clean skirt and blouse over her shoulder, Jess tried not to feel guilty for having been so quick to put off ringing home.

CHAPTER 22

Lucy was trying to remove a stubborn bit of burnt-on grease from the roasting pot when the telephone started ringing.

'Can you get it Mama?' she called, trying to make herself heard above the noise of the television in the next room. She waited.

'MAMA. PHONE.'

The game show continued to blare.

'OHHH!'

Dropping the dish back in the water, she rolled a shoulder to wipe perspiration off her face, dried her hands on her apron, and stomped through into the hall.

'I'LL GET IT,' she shouted through the living room door.

'WHAT?' came the reply.

A flyer was hanging out of the letterbox. Lucy snatched at it as she grabbed the handset off the hall table.

'Hello?' As she waited for a reply she glanced absently, at the paper. Something to do with roof repairs, the disclaimer, *WE ARE NOT TINKERS*, in a box beneath.

'Is that you Tamara?' A woman's voice, heavily accented.

For some reason, Lucy imagined her as old, frail. 'No. This is her daughter, Lucine. Who is this?'

'Ah, Lucine. Yes. I remember. You were only a child when I saw you last. This is Nunofar, your mother's cousin, from Cyprus.'

'Cyprus?' Lucy vaguely remembered her mother speaking about family there one time. As far as she knew there had been no contact for many years. Certainly not since they'd arrived in England. 'Hang on. I will get Mama.'

'WAIT LUCINE.'

The abrupt way the woman barked out the command took Lucy by surprise. How rude, she thought.

'I am sorry,' the woman said. 'I did not mean to shout. Are you still there? Lucine?'

For the first time, Lucy heard the anxiety in the woman's voice. Something was wrong. 'Yes. What is it?' But she was already thinking someone must have died. At least it shouldn't be too hard on her mother. They couldn't have been that close.

'First, please tell me. How is your mother?'

Lucy frowned. What to say? How much does this Nunofar know?

'She is not too bad… but getting older, you know? She does not get out much.'

The woman didn't seem surprised. 'No. She was never strong….' There was a moment's hesitation. 'And… your father? Is he…?' Lucy's heart skipped a beat. There seemed to be something more than just family interest in the voice. 'Is he still… alive?'

Lucy swallowed. 'Yes.'

'Ahh….'

'What is it Nunofar? Why are you calling? Has

something happened?'

There was a long sigh, then. 'Yes Lucine. Something has happened. Something very bad.'

Lucy's stomach started to flutter; a feeling of dread beginning to take hold.

'Tell me what is wrong, Nunofar. I will tell Mama. What is it?'

There was a pause as the woman spoke with someone - a man's voice - in the background. The voices were muffled, like her hand was over the mouthpiece, but Lucy thought she heard, 'Does she know?' Eventually Nunofar came back on the phone.

'It is probably best if I tell you. Are you sitting down Lucine?'

'I am alright. Just tell me.'

The woman took a deep breath. 'I have-.' She started again. 'Your mother and I, we have-. We *had* another cousin. Ashken. She and your mother used to write.'

Lucy thought she remembered the name from when she was young. Before they left Armenia. 'What about her?'

There was a long sigh. 'Ashken has been... killed. Her husband too.'

Lucy dropped into the chair next to the table.

Not *died. Killed.*

'I only heard from the police yesterday.' Nunofar's voice started to tremble. 'It is terrible, Lucine. You must tell your mother.' Her voice became urgent, a note of panic entering. 'You must *warn* her.'

'Warn her? About what Nunofar? I don't understand? How did your cousin die?'

The woman started wailing. 'Oh poor Lucine. May God protect you and your family.'

Lucy's heart froze as the woman's wails increased in pitch and she started babbling in Turkish, almost hysterical now. Lucy breathed deeply, forcing herself to stay calm. She needed to know what had happened.

'Nunofar,' she called down the phone, trying to draw the old woman back.

There was a scramble at the other end, shouting, followed by Nunofar's wails, only now she was in the background. A man's voice, gruff, determined said, 'Are you the daughter?'

'Yes.' Lucy was scared now. What was going on?

'You must listen to me.'

More wailing, then Nunofar calling into the phone. 'I will pray for you Lucine.'

'GET AWAY WOMAN,' the man shouted. 'I told you to leave it to me.' Lucy heard a sharp 'crack,' and the wailing stopped. 'Are you still there girl?' the man said, calmer. Like he knew he would not be interrupted again.

'Yes. Please, just tell me what has happened.' Lucy was almost in tears, the waiting too much to bear.

'Ashken and her husband were murdered. Worse than that. They were *butchered*.'

Lucy's hand went to her mouth. *Oh Great God no. It cannot be.*

'Now listen closely Lucine. Your life, and those of your mother and that bastard father of yours, may depend on it.'

CHAPTER 23

By the time Carver parked his Golf under the ramshackle car port that had once been a stable at the back of the house, he was expecting he would be walking into a war-zone.

He was surprised, therefore, when he stepped from his car and the evocative strains of, *'Povo Que Lavas No Rio'*, came to his ears. The kitchen window was open, allowing Rosanna's voice to echo around the courtyard, enveloping him like a warm duvet in winter. Instantly, he was back in Barco-Negro's smoky depths.

Lisbon's famous back-street nightclub was where he first came across the flame-haired beauty whose rendition of the heart-rending ballad – not that he understood a word – rooted itself in his memory and stayed - unlike the rest of his and Gill's abortive, make-or-break holiday. They'd parted soon after. *'Povo'* was also the one she was singing when he chanced upon her again a couple of years later. It was in the aftermath of the Hart case. A well-meaning lady police doctor friend decided it was time he re-entered the real world and dragged him out to a Liverpool Music Festival event - something called The Fado. He didn't make the connection until he saw Rosanna.

He'd always remembered her, but that evening, in a

sparkling white gown split dramatically up the side, she looked stunning. Like everyone else he couldn't take his eyes off her and afterwards waited at the side door, feeling a bit like a stalker. But he managed to catch her eye as she came out, and when he mentioned having seen her in Lisbon she was interested enough to join him for a drink, the following night, dinner. The memory of her face next to his on the pillow the next morning was one he hoped would remain with him forever.

Since then the only times they'd been apart were when he couldn't get out of some training course, or her recitals took her too far away to get back home the same night. One of only a handful of *Fadistas* in the UK, Rosanna never refused an invitation from the surprisingly numerous groups of ex-pat Portuguese living in Britain.

The music stopped, and as the sound of clapping and the children's excited voices broke the spell, he crossed the cobbles to the back door and walked in.

She was standing in the middle of the roomy, unfinished lounge, looking radiant in the trailing, red dress that was his favourite. The three children were sitting in line on the sofa, still clapping. It brought the fleeting thought that he had wandered onto the set of some Sound of Music revival.

'Uncle Jamie,' Patsy squealed, sliding off the sofa to run to him. 'Rosanna's been singing for us. She's *ace*.' The two boys came to join them and as the children bombarded him with questions; 'Would you like Rosanna to sing one for you Uncle Jamie?' 'Are you staying home now Uncle Jamie?' 'Where did you and Rosanna meet?' 'Can we play football?' – the last from

Jason - he looked across at her, and raised a questioning eyebrow. She gave a resigned shrug of her shoulders.

'It was the only way to calm them down. I am glad you are home. I was running out of songs.'

He went to her and put an arm round her waist, feeling the stiffness of the dress's brocade, wondering what she was wearing underneath. He kissed her, lightly, on the lips. 'I'm sorry. You know how it is, sometimes.'

The green eyes flashed. 'Yes. I *do* know how it is.' She turned towards the stairs. 'And now you can entertain them while I change back into something comfortable.'

He tried to placate her. 'Do you have to?'

Stopping on the bottom stair, she threw a glance at the children. Having realised the impromptu concert was over they were already arguing about which movie they would watch next. The look she gave him was pointed. 'Definitely. And next time please give me some warning if I am going to be nanny for the day.'

As she disappeared up the stairs - at least the new handrail still seemed solid - Carver let out a sigh. There had been a time when her arousing home 'recitals' were the prelude to an evening of fine wine, good food, and other things - not necessarily in that order. But it hadn't happened since they'd moved out of the city flat that for eighteen months had served as their temporary home. And for all the lengths she'd gone to to entertain the children, he could tell she was still simmering. He didn't look forward to conversation after the children were in bed.

He turned, eyes searching for the TV control.

'Right, what's it to be? Toy Story, or Shrek?'

CHAPTER 24

Soon after they'd arrived at the restaurant, Mikayel Kahramanyan found himself thinking of poor Gadara. Of how she would have enjoyed being there, what she would have made of it all, what they would have talked about. But as if she somehow sensed what he had been through and was ready for it, Jess skillfully diverted his attention away from the dark reflections that threatened to cast a shadow over the evening.

Now, half way through a juicy peppered steak, Mikayel had to admit that he couldn't remember the last time he'd relaxed in the way he had the past hour. So what if Finnegan's Grill on Lowry Warf was only a, 'Family Restaurant,' as Jess described it? By the standards he was used to, it was most agreeable, whilst the food, hearty and plentiful, was mouth-wateringly delicious. And thanks to his interesting - not to mention attractive - dinner partner, he wasn't missing Carver's company one bit.

During the afternoon he had sensed that something in the detective had changed since their first meeting. On that occasion, Carver had been full of under-stated confidence, engaging easily with his audience, whether to clarify some point he had made or to respond to a delegate whose experience was at odds with his own.

Carver's reaction was always the same, pointing out that he was a detective, not an academic, and that he wasn't suggesting that his approach to the investigation of 'Series Crime' was necessarily scientifically valid. All he knew was, that in his experience of Repeat Offending - which Kahramanyan gathered was wider than most - he had identified some common threads. And if he became involved in such cases again he would make sure he paid them special attention.

Mikayel recalled how Carver's low-key delivery imbued his ideas with an authority they may not have had had he been more forthright in his approach. Certainly, his well-documented experience only served to enhance his reputation in the eyes of those present as, 'Someone who should know what he is talking about.'

But since meeting with him again, Mikayel had concluded that something must have happened to knock him back. He wondered whether Carver's present, non-operational role was the cause, or the result. After his presentation that afternoon he had picked up snippets from a couple of detectives that hinted Carver was working under constraints. He had been noticeably reticent to contribute anything to the question and answer session that followed Mikayel's presentation, and the psychiatrist was surprised when it was Carver himself who drove him to his hotel, leaving the others to work on.

Taking advantage of the lull in their conversation, Mikayel sneaked another glance at his dinner partner as she tucked into her Dover sole. It was strange how the change in her was the almost exact opposite to that in Carver.

When he first met her, she and Carver hadn't worked

together long. He remembered how she had then seemed in thrall to her more experienced boss. 'Just learning the ropes,' she admitted to him. But now she was much more self-assured, carrying herself with a cool haughtiness he found intriguing, both as man and psychiatrist.

Nor was he the only one, judging by the reactions he'd observed in some of the detectives that afternoon. Apart from the way some of them eyed her now and then, there was always a respectful silence whenever she spoke. It surprised him. He had come away from his previous visit with an impression - mistaken he now realised - that the British Police Service was heavily sexist, and that women may struggle to make an impression. Now as he watched her, poised and confident, he found himself wondering what kind of experiences had wrought such differing changes in the two.

But it was clear she and Carver were still close. Their body language said as much, the way they kept checking each other out as he was speaking, their mirroring behaviours. Had it not been for his training, he doubted he would have noticed most of it. And though he still didn't know if there was anything more to their relationship than work, he was in no doubt that if she had a mind to do so, Jess would be able to explain exactly how and why her former partner had changed.

As he leaned across to top up her glass – she had declared herself happy to share his Merlot with her fish - she put her hand over it.

'That's enough for me thanks, Mikayel. I'm driving.'

He settled for pouring himself a refill, and sat forward.

'I must thank you for postponing whatever you had planned for this evening to look after me. It is very good of you to step in for Jamie.'

She waved it away. 'No problem. Besides, I like it when a man owes me one. It gives me power over him.'

As she said it, he wasn't sure if he caught a mischievous look and he blinked, uncertain if the interpretation that had popped into his brain was what she intended. *Don't be stupid.*

'Nevertheless, I am sure there are other things you could be doing rather than looking after some boring old Armenian.'

Stopping her fork halfway to her mouth, she gave a look that said she wasn't taken in by his attempt to run himself down. 'Hardly *that* old, Mikayel. And definitely not boring. I'm always interested to hear about other parts of the world. Armenia sounds fascinating, if maybe a little, under-developed for my tastes.'

He smiled. 'Under-developed is a good phrase.' He drank some wine. 'Still, it is a pity that Jamie could not be with us.' She nodded her agreement. As he watched her working at filleting the rest of her fish, he dipped a toe. 'Jamie is, erm, a friend, as well as a colleague perhaps?'

She paused in her eating again long enough to peer at him through long lashes.

'A friend, yes. But nothing else, if that is what you are asking.'

He pretended innocence, and she smiled before returning to her surgery.

'It is nothing serious that prevented him being with us I hope?' He caught the flash of another, suspicious, look before she answered, straight-faced.

'A home commitment that's all. I think his life's a bit up in the air at the moment.'

Sensing an opportunity, Mikayel made a point of showing understanding. 'I get the feeling he is under some pressures.' She didn't respond. 'Is it his work, may I ask, or…?'

She finished chewing, washed it down with the last of her wine, then dabbed her napkin to her mouth before sitting back in her seat and pinning him with a stare. It was a carefully executed sequence and Mikayel had no choice but to respond as was polite.

'I am sorry. I am asking questions about things that are none of my business. Please forgive me. I find it hard these days to switch off.'

Thinking he'd seen a twitch of amusement in her eyes, he fought to stop himself smiling. She was as adept at conveying meaning without speaking as anyone he had met. For several seconds she regarded him through half closed eyes, as if weighing him up. She pushed her glass forward.

'I will have another wine after all, if you don't mind, *Doctor*.'

He waited while she took a few sips. *Deciding how much to say*? It was something he had seen many times. Once people realised he was happy to talk, they often found the opportunity for a free consultation too good to resist. The interesting thing was, they invariably talked about others. People like to assume they are normal.

'What makes you think Jamie is under pressure?'

He shrugged, remembering to keep it casual. 'He is different from when we last met. He seems… restrained, as if he is holding himself back.' He saw her bite her lip, hesitant. A loyal friend. She would need a push. 'He is not happy in this work he is doing?'

She gave a shrug. 'I don't think it's that. He's done this sort of work before, was good at it too. It's more to do with… other things.'

He let his puzzlement show. She drew a deep breath.

'Jamie has been through… difficult times. A couple of his cases weren't easy. It… affected him. He's made a promise not to get involved like that again.'

'Who has he promised?'

'Himself. His boss. His girlfriend.'

'Girlfriend?'

She told him about Rosanna.

As he listened, Mikayel's suspicions grew and his instincts took over. There seemed more than he had first imagined. But it would not be the sort of thing a friend would reveal to a relative stranger. He leaned forward.

'I do not usually pry, but I can see you are worried about him. I suspect Jamie is not someone who would rush to seek professional help, even if he needed it. If an opinion would help… I am very discreet.'

The way she looked straight at him, eyes flaring, he thought for a moment he had gone too far, had offended her. But then she shifted her attention to her glass, turning it as she stared into its plummy depths. Suddenly she lifted it, drained its contents then poured herself more. Putting the glass down, she glared at him.

'How much do you know about Jamie's previous cases?'

'Not a great deal. When I was at the seminar where we met previously, they played the video of the TV programmes about the murders of those escort girls. It was in the news at that time because the man responsible….' He clicked his fingers.

'Edmund Hart.'

'Him. He had hanged himself in prison not long before.' As he spoke, Mikayel recalled the evening he and several other overseas delegates sat through the videos of the documentary series that had been made about the case, the animated discussions that followed. A couple of English police officers present had some fringe contact with the investigation and claimed to have 'insights' they were happy to share. The programme was apparently originally intended as an exposé of racism within the British CID, but when the body of Hart's third victim – they were all high-class 'Escort' girls - turned up on the area where the programme makers were filming, they re-wrote their plans to follow the investigation, fly-on-the-wall style. Not shown until after the trial, the series gave a fascinating, but often harrowing insight into never-before-seen Major Crime Investigation procedures. It proved popular with viewers. In particular Mikayel remembered the way the programme makers credited the quietly-spoken Detective Inspector who only joined the team after the fourth murder with turning the investigation round - something Carver was quick to deny during his talking-head spot.

'I didn't do anything special,' Mikayel recalled him insisting. 'Some of the stuff I picked up during a stint with the FBI's Behavioural Science Unit was useful later on, but everyone worked bloody hard on that enquiry. I just happened to come in at a time when things were starting to move.' He didn't disclose what the 'things' were but another of the detectives interviewed was more candid.

'The enquiry was going nowhere until DI Carver

joined us. It was him who came up with the information that led us to Hart.' But what that 'information' was, no one would say.

Interested to know what Jess had to tell, Mikayel gave her his full attention.

'Jamie had some problems after that case. The truth is he got a bit more involved with a witness than perhaps he should have. The night they arrested Hart, he raped and nearly killed her. Jamie blamed himself. It took him a while to get over it. It certainly knocked his confidence for a time.'

'A breakdown of some kind?'

Jess rocked a hand. 'Something like that.'

'This witness. She was one of these escort girls?'

Jess hesitated. 'Yes.'

'They are no longer involved I take it?'

Jess shook her head, cast her gaze down. A darkness seemed to envelop her. She took a deep breath. 'Are you aware of what happened after the Hart case? The Worshipper killings?'

The psychiatrist looked blank. 'These past years, I have barely kept up with what has been happening in my own country, never mind the rest of the world.'

Jess nodded. For long seconds she hesitated, as if ordering her thoughts. Raising her glass she took a couple of sips, readying herself. Then she began.

Over the next ten minutes, Mikayel listened as Jess told of the events that had dominated Jamie Carver's, and to some extent her own life the past three years. She began with the Worshipper Killings themselves, and the decision to enlist the aid of someone the investigators thought may point them towards the killer, what happened after. As Jess told it, the horrific murder of the witness who had so narrowly escaped murder at Hart's hands the first time, was undoubtedly the worst part. Mikayel saw at once the effect such a horror could have on someone, even a hardened detective. But there was more. The killer also claimed one of Carver's detective colleagues and, right at the end, tried to kill Carver himself and his girlfriend. As Jess went on to describe the trail of murder, death and conspiracy that continued in the wake of the Worshipper Killer's arrest and conviction, through elements in the British Government and higher echelons of the Police Service, and on to Paris, Mikayel had to make a conscious effort to stop his jaw dropping, several times. When she told of what had happened in Paris - more death, more personal loss for Carver and another, horrific final encounter - Mikayel wondered how he had managed to never hear any of it. But at that time he was struggling just to acquire the basic food and medical supplies he needed to keep his charges in the Institute alive. Jess concluded by telling of how she had to go to Paris and more or less physically drag Carver back to the UK. He was on the verge of dropping out altogether, ridden with guilt, self-doubt and grief. She finished with, 'Afterwards, he went through another course of rehab and finally managed, thankfully, to pull himself back together. Enough to get back to some sort of work at any rate. Which is where you now find him.' Settling back in her seat, she reached again for her wine.

For almost a minute, Mikayel stared at her. Images of what Carver must have been through, the pressures he must have suffered, swirled about his psychiatrist's brain. It did not take long for the pattern he knew was there to show itself. He had seen it before, many times.

'My God,' he said, eventually. 'I had no idea.'

'No,' Jess said. 'You wouldn't'

Mikayel took up his own glass and also sat back, reflecting on all he had heard. It was an astounding story, one that fitted with what he already knew about Carver, and what he had seen for himself since his return to the UK. After several minutes he glanced up at Jess. She was staring into her glass, still dwelling it seemed on the matters he suspected were never far from her mind.

'Now I understand,' he said.

'Understand what?'

'His problems. What he is going through.'

Jess's eyes narrowed. 'You think he has problems?'

'Don't you?'

She stared at him. She and Carver were more than just colleagues. It would be hard for her to admit it to anyone, never mind a psychiatrist. But eventually the hardness in her face softened. Acceptance flooded in.

'I suppose if I'm honest, yes. He does have a problem.'

'Not just one. Several I suspect, given all you have told me. And no wonder. What he has been through, it is enough that even the strongest-minded person might struggle to cope.'

Jess looked wary. 'You think he's not coping?'

About to answer, Mikayel hesitated. Unwittingly, he had manoeuvred himself into a delicate situation. Carver was not his patient, even so, using his professional knowledge to speculate with another about a third party's mental health made him uncomfortable. Apart from anything, it raised ethical issues. But then it was clear that Jess only had Carver's best interests at heart. If by talking, it may help her to help him, then why not? It wasn't as if he planned to remain in the UK long enough for there to be any come-back on him. Jess seemed to sense his dilemma.

'Don't worry, Mikayel. Anything you say will stay between us, no one else.'

It decided him.

'You must appreciate, this is only my observation, not any sort of diagnosis,'

'Of course. Go on.'

'I would say that in one sense he probably is coping, but only by avoiding.'

'Avoiding what?'

'Himself. His own instincts.'

She stared at him, waiting. He continued.

'From what I have seen, I believe Jamie is the sort of man who would normally do what he thinks is right, rather than worry about consequences, yes?'

Jess thought on it. 'When he was in Paris, he ignored a recall so that he could stay and save a girl's life. He didn't hesitate.'

'Just so. And this case I have brought you today. This Vahrig Danelian. I suspect that Jamie has exactly the sort of knowledge and experience needed to find him?' Jess nodded. 'And yet, he seems willing to stay out of it.'

'But only under orders from his boss.'

'You think that would stop him?'

'Well, also, it could cause problems for my boss, Mr Morrison.'

Mikayel weighed it. 'But we know people's lives are at risk if you do not find Vahrig in time. Do you think the Jamie Carver you first met would stay shut up in an office when he knows he might prevent such a thing happening?'

After several seconds she said, 'No.'

'And nor do I.'

'So why is he?'

'Guilt. And fear.'

'About what?'

'You have already said. His last few cases, people close to him died. His girlfriend nearly lost her life. I would think that could cause anyone to wonder if they were to blame. And I can well imagine they would worry about such things happening again, in the future.'

'Which is why you think he isn't pushing to be involved in the hunt for Danelian?'

'Yes. I suspect he does want to, but fears doing so, for the reasons I mention.'

After another short silence, Jess heaved a sigh. 'So what would you advise, Doctor? From what you are saying, it seems to me that unless something happens to break him out of it, things will only get worse.'

'I have to agree,' Mikayel said. 'As to what can you do? I can only say that if he were a patient of mine, I would start by encouraging him to confront his fears. Only when he realises what drives them can he deal with it. In the end, it comes down to the old analogy. After falling off a horse, the thing to do is to get right back in the saddle.' Seeing her doubtful look, he shrugged. 'I am sorry, that probably sounds... over-simple? But I see it many times in those whose profession brings them close to danger.'

His questions concerning Carver answered - at least for now - Mikayel sensed he'd already drifted further than he'd intended into murkily-unethical waters. A few minutes later she too seemed grateful when he steered conversation to how some of the better East-European wines compared with those from the New World.

'I wasn't aware East-Europe had any, 'better wines',' she laughed.

Sensing an opportunity of an altogether different kind, Mikayel hailed a waiter and asked for the wine list.

'Then let me educate you,' he said. 'I doubt this place will have anything from my part of the world, but I am sure there will be others we can consider.'

It was past midnight by the time Jess watched the taxi that dropped her off depart to take the cheerfully-sozzled psychiatrist back to his hotel. Wine had won out, and she had decided to pick her car up on the way in the next morning. She hadn't intended to stay out late, but after the wine tasting, Mikayel had insisted on her demonstrating some of the niftier features of her new Samsung mobile. More advanced than anything he'd ever had access to, and being something of a gadget freak it turned out, he'd seemed fascinated with it.

As she turned towards her apartment block, her thoughts went back to their conversation about Jamie. Since then, part of her brain had been mulling over it, trying to digest what the psychiatrist had said. What he had said certainly seemed to make sense. In truth, if confirmed much of what her instincts had been telling her. But until she gave it further thought, she wasn't sure there was anything she could, or even should, do. And by the time she stepped out of the lift, the clear night air having hit her, she knew there was no point trying to go over it right now.

As she entered her flat she saw the flashing red light that told her she had messages.

The first was from Howard Leather.

'Please forgive me for leaving a message, Jess. I was ringing to see if you might be free for, erm, dinner, in the next couple of weeks? I rang a couple of times earlier this week, but it seems I wasn't able to catch you. You have my number if you'd care to come back to me.'

She smiled as she imagined his dilemma. Worried in case he incurred her 'displeasure'. She would have to let him know it might be a while before they got together again. He wouldn't argue. The second message was from her mother, speaking in her usual faux-posh telephone sing-song.

'Just ringing to ask if you will be coming down any time soon, Jessica. Only Derek and Marjorie are back in the country for a few weeks. They are staying with Alistair. You remember Alistair don't you, dear? Apparently he has moved to new chambers in the city, and is doing very well for himself. I *was* wondering whether to invite him to-.'

Jess's finger hit the 'stop' button.

'Oh bugger off Mother.'

CHAPTER 25

The man who opened the door of the well-kept bungalow on the outskirts of Stockport was in his late fifties. Paunchy and with thinning grey hair, Carver thought he had the comfortable retired look he'd seen many of his former colleagues attain once they started drawing their index-linked pensions.

'Ron Gover? Jamie Carver. We spoke on the telephone.'

Carver put a hand out and the man took it. His grip was firm, warm, but slightly damp.

Gover invited Carver in and led him through to a back living room that was too chintzy for Carver's tastes. A picture window, so big it made Carver wonder about heat loss in winter, looked out onto a well-stocked garden with an immaculately manicured lawn. Somehow, the ordered regimentation of the flowers and shrubs was just as Carver would have expected from an ex-Scenes Of Crime Officer. Gover offered coffee but Carver declined. Four in one morning would be too much for even his caffeine-acclimatised system.

'You sounded rather mysterious on the 'phone Mr Carver,' Gover said as he indicated Carver to take a comfortable-looking armchair facing the window. 'Mind telling me what this is all about?'

Carver told how he was reviewing some old cases in which Gover had had some involvement, but had come across some anomalies he hoped he may be able to help him with. As he spoke Carver dug himself out of the cushions he had sunk into and perched on the seat-edge. He didn't want to be too comfortable to discuss the matters that had brought him.

'I'll help any way I can,' Gover said, sitting forward to receive the folder with papers Carver took from his briefcase and passed across. As he glanced at the covering, Investigating Officer's Report, with the name of the SIO and the case reference at the top, Carver thought his features darkened, just a little.

'Do you remember?' Carver said. 'It was back in the late eighties. A spate of rapes and bad indecent assaults around Salford and Eccles. They were never cleared up. You were Exhibits Officer.'

Gover spent some time leafing through the papers before nodding. 'Yes. I remember them, vaguely. What's the problem?'

'Some of the exhibits are missing.'

Gover straightened in his chair. 'Well it was a long time ago. You know what it's like. Things tend to go astray over the years.'

Carver nodded. 'That's true. But I've spoken to a few people at Salford nick. Many of them remember you. They all say you were the most meticulous SOCO around at that time. And I've been through your exhibit books and indexes. They're the most thorough I've ever seen. All the movement logs showing stuff going to and from the lab are complete right up to the time you boxed everything up when the enquiry was wound down. Everything's accounted for up to that point. I'm wondering if you have any idea how things could have gone missing since.'

Gover shrugged and spread his hands. 'I'm sorry. I retired some ten years ago. I don't remember anything about it since I put everything in the SOCO store.'

'Do you recall anyone taking an interest in the case after?'

Gover shook his head, looking regretful. 'I'm sorry.'

'No problem. Can you remember if there were ever any suspects?'

'Doesn't it say in the IO report?'

'I'm asking you.'

Carver knew it was the sort of come-back he would more usually put to a suspect and for a moment Gover looked as if he might challenge it. Instead he got up and crossed to a sideboard where he took a small cigar from an ornately decorated box. He lit it and blew smoke into the air before returning to his chair. 'No. I can't say I ever remember there being any suspects.'

Carver nodded slowly. 'What about Paul Murphy, the SIO? Did he ever contact you about it afterwards?'

'Not that I recall. But as I say, it was all a long time ago.'

For several minutes Carver questioned the retired SOCO further about the procedures he and his then colleagues followed to ensure the exhibits were safeguarded once they were in storage. As Carver expected, the system was rigorous. Anyone trying to access old case exhibits needed to go through the SOCOs themselves, who kept the keys for the store. And if the relevant SOCO wasn't around at the time, his or her colleagues would only grant access after checking with them first. Unauthorised handling of exhibits could sound the death-knell of a case in court and SOCOs always took their Exhibits Officer roles most seriously. Gover apologised again for not being able to account for the missing items. 'But if anything's gone astray it must have happened after I retired.'

Eventually, thanking him for his time, Carver rose to leave and Gover held out the case-folder to him. But as Carver reached for it, Gover suddenly pulled it back as if something had occurred to him. He re-checked one of the papers.

'I've just realised. One of the victims was a Sarah Carver.' He looked up at his visitor. 'Is she….?'

'My sister.'

Gover looked stunned. 'I… I'm sorry. I didn't realise.'

'No reason why you should.'

The older man's eyes seemed to glaze over. 'That's why you're reviewing it?'

Carver nodded. 'She's had a few problems.' He delved into his wallet and took out a photograph, showed it to the man in the chair. 'They're her kids. Ten and seven. Things are rough for them. I'm trying to put some things right.'

Gover gazed at the young faces. 'I've a couple of grandkids about the same age.' He handed the photograph back. 'I'm sorry I can't help.'

'So am I,' Carver said.

As Carver's Golf passed out of sight, Gover let the net curtain fall back in place and sighed. For several minutes he stared out through the gauze, seeing nothing. Eventually he turned and walked back over to the sideboard. He was about to take another cigar when his eyes lit on the framed photograph next to it. It showed the happy faces of two young children, smiling into the camera. He picked it up, gazing at it lovingly, the way grandparents do. Forgetting about his smoke he returned to his chair and sat down, cradling the photograph in front of him. But he was remembering two other faces, the ones in the photograph Carver had shown him. He stayed that way for several minutes then, slowly, he lifted his head and gazed towards the window again. After a while his shoulders hunched as he doubled up and buried his face in his hands.

Of the several voice-mails waiting when Carver got back to the office, he responded to Jess's first. Her, 'Call me soon as you get this,' sounded urgent, though she'd been fine when he'd rung her first thing to find out how she got on with Kahramanyan. A cryptic, 'It was an interesting evening,' was all he could get out of her at the time, leaving him wondering what - or who - the main topic of conversation was.

'Have you heard from The Duke?' she said when she realised it was him.

'No. Why?'

'It's Cathy. The hospice rang just after he got in work and he's rushed off to be with her. Looks like nature may be shaping up to take its course a bit earlier than expected.'

'Oh God,' Carver sighed as the sadness he had been keeping in check until the time was right broke through. His free hand went to his forehead and he hunched over the phone. 'God,' he repeated. After a lengthy silence he became conscious neither of them was speaking – not that there was anything to say.

'I'll give him some time then ring him.'

After sharing commiserations for the The Duke and his dying wife, Carver mused aloud on what the Head of SMIU's plans might be.

'Let's put it this way,' Jess said. 'I don't think we'll see him back here for a while.'

Carver agreed. The Duke had spoken about staying with Cathy once the end was in sight. He wondered how long it would be and how it would affect the man he respected above all others. Despite his, 'Man's man,' persona, The Duke was a romantic at heart and loved his wife, deeply.

'It's going to hit him bad,' he told Jess.

'I know.'

Eventually talk turned back to work and Carver voiced the question that was next uppermost in his mind after concerns for his ex-boss.

'Has anyone said who'll take over while he's away?'

'Looks like Terry West,' Jess said. 'That was always the plan. We're just waiting for ACPO confirmation.'

'What about the Danelian thing?' Carver asked.

'As far as I know he'll be running that as well.'

Carver gave an acknowledging, 'Uh-huh,' but avoided further comment. He'd worked with the former Merseyside Crime Squad DCI on a series of armed, cash-delivery robberies around the region a couple of years before. West was an excellent thief-taker and it was largely thanks to his sources within the Merseyside underworld that seven of the gang responsible eventually received lengthy prison sentences. But Carver knew Terry worked best as a street detective, dealing with criminals, carrying out surveillance and evidence-gathering operations. Carver had witnessed his running of a Major Enquiry and thought it wasn't where his strengths lay. He would come good in time, Carver was sure. But it was a big ask to expect someone to take charge of the new unit, work with staff he hardly knew, *and* run an Operation like Aslan - the designation given to the hunt for Danelian after Alec Duncan kept referring to Armenia as, 'Narnia'. To Carver's mind, Jess would have been the safer pair of hands. But whatever her abilities, she was still too junior and, on paper at least, could not demonstrate she possessed the levels of experience SMIU's Chief Officer overseers would look for in a temporary Unit leader. As he mused on it, Jess must have heard him sucking air between his teeth.

'Don't say anything. I said you should have accepted The Duke's offer.'

Not wanting to go there, Carver told her he would catch up with her later and rang off. But another minute passed before he realised he was still musing on Terry West's likely appointment as The Duke's stand–in.

'It's nothing to do with you,' he reminded himself. 'Just forget it.'

He turned his attention to his growing in-tray. But after spending fifteen minutes reading and re-reading an analysis on the burgeoning East European Sex-Trade problem, he closed the file, returning it to the pile with an annoyed grunt of frustration.

Apart from not being in the right mood for the Intelligence-Assessor work that was the other side to his 'Organisation Transition Management' role, his interview with Gover and Jess's news about The Duke kept intruding.

After getting up to refill his coffee mug – he decided

to suffer the jag - Carver returned to his desk. Picking up his document case, he took out the papers he had showed Gover that morning and spread them in front of him, letting their graphic contents focus his mind on something he might at least be able to do something about.

It hadn't required any conscious mental effort on Carver's part for him to conclude that Ron Gover had lied. Carver's wizarding instincts kicked in the moment he felt the man's damp palm. And Gover's attempts to stifle the instinctive physical responses to the act of telling a lie – altering his posture, getting up to light a cigar, trying to keep his face from reacting the way it should have done – were tell-signs any half-decent detective would have spotted, never mind one who's lie-detection capabilities put him within reach of the percentile of those sometimes labelled, 'wizards'.

It was Professor Maureen O'Sullivan of the University of San Francisco who first ascribed the term 'wizard' to those one-in-twenty-thousand people who possess the innate ability to tell when someone is lying. Her pioneering late-nineties research into the psychology of lie detection and facial analysis demonstrated how 'wizards' are adept at reading the involuntary micro-expressions - invisible to most of the population - that invariably accompany the act. O'Sullivan also showed that the most gifted wizards are more than capable of consistently outperforming polygraph machines. And it was during a National Crime Faculty-sponsored exchange-trip to the FBI's famed Behavioural Analysis Unit at Quantico when Carver first discovered that his ability to 'read' people placed him within the top twenty percentile of identified 'wizards' worldwide – according to O'Sullivan's strict criteria.

But far from being the boon most people assumed such an attribute was for someone in Carver's position, he had long ago realised it was nothing of the sort. Most experienced detectives can tell when someone is lying, the difficulty, usually, is proving it. Following his back-slapping return from the US and after the first wave of 'parlour-trick-curiosity' died down, Carver soon discovered the drawbacks. Many people, especially those with secrets – which means most - are suspicious to the point of avoiding once they realise that the person they are talking to really can tell when their words don't quite fit with the reality they are purporting to describe. Social and, in particular, work gatherings were a nightmare. It explained why Carver's attendance record at the sort of events senior officers were sometimes expected to be seen at was so poor as to occasionally draw comment. Nevertheless he always made a point of showing up at the retirement functions of those he respected.

But even without the behaviours that had evidenced Gover's discomfort, the ex-SOCO's failure to mention that there had in fact been talk of a suspect – a couple of still-serving officers around at the time remembered as much though there was no mention of it in the IO Report – together with his apparent lack of interest in which exhibits were missing would, in any case, have raised Carver's suspicions.

The real questions were, *why* had he lied, and *what* did he know? So far there was nothing to show who would have had an interest in losing some of the exhibits, or why. And with so little to go on, it was too soon to start putting people like Gover on the spot. All he had to do was play innocent. There wasn't even enough – yet - to arrest him on suspicion of perverting the course of justice, the favoured tactic of many cold-case investigators. And there was certainly no point trying to tackle the SIO at the time, Murphy, directly; not without something concrete to put to him. Carver needed more, though at that moment he wasn't sure where it would come from. He had to dig deeper.

Gathering up the papers, he returned them to his bottom drawer and locked it. Then, with a sigh, he decided he ought to give his in-tray another try, and pulled it towards him.

CHAPTER 26

As the enquiry-desk buzzer sounded again, Lucy glanced up from her screen. Her colleague, Emma, was still on the phone, looking helpless and apologetic, as if talking to a legitimate enquirer she couldn't get rid of. Not convinced for a second, Lucy sent her an admonishing look as she rose to see to who was at the desk. The two women who were the College's Administration Support Unit rotated Enquiry Desk duties between them, hour on, hour off, but this was the third time Lucy had had to cover for Emma while she was 'tied up' on the phone. The way she'd been talking, in mainly hushed tones, Lucy was pretty sure who it was. When she'd arrived that morning Emma seemed out of sorts and had mentioned something about having had a 'bad night' with her boyfriend.

Despite her annoyance, as she walked round the frosted glass screen to the enquiry window, Lucy managed to stitch a smile to her face.

'May I help you?'

He was standing with his back to her, hands thrust into the pockets of his long black leather coat, which is why she didn't recognise him. But as soon as he turned she remembered. The man from Starbucks. The one with the strange eyes. As he saw her, his face registered, in quick succession, puzzlement, surprise then finally, recognition. A smile came into his face which she struggled to not return.

'Hello again,' he said. 'I did not know you work here.'

Caught off guard, she wasn't sure how to respond so as not to give off the wrong signal. But with no time to do anything else, she settled for a quick, confirming nod and a garbled, 'Oh, yes.' Then she stood there, waiting, remembering to keep her face straight in case he got the wrong idea.

As the silence lengthened – he was just standing there, staring at her - she felt herself starting to redden. *Oh for goodness sake*…. Eventually he spoke.

'I am interested in enrolling on one of your English-language courses,' he said. 'Do you have a prosec… prosp-ec…?'

'Prospectus?'

He nodded. 'Yes. A prospec-tus. Thank you.' His eyes were still rooted on hers.

'One moment.' She stepped back around the glass, grateful to be out of his sight while she attended to his request. Her heart was already pounding as she tried to take in the coincidence of him suddenly turning up there. What did he want with a language course anyway, she wondered? His English seemed fine to her. But even as suspicion formed, she realised she was being stupid, and admonished herself for over-reacting.

Ever since the call from Cyprus – she was yet to tell her mother, still worrying about what it would do to her - she had been on tenterhooks. Wary of strange faces. Afraid to answer the telephone. Suspicious of anyone she didn't know looking her way. But apart from that one time at Starbucks, she had definitely never seen the man before. There was no reason whatsoever to fear him; at least not in *that* way.

As Lucy passed Emma's desk, making her way to the cupboard where the prospectuses were kept, Emma put her hand over the phone. 'Are you alright, Luce? You look like you've seen a ghost.'

Lucy glared at her over her shoulder, mouthing, 'Sshh,' while flapping her hand, wildly. *Tell the world why don't you?*

Emma pulled a, 'Get you,' face and leaned sideways so she could check out who had sent her co-worker into such a spin. As she pulled back, she shot Lucy another glance. This time her face read, *Impressed.*

After rooting through the cupboard, Lucy returned to the window, throwing Emma another warning look as she passed. Emma grinned, hand still over her mouthpiece. Lucy could hear the man on the other end of the line calling, 'Emm? Are you still there? Emm?'

'These are all our language courses,' Lucy said, remembering to keep her eyes down as she placed the pamphlet on the ledge that served as a counter. 'Can I help you with anything else?' A pale-skinned hand with nails bitten right down slipped into her range of vision and took the booklet.

As it disappeared he said, 'Just one thing. Do you do muffins and coffee here?'

Not sure she had heard him correctly, she glanced up. 'I'm sorry? What?'

He was staring at her again, but now wearing a wide grin. Not the best of teeth either, she thought. Nevertheless there was a boyishness about him that, along with the eyes – what was it about them? – was hard to resist. She started to smile back, but then realised and caught herself.

'I said, 'Do you serve muffins and coffee here.' Or must I take you somewhere?'

She started to panic, unsure if he was making fun of her. *Or was it something else?* 'I'm sorry,' she said, conscious she was repeating herself. 'I don't understand.'

'Yes you do,' he said, letting the grin slip, so it was less obvious he was chatting her up. 'But if you want to pretend, that is all right. I do not want to upset you again.'

Lucy wasn't sure if he had intended to make her feel guilty, but she had been brought up to always be polite, even to strangers. And remembering the first time they had met and all the college memos she'd read about the need to be careful when dealing with people from minority groups, she worried in case he interpreted her reticence as some sort of prejudice.

'You haven't upset me. It's just-.'

'In that case let me take you to lunch. I can act as first slip in case you drop it again.'

She hadn't a clue what he was talking about and his confident use of English made her wonder again why he was interested in language courses. But by now she was aware that Emma had moved from her desk and was pretending to be doing something just behind the glass partition. Her panic increased. A bell rang, signalling the end of the first afternoon period.

'Alright,' she said. *Anything if you'll just go.* 'I'll be there, tomorrow. About one.'

'I will look forward to it.'

With that he turned, prospectus in hand, and headed

away down the corridor that was now filling, quickly, with groups of students. Lucy noticed that as he neared them they parted, as if by magic, to let him through. He didn't acknowledge them, nor did he look back.

'Well you dark horse,' Emma said as Lucy returned to her desk. 'Are you going to tell me or what?'

'Sorry?' She was still thinking about him. Who was he? Where was he from?

Emma gave her an exasperated look. 'Alright,' she said. 'Keep it to yourself. But I'll want chapter and verse after lunch tomorrow.'

Lucy showed her annoyance. She *had* been listening. And she wasn't finished.

'Just remember to put on some make up. And for goodness sake, do something with your hair. Like you did for the Christmas do last year. You looked really sexy then.' Lucy blushed. 'And don't forget to ask if he's got a brother. I could quite go for one of these exotic-foreigner types.'

Trying not to smile - it would only encourage her shameless colleague - Lucy shook her head and turned her attention back to the timetable she had been working on when the buzzer sounded. But as she sat looking blankly at the screen, her mind was racing. For all that the shadow that had fallen over her life recently was still there – and needed to be dealt with, soon - she was conscious of a feeling she hadn't experienced in a long while. A tingle that came from thinking that, after all this time, something might be about to happen that might – just might - interrupt the plodding sameness of her otherwise humdrum existence.

She pursed her lips so Emma would not see how excited she was, and started to attack her keyboard.

CHAPTER 27

Carver checked his watch as he waited for Sarah to come down from the bathroom. He was conscious that time was running away from him – again - and that Patsy and Jack would soon be home. But at least his impromptu visit meant that they would find their mother in a better state than they would have done. Images of Social Services intervention loomed in the back of his brain and it depressed him to realise she was slipping back again. He had hoped he was seeing signs that with him and Ros taking the kids now and then, and the occasional visits from Joyce, she was close to getting back on her feet.

Wrong.

He hadn't actually asked when she'd last showered and put on freshly-cleaned clothes, but her dishevelled appearance when he'd arrived an hour earlier told its own story. Entering via the back door, having got no answer at the front, he'd found her asleep on the couch, an empty wine bottle and a glass on the floor next to her. It was two o'clock in the afternoon. The day's post lay next to the bottle. She had only opened one letter. It was a summons for non-payment of council tax.

Now, as he waited, knowing he was supposed to be elsewhere, he was conscious he was guilty of abusing the freedom his present position afforded him; the freedom to come and go as he pleased, and to attend to personal matters - at the expense of the professional. It was something he'd long abhorred in some of those with whom he'd worked over the years. But right now he was glad he'd decided to visit, prompted by her not answering her mobile the past twenty-four hours. And besides, it wasn't too far off-route to his meet with Alec Duncan, whatever that was all about. Alec had rung mid-morning requesting a meeting. And there'd been more than a hint of conspiracy in his response to Carver's asking why. 'Just a couple of things I'd like to run past yeh,' he'd said. Carver's best guess was, it concerned Aslan in some way. Things had gone quiet on that front since The Duke's enforced absence. His instincts told him not much progress was being made. If it were, he'd have heard. But first there was Sarah.

On cue, he heard her tramping, unevenly, down the stairs. A few seconds later the door opened and she came in. Her hair hung in rat's tails. But at least he could smell shampoo. He'd worried she might just splash water over it to try to fool him. And while the pink and black jogging suit hadn't been ironed, it looked clean.

'Here,' he said, thrusting the mug of tea he had waiting at her.

Taking a sip - 'Not enough sugar,' – she went and sat in the chair next to the gas fire where she wouldn't have to look at him. She lit a cigarette.

'How are you feeling?' he said.

She blew smoke up into the air and sniffed to clear her sinuses. 'Bleeding brilliant, what do you think?' But after a few seconds she turned to him, her features softening. 'Sorry.'

'S'alright.'

For a moment he wrestled over what to say. Things couldn't go on like this. But he could see she was embarrassed, and with the kids due home soon, now was not the time to start getting into it. 'Will you be okay?'

She looked at him over the rim of her mug. 'I'm not going to let them roam the streets in their bare feet if that's what you are worried about.'

'I didn't mean the kids. I meant this.' He held up the summons.

She looked at it for a moment, then shrugged. 'What are they going to do, lock me up?' He gave her an even look he hoped would mask his thoughts. Then he folded the papers and stuffed them inside his jacket.

'What the fuck do you think you're doing?'

'I'll sort it.'

'Like hell you will. Give it back.' She held out a hand.

He leaned down, bringing his face close to hers. 'Don't argue. Call it an early birthday present.'

Another time she might have tried harder, but he could see she was tired, out of options. As she turned away her eyes began to glisten. Carver shook his head. For all that she was struggling, the old Carver arrogance was still there. Only in her case it manifested itself in the way she refused offers of help, especially those that came regularly from their parents. Carver still had no idea what lay behind their estrangement, particularly from her father. He had tried asking, but none of them were saying. His suspicion was that the retired Chief Constable had probably tried 'pulling rank' in an attempt to bully some sense into her - something he could well imagine her resisting to the point of cutting him out. If he was right, it wouldn't be the first time. Something similar had happened just after Patsy was born. It lasted a couple of years.

Now, as he watched her staring blankly over her not-sweet-enough tea, he decided to voice the thought that had come while tidying up the sitting room - God knows when she'd last given the vacuum a run-out. He would just have to talk Rosanna round.

'Look, Sis.'

She looked.

'I was going to ask you this anyway…. I mean before I found you…. I mean-.' *Bollocks to it.* 'The half-term's coming up. Why don't you all come to us for a few days? Patsy and Jack enjoy it out there and you could do with a break as well. Make a mini-holiday of it.'

She eyed him suspiciously. 'What would Rosanna say?'

'It was her idea.'

She thought about it a few seconds. Then a miracle occurred. She smiled. For a fleeting second Carver caught a glimpse of something he had never expected to see again. But before he could be certain, it was gone, the suspicion came back again – the response programmed by years of discovering that something sounding too good to be true usually turned out to be exactly that.

'I thought Rosanna didn't like me.'

'What gave you that idea?' He knew damn well. 'She'd love to have you.' *She'll kill me.* 'You'll just have to remember. No smoking in the house.'

She thought on it some more. Eventually she looked

up at him. The smile again, steadier this time. 'I would like that.'

'Great.' But as he returned it, he was thinking he may as well stop at the riding stables he passed on the way home and pick up a riding crop. *So she can flail me alive.*

For the next few minutes they talked about when and how. Sarah didn't drive and started talking trains and buses.

'No need for that. I'll pick you up on my way home on Friday night.'

'Will you be able to get any time off?' Already she seemed excited by the idea.

'I'll see if I can get a couple of days. We could have a run out to Portmeirion.'

Her eyes lit up. 'I haven't been there since we used to go with Mum and Dad. I thought it had closed down.'

'Not at all. Apparently it's doing really well since they started re-running The Prisoner on subscription.'

'Patsy and Jack would love it there.'

'That's why I suggested it.'

He checked his watch again. 'Look, I'd love to stay and see the kids. But I'm supposed to be-.'

'It's okay. You get off. They'll see you soon anyway.'

Seeing her brightening, Carver's memories stirred. There was a time she'd always been first amongst the Carvers to laugh and smile, before it all stopped. A fuzzy-warm feeling started in his stomach.

'And thanks for coming round. I'm sure there're all sorts of important cases you're supposed to be solving.'

He made a mock-sad face that wasn't all that mock. 'I'm just a desk man now, remember? But there's something brewing I need to deal with.'

'Anything exciting? I'm always the last to hear of these cases you keep getting involved in. If it's going to be on the news you have to tell me first.'

'Don't worry I'm not going to be on the news. And no, it's nothing exciting.' He thought about it. 'Well, not unless you count an escaped Armenian nutcase exciting.'

She started. 'Armenian? Bloody hell.'

He nodded and stood up. 'I'd better whiz. I'll ring you.'

As he came away he congratulated himself on his success. Then he remembered about having to tell Rosanna, and his mood darkened again.

CHAPTER 28

About to bite into the ham and cheese toastie Alec Duncan had waiting for him, Carver looked across at the Scottish detective. 'You talk, I'll eat,' he said. He was half an hour later than the 'Ten minutes,' he'd said he would be when he rang to tell Alec he was on his way. Traffic through Salford had been a nightmare.

They were meeting in The Great British Pride again. As Carver pulled a rubbery strand of cold cheese off his chin, he saw Alec hesitating, unsure it seemed where to start. He was clearly uncomfortable. Carver thought he could guess why. A couple of times in his career he'd found himself having to confide personal doubts over an investigation-in-progress to another SIO. It always smacked of treachery.

'We've known each other long enough, Alec. Just spit it out.'

The Scotsman turned a grave face to him. 'I'm not sure I'm doin' the right thing here. It's probably well out of order-.'

'Tell me about Aslan.' Carver tried to make it sound like an order. He didn't want to have to spend the rest of the afternoon talking the man who was about the most moral detective he knew into putting his ethical principles to one side. That Alec didn't argue, Carver took as signalling the depth of his disquiet. The DS took a deep breath.

'The rate things are going, we're never going to catch this Danelian character before he finds his family, assuming that's who he's looking for. There're things we ought to be doing that aren't getting done.'

'Such as?'

'Such as getting into the Armenian community and doing some digging. West has got half of us reviewing the Durzlan case and the other half going through immigration records. Someone ought to be *oot and aboot*. On the street.'

Carver nodded, wondering if it was the result of the two years they worked together that Alec's instincts mirrored his own or just that they shared the same basic philosophy - that proper detective work involves wearing out shoe-leather and knocking on doors.

'Have you said anything?'

Alec nodded, glumly. 'And so's Jess. But he insists he wants to do it his way. He says there must be a link between the Durzlans and the Danelians. He thinks if we find it, it'll turn them up.'

'And he may be right,' Carver said. 'But only if you find it in time. We spent weeks reviewing the Durzlan case on Chainlink and never came up with anything. Okay, we didn't know about Vahrig Danelian back then, nevertheless….'

'That's what we told him. But he did'nae seem impressed.'

'You told him that I'd reviewed it?'

Alec nodded. 'Should I not hae done?'

Carver shrugged. 'It shouldn't be an issue, but knowing Terry, he'd probably love to find something I'd missed.'

Alec supped his pint. 'That's what Jess and I wondered.'

'What about the immigration side? How's that going?'

'We've got a team down at the Immigration Office, going through all their records for the year before and after the Durzlan family were killed.'

Carver pulled a face. 'There won't be a record. From what Kahramanyan said, I'd bet my wages the Danelians came here illegally.'

'We told West that as well. But he said we can't do everything. 'One thing at a time,' he said.'

Carver pursed his lips. 'Normally I'd say the same. But when you're up against the clock you've got to be looking at everything.' A thought occurred to him. 'Has he put in for more staff yet?'

Alec shook his head. ' Jess thinks that with the Duke only just having departed he's holding off. In case they think he can't manage.'

Carver shook his head, letting his exasperation show.

'People worry too much about what others think. There's a bloody killer out there needs to be caught.' But from the look on Alec's face Carver could see he wasn't saying anything the older DS hadn't already considered. He'd come looking for advice.

A thought occurred to him.

'Does Jess know about us meeting?'

Alec looked abashed, then shook his head. 'She said I wasn't to involve yeh. Under any circumstances. She said if I did, you could end up in the shite.'

'Oh, thanks. You're not bothered about me getting in

the shite then?'

Alec smiled. 'Och, I know the way yeh operate. If I thought you was going to drop yerself in it, I would'nea be here.'

Carver gave a sarcastic nod of appreciation. 'Thank you for that vote of confidence.'

As they paused a moment to give their attention to their beers, Carver mused on how closely it matched with the concerns he'd been having. The day Kahramanyan briefed them on Vahrig Danelian, his instinct had been that if the Danelian family were here, the best way of finding them would be through the Armenian community itself. But that would need a lot of leg work and not a little luck. Once they arrive in this country and are absorbed into their own community, illegals are notoriously difficult to track down – particularly if they are otherwise law-abiding. He recalled the recent intelligence assessment he'd seen estimating the true number of illegal immigrants into the UK over the past five years - part of what people referred to routinely now as, 'Under-Britain.' The numbers were staggering. It was one of the reasons why Carver and others with access to the sort of information politicians never dare release into the public arena were so strongly in favour of Identity Cards. But from an investigator's point of view, the trouble is, such communities are fiercely protective of their own and easily capable of running the most intense police enquiry into the ground - as Carver had discovered during the Ancoats Rapist case. Despite it being the Asian community's women being attacked, it had taken all of Carver's diplomacy skills, along with help from elsewhere, to break down the barriers of suspicion that held the investigation back in the first few weeks.

'So what are yer thoughts?' Alec's question pulled Carver back to the problem at hand. 'I was wonderin' whether to have a word with The Duke in case-.'

'No. Leave him out of it. He's got enough on his plate. And I need to think things through before doing anything. I don't want to drop you or anyone else in the mire by letting on we've spoken.'

Alec shook his head, sadly. 'Fuckin' politics.' He said it in his deepest brogue. 'This case wid be right up your street. And this nutter we're lookin' for is just the sort of bastard you're guid wi'.' Then he added, 'I mean that as a compliment.'

Carver smiled.

But as he left the pub to head back to the office, Carver was conscious it wasn't just politics he needed to consider if he was going to come up with something to accelerate Aslan's progress. Then he remembered. There was another matter he needed to front. He rang Rosanna and told her about his visit with Sarah.

'And?' she said, waiting.

'And what?' he said.

'You would not ring just to tell me you have seen Sarah. What is it?'

He grimaced before he said it. 'What are your plans for next week?'

CHAPTER 29

The next morning Carver was at his desk early, so he could do what he wanted to do before some nosy-parker bounced in and hit him with an awkward question. Such as, 'So what, exactly, is the NCA's interest in the Manchester-Armenian community?' But by the time everyone started arriving, his enthusiasm for the task was already draining.

The previous evening, after Rosanna stopped talking to him, he had gone on line, just to see what there was on the UK Armenian Community. His first search - "UK Armenian Community" - turned up fourteen million results. A quick scan showed they covered a huge range of topic; religion, history, community, business, and more. He tried narrowing his search by changing it to "Manchester Armenian Community". The results increased to twenty million. 'What the f-?' After going to bed, he fell asleep thinking about where to even begin looking.

Since arriving at work, he had searched again, digging deeper into what came up. So far, nothing was jumping out as a possible start point. Many entries he clicked on simply took him to sites signposting restaurants, bars, and specialist food and other goods targeted at the Armenian community. Other sites seemed almost like clones of each other, but offering subtly differing slants on the topic around which most were centred - Turkey's attempt in nineteen-fifteen to wipe out the remnants of the Ottoman Empire's Armenian population, commonly referred to as the Armenian Genocide. After searching through the umpteenth site that appeared little more than a vehicle for some fringe-group's rant against Turkey's continuing failure to officially recognise its responsibility for the atrocity, Carver tutted loudly, pushed himself away from the desk and turned towards the window.

As he sat looking out at the several, unmarked business units that always made him wonder how the Post Office knew which was which and who was who, he derided his naïve optimism that made him think he would find answers on-line. The world-wide-web is wonderful in many ways, but it hadn't yet reached the point where detective work can be conducted from behind a desk. His thoughts turned again in the direction they had taken the previous afternoon, speaking with Alec. But almost immediately, other thoughts crowded around, stifling him with their suffocating warnings about 'consequences.' Carver rubbed at his forehead, where the tension was growing again. Each night of late as he lay in bed, it seemed to take longer to disappear.

Worrying, or even just thinking about consequences, had never come easily to Carver. Since his early days in CID he had learned to trust to his instincts and let the investigative process take him where it would. It could be some backstreet dive frequented by gangsters and junkies where the police nowadays only ever patrol in numbers. Or it may be a leafy, city suburb where criminals disguise their activities under a cloak of respectability. Either way, his willingness to go with the flow had always served him well. If it meant venturing, occasionally, into territory a more cautious detective may think twice about, then so be it. What's the saying about not making omelettes without breaking eggs? Musing on it, he was aware that at least his approach meant that the only person's safety he had to worry about, was his own, though there was the odd occasion when he needed to be mindful of the fall-out that can follow when some notable figure becomes drawn into a sensitive police investigation, as in the case of the late Alistair Kenworthy MP. But right now Carver was operating under constraints with which he was entirely unfamiliar.

Never before had he held back simply because someone in authority had told him that not doing so might be bad for his career. Even during his short-lived marriage to Gill, he had never experienced the feeling of unease that came whenever he thought about how Rosanna may react if he were to mention escaping from the frustrations of his present role.

'Jesus, Carver,' he said aloud, conscious his mind was beginning to loop around the problem in the way it had been doing for days. 'What's wrong with you?'

'I am not sure. Perhaps we should talk about it.'

Carver spun round. Mikayel Kahramanyan was in the doorway, nodding his thanks to Shiela for showing him in as she turned to make her way back to her desk.

'Mikayel,' Carver said, glossing over the embarrassment he felt at having been overheard. 'Good to see you.' Coming round the desk, they shook hands.

Carver had seen relatively little of the psychiatrist

since his arrival. Most of the past two weeks he had been ensconced with one or other members of the SMUI team, trying to help them anticipate Vahrig Danelian's intentions. During that time, there had only been time for the occasional coffee or snatched lunch.

'I am just letting you know, I will be leaving tomorrow. I have to get back.'

'Problems?' Carver said. The man's face spoke of his regret at having to leave before Danelian had been found.

'Some of the inmates that escaped the Institute are starting to turn up again. My colleagues need my help in re-settling them.'

'I don't envy you,' Carver said.

Kahramanyan had said only little about what had happened the day the Institute was destroyed. But it was enough that Carver sensed there was a deal of pain there that the Armenian preferred not to dwell on. But he had mentioned how most of the Inmate Records had been lost, burned or scattered to the winds. In many cases it meant the authorities were having to start from scratch in re-mapping the individual's profiles.

'And I don't envy you either,' Kahramanyan said. 'It is frustrating watching others do what you want to do yourself.'

Carver blinked, taken aback by the psychiatrist's directness. Then he remembered. Jess and he had been spending a fair bit of time together. Suddenly wary, Carver crossed to his coffee pot and held it up. Kahramanyan nodded. He poured two mugs then returned to his chair. Cradling his in his lap, he was careful in the way he framed his response to the psychiatrist's observation.

'Yes, it is frustrating. But that's something we all have to live with now and again.' He intended it to sound casual, and was surprised when Kahramanyan seemed to read something into it.

The Armenian sat forward. 'And can you?'

'Can I what?'

'Live with it.'

Carver's brow furrowed. 'Well I'm not suicidal or anything.'

'I'm not suggesting you are. But please, forgive me for saying this, but you do not seem happy with your present situation.'

Unsure whether it was a statement or a question, Carver felt unsettled by the psychiatrist's smooth segue into professional mode. But to his surprise, instead of steering the conversation elsewhere, he found himself responding.

'No, I'm not happy with the situation. But I can't do much about it.'

'Cannot, or do not want to?'

His response came back so quickly Carver wondered if Kahramanyan had been anticipating it. *What the hell's he doing?*

'Forgive me Mikayel. I'm afraid things are complicated right now. There're things happening you're not aware of. I'm restricted as to what I can get involved in. Organisational stuff, politics, you know.'

Again, the psychiatrist didn't hesitate. 'I am not sure a loss of confidence can be blamed on organisational influences alone.'

Carver stared at the man across the desk. He'd been right. He and Jess *had* been talking.

'Who said anything about a loss of confidence? It's

just that as I'm not part of SMIU, this Danelian thing is not my responsibility.' Though Kahramanyan's face didn't change, Carver was in no doubt what he was thinking. *Liar*.

The psychiatrist changed tack.

'I believe the last couple of years have been hard for you. Some difficult cases, yes?'

'Where have you heard that?' *Just you wait, Jess.*

'Oh… around. Is it true?'

He hesitated. *Should I even be talking about this?*

'Yes.'

'I believe some people you were close to died.'

Carver gave a slow nod. 'Yes.'

'I am sorry to hear,' Kahramanyan said.

'Thank you. But that was all a while ago. In the past.'

'Is it?'

'Is it what?'

'Is it in the past, or is it here, in the present?'

'What are you getting at, Mikayel?'

Kahramanyan looked nonchalant. 'Nothing in particular. It is just that, some people like to think that because things happened long ago, they are no longer affecting us. When in fact they are.'

Carver stared at him, uncertain as to what was going on. But before he could say anything the man continued. 'Take these people you knew who died. I suspect you felt their loss greatly.'

Carver took a moment before replying. 'Yes, I did.'

'And not just grief, perhaps?'

'What do you mean?'

'Perhaps some guilt also? Misplaced guilt I have no doubt, but guilt all the same.'

Carver felt his chest tightening. 'Some.'

'And would you say that guilt is still with you?'

Carver hesitated. He knew now this was no casual conversation about life in general or the sort of problems a stressful job can sometimes throw up. This was about *him*. And though part of him wanted to shy away from it, another said, *Stay with it*, he wasn't sure why.

His gaze stayed on Kahramanyan as he answered his question. 'Some of it may be.'

'Only, *some*?'

Carver shrugged. 'Some of it, all of it, who knows? How do you gauge these things? Some things you can just never forget.'

'This is true, but it *is* possible to remember things from the past, without letting them impact on the present.'

Carver frowned. 'What is it you are trying to say, Mikayel. Has Jess asked you to do a number on me or something?'.

He waved it away. 'Absolutely not. I would not allow such a thing to happen.'

'Then why-'

'Because I think you are suffering, my friend.'

'Suffering? Suffering how?'

'I do not know. You tell me.'

For several seconds, snatches of half-formed thoughts raced through Carver's mind. But it seemed that each time he tried to grab at one so that he could hold it and see it clearly, it leapt away, evading his grasp. Kahramanyan seemed to sense his difficulty.

'Are you having difficulty sleeping?'

'Some nights.' Then, 'Most nights.'

'Would you rather be doing other work than the work you are doing right now?'

'Well like I said before, it can be frustrating-'

'Personal relationships?'

'What about them?'

'Would you say there are difficulties there?'

An image of Rosanna formed. Sarah. His parents. Jason and his grandparents.

'In some areas, maybe.'

'Difficulty making decisions?'

He thought about recent conversations with The Duke, about him switching to SMIU, around whether he ought to be applying for another promotion board. With Rosanna, about their future together, and Jason. Decisions avoided, or postponed.

He nodded, saying nothing.

Without warning, Kahramanyan switched tack. 'Tell me again about Operation Aslan, why you are not involved in it.'

'Like I said, I'm under orders to stay out of it.'

'And the approach they are taking. Is it what you would do?'

He stifled a snort. 'Not exactly.'

'You would do things differently?'

'Some.'

'And what will happen if they do not catch The Monster in time?'

'He will probably kill his family. Others as well perhaps.'

'You think you could prevent this happening if you were involved?'

'I'd have a bloody good go.'

'So why aren't you? *Having a bloody good go*, I

mean?'

'I've told you. They won't let me.'

'And that is the only reason?'

'What other reason could there be?'

'Guilt. Fear.'

'What sort of guilt? And what's there to be afraid of?'

'Guilt over the fact that in the past you weren't able to save people you cared about from being murdered. Fear that if you get involved someone else you care about may die.'

'That's ridiculous.'

'Is it? People tell me that you have always done what you think needs doing, rather than obeying your superiors, is that true?'

'Probably.'

'So what is different this time? You think you could probably help save a family, yet here you are, staring out of the window, talking to yourself.'

By now Carver could feel his heart pumping. He knew that if he raised a hand to his brow, he would find beads of sweat. He hadn't felt this way since those sessions he'd attended after Edmund Hart's trial. And Kahramanyan had a point. What *was* different?

'It… It's not that simple.'

'Isn't it? I think it is.'

'Yes, well you're not sitting where I am sitting.'

'No I'm not. But I'm not sitting at all. I came over here because I thought you are the right man to catch this monster. I still think that.'

'So what are you thinking I should do? Tell them all to fuck off and start my own operation?'

'Is that not what you did in Paris?'

'That was different.'

'Was it? My understanding is that a killer needed catching or else people would die, is that right?'

'Yes.'

'So. No difference at all then.'

Carver said nothing. He wasn't sure what he was supposed to say. Maybe it didn't matter what he said. Maybe what mattered, was what he did. He thought about what Kahramanyan had said, about things being simple. Were they? *Really?* At that moment an image came to him. It was of the yet-to-be-identified Danelian family, arranged as in the photographs Kahramanyan had bought with him. And like the Durzlans. Butchered.

He looked across at the psychiatrist.

'You're very good Mikayel.'

He didn't smile. 'I am just a poor psychiatrist.'

Carver shook his head. 'So you think I ought to throw caution to the wind and just jump in?'

Kahramanyan put his hands up. 'Oh, it is not for me to tell you what to do. I am not a policeman. You must do what you think is right.'

'But if Vahrig Danelian kills his family, and I haven't tried, you think I'll suffer more guilt, right?'

The other man gave the sort of shrug a Frenchman would have been proud of. He seemed to give it some thought.

'Sometimes people choose to do or not do something because it is the easiest option. It is only later that they come to wish they had made a different choice. It is why people continue to smoke cigarettes when they know it is killing them is it not?'

'I guess it is.'

For the next few minutes they drank coffee and, to

Carver's relief, spoke about matters other than himself. But when Jess's name came up, Carver wasn't sure if the psychiatrist wasn't trying to make a point when he said, 'Now there is a young woman who does not lack confidence.'

Carver gave him a sideways look. 'No, indeed.'

'And what does she think about the matters we just discussed?'

Carver returned him a pointed look. 'Something tells me you already know the answer to that question, Mikayel.'

Kahramanyan smiled. *Touché*.

Having finished their drinks, conversation began to wind up. As Kahramanyan made ready to leave, Carver asked the question that had been forming.

'Just answer me this. In your experience, what happens to people who deny themselves what they really want to do. Deep down I mean?'

As before, there was barely any hesitation.

'They wither. Then they die.'

After Kahramanyan had left, Carver stared out the window for a long time, letting his voicemail do its work. Eventually he reached into a drawer and took out the Manchester Force's Internal Directory. Finding the number, he dialled it.

After a few short rings a woman's voice, slightly breathless, said, 'Community Affairs, Constable Skelton.'

He was in luck. Carver imagined her having rushed across the office to pick up. Voicemail isn't popular with uniform staff.

'Hello Bones. It's Jamie Carver.'

'Mr Carver!' She managed to make it sound like she was excited to hear from him. 'Are you a Chief Super yet?'

'Still only a lowly DCI I'm afraid, Padma. As I'm sure you know.'

'What a shame. But don't despair. It can only be a matter of time.'

He chuckled, amused by her teasing. She hadn't changed.

'What can I do for you?'

'There's something you may be able to help me with. Are you busy?'

CHAPTER 30

Like Warrington, Harpurhey Police Station is an old, Victorian nick, one of the few the Manchester force retains within its estate and a throwback to the Dixon of Dock Green era. Once a Divisional Headquarters, today its warren of hidden rooms and endlessly twisting corridors house a disparate array of specialist squads and Area Support, including the Neighbourhood Policing Team. Ridiculously cramped for the number of officers posted there, the inhabiting factions wage a continuing battle for office space. Of its three floors - rumoured to stretch to four in the more remote parts – the third is the most sought after. Visiting Senior Officers rarely trust themselves to wander above the second, either for fear of what they may come across, or never finding their way out again.

The Eastern Area Community Affairs Department occupies one half of the floor and consists of three offices. The unit's complement of constables and sergeants, and the pair of job-share support staff occupy one each, whilst the Department Inspector's desk fits snugly into what is little more than a cubby-hole at the end of the corridor. The story is it used to be the 'upper larder' in the days when most of the floor was given over to the Senior Officers' Dining Room.

As he waited, Carver studied the montage of posters, pamphlets, bulletins, community newsletters and other paraphernalia that covered every inch of wall space. Printed in a range of languages and dialects, they attested to the diversity of the department's work, though Carver thought he remembered many from his last visit, which had to be over a year ago.

One section was new. A green felt notice board bearing the legend, 'Department Performance Monitoring' hung behind the door. Pinned to it were a range of coloured graphs, bar-charts and league-tables. Each one corresponded to some performance measure or target, comparing data-set periods. The targets covered areas such as the number of Community Contacts made, School Visits carried out, Neighbourhood Forums attended, and a host of others. Carver shook his head at the thought that some still believed that a nebulous field such as maintaining good Police-Community relations, lent itself to the sort of Target-and-Measure nonsense that afflicted most of the service these days.

'Hope you're impressed,' the officer said as she came back into the office.

Community Constable Padma 'Bones' Skelton was carrying two brightly coloured mugs. They were both emblazoned with a cartoon-like figure showing a badger wearing a police uniform and bearing the logo, 'Bobby Brock says, Never Go With Strangers.' She offered one to Carver. Taking it with a smile, he settled himself on a desk while the woman he had come to see took one of the metal-framed office chairs that looked like it may have been saved from landfill.

As she sat down, Carver noted that she had barely

changed since their last meeting. As slight and slim as ever and with a burnt-coffee complexion that was somehow ageless, she could still pass for a probationer. Of Indian extraction – 'Bones' was a play on her surname – Carver knew that she was in fact mixed race, her tiny, Kolkata-born teacher-mother having somehow ended up married to a Lancashire dairy farmer. Carver had once met her parents at a Community Officer Of The Year ceremony where Padma's work with Manchester's diverse communities was finally given the recognition it deserved. Possessed of her mother's beauty and her father's down-to-earth manner she was, in appearance at least, the antithesis of what some - the more traditionally-minded - may imagine in a British Community Bobby. She also happened to be the most gifted community mediator and ablest informant handler Carver had ever come across.

Carver first met Padma during the Ancoats Rapes Enquiry where, almost single-handedly, she managed to bring the local Asian population round to cooperating with the investigation. He had made use of her skills several times since, mostly in cases where he needed to establish trust within communities where there was none, or to garner information from those whose opinions of the police might prevent them coming forward. Commended, several times, by her Chief Constable, Padma had been feted at the Home Office for her community work and details of her initiatives were constantly being cited as good practice. Years before, Carver had initially taken it as a personal failure when she rejected his implorings to join CID. Since then he had come to realise that she was one of those police officers who were increasingly rare - ideally suited to her role and with no interest in promotion. The time she stood up before an assembly of Senior Officers and berated them for their collective ignorance of both Islam and prevailing attitudes towards the police amongst Manchester's Muslim population, had passed into legend.

She raised her mug. 'Cheers.'

'Cheers,' he answered.

As he savoured the coffee's rich, dark flavour Carver purred his pleasure.

'Glad to see CAD still makes the best coffee on the force. Eusebio's?'

Padma nodded into her mug. 'His son took over the shop last year, but it's not changed.'

Carver made a mental note to call in on his way back. Eusebio's Coffee House, just off the main Rochdale Road, stocked the widest range of coffees he had ever come across. The chance to replenish both his home and office stocks with something more substantial than the supermarkets' 'so-called 'premium blends' he'd fallen back on of late, was a rare opportunity.

'So what are you after, boss? I heard you'd given up CID for a desk job?'

Seeing the mischievous twinkle in her blue eyes, Carver thought again on how her broad Lancashire accent belied her exotic looks. But though she was probably closer to the truth than he cared to admit, he responded to her dig by sending her a look that was part admonishing, part weary.

He briefed her on Aslan, and its background.

'Armenia?' she said when he finished. 'That's a bit different.'

'How so?'

'They're not like some of the other communities around here. When they started arriving here, mostly in the eighteenth century I believe, they never settled in any particular part of the city. Physically and geographically, they integrated with the rest of the population, though there's a thriving cultural community, mainly based around the Holy Trinity Church in Upper Brooke Street.'

'I know it,' Carver said, impressed but not surprised by her ability to speak with authority about a community he had mentioned for the first time only moments before. 'So what if I wanted to trace a particular family?'

'Well… I might say the church would be a good place to start, but….' She gave a guarded look.

'But what?'

'I take it you are talking about a family that might not want to be found?'

He nodded. 'Quite possibly.'

'Illegals?'

His eyebrows jerked upwards.

She thought about it. 'How long ago you say?'

'Ten years. Thereabouts.'

She thought some more. 'The church is no good then. They're very cagey and wouldn't openly admit to having illegals within their congregation. Even to me. We need someone closer….' She stood up so suddenly he jumped, nearly choking on his coffee. 'What are you driving these days?'

He coughed. 'A Golf. Why?'

She looked disappointed. 'A Golf? Where's the ruddy BM?' He tried to look hurt. 'Never mind, it'll do. Come on. Take me for a ride.'

She was already heading out the door as he rushed to gulp down what was left of the drink he'd been enjoying. 'Where to?'

'You'll see.'

CHAPTER 31

Half an hour later, Carver pulled up outside the block of shops Padma had indicated. Though he had driven through Openshaw many times, he wasn't familiar with this particular part of the East Manchester district or the estate to which Padma had directed him. But the iron shutters over the windows, the graffiti and the stripped-out cars littering some of the open spaces around told their own story.

'Here we are,' Padma said, slipping off her seatbelt.

Carver surveyed the row of tired-looking shops. 'Where's here?' he said.

She pointed to a grocery next to the hairdressers on the end. The shop's frontage was stacked full of produce boxes, almost to half the height of the front window. 'The place everyone comes when they first arrive,' she said.

'Don't tell me. Tea bags and cabbages are the first thing a family of illegal immigrants need when they get here, right?'

She threw him a lop-sided grin as she got out. 'Something like that.'

Inside, the shop was cramped, with closely-packed rows of shelves running down its length. With the boxes out front shading the window, it was even dimmer than it looked from outside. Padma exchanged nods and smiles with a young girl on the till at the front door before leading Carver through towards the back. As they made their way down the aisle, Carver checked the display lining the wall to his right. Blue plastic baskets overflowed with every kind of vegetable he knew, and many more he did not recognise. To his surprise, they all looked fresh, clean and succulent. At least they eat well around here, he thought.

At the back of the shop, a slim, dark-haired youth who looked like he might be the girl on the till's brother, was carrying boxes through from a storeroom. Their dark features put Carver in mind of the various Balkan factions he kept coming across and whose prominence in the city's underclass had increased so dramatically in recent times. The young man beamed when he saw Padma, but the smile vanished as he spotted Carver.

'Hello Eric,' Padma said. 'Is your Dad about?'

The youth eyed Carver with suspicion before nodding over his shoulder. 'In the back. But he's with someone.'

'That's okay. No rush.'

Padma squeezed passed him and as Carver followed, he was aware of Eric's attempt at an intimidating stare. Another time he would have met it. But this was Padma's territory. It wasn't for him to fall out with her contacts. Nevertheless, he gave the lad a wink as he passed.

As they came through into the storeroom, a heftily built man with a full beard and who was perched on a stool outside a door to a small office, dropped the paper he was reading and stood up, unwinding himself to display his considerable bulk. But even as a huge hand balled into a fist and the other reached inside his jerkin, Eric called to him from behind. He said something in a language Carver didn't recognise and the man relaxed. Retrieving his paper – it was in Coptic Carver noted - he returned to his post.

Eric came forward and knocked. A man's voice, gruff and impatient, sounded from within. Eric spoke through the door. Carver heard mention of Padma's name. The voice inside shouted something back, the tone softening noticeably.

'Give me a minute, Padma,' he called through the door.

As they waited in silence – the gorilla on the stool was engrossed in his paper again - Carver checked out the shop's rear door. As he'd expected, it was made of steel, which he guessed would be reinforced. Bolts fitted to the door itself and sturdy looking hinges fixed to the brickwork around the frame indicated that the back of the shop could be locked-up as tight as Fort Knox. Whatever goes on here, Carver mused, it's not just selling tins of chick-peas.

Carver's first thought had been drugs, but he ruled it out immediately. Padma hated the dealers who dealt death and misery within the communities where she worked. She would never even pretend to be on as friendly terms with these people as Carver had judged from the reactions he'd seen so far - King Kong excepted. But if not drugs, what then?

The sound of latches being drawn and keys in locks sounded through the office door. A moment later it swung open. An elderly couple, vaguely Mediterranean in appearance and formally dressed in a Sunday-best kind of way, were ushered out by a small, balding man with a thick black moustache. Again Carver was surprised. From the voice, he had expected someone bigger. As the couple made to leave, there was much hand-shaking and smiling. Several times they joined hands, as in prayer, and nodded their respects to the man. It put Carver in mind of a scene from, 'The Godfather.' Realisation began to dawn.

Eventually the man managed to get the couple to desist and, as they turned to leave and saw Padma and Carver, they fell silent. Their heads went down and they scurried out through the shop, the man pulling his coat round him to conceal the package he was carrying under his arm.

The man with the moustache turned to Padma, smiling widely. 'My Little Jewel.' Placing his hands on her shoulders, he kissed her on both cheeks before enveloping her in a fatherly embrace. Letting her go he turned to Carver.

'Radi Maleeva,' Padma said, 'This is Detective Chief Inspector Carver. But you can call him Jamie. He is a good friend of mine.'

'Then you are most welcome, Mr Jamie,' Radi said. As they shook hands, Carver noted that though much smaller than himself, Radi's grip was the fiercer. The way his dark eyes held Carver's made no secret of the fact he was appraising him and Carver returned the gaze evenly. Apparently satisfied, the man turned and called to the youth still hovering near the doorway.

'Eric. Coffee and schnapps for our guests.'

It was clear now to Carver that they were father and son and that the shop was a family concern, like many such small businesses around the city.

Radi pushed open the door that had sprung shut as

he'd shown the other couple out. 'Please. Come in.'

As they entered the office, Carver just caught Radi's slow shake of his head to the sentry on the stool and the man's confirming nod. He read it as, 'No interruptions.'

Inside, Radi made sure the door was firmly closed and locked – force of habit Carver guessed - before turning to address them. 'Please, sit.'

Carver took in his surroundings. It looked and felt like an ancient accountant's office, ledgers and books stacked on shelves everywhere. In the far corner was the biggest, oldest safe Carver had ever seen. Dark green and embossed with the name, 'Hall and Hall,' it confirmed Carver's growing suspicions.

'Now then, my little Indian ruby.' The ripple of delight that passed through Radi marked his pleasure at seeing her again. 'You have been away too long. I am so pleased to see you.' Then, remembering his manners he turned to Carver. 'And to meet your friend.' Carver nodded back, amused, but also impressed by the man's open display of affection. Would that more people felt that way about their local police.

For a couple of minutes Radi and Padma talked family. Radi asked after her work and parents. She enquired as to his wife, son and daughters and how business was doing. Carver wasn't certain which business she meant. After being let in by Radi, Eric delivered a tray laden with coffee in small cups which Carver knew would taste foul, a bottle of Rakija, and glasses. As he laid them out Eric's eyes hardly left Carver, but he said nothing. When he'd gone, Radi locked the door behind him.

'Drink,' Radi said, sweeping his hand over the tray.

Carver took his coffee and sipped at it, fearing the

worst. It was wonderful, not too sweet and full of flavour, Nothing like the ground-earth bitterness that characterises most Greek-Balkan brews. It drew him to exclaim, 'This is really good.'

Radi showed surprise. 'You think I would serve shit to my guests?' Carver glanced at Padma who chuckled in a way that showed her natural charm. She was clearly at home in these surroundings. Radi poured them shots of the Rakija. As Padma took hers and knocked it straight back, Carver's estimation of her went up another notch.

The drinks ritual completed, Radi brought his chair round and sat down in front of Padma, eyeing her, slyly. 'Now, be honest with your old *bunic*. What is it you are wanting from me?'

Padma smiled. 'What makes you think I have not come just for the pleasure of seeing you again?'

Radi scoffed. 'Well first of all, I am old and wrinkled, while you are young and beautiful. Secondly, with all respect to your friend,' he nodded politely to Carver, who returned it. 'You would not bring someone so important here unless it was business.'

Padma gave a wry grin before accepting defeat. 'Mr Carver - Jamie - is trying to find some people. An Armenian family. I thought you might have had business with them.'

Radi's put on a serious face, giving her a pointed look he did not share with Carver. 'Business?'

She nodded, matching his seriousness, look for look. 'Business.'

Sitting off to Radi's left, Carver just caught the way Radi's eyes flicked in his direction before returning to Padma.

'It is alright, Radi. Jamie is okay.'

Carver wasn't certain what, exactly, Padma's 'Okay' was intended to convey to Radi. He assumed it was something to do with trust, and that Radi could talk openly about his 'business' without having to worry that Carver would react the way some senior police officers might upon hearing about certain, unregulated activities. Whatever it was, it had the desired effect. Radi turned in his chair to face Carver squarely, arms stretched out in front so his hands rested upon his knees. For several moments he explored the detective's face, before speaking.

'So, Mr Jamie. Our mutual friend Padma vouches for you. You are therefore my trusted friend as well. She has told you about me, yes?'

Carver shook his head. 'Not a word.' Radi turned to Padma, surprised.

She shrugged. 'It would not be right for me to tell him without your permission *bunic*,'

Radi studied Carver one last time. 'Then you have my permission.'

Padma turned to Carver. 'Radi is a banker. At least he was in his own country.' She turned to the older man, as if to apologise in advance. 'Now, I suppose he would be called, a money-lender.' Radi shrugged his acceptance of the term.

'That is correct Mr Jamie. I am from Bulgaria, and for, *ahem*, various reasons would not be given a license to bank in your country. Unfortunately there are many people who need money, but dare not use the banks here because-' He hesitated.

'Because they aren't supposed to be here,' Carver finished.

Radi pushed his bottom lip out and spread his hands in a, 'What can I say,' gesture. But he was quick to clarify.

'Please do not think that I deal with the criminals Mr Jamie. The drug-peddlers and money launderers. Nor am I one of these usurers who bleed people to death with their squeezing interest rates. I run a co-operative, on behalf of the peoples of many communities, not just my own. And we charge only as much interest as we need to keep things going.' His hand swept out, gesturing beyond the walls. 'As you can see, I am not a rich man. I have to work for a living, like other people.'

Carver had never met a banker prepared to admit to being rich, but tempered his scepticism. In the short time he had known Radi, his wizarding skills had been working flat out. So far, he had seen or heard nothing that suggested the man wasn't saying anything he didn't truly believe. And by admitting even the little he had already, Radi had shown a degree of trust that Carver felt duty bound to return. Besides, Carver had met some like him before. People who genuinely see it as their responsibility to do whatever they can to help others within their community, whatever their status.

'I believe you,' Carver said.

'Good. So tell me, Mr Jamie. Who is this family you are looking for?'

Carver told him about Vahrig Danelian, and the urgent need to find his family.

Radi looked troubled when Carver told of their fears as to what Vahrig intended. He asked what Carver knew of them.

'All I can tell you are the names they went under in Armenia and their approximate ages.' He handed Radi the sheet of paper he had brought with him.

'Photographs?' Radi said.

'Only of Vahrig, I'm afraid.' He dug one out and passed it across. Radi looked at it blankly, before placing it on his desk. 'All the ones of his family appear to have been destroyed I'm afraid.'

'Ach.' Radi shook his head, gravely.

Carver glanced towards Padma for confirmation before asking his next question. 'Do you think it likely the family might have turned to you?'

Deep in thought, it was a moment before Radi replied. 'I am sorry, what? Oh yes. If they are Armenian, almost certainly.' Carver's heart did a little skip. Radi continued. 'The only ones who do not come to me are the Chinese and Africans. They like to handle their own affairs. And people nearly always come to see me first. There is nowhere else they can go you see. Even if they have money, where can they change it?'

Carver considered it - how obvious - and wondered why he had never thought about it before. He resolved that the next time he needed to track down 'illegals', the first people he would turn to would be the money-lenders.

Without saying a word, Radi got up and went across to a shelf that ran the length of the wall behind his desk. It was packed tight with ledgers and journals. He ran a finger along them as if hoping to magically coax out one that might contain the information Carver needed. On his way back, he stopped a third of the way along, and pulled out several ledgers. They were all thick, and dusty. As he opened one up, checking the dates, Carver caught a glimpse of the columns of entries. Each journal had to contain several hundred transactions. Unless

Radi already remembered something, it didn't look like it was going to be easy, or quick.

Radi stacked the ledgers on his desk, brought his chair back round and sat down. He looked first at Carver. 'I will try to find who you are looking for.' Then he turned to Padma. 'I will ring you when I have something.'

As he let them out, Carver and Radi shook hands again. 'Thank you, Radi,' Carver said, noting from the corner of his eye that Radi's minder was off his stool and in the alert position again. He wondered how much cash was in the safe.

Padma leaned forward and kissed Radi on the forehead. 'I am grateful, *bunic*. I will be in touch.'

As they left through the shop, Eric was re-stocking shelves and Carver felt the young man's gaze follow him all the way out the front door.

Back in the Golf, Carver turned to Padma. 'An interesting character. How did you get to know him?'

For a second she looked at him strangely, then she said, 'Through my own *bunic*. My grandfather on my mum's side. Apparently he and Radi did business together when mum's family first moved here.'

Carver blinked. 'You mean your mother's family was....' But the look on her face told him he should drop it. He turned the engine. 'Bloody hell.'

Carver waited, letting a couple of cars pass before pulling away. Checking his mirror, he just caught sight of the dark figure who came out of the newsagents, a couple of doors down from Radi's. Given the time of year, his long black coat seemed out of place. Unsure if his first impression was correct, Carver watched as the man stepped further out onto the pavement, as if following their departure. Though certain he had never seen him before, Carver had no trouble recognising that they had been made.

'Your friend Radi may be sound, but I think some of his fellow countrymen round here aren't too keen on the likes of us hanging around.' He jerked a thumb behind him.

Padma turned to look but when Carver checked again, the man had gone.

'I never suggested this was a crime-free area,' she said.

Carver chuckled. 'And how right you are.'

Back at the NCA, Carver was heading down the corridor to his office when he met Terry West coming the other way. He had never seen West this side of the divide before and the way he reacted when he saw Carver made him wonder what he was doing there.

'I'm looking for Jess,' West explained, too quickly. 'Thought she might be with you.'

'A phone call would have done it,' Carver said.

'Thought it was time I saw how the NCA operates,' Terry said.

Carver half-turned back in the direction of the main office. West would have passed it to get this far. The Merseysider didn't flinch.

'Nice set-up,' he said. 'But I'd better leave you to it. You're obviously busy.'

Carver watched as West re-traced his steps down the corridor and out through the dividing door, before making his way to his own office.

On entering he checked around but couldn't see anything that looked like it had been disturbed.

Thinking he was being paranoid, he dropped into his chair - just as his monitor went to screen-saver. It was set up to kick in after an annoyingly short three minutes and Carver had never got round to adjusting it. He stared at it for a few seconds, then moved the mouse. The web-browser came back up, still showing the home page of the Armenian Community and Church Council of Great Britain, the last place he'd trawled for inspiration before heading out to meet Padma.

He looked up at the door through which Terry West would have left some three minutes before.

'Damn,' he said.

CHAPTER 32

The porcelain cup rattled on its saucer as Radi Maleeva handed it across to his visitor. As he did so, the moneylender took heart from knowing that Ishvan was at his post, only a few short feet away.

Radi could not remember ever leaving the office door unlocked while he did business, not even the time he was visited by those two Romanians seeking to discuss 'insurance.' But having seen the cold look in his visitor's face when he invited him to take coffee, Radi decided he would be happier knowing Ishvan could respond to any summons instantly, without having to worry about him getting through the door.

The man in the black coat's arrival – only minutes after Padma and Carver left - had caught Radi unprepared. He had anticipated that after the officers had gone, he would have time to think it all through, to decide what to do for the best before dealing with the man in the black coat again. Instead, he was having to work hard at not letting his nervousness show.

There was definitely something different about the man this time. An edginess that was not there when he first showed up claiming to be an Armenian undercover police officer seeking an escaped killer. Though initially suspicious, as Radi always was of people who refused to say how they'd learned of him and the services he provided, Radi eventually accepted the man's story. That the Armenian authorities wished to keep the British Government in the dark concerning the extent of their security and border failures had the ring of truth about it, particularly as Radi was only too aware of certain members of the Armenian Governments' complicity in the illegal trafficking of people, especially young women, from that area. To Radi, a man working on his own, with a brief to detain an embarrassing escapee and arrange for his 'unofficial repatriation' sounded plausible. No fuss no bother.

It was only later, after the man had left, that Radi thought, why go to the trouble of returning such a man at all? If this, 'undercover officer', did manage to track his man down, why not deal with him there and then? What good would it do taking him all the way back simply to incarcerate him for the rest of his miserable life? No. Far simpler to end things here. A knife in the night and it was done. Even if the body were found, so what? The local police wouldn't have a hope of identifying him, or tracing his killer. He would just be one more dead illegal amongst the increasing number the English police had to deal with these days. It wouldn't be the first time such action had been taken on English soil by foreign governments. And unless Radi's ability to judge character had suddenly waned, his visitor was possessed of all the qualities such a solution required, and in ample measure.

But following Padma's visit, Radi was confused. The undercover man – he gave his name as Garo – had insisted that his mission and the background to it were not known to the British authorities. So how was it

Padma and her colleague were looking for the same man? The detective, Carver, had spoken of someone from Armenia's Health Ministry assisting him. That did not fit with any supposed 'undercover' operation.

So what was going on?

It was only Radi's natural wariness of being too open with the police - his experiences in his home land had conditioned him to exercise caution in such matters - that prevented him from telling Padma about this other fellow as soon as he heard they were looking for the same family. And the way his visitor was now pumping him, Radi was beginning to wish he had done.

'Are you certain, Radi?' Garo said, as he sipped at his coffee. 'They made no mention at all of the matters that interest me?'

Radi feigned indifference. 'As I have told you, it was to do with a gang fight in the city. A man was stabbed. They have information it was someone from around here. They thought I may be able to help.'

As he spoke, Radi avoided the man's searching gaze by pretending to be looking for something amongst the papers strewn over the desk. Nevertheless he was conscious of the man's scrutiny. When his casual explanation was met only with silence, he glanced up to see Garo's eyes roaming the desk, as if looking for what could be of such importance as to distract Radi from giving him his full attention.

'And what did you tell them?' Garo said, eventually.

Radi shrugged. 'What I always tell them. That I will make enquires and contact them if I hear anything.'

'And will you?'

'Of course not.'

Garo nodded, beginning to seem less agitated than he

was when he arrived. 'This is wise. A man in your position should not be seen to be cooperating with the police here against your own kind. It would not be… acceptable.'

Radi was quick to concur. 'My view also.'

'Of course the same does not hold for myself. After all, we are compatriots.' The way Garo looked at him, Radi was in no doubt as to his meaning. 'So what do you have for me? Have you found out what I asked?'

Radi showed regret. 'Alas, not yet, Inspector. It seems that the family keep very much to themselves these days. If they ever had a son back home, no one knows of it.'

The man drew himself up in his chair and let out a long sigh that sounded like disappointment. The way he looked at him, Radi thought for a moment he was about to tell him he believed none of it. He prayed that Ishvan had not chosen that moment to relieve himself. But the man seemed simply to be considering his options.

'What about the daughter? She goes out doesn't she? She must have friends, people she talks to?'

Radi shook his head. 'Her father is crippled and her mother ailing. She spends most her time looking after them. She does not seem to have a life outside her home.' For a moment, Radi forgot about his own dilemma. 'It is a great shame. Such a lovely girl.'

As Radi spoke of her, wistfully, he saw Garo's gaze become unfocused. For what seemed a long time he stared out into empty space, as if his mind had suddenly wandered elsewhere. And for some reason the leering half-smile that played around his mouth, made Radi's flesh crawl. With a shake of his head, Garo returned and, to Radi's relief, stood up. But as he made ready to leave, he fixed Radi with a cold look and when he spoke, his voice had dropped an octave.

'You must try harder, Radi. I must know if this is the family I seek before I do anything. No one else must learn I am here. You must *promise* me.'

Radi swallowed. 'Of course, sir. I will do everything I can. I swear.'

'Good. Thank you for the coffee. It was excellent.'

As the man left the shop, Radi saw him nod and smile to Nadia on the till. A chill ran down his spine, making him shudder.

It was only when he returned to his office, after making sure Ishvan was going nowhere and locking himself in again that he saw it. On the desk, near to where Garo had sat, right where the English detective had left it. The photograph of Vahrig Danelian, was half-obscured by the papers he had shuffled round. But it was visible enough for someone to make out the face if they already knew it. And as Radi remembered Garo's eyes wandering over the desk – might he have missed it? - a feeling of dread took up residence in his stomach, and refused to leave.

That evening as they drove home, Nadia in the back seemed to notice her father's distraction.

'Why do you keep looking in your mirror Papa? Is something wrong?'

He glanced at her reflection. 'No daughter. It is just that…. I keep thinking I see….'

In the passenger seat, Eric knew enough about his father's business to turn round for a better look. 'What is it?'

'I'm not sure,' Radi said. 'Do you see a silver car? A Corolla I think.'

Eric looked. 'There is much traffic, but I cannot see one.'

Radi relaxed a little. 'It must be my imagination.' He smiled up at his daughter. 'Nothing to worry about, Nadia. It is just your old father's mind playing tricks.'

Nadia shook her head and gave him the sort of scolding look she knew her mother would have done. 'Too much work and not enough rest, Papa.'

Radi chuckled. The beautiful young girl he had sired was, without doubt, her mother's daughter.

But after a few minutes had passed, the edgy feeling returned and as he drove through the evening traffic – still checking his mirror every now and then – he thought about the afternoon's events. He still wasn't certain what was going on, but things were becoming complicated. If he wasn't careful, he would end up stuck in the middle of it.

The rest of the way he reflected on his options. By the time he turned into the leafy avenue where home lay, he had made his decision. 'Yes,' he muttered to himself. 'That is what I must do.'

But as he glanced up to check behind one last time, he saw Nadia's worried face staring at him. She must have been watching as he ruminated. She would have seen the conflict reflected in his features. He tried throwing her another smile, but he knew it didn't work.

CHAPTER 33

Standing next to the hearth, Rosanna's eyes blazed, though no fire was lit in the grate. Carver reminded himself to be careful.

'I'm sorry, Ros. I don't have any choice.'

'Of course you have a choice.' She all but spat the words out. 'It is not even your job. Just because this man from some Armenian prison-.'

'He's a psychiatrist.'

'...Fills your head with stupid ideas, why do you have to get involved in something that is nothing to do with you?'

'They're not so stupid. And besides, there's more to it than that.'

'Like what?'

'Like me sitting here with my finger up my arse when I should be helping to catch this nutcase. It's like Mikayel said. If I don't do something and someone dies, what'll I feel like then?'

She folded her arms and glared harder, one foot tapping against the reclaimed Welsh Slate fire-surround Alun had finally got round to fitting the weekend before. As he took in her thunderous expression, Carver thought that had a fire been raging, it wouldn't match the heat coming from her.

'And what will happen if you become ill again?' she said.

'I was never ill,' he countered.

Her eyebrows arched at his denial. And as he took in the haughty look, he tried to banish the familiar, conflicted feeling. For all that he hated arguing, especially about work, there was something compelling about her when she was angry.

'If you were not ill, why did you have to see that counsellor?'

It was a cutting blow and Carver winced. 'You know why. After what happened, I was- was….'

'Ill?'

'No. I was close to… giving up.'

'On us?'

'Of course not on us. On work.'

'So why are you ready to give up on us now?'

'I'm not. My getting involved isn't giving up on us. Just the opposite. It's because of us that I'm doing it. If I don't, I'll be giving up on myself. You wouldn't want me to do that, I'm sure.'

She waved her hands in the air, exasperated, eyes glistening.

'How do you know what I want? Do you ever ask?'

'That's not fair, Ros, and you know it.'

'Not fair? Did you ask me when you moved us up here?'

'I didn't, *'move us up here'*. We discussed it, remember? It was a joint decision.'

'Only after you had already spoken to the estate agent. And the building society.'

'That's not true. If I'd thought you were against it, I would have stayed in the city.'

She gave a sceptical look. 'I think you remember how you like to remember. We moved because you did not like to live there anymore.'

About to remind her of certain events, what he'd gone through, he thought better of it. 'We moved here for a fresh start.'

'For you maybe.'

'Jeez, Ros, you make it sound like I dragged you up here kicking and screaming.'

She gave him a look that made him wonder if it wasn't exactly what she thought. Suddenly he wasn't so sure of himself. Up to now, he had always thought of it as a joint decision. That they both needed to get away from the memories that seemed to be around every corner. Had he been deluding himself? But, recognising that if he went into it any deeper he risked opening up a whole new bag of worms, he decided it best to leave it for another time. She opened her mouth to say something, but then closed it, as if maybe thinking the same thing. Having been down this route before, they both knew where it might lead. And it wouldn't be much fun for Sarah and the kids if he and Rosanna weren't speaking.

On cue, there was the noise of the back door opening, children's voices. Sarah called through.

'We're back.'

As Carver listened to his sister reminding Patsy and Jack about their boots – it was amazing how just two days in Rosanna's company seemed to have wrought a change in her – he and Rosanna stared at each other. Then, with a final shake of her head she turned and went through the connecting door to the kitchen. She had mentioned earlier about the number of times already she'd had to mop the floor.

As the door closed behind her, Carver let out a long sigh.

After a beans-on-toast supper – Patsy and Jack had badgered Rosanna all day until she finally agreed to try her hand at their favourite – the children disappeared outside again and Rosanna took herself off upstairs. For the first time since she'd arrived, Carver found himself alone with his sister. Tidying away some of the children's things – another first, of sorts - she turned to him.

'I just want you to know, Jamie, I'm really grateful to you and Rosanna for having us.' He waved it away but she persisted. 'No, I mean it. I know things aren't too good with you two at the moment.' His ears pricked up. 'And I know I'm not always the easiest person to live with-' *An understatement.* 'But if there's anything I can do that would help, you only have to ask.'

'Thanks, Sis. I'll let you know.' But as he looked at her he saw the doubtful look in her eyes.

'If it's me…. Or the kids, then we'll-.'

'It's nothing to do with you. And despite how she sometimes seems, Rosanna loves having the children around. It's just my work. We'll sort it out.'

'This Armenian thing?'

He showed surprise. 'What?'

'You mentioned the other day about some Armenian bloke and his family that you're looking for. Is that what she's not happy about?'

He gave a weary sigh. He hadn't realised he'd mentioned it. 'Partly. But not all of it.' To his surprise, she nodded as if she understood.

'Rosanna told me she's just worried about you

getting hurt again.' Carver started. They'd been *talking?* 'And after last time, I suppose that's understandable.' He gave her a wary look. He couldn't remember ever talking to her about what happened, not in detail at any rate. She had enough problems of her own.

'Maybe so, but if I don't do something, someone could end up dead.'

'This bloke's family?' He nodded. 'Do they live around Manchester?'

'We think so. But we're struggling to find them. They may be illegals.'

'Have you got a name?'

'Danelian, but they've probably changed it to something else.'

'When did they come here?'

'About ten years ago.' He looked at her. 'Why the interest?'

'I once worked with someone from Armenia. But her name wasn't Danelian.'

He nodded. 'There's a big Armenian community around Manchester. I've put out some feelers.'

'And that's why Rosanna's upset?'

'More to do with where it might lead if I get too involved, I think.'

Sarah nodded thoughtfully. 'Well you know how mum mixes her metaphors.'

'What?'

'May as well get hung for a penny as a pound?'

'Thanks Sis.'

'You're welcome.'

His phone rang. It was Padma.

'Radi's just rung. He says there's something he needs to tell us. He wants to see us first thing tomorrow.'

He asked what time Radi opened up.

'Seven-Thirty.'

'I'll meet you at your office at seven.'

As he hung up, Carver was starting to feel the familiar tingle, when a noise at the top of the stairs made him look up. Rosanna was standing there, looking down at him. But before he could say anything she turned on her heel and headed back to the bedroom.

He looked across at his sister and gave a shrug. *What can I do?*

Sarah shook her head and went back to her tidying.

The next morning Carver was up and out early for his meet with Padma, leaving no time for anything between him and Rosanna other than a strained, 'We'll talk later.' Then he was away along the coast road, deploying the camera-avoidance techniques that would continue all the way into Manchester.

Padma was waiting and they wasted no time heading for Radi's. The rush hour traffic was as bad as ever and it was past eight by the time they rolled up outside the shop. It was closed, the steel shutters still locked in place.

'That's not like Radi,' Padma said, digging out her mobile.

It was a while before someone answered and when they did, Carver saw Padma's expression change.

'Hello? Is Radi there? This is Padma Skelton, I'm a Community Police Officer at Harpurhey. No, a friend of the family. Who is this?' As the reply came she threw Carver a concerned look. 'What has happened?' Some of the colour drained from her face. 'Oh my God. Oh my God.' Her face twisted in anguish and she thrust the phone into Carver's hand as tears started to flow.

'This is DCI Carver. Who is this?'

'Jamie? It's Tom Sullivan.' Carver recognised the Cheadle Hulme DI's voice at once. 'I'm sorry if I upset the young lady. We've got a Number One here.'

'Ahh, Jesus.' Carver glanced across at Padma. She was distraught. 'Who is it Tom? The father?'

There was a moment's hesitation before the DI replied, and when he did the words hit Carver like an express train.

'Not just him. All of them.'

CHAPTER 34

During his years of service, Carver had come across many sights for which the word 'horrific' barely did justice, some in the flesh, many more on video or in photographs. But the scene in the Maleeva family's gaudy lounge was of a different scale to anything he had seen before. Even the pictures of the Durzlans, and those Mikayel had brought with him showing Vahrig Danelian's exploits in his home country hadn't prepared Carver for the experience of encountering, first hand, something human eyes were never meant to witness.

Jess was standing to his left. He checked her out. Like him, she was wearing a white scene-suit and protective mask. Blood was everywhere; floor, walls, ceiling. Her eyes were wide and the face above the mask flushed. But though Carver could see she was horrified by the sheer depravity of the tableau before them, her breathing was steady and she seemed to be holding it together. Of course her experience had widened, considerably, since the first murder scene they'd attended together. On that occasion she had hidden everything so well it wasn't until during an evening of drink-fuelled reflection almost a year later that he became aware of how hard she'd found it. But despite her involvement in several murder investigations since, he was certain she would never come across anything remotely like this.

Apart from Jess and himself, two others were present. Across the other side of the room, Terry West was playing the dispassionate SIO, face set firm, hands thrust deep into his trouser pockets. It was a method Carver knew well. Whilst giving the appearance of complying with the old adage – 'At a murder-scene stay HIP - Hands In Pockets;' it also lessened the chances of anyone noticing the fists, clenching and unclenching.

West was watching the stocky, bearded figure crouching before the bodies. Andy Gibson was the on-call Home Office Pathologist and he was going about his business with a grim determination. Nevertheless, Carver couldn't but be aware of the incongruity of his presence at such a scene. Under the white suit and mask, Gibson, white-haired and full-bearded, bore more than a passing resemblance to Santa Claus.

But even as Carver turned his attention to the pathologist – he was examining that part of the tableau comprising Radi's wife and their son - he stood up. The cracking from his knees broke the cloying silence. He turned to look at the detectives, meeting their gazes one by one, starting with West and finishing with Carver. He lifted his mask for a moment, to let in some cooler air.

'I hope to God you're going to tell me you know who did this.'

Carver had never worked a job with Gibson, but they had met. He had a deserved reputation for gallows humour, though on this occasion, he was keeping the trait firmly in check.

'We think so,' Carver said, evenly. He nodded towards Jess and West. 'My colleagues are on the case.'

Gibson eyed them warily. 'In that case do me a favour. Catch the bastard before I have to see another like this.'

Given that pathologists usually affect immunity from the angsts some murder scenes invoke in the uninitiated, Carver thought it a telling remark. He was aware that Gibson had children, probably about the same age as Eric and Nadia. The scene would cause many a parent to suffer sleepless nights for a long time to come.

'That's exactly what I intend to do,' West said, answering the pathologist's appeal. 'But before we get on it, can you give me an interim cause of death? It would help.'

The pathologist turned back to the entwined, bloody bodies.

'Most likely as it appears, I'd say. Blood loss caused by severing of the carotid arteries. Father and son also show signs of head trauma which I suspect were disabling injuries. Mother has bruising around the mouth. Probably the same thing.' He demonstrated by raising a hand to his face, mimicking the assault on her. 'She must have put up a hell of a struggle.'

'Who wouldn't under the circumstances?' Jess said.

Carver looked across at West. Prior to the temporary head of SMIU's arrival, he'd had time to check out the rest of the house.

'It fits with his MO, Terry, taking out the members of the family one by one and restraining them before bringing them back together.' The reference took their eyes back to the bodies in front of the hearth before Carver continued. 'The blood in the hallway will be where he hit whoever answered the door, the son probably. There's more in the downstairs study. That'll be where he got Dad and there're signs of a struggle in the kitchen where he surprised mother.' He lowered his tone even more. 'And judging from the state of the daughter's bedroom… it looks like he found her there.'

West caught the hint. 'Raped?'

'Possibly.' Carver turned his gaze on Gibson who nodded back.

'I'll start with her when I get them back to the mortuary. I'll let you know.'

Jess moved around the large sofa to get a closer look but had to stop where the blood stain was still spreading through the carpet's thick pile. 'I still find it hard to believe that one man can arrange four people on his own like this.'

'If they're properly restrained and you are ruthless enough, it wouldn't be too much of a problem,' Gibson said. He leaned towards where Nadia's tied body knelt before that of her father – held upright by the web of ropes strung between wall-light fixings and anchored to the mantlepiece. They were both naked. Using his little finger, the pathologist tracked the secondary cuts and livid-blue grazing to her throat, seemingly oblivious to the depraved act she was forced into committing as she died. 'I would imagine this is where he held the knife. To ensure compliance from the others.'

Carver saw Jess give a shudder.

'My God. What must have been going through their minds?'

As they all lapsed into silence once more, Carver read the signs. He had seen enough. 'I need some air.'

'Me too,' Jess said.

West said nothing but didn't take long to follow.

Out on the driveway at the front of the house, West

lit up a cigarette, drawing the smoke deep into his lungs. The banging of van doors and the sounds of cars pulling up heralded more elements of the circus arriving. Jess offered Carver a stick of spearmint gum. As he popped it in his mouth, Alec Duncan came up the drive together with Mikayel Kahramanyan. The psychiatrist was due to fly home that morning. Alec must have rung in on his way to the airport. Ashen, Mikayel could barely wait to ask Carver.

'Is it...? Was it... him?'

Carver looked at West who stared back at him, then nodded.

'Father, mother, son and daughter.'

'So he *is* here.'

Carver regarded the psychiatrist with surprise. He sounded almost like he'd been harbouring hope that their theory about Vahrig Danelian making his way to England was mistaken. For his part, he'd never doubted it.

'Oh he's here alright,' West said, forcefully, as if to remind them all who was in charge. 'What we don't know is how he came to target this family.' Slowly and deliberately, he turned his gaze on Carver. Carver readied himself.

But Jess seemed to sense what was coming. 'Come on Alec,' she said. 'We'd better check where Forensic are. You come along as well Mikayel. I can fill you in.' Looking slightly bemused, Kahramanyan let her lead him back down the drive towards the gate.

'Right,' West said as soon as they were gone. He took another long drag on his cigarette, winding himself up, before flicking it away into the hedge. Carver noted where it landed, so he could tell whoever was in charge of the Ground Search Team later. 'I want to know what the fuck's going on. How did you and this PC come to be involved with Maleeva without me knowing?'

Carver nodded. Under the circumstances it was a fair question, and he met West's gaze squarely. 'I was looking to see if there was another way of finding the family apart from trawling immigration records.'

'On whose authority?' West's voice rose in pitch. 'I thought it had been agreed you aren't involved in this investigation?'

Carver checked his response. They both knew there was nothing particularly unusual in an officer not involved in a major enquiry putting out feelers. So long as it didn't cut across an existing line of investigation, most SIOs put up with it, happily. It was an extra resource, and a break from any source was still a break. But West would know that Carver had ignored his own boss's instructions. Okay, that was a matter for him, not West, but the obvious inference was already bouncing around his head like a pin-ball machine, and West would be aware of it. *Am I in some way responsible for all this?*

'I'm not involved. It was just something I thought I could help with.'

West couldn't resist the opportunity. 'Tell that to those poor sods in there.'

It was savage comment and for a moment Carver thought about responding. Despite what had happened, he hoped that once he'd thought about it, he would know that his attempt to use Radi Maleeva as a source was legitimate under the circumstances. There were always risks in such things, but if detectives weren't prepared - encouraged even - to take them, half the murderers serving time in the country's prisons would still be on the streets. But he wasn't about to disrespect the memory of the family Padma had been close to by getting into an argument with West about it, not here. Besides, it was time he found out how she was managing. He'd left her sipping tea in next door's kitchen, rapidly turning into the scene's unofficial cafe. The snippets picked up by the lady of the house would ensure her popularity around the morning coffee circuit for weeks to come.

'Look, Terry-' Carver began, but as he saw the look on West's face he knew that nothing he said would dissuade his ex-colleague from making the most of it. He suspected he would be hearing from Nigel Broom before long. He gave a resigned look. 'Forget it. Let's just say it was a bad idea. Just get on and catch the bastard.' He turned on his heel.

'Hang on, I'm not finished yet,' West said to his departing back. 'I need to know what this Maleeva bloke told you.'

Carver stopped and turned. 'Nothing. He wanted to see us this morning to tell us something. But we'll never know now, will we?'

Ignoring West's demands to come back, Carver strode out the gate and turned right, heading for the neighbouring drive just as Jess, Alec and Mikayel appeared from it.

'How's Padma?' he said.

'Getting it together,' Jess said. 'How's he?' She flicked her head in West's direction.

'Chunnering. I've left him to it.'

'So what's the connection between Danelian and the Maleevas?' Jess said. She had arrived with West and it was the first chance they'd had to speak alone. 'This can't be a coincidence.'

He filled them in on Radi's business, what he'd hoped to learn.

'But why kill them?' Alec said. 'If Vahrig's already here, wouldn't he go straight for his family rather than alert us by this?'

Carver shrugged. 'We can't be sure of his intentions yet, Alec. Maybe he's got another agenda.'

'DI GREYLAKE?'

West's shout signalled his impatience to get on with things. Jess's conflicted look as she looked at the tall hedge between the two houses then back to Carver spoke of her concern as to what her former partner might be planning.

'So what're you going to do now?'

There was a defiant look in Carver's face as he stared through the hedge. 'My mum had a saying. Might as well get hung for a penny as a pound.'

Jess blinked her confusion, before letting it go and glaring at him. 'Aren't you in enough trouble already?'

Carver's eyes bore no trace of conflict as he turned from Mikayel to her. 'People are dying Jess. I'm going to do my job. I'll catch up with you later.'

Repeating the goodbyes he'd made the previous day to Mikayel - 'I'm sorry this had to happen just as you are leaving,' - he shook the psychiatrist's hand before disappearing round the side of the house to find Padma.

Jess turned to Alec and Mikayel. 'Great. Jamie and Terry West trying to score points off each other is all we need.' But as she saw the look on Mikayel's face, her thought was that he seemed strangely unaffected by the apparent conflicts he had just witnessed. She had seen what seemed a meaningful look pass between him and Jamie as the two men parted.

The Scotsman also seemed sanguine. 'Och, lassie, they're big boys, leave them to it. An' speakin' personally, I'd rather the boss was working with us, even if it has got to be unofficial.'

Jess turned to him. 'It's alright for you. You aren't the one who's going to be getting the phone calls from Rosanna.'

' JESS? ARE YOU THERE?'

She gave the two men a resigned look. 'You'd better get Mikayel to the airport while I start getting this scene sorted. We'll speak about Jamie later.' She turned to Mikayel.

'Goodbye again, Mikayel. Hopefully when we meet next this will all be over.'

'I hope so too,' he said. 'But at least you can keep me informed how things are going now.' He took the leaving present she had given him the night before from his pocket and waved it, to show him how chuffed he still was. The Samsung's silver and black case glinted in the morning sun.

'Don't lose it,' she said.

'I won't,' he promised.

Half an hour later, Carver headed away from the scene, leaving Padma to brief the just-arrived Family Liaison Officer - something positive she could do. As he drove, he fought to keep at bay the doubts that had been threatening to form since his face-off with West.

It *wasn't* his fault, he told himself. It couldn't be. Radi meeting his death the day after they had met would be too much of a coincidence. Something had happened to mark Radi and his family as targets beforehand. But what?

As he headed back into the city, determined to find out, his seat belt pressed against the bunch of keys he'd taken from the desk drawer in Radi's study. Reaching into his pocket he pulled them out and tossed them onto the passenger seat before checking his watch. It was already gone noon. The day had disappeared quickly following the discovery of the slaughter and there were things that needed doing before it was over.

He turned his attention back to his musings and drove to his destination mainly on auto-pilot. Which was why he remained unaware of the silver saloon that always managed to stay at least two cars behind him.

CHAPTER 35

Lucy peered, expectantly, out of Starbuck's window, scanning the passing shoppers and office workers as she sipped her latte. The day before, after lunch, he'd seemed uncharacteristically vague as they parted. 'Maybe see you again tomorrow,' was all he offered.

Now she was embarrassed to admit that though she had been telling herself all morning she was being foolish she had, deep down, assumed he would show. But half an hour had passed already and still there was no sign.

She kept trying to convince herself that it was probably just some work commitment that had detained him. He hadn't actually said what he did, mentioning only something about some 'project' he was involved in when she asked. But the thought was beginning to settle that her ridiculous nervousness had finally seen him off, like all the others.

'You stupid, stupid, woman,' she scolded herself under her breath. Then, realising the young man on the stool next to her was glancing, warily, her way, she continued the dialogue in her head.

Why can't you just be natural? No wonder they never come back, the way you respond to their every question with suspicion. Isn't it normal for a man who is interested in a woman to ask about where she comes from, her family, their background? It is time you learned to trust people. But then she remembered the reasons why she didn't trust people. Her family's past. What the future may yet hold for her. The telephone call from Cyprus - she was still to mention it to her mother, though was planning to do so that evening. But why should all that stop you behaving normally with someone who knows nothing about such matters? He was just doing what any man does who wants to get to know a woman better. Where is the harm in that? Oh no. You have to make a big thing out of it, like he is about to ask to meet your parents or something, as if it were the prelude to a proposal. *Stupid woman.*

'Hello, Lucine.'

She gulped, nearly choking on the coffee she was swallowing as he'd said it. How the devil had she missed seeing him come in?

'H-hello,' she stammered. 'I didn't think you were coming today.'

'I am sorry, I am running late. Busy morning.' He was red in the face, like he had been jogging.

'I don't have much longer I'm afraid,' she said, trying to keep the disappointment out of her voice. She checked her watch. 'I am due back in a few minutes.'

His face fell. 'What a shame. I was looking forward to lunch. I, er-.' He looked at her in a way she thought was almost sheepish. 'I enjoyed talking to you yesterday. I was hoping….' As she gazed up at him, waiting to hear it, she willed herself not to flush. *Don't turn red. Don't you dare turn red.* 'I was hoping we might be able to repeat it sometime.'

Lucy felt her ears warming. 'Well, I'm here most

days-.'

'I don't mean here,' he said, quickly. 'I thought we might…. I wondered if….'

Her heart began pounding.'Yes?'

He took a deep breath. 'I wondered if I could take you somewhere? Dinner perhaps?' He must have read her face. 'Or maybe just a drink, if dinner is too much?'

She felt her stomach tying itself in knots, the familiar panic. But as she fished for the usual excuse, she remembered her one-sided conversation of a minute before. *So. Is this the way it will always be, or are you going to stop it, right now?*

'I… I would like that.'

He beamed. 'How about tomorrow? I could call for you. Maybe around, seven-thirty?'

She thought a moment. She needed time to help her mother settle Dadda. 'Well… Could you make it eight?'

'Eight it is.'

She slipped off her stool, eager to leave before she made an even bigger fool of herself.

Suddenly she stopped. 'I've just realised. You don't know where I live.' His mouth opened as if to say something, then closed again. She delved into her bag, took out a pen and scrap of paper and scribbled her address. 'Here,' she said, handing it to him. He barely glanced at it before slipping it into his coat pocket.

Heading back to work, Lucy suddenly remembered the phone call she had resolved to discuss with her mother that evening. She had been putting it off, knowing how her mother would likely react. She knew there would be no going out for a while once she did. Time was drifting and she had already left things longer than was probably wise. But events of the last few minutes had emboldened her. No matter, she told herself. Another day or so cannot harm. In any case, it would give her a while longer to think over their options.

In lighter mood than she had been for a long time, she returned to her altered schedule. And as she made her way back to the office, it was all Lucy could do to stop herself from skipping along the pavement.

CHAPTER 36

Carver's gaze roamed the dead moneylender's cluttered office. He had half-expected to find it ransacked, but the shop was still locked when he arrived, and there were no signs anyone had been there before him.

Though he had chosen, quite deliberately, not to dwell on it, Carver knew he was now going far beyond the bounds of, 'putting out feelers'. By searching the victim's office without authority - legal, investigative or otherwise - he was leaving himself open to accusations of, 'undue interference', and was in no doubt West would not hesitate to make them. But the clock was running and he knew the way West liked to operate, slow and methodical. It would be hours before he got round to thinking about searching Radi's business premises.

Carver knew better than to look for rationality in any of Vahrig Danelian's actions, and he wasn't about to assume that the slaying of the Maleeva family would slake the killer's thirst for blood. On the contrary, he read it as a sign that the man they were after may be throwing caution to the wind, and that any further murders – if that was his plan - may follow quickly. It was why he had decided to put aside the doubts and fears that had been dogging him, and to now do whatever he could to find Vahrig Danelian. And if not Danelian himself, he may at least prevent another slaughter by finding his family. He would think about Rosanna later.

On his way to the Maleeva grocery, he visualised the action-list he would put into the Major Incident Room once it was up and running. Even now members of GMP's Major Incident Team would be swarming over Cheadle Heath Police Station – the force's Western Area 's designated MIR site – racing to establish the room within their 'eight-hours from notification' target. At the top of the list was tracking down and speaking to Radi's gargantuan body guard – if only he had been around the night before – though depending on what he found here, Carver hadn't ruled out taking that one on next.

His thoughts returned to the here and now, and his gaze came back to Radi's desk. It was tidier than the day before. He must have cleared up after he and Padma left. But one of the journals he had seen Radi take down from the shelf was still there, though the others were back in place.

Crossing to the desk, he picked the book up and saw at once the slip of paper marking a page halfway through the thick volume. He turned to it. It took him a minute or so to get his head round the dead banker's elaborate script, but once he did so, he read quickly, running a finger down the list of names. He found it three quarters of the way down. It was a one-line entry against the name, "Danelian". Like the others, a line was drawn through it, presumably denoting the debt was discharged. But the entry consisted only of figures and dates. From his reading it showed that Maleeva had loaned the family three thousand pounds. The final figures, dated almost three years later, showed three thousand eight-hundred pounds repaid. But there was no address.

'Bugger,' he said.

For a moment he stood there, thinking. Then he started checking through various other ledgers. None of them contained addresses. Carver wasn't surprised. He had dealt with many people who operated businesses that fell somewhat short of 'legal'. Only the most stupid kept their clients' addresses along with their other records. There would be a list, somewhere of course. But it wouldn't be around here, and it wouldn't be easy to find. He imagined another safe somewhere - Maleeva's home probably. But it would almost certainly be concealed, and he didn't think he would get far if he headed back there and demanded West give him free access to look for it. And that was assuming an address list even existed.

Disappointed and temporarily out of ideas, he tutted and turned back to the original journal, still open at the Danelian entry, intending to return it to its place on the desk. But as he slipped the marker-paper back into the page, he realised there was something written on the other side. Turning it over, he saw a name, 'Lucine', along with a Manchester district telephone number, the Prestwich area if his memory served.

For a moment he thought about it, trying to imagine the moneylender's actions after he and Padma left. The journal entry was close to ten years old. The family may have re-settled in that time. He imagined Radi ringing round his contacts for up-to-date information, noting names and telephone numbers. He looked at the piece of paper again and wondered. It could of course be nothing; just a scrap Radi retrieved from the waste bin to mark the page. He looked down. The waste bin was empty.

'Then again….' He took out his wallet and slipped the paper between its folds. Then he closed the journal and put it back in place on the desk.

As he turned to leave, a noise sounded outside the office and he stopped. It had sounded like the beaded curtain separating the back of the shop from the front being brushed aside. Then he remembered. While he had closed the shop's front door, he hadn't locked it. Even if news of the Maleevas' murders hadn't yet reached the streets, the shutters and drawn blinds would signal the shop wasn't open for business. Stepping quickly behind the half-open door, he pressed himself to the wall. For several seconds there was only silence, then he heard soft footfalls outside the room, another pause, then the door began to open, slowly.

Carver's first thought was Radi's bodyguard, but as he glimpsed a man's bulk through the door's hinge gap, he saw that, whilst reasonably tall, he wasn't as big as the giant he had seen the day before. Nevertheless he recalled Vahrig Danelian as being just under six foot - and at that moment could think of no one else who might be interested in searching Radi's office.

He waited a second more while the figure stepped into the room, then hurled himself against the door so that it battered the intruder against the door frame. There was a guttural grunt of pained surprise as the man bounced off it then staggered back into the darkened storeroom. Off-balance he crashed down amidst a pile of discarded cardboard boxes. Wrenching the door open, Carver didn't hesitate but threw himself at the figure now struggling to regain his feet. But even as he fought to get a restraining grip on the man, Carver realised that while he lacked the bulk of the bodyguard, he was big enough, and strong. Knowing he had to get the upper hand quickly or risk being overpowered, he was about to plant a fist into the middle of the face emerging from the cardboard boxes when an anguished cry stayed him.

'DON'T, MR CARVER. It's me.'

For a moment Carver couldn't place it, but as he hesitated and backed off to let some light in, he recognised the cowering figure beneath him.

It was the retired SOCO, Ron Gover.

For several moments Carver stared at the man in mute surprise. Having expected Vahrig Danelian, or at the very least some shady associate of Radi Maleeva, he was thrown completely by the retired SOCO's presence. *Was he connected with Maleeva in some way?* With adrenalin turning his surprise quickly to anger, he reached out for Gover's jacket and hauled him to his feet.

'What the hell are you doing here, Gover? I could have hurt you, dammit.'

'I'm sorry, Mr Carver,' Gover gasped, still shaken. 'I wasn't sure where best to approach you. But I knew you were on your own so I came in.'

Carver was having difficulty putting it together. 'Approach me? How the hell did you know where to even find me?'

Gover looked abashed. 'I, er, I've been following you. I picked you up on the way into the city this morning.'

'What?'

'Someone I used to know said you live out in North Wales, so I guessed you would come in along the 'fifty-six.' Seeing Carver's look of astonishment, he added. 'I was Regional Crime Squad in my early days. I'm a bit rusty but the basics are still there.'

'Jesus.' Carver made a mental note to revise his surveillance-awareness techniques at the next opportunity, if it had been Danelian… It made him think of Rosanna, and a wave of panic shot through him before he realised he was confusing past and present. Nevertheless, it was a reminder and he set himself another prompt to phone her and tell her to be careful. Things were happening he didn't fully understand. It may be an overreaction, but better safe than sorry.

'I'm sorry if I-.' Gover began, but Carver put out a silencing hand.

'Hang on, Ron.' He took a deep breath to clear his mind and flush away the remains of his scare. 'I don't understand what you're saying. What's the problem with you approaching me? And why go to all the trouble of picking me up on my way into work? I gave you my office number, why didn't you just call?'

Gover's sheepish look faded, giving way to something more serious. He pulled at his jacket, still straightening himself after his mauling. 'No, I couldn't. It would have been too risky.'

'Risky? Why would it be risky? What are you talking about?'

Gover stared at him, blankly, for a long time, like he was weighing consequences. Eventually his face broke and he gave a resigned sigh. 'I've something for you….'

CHAPTER 37

After initially sounding like she wanted to be helpful, the woman who had answered Carver's call with, 'Tesco Prestwich. May I help you?' was apologetic when she returned to the phone.

'I'm sorry, I've checked our personnel system, but there's no record of a Lucine Danelian. And I've asked around but no one here now remembers anyone by that name. Unfortunately we have quite a turn-over of staff, especially young women. They tend to come and go a lot.'

Carver pulled a face. *Sod's law.*

'Well thanks anyway,' Carver said. He gave her his number, asking her to ring him back if anyone remembered anything.

'Will do,' she said brightly. But as Carver put the phone down he had a feeling he would never hear from her.

'Damn,' he said. He stared at the name and number on the slip of paper, wondering what it was his instincts were trying to tell him. He still didn't know if the name, 'Lucine' held any significance, but he couldn't think of any other reason why the murdered moneylender would have jotted her details. He scratched the back of his head. Something was bugging him, but he couldn't think what.

'Come on,' he urged himself as he re-played the phone conversation in his head.

He was doing so for the third time when the telephone rang.

It was Nigel Broom and the way he barked, 'Carver?' down the phone as soon as he picked up, Carver knew what it was about. *You bastard, West.*

'Yes, sir?'

'What the fuck are you doing?' Carver moved the phone away from his ear. 'I thought I made it clear you were to stay out of this bloody SMIU investigation?'

'You did. I–.'

'So why have I got a DCI West onto me telling me about you visiting a potential source, and now he and his family are dead?'

Carver bit his lip at the inference that West had described Radi Maleeva as a potential source, as if he had already figured in the enquiry. He wondered what else his former colleague had sold to Broom.

'I was looking to see if I could speed things up a bit. West has got half his team wasting their time trawling immigration records and-.'

'That's his prerogative. He's the SIO so it's his shout. It's bugger-all to do with either you or NCA. You know what I told you.'

'I do, sir, but someone on his team was expressing concern that-.'

'Who? Your friend Ms Greylake I presume? If you can't stay away from her, Jamie, then you'd better-'

'It wasn't her. And even if it had been, it makes no difference. This Armenian guy is looking for his family and if he finds them he's going to do to them what he did to the family we found this morning. The information came to me in the first place, and I know how you feel, but I'm sorry, I can't just sit on my hands and wait around until more bodies turn up.'

Even down the phone, Carver heard Broom's long intake of breath. 'There are plenty of officers around just as committed as you are. You're not the only detective capable of catching murderers you know. And if you aren't prepared to follow my instructions, then you leave me no choice but to re-consider your position with NCA.'

'I didn't say I'm not prepared to follow your instructions. It's just-.'

'I'm sorry Jamie. You know I have a lot of respect for what you've achieved, but when I agreed to take you back onto NCA - remember, when you needed a break?' Carver remembered, but decided against pointing out it was Broom who telephoned him with his offer. 'Well it wasn't charity. I shouldn't have to point out that we're still trying to put our own house in order. That's what I took you on to do.'

'I thought it was for my practical experience.'

'Don't be smart with me. You know exactly what I mean. Now I'm telling you one last time. Back off. May I remind you I'm still waiting for the North West office's contribution to the new NCA Strategy document. It was supposed to be with me by the end of last week.'

Carver's gaze wandered to the middle tray of the three-stack right in front of him. The buff folder containing the half-completed analyses and Crime-Trend Projections seemed to have sunk even further down the 'pending-not-urgent' pile than the last time he'd thought about it. He remembered he was off that coming weekend.

'How about if I-.'

But Broom wasn't for having any. 'I'm not negotiating with you Jamie. Either do as I say, or get yourself fitted for a uniform. I'm sure there are plenty of DCIs who would welcome a respite from the pressures of area work.'

Before Carver could respond the line went dead and after a few moments holding his breath, he let it out with a sigh - of relief as much as anything. He didn't take well to threats, and had felt the onrush of blood that would no doubt have fuelled whatever would have come out of his mouth next. He let it go. 'Thanks for your understanding,' he said to the telephone.

'I take it that was Broom?'

Carver glanced up. Jess was in the doorway, looking drawn. He made a rueful face.

'I'm sorry,' she said. 'Terry was on to him, blowing you out as soon as we got back. I tried to ring but you were engaged so I came round to warn you. Looks like I was too late.'

Craving the sanctuary of caffeine, Carver nodded as he rose from his chair. 'I was expecting it from the moment I heard about the Maleevas.' He waved a mug. She declined. 'But I'm not blaming anyone. I knew the risks when I rang Padma.'

As he returned to his seat, Jess closed the door and took the chair at the side of his desk. 'Okay. What else didn't you tell Terry at the scene?'

Carver told her more about his visit to Radi the previous day and his request for a meeting that morning.

'So you think he was going to put you onto the Danelians?'

'I'm positive. And if that idiot West had bothered to ask, I'd have told him to go through Radi Maleeva's house and business records with a fine-tooth comb. There's an address somewhere. It's probably why he was killed.'

'So why did he kill the rest of the family?'

Carver gave her a resigned look. 'Remember what Mikayel said? It's what he does.'

She pondered on it, nodding, but then remembered something else.

'I rang earlier, from the mortuary, but you weren't in and you weren't answering your mobile . Where were you?' He twitched an eyebrow. 'Jamie…? What are you doing?' It twitched again, and swung his gaze towards the note on his desk. 'Oh God, you're still on it aren't you?' She came around the side of his desk, twisting her neck so she could read the scrawl. 'Lucine? Who is Lucine?'

'That's what I'm trying to find out. I think Radi wrote it before he died.'

Jess gave him one of her scolding looks. 'Broom'll have you put back into uniform the moment he finds out. And he will. West will see to it.'

He shrugged. 'But at least by then we may have found the Danelians.'

'Tell you what, let me follow it up.' She reached towards the note. ' At least then he can't make anything out of it.' But about to pick it up, he caught her wrist. She looked up to find his dark eyes burning into hers.

'Not this time, Jess. I'm going to see it through.'

Her brow furrowed. 'But why? What's the point?

It'll only lead to trouble.'

'And it'll be my trouble. No one else's.'

She looked at him pityingly. 'So that's it is it? A man's got to do what a man's got to do? Who do you think you are, Gary Cooper in High Noon?'

The cinematic reference – usually his trick – almost brought a smile. 'I'm just saying, I'm not hiding anymore. If it needs doing then I'm going to do it. And bollocks to anyone who tells me otherwise.'

The look in her face turned to exasperation and as she shook her head, her hair shook and glistened under the light. 'Men. You can be so immature sometimes.' She returned to her seat. 'So what's the number?'

'Tesco.'

'Tesco?'

'At Prestwich. But no one there remembers a Lucine and they can't find any records.'

'So what next?'

'I was working on it when you came in.'

'Sounds like you need to find someone who worked for Tescos and might remember…. Jamie?' His eyes had glazed over.

' Jamie?'

He came back to her with a start but instead of speaking he just lifted a hand to his mouth as he pondered on the thought that had come to him, responding - at last - to the itch.

'What is it?' Jess said.

Still silent, he checked his watch. It was nearly three already and he'd promised the woman he'd arranged to see he would be there by half-past. He picked up the phone and dialled home. He let it ring for a long time in case they were outside. Jess stood there, watching.

Hanging up, he tried Rosanna's mobile, assuming she would be with them, wherever they were. As the robotic voice he'd grown used to hearing kicked in, he hung up before she could tell him, 'The person you are calling is unable to take your call.'

'Damn.'

He imagined them all, half way up a Welsh mountain-side and wondered again why, in this day and age, mobile phone networks still can't cope with hills. No telling when they would be back. But he could keep trying on his way.

He grabbed his jacket off the back of his chair. 'Sorry Jess. Things to do. Ring you later.'

And he was gone.

CHAPTER 38

The slightly-built woman with short black hair spread her weight on her hands and leaned over the glass-topped examination table. From a distance, her gaze seemed steady, unreadable, but across the room Carver could just make out the minute eye movements that reflected the feverish activity going on behind them. They had begun the moment he stopped talking.

Without moving her hands off the table she swivelled her head round, slowly, looking over her shoulder. Above waist height, the walls were of glass through which the technicians and scientists who made up her team could be seen, going about their work with the methodical deliberation their calling demanded. No one was paying Carver and the dark-haired woman the slightest attention. Why would they? Investigating Officers visited the Forensic Services lab just outside Chorley every day. And while many knew Carver and had worked with him, they also knew he liked, whenever possible, to engage Senior Analyst, Claire Trevor, to work on his cases, just as he was seeking to do now.

Eventually Claire stood upright and wandered, casually, to the door, nudging it with a foot so that it closed, slowly and quietly. No one looked around.

Carver knew that many of the Lab-Rats, as he enjoyed calling them, kept the doors to the individual Inspection Rooms closed while they worked. They claimed it reduced the risk of contamination, but seeing as they worked in an environment that was pretty much sterile anyway, Carver suspected they just preferred peace and quiet - not that a place where the decibel level seldom rose above library pitch could be described as 'noisy'.

Claire returned to the counter and pinned him with the stare again.

'You've got to be kidding me.'

He held her gaze for several seconds, arms folded, before shaking his head.

She looked down at the collection of plastic bags in front of her. 'Who knows?'

'No one.' Then he added. 'Yet.'

'If I don't find anything?'

'Then it won't go anywhere and I was never here.'

'And if I do?'

He took a deep breath. 'I'll take full responsibility.'

The guffaw was as low as she could keep it. 'Oh yeah. Like my Director won't be, "Tell me, Ms Trevor, on whose authority did you accede to DCI Carver's request when there was no SR?"'

He ran his tongue round his lips. 'If you want a Submission Report, I can let you have one. It may just be a little… imaginative.' He sent her a wink. It earned him a ticking off.

'Don't do that. I'm not one of your floosies in some city-centre dive.'

It was his turn to pretend. 'Excuse *me*. What sort of people do you think I mix with?'

'I know what sort of people you mix with. You showed me once, remember?'

He did. It was at the height of the Ancoats rapes investigation. Claire had wanted to see for herself exactly how the 'entirely innocent' contact-and-transfer process he'd been hypothesising about might work. Carver claimed it could account for the multiple DNA traces - from differing sources - she had found on some of the victims' outer clothing. After failing to dissuade her and settling for warning her as best he could, he took her to the Neptune, then the dingiest, most low-life nightclub in the City. After an hour spent observing what went on in the toilets - ladies *and* gents, -swapping seats around the club's less-than-salubrious lounge area, and letting her experience the fun of the crush around the bar – 'I'm sure that bloke with the tattoos was trying to have sex with me,' - Claire could stand the noise, atmosphere and groping no longer. 'Get me out of here,' she begged.

He was happy to oblige.

As he drove her home, and after she got her breath back, she swallowed her pride enough to acknowledge that there might be something to his suggestion after all. For weeks he had been imploring her that the Forensic Service industry was long overdue in reviewing some of the assumptions that still underpin many scientists' 'expert opinion' concerning presence and origin of body-fluids on victim clothing.

Now, he didn't waste time disputing her assessment of his social circle, but let her muse on all he had told her. And he knew he didn't need to press his argument. He'd worked with Claire enough to know two things about her. One was she relished a challenge, which was exactly what he had bought her. Second, Claire was different to many in her profession who wouldn't dream of going near an exhibit unless every administrative 'i' was dotted and 't' crossed. She preferred to focus on making sure that any analysis undertaken by her and her team was done in a way and within a time-frame that met the needs of the investigators. Right now he was hoping that her silence signalled she was just buying time before agreeing to stick her neck out.

'How long ago you say?' She picked up one of the bags and peered through the plastic at the flimsy gold top Carver remembered so well.

'Twenty years.'

She let out a low whistle. 'That's a long time.'

'But it doesn't deteriorate, right?'

'Degrade,' she corrected him. 'Organics degrade. And no, for our purposes and over a relatively short time scale as that, it doesn't.'

She dropped the bag and looked across at him. 'You're sure you want to do this? There's no going back if I find something. And if what you told me is true, I imagine things could get very messy.'

He stared at the small pile of bags, remembering what it stood for. A life not lived.

'Believe me, nothing would give me greater pleasure.'

She nodded slowly, casting her eyes over the table, weighing the task. 'Give me a couple of days. I'll call you when I have something.'

Back in his car, Carver made two calls. The first was to the office of one of the handful of senior officers he knew above the rank of Superintendent in whose integrity he had absolute faith. When his call fell into voicemail, Carver left what he thought would be just enough information to guarantee the man would call him back as soon as he picked it up.

The second call was to home again. He'd tried several times on the way to the lab. This time Rosanna answered. *At last.*

'Is Sarah there? I need to speak to her.'

He pretended not to notice the frosty hesitation, and a second later the clatter indicated the phone being put down on the table. After half a minute his sister came on. ' Jamie?'

'You told me you once worked with someone from Armenia. A girl I think you said. Was that when you were at Tesco?'

'Yes. Why?'

He tensed. 'You don't by any chance remember her name do you?'

She blew air. 'She wasn't there long. Erm, let me think.' But after a moment's hesitation, she twigged. 'Is she something to do with this case of yours?'

'Just try to remember, sis. It's important.'

For what seemed a long time, Sarah umm-ed and ahh-ed. 'I'm not sure I'd know her family name if you said it now. But I'll know her first name. Lin-da? Ssss-usan?' He was about to give her a prompt when it came. 'I've got it. Lucy. No, something like that. Erm.'

'Lucine?'

'Lucine, yep. Is she the one you're looking for?'

'That's what I'm trying to find out. Where did she live?'

Her voice fell. 'I'm sorry. I never knew her address. Somewhere in Miles Platting, I think, or it might have been Fallowfield.'

'Damn.' His spirits started to plunge again.

'Hang on though-.'

'Yes?'

'I remember she left to take a job at one of the colleges….'

Carver waited, hardly daring to ask the question. There were scores of colleges around Manchester. He didn't have to worry long.

'I'm sure it was a language college. She was good at languages.'

'Do you know which one?'

Another hesitation, then, 'I think it was the City College of Language. I remember being dead impressed.'

'Great. Keep thinking about her. I might need more if you can remember anything.'

'Er, Rosanna wants a word.'

Oh-oh.

'What are you doing, Jamie?'

He took a deep breath. 'What I have to, Ros,. Don't worry I'm not going to let it harm us.' There was only silence. 'I need you to bear with me, Ros. Please.'

He waited.

'Be careful,' she said, and hung up.

He let out the breath he'd been holding, then started Googling the Manchester City College of Languages.

CHAPTER 39

As the young administrator with the blonde hair returned to the office, Carver stood up, hoping.

'Just caught her,' she said, smiling. She nodded back over her shoulder.

Seconds later, a tall, young woman with dark features, long dark hair and wearing a puzzled expression followed her in. Carver wasn't certain but he thought he'd caught a glimpse of her amongst the throng of departing students and lecturers he had passed in the corridor a few minutes earlier. He remembered the hair and coat. But he hadn't seen her face, not close to. If he had, he would have approached her directly. For the face now staring at him, whilst attractive, also bore unmistakable similarities to the one in the photograph in his inside pocket. The slight almond shape to the eyes, though in her case devoid of the sinister darkness. The high cheekbones. The fullness of the lips. Carver was in no doubt. She had to be Vahrig Danelian's sister. He was grateful her colleague had been able to catch her, a few minutes later he'd have missed her altogether.

He'd taken a risk not ringing ahead, but thought that advance warning of his coming might panic her into disappearing. Luckily, the girl on reception downstairs knew exactly who he meant when he asked after an

Armenian girl named Lucine.

'You want Lucy Donovan,' she'd said. 'She works in Admin Support.' As she directed him to the Administration Unit's second-floor offices, Carver mentally congratulated the family on their choice of alias, Danelian-Donovan. Sufficient to forge a new identity, but with enough echoes of the past to recall the original.

Lucine's husky-but-sweet accent dragged him back to his mission.

'You wanted to see me?'

About to speak, he saw her colleague hovering behind, not even trying to be discreet about showing her interest. When he'd arrived at the office, he had purported to be a prospective mature student in urgent need of Lucy's advice. The way Lucy was now looking at him, he guessed she was already seeing through the sham.

'Is there somewhere we can talk?' He shot a glance over her shoulder to where her friend still lingered. 'Privately.'

An uncertain look passed across her face and she turned to check it out with her friend before coming back to him.

'I assure you, I'm perfectly safe,' he added, and gave her the smile Jess had once told him was his most disarming. It seemed to work, at least as far as the blonde was concerned.

'Mr Hedley's already left, Luce. You can use his office.'

As Lucy showed him through to the Deputy Principal's office, Carver caught the ferocious glare she threw her blond colleague. The girl sent back a grin that was equally fierce.

Carver waited while she shut the door and settled herself in the chair facing the one he had taken before starting.

'My name is Jamie Carver and please, don't be nervous, but I'm a police officer.' Her dark skin paled and, as he leaned forward to show his warrant card, he saw the way she clasped her hands together, tightly. Nevertheless she took the time to compare his photograph with his face, something most never do. As he looked up so she could study his features, he had no trouble sensing her fear.

'Wh-what do you want Mr... Carver?'

'Please, you can call me Jamie.' She didn't nod, or smile. 'I just want to ask you a few questions. If that's alright?'

'What about?'

He hesitated, knowing it could go one of two ways. 'Now don't worry, I'm not anything to do with immigration or anything like that, but I'm trying to trace an Armenian family by the name of Danelian. I think you may be able to help me.'

Her reaction confirmed what her appearance had already told him. A look of panic came into her face, she squirmed in her chair and a shiver rippled through her body. At that moment Carver knew without any shadow of a doubt he had found the family they were looking for. A wave of relief swept through him that he had done so in time. *Thank God.* But as he sat forward, not too much, just enough to establish who was in charge, a remarkable thing happened.

From her initial reactions, he had anticipated that in the next few seconds – certainly as soon as he hit her with a couple of direct questions - she would cave in and tell him everything he needed to know - about her, her family and, if she did know anything, her brother. He had seen it countless times in people who had borne burdensome secrets for a long time and now faced exposure, total and utter capitulation. But instead of collapsing, Lucy closed her eyes, gathered herself, and drew herself up in her chair. When they opened again there was a strange serenity there that had been absent seconds before, and she didn't try to avoid his searching gaze as she said.

'I'm sorry Chief Inspector, I've never come across a family of that name.'

It was one of the most blatant lies Carver had ever been handed. For several seconds he was so shocked he wasn't sure what to make of it. His normal response would be to hit her with some quick-fire questions, shatter her defences and open her up. And though the lie had taken him by surprise, he was still certain he could do it. But some other instinct – he wasn't certain which one – stalled him. Lucy wasn't a criminal. She and her family were, as far he was concerned, potential victims. And whilst he knew nothing about them, the fact they had been driven to seek refuge from their past in a foreign land drew his sympathy. Nevertheless, he needed to get to the truth.

For several seconds more he stared at her, thinking on which line of questioning would bring her round most quickly. Again to his surprise, she sat quiet and calm, returning his stare with no trace of self-consciousness or embarrassment. If he had allowed himself to acknowledge it, the look in her face would be saying, 'Whatever you ask, I will deny it.' Which was exactly what she proceeded to do.

Over the next twenty minutes, first sensitively, then cajolingly, eventually more directly, Carver tried to get her to admit she was Lucine Danelian. He stressed again he was nothing to do with the immigration authorities and that his only interest was in keeping her and her family safe. In so doing he shared with her everything he knew about her brother and the terrible plight her family had found themselves in all those years ago, and which had culminated in their flight to the UK. He recounted what Mikayel Kahramanyan had told him about what had happened in the asylum and her brother's escape. He showed her his photograph, described his trail through Turkey and Cyprus, and referred, in not too much detail, to the Maleeva family slayings that only that day had confirmed her brother's presence on these shores. But through it all, Lucy maintained total ignorance, though she remembered to show the appropriate level of disquiet and horror on hearing of such awful events.

Even when, exasperated to the point of disbelief, he accused her, outright, of lying and what was more, she *knew* he knew she was lying, she kept up the distant front that, for some reason Carver could not begin to imagine, she had decided to put up. When he threatened to take her into 'protective custody' - not that such a thing exists for adults - she called his bluff and simply asked to be allowed to speak with a solicitor.

Eventually, Carver sat back in his chair, nonplussed. In all his experience he had never come across anyone so determined to not only deny the obvious, but also to not even acknowledge, to the slightest degree, she may be lying. Her performance was so bare-faced it would, in other circumstances, have bordered on the comical. Even the most hardened criminal lets slip a sly smile now and then when expressing their shock/horror/disappointment that someone should think them capable of the heinous crime for which they had been arrested.

And as he sat looking across at her, forced into having to reassess every assumption he had made concerning how things would proceed once they found Vahrig Danelian's family, Carver realised. Lucy Donovan wasn't simply a woman scared to admit who she was. During his vain attempts to draw her out, he had given her every assurance he could think of. Her family would be protected. Their status as immigrants would be ratified so that they could remain in the UK; after such a long time and given their history, he was certain it would pose no problem. That despite her brother's horrific crimes there was no reason Lucy or her family should harbour feelings of guilt. None of it had any effect. *There's got to be something else*, he reasoned. But what? Whatever it was, it had to be pretty major.

'You're making a big mistake, Lucy.' He said it matter-of-factly, with no hint of implied threat, as if ready to accept defeat. Even that didn't work.

'I am sure you think that most genuinely Chief Inspector, but as I have said, you are mistaken in this matter. I am sorry I only wish I could help. It sounds like this poor family needs your protection badly.'

He heaved a long sigh. Though there were grounds on which he could, if he so wished, arrest her – her suspected illegal status for one – something nagged at him, making him hesitate. Clearly intelligent, she had to know, deep down that he knew full well she was lying.

And that he wasn't going to let things rest here. His next step would be to visit her at home and either there or through her, find the rest of her family. It wouldn't take him long, and she would know that too.

So why continue with such a transparent deception?

There was only one thing he could think of in such a situation. Without saying anything further, he slipped into a reflective silence, eyes staring in her direction but without focusing, as if seeing off into the distance. As he drifted away, a puzzled look came into her face, and for the first time since putting on the mask, she looked uncertain.

'Chief Inspector? Are you alright?' When he didn't answer, she sat forward in her chair, as if undecided whether she was free to leave or not. After a few more seconds he returned. His eyes focused on her once more, but now there was a certainty in them that had been absent before.

He reached over to the desk for a piece of paper and took out his pen. Putting them down in front of her he said simply. 'Your address. The right one please.'

She looked at him uncertainly, then wrote. As she put the pen down he snatched the paper up so quickly she jumped and the look in her eyes was almost disbelieving as he glanced at it once, then tucked it away inside his jacket. Next he dug into his wallet, took out his card and wrote his mobile number on the back. He handed it across to her. 'Take this. When you've thought about it, done what you have to do, call me, any time, day or night. There isn't much time.' He stood up.

She looked up at him, surprise evident in her face. It was the closest he had come to unsettling her. 'I- I'm free to go?'

'Why should I detain you? You say you aren't the person I'm looking for.'

She rose, hesitatingly, her eyes never leaving him, as if expecting he might suddenly produce a pair of handcuffs and detain her after all. When he stepped away, clearing a path to the main door - not the adjoining one they had come in by - he sensed the relief, and disbelief, within her. She had been expecting she would be arrested.

As he moved aside to let her pass she stopped and turned towards him. Their eyes met and it was as if she was seeing him for the first time. She opened her mouth to say something, thought better of it, then turned to go.

'Lucy.'

She stopped in the doorway but didn't turn.

'Don't leave it too long.'

She stood there for a few seconds, then completed her exit. Carver listened as her heels marked a quick-tempoed staccato down the corridor. He wouldn't have been surprised if she had started running.

He gave it a couple of minutes, getting his head round what he had to do next, before taking out his phone and ringing Neil Booth at the NCA's Longsight office.

'I hope you're not ringing to tell me you've got another of those bloody newsletters,' Neil said on hearing Carver's voice. 'The last one gave me earache for a week.'

'I need a baby-sit job, Neil. And tooled up.'

The reference to an armed operation swept Neil's domestic concerns away. 'Just a minute. PEN, SOMEBODY.'

Quickly, Carver briefed him on Operation Aslan, the

Maleeva family murders that morning – 'I heard,' Neil said. 'The force is buzzing over it.' - and Lucy Donovan.

'You mean now?' he said as Carver finished and he realised what he was being asked to do.

'Yesterday, preferably,' Carver said. 'We've no idea where he is or what he's planning next. He could try to get to them any time.'

'Jesus Christ, Jamie, you don't want much do you?' Carver didn't bother responding. Neil knew him well enough that he wouldn't need further justification, and he was the best Carver had ever seen at organising rush jobs. Sure enough, his next words were, 'What's the address?'

After admitting he wasn't sure whether the rest of Lucy's family were there or not, - 'It's another reason why I need the surveillance,' – Carver wound it up. He needed to get back to SMIU, asap. 'Can I leave the authorities to you?' he said, referencing the need for Chief Officer approval for pre-planned armed operations.

'Tell you what. Give me a brush and I'll stick it up my-.'

'Thanks Neil. I owe you.'

'If you don't hear back, assume we've got the green light.'

Carver rang off then tried SMIU. Jess answered, just back from the mortuary.

'Is West there?' Carver said.

'He's talking to Charlie Brook about who's running the MIR.' Brook was Greater Manchester's Assistant Chief Constable - Crime.

'I thought the SLA says SMIU takes precedence?'

Carver remembered being surprised that, for once, a Service Level Agreement was actually clear about where responsibility would lie for running a Murder Incident Room.

'It does. Brook hasn't got round to reading it yet.'

Carver shook his head. Typical. 'Well tell Terry not to go anywhere. I need to see him.'

'I'm not so sure he'll be that keen on seeing you right now.'

'I've found the Danelians.'

'WHAT? Where? How?'

But Carver had gone.

CHAPTER 40

Lucy felt a touch on her arm and looked around. The West Indian gentleman sitting next to her was staring at her strangely, pointing a finger, ahead. 'I think he's talking to you.'

Following his direction she turned to see a black face she recognised, looking back at her. It was the man who often drove the bus on the route home. Then she realised. She was *on* the bus. Another panic took her, the latest of many she seemed to remember. As she looked around, her thought was, *How did I get here?*

The driver's voice drifted down the aisle and she turned again in his direction.

'This is your stop isn't it, Miss?'

Spinning round, she looked out the window. It *was* her stop. She jumped up from her seat as if she'd been electrocuted, causing the man who'd nudged her to regard her with some apprehension. Disoriented, she started towards the door then stopped to look back at the man who was just beginning to relax. The apprehensive look returned as she spoke to him.

'Did I… did I have any bags with me?'

'Bags? What sort of bags wom-an?'

She tried to remember, couldn't and gave up. 'Never mind.'

As the bus pulled away, she stood at the kerb, trying to get her bearings. She knew where she was now. Her street was just fifty yards along the road. But everything seemed strange, out of place. It made her wonder if it was how dementia sufferers feel when they first start to lose track of themselves.

She couldn't believe she couldn't even remember getting on the bus. In fact thinking about it, she couldn't remember anything from the moment she left the DP's office. My God, she thought, what is happening to me? She remembered speaking to the policeman of course, how could she not? And she knew what she had been thinking about since - recalling every word he had said so she could play it back to herself later and decide what to do. Now, after going over it several times, it was all as clear in her mind as if she had transcribed it from dictation.

It was the journey home she couldn't remember.

Gradually, it came to her what had happened. Absorbed, totally, in re-living the nightmare of her meeting with the detective, she must have left college, walked to the bus stop, got on the bus, shown her pass, and ridden home, without any of it registering in her consciousness. The thought she could do such a thing scared her, but having realised what had happened she relaxed a little. But not about the other things. The other things she was still panicking over.

She still didn't know how she had managed to withstand his questions. But she recalled, painfully, the vision that came to her the moment he mentioned the name Danelian, a name she had not heard in a long, long time. And in that vision she saw, with crystal clarity, what would happen if she ever hinted at there being so much as a grain of truth in what he was saying. It would be too awful, too much for them to bear, for her mother to bear. There was only one possible way to deal with it, to pretend that he was wrong and, that for as long as he was going to speak with her, she was not Lucy Donovan - at least not the Lucy Donovan he was seeking.

If it had not been for her past experiences she would not have been able to keep it up. Not for so long at any rate and certainly not against someone as persistent as that detective. For Lucy had had long experience of denial, half a lifetime's in fact.

In the months after she first discovered the truth, pretending something to be true that was patently not, had not come easily to her. Despite everything, her mother had brought her up to be truthful and honest. But as the weeks and months passed, she learned how to make it easier for herself. She learned to imagine that the way she wished things had been, was the way they *had* been. That the way things actually were, was just some nightmare she had once dreamed and could therefore confine to history, the way a child's favourite book initially stays bright in the memory, but as the years roll by it dims until it is just a story they once read.

In this way, Lucy had learned to live with the horror that had been part of her life for so long. And it was the means she used to withstand the detective's questions. Remembering him again, she even began to feel a little sorry for him. He had been easier on her than she had expected the police might be if they ever came calling, at least to begin with. Later, he did begin to show his frustration, including raising his voice. But it was only the once, and she wouldn't hold that against him. In fact, to her surprise she had almost believed him when he said she could trust him. It made her wonder what she would do if things were different, if... She put the thought out of her mind. Now that he wasn't there she could admit to herself that things *weren't* different. It was just unfortunate for him he had no way of knowing he was never going to get anywhere. That he could have continued to question her as long as he liked and still not broken her. Because for all the time he was talking to her, right up to the moment he stood up and told her she was free to leave, she was not *that* Lucy Donovan, but the other one. The Lucy Donovan she had learned to become all those years ago when the only way to stop herself committing a mortal sin that would damn her to Hell forever was to imagine a life other than the one she had lived. And the family that went with it of course. The oh-so-happy family every young girl had a right to wish for. No, the detective never really had a chance. He could even have-.

She stopped. It had happened again. She was at her front door, key in hand, with no recollection of walking from the bus stop. It worried her, but she didn't have time to dwell on it. From now on she needed a clear mind to do what must be done.

She turned the key in the lock, took a deep breath, and stepped inside.

CHAPTER 41

Driving back to Salford, Carver couldn't get Lucy or what he had witnessed her do, out of his mind. In all his service he had never come across anything like it. The part of him that was interested in such things wanted to understand more about how she had done it, but right now it didn't matter. What mattered was, it was clear there were things going on in her life he neither knew of nor understood. More to the point, they were things she didn't *want* him to know - over and above the fact she was Vahrig Danelian's sister. Harper Lee had told him that much, at least.

Carver could never understand why people who claimed to have read Lee's one-off classic, To Kill A Mockingbird, showed surprise when he credited it with being the bedrock for much of his investigative technique. Then again, while the novel is fascinating in the way it tells its story through the eyes of its eight-year old narrator, it probably isn't the one most would think of if asked to name one that could inspire someone to become a detective.

After reading it when aged thirteen, Carver never forgot the words of Atticus Finch - the narrator's indecently-wise lawyer-father. Entreating his young children, Scout and Jem, to understand why other people behave the way they do, he advises them, 'Put on their clothes and walk around in them a bit.' It summed up, perfectly, the technique Carver fell into using during his early years in the police. He had been refining it ever since. And it was the means by which he came to understand how and why Lucy Donovan was holding out against him.

Given that he barely knew her, anything the technique revealed was only ever going to be sketchy, at best. Nevertheless, the short time he spent, 'walking around in her clothes' was enough to make him realise that other than arresting her and subjecting her to physical torture, Lucy Donovan was not going to admit who she was. Not today at any rate. Which was why he gave up on the job and let her go. He knew who she was and where she lived. For the time being, that was enough.

He still wasn't entirely certain what it was he saw during his brief 'walkabout'. Several things came to him, not least that the main fear driving her denials, was nothing to do with the threat of being revealed as Lucy Danelian. It would take something of far greater consequence than having to deal with the immigration authorities to force someone who had been through what she had been through to stop being herself for a while. The only people Carver had ever come across capable of such a feat were the multiple-personality sufferers he'd once researched at the National Crime and Ops Faculty. And Carver was pretty sure Lucy Danelian was not suffering from any mental dysfunction.

His phone rang.

' Jamie? Just got your message.' It was the man for

whom he'd left the message after leaving Claire's lab.

For the next few minutes, Carver talked while the other listened. Apart from the occasional, 'Uh-huh,' he remained mostly silent, his only reaction coming when Carver mentioned the name at the centre of things. 'Oh,' he said simply. He was used to hearing stories that would send many senior officers into a flat spin. When Carver finished there was a lengthy silence, but he could tell the man was still there. He could hear his heavy breathing. Eventually he said. 'I'll need to see you. First thing in the morning.'

Twenty minutes later, as he pulled into his parking bay, Carver was still musing over how it was that whenever you had two jobs running in parallel, you could guarantee that when one broke, so would the other.

Heading straight into SMIU, Carver found it buzzing with detectives shouting down telephones and wading through murder boxes. Terry West was waiting for him in Jess's office. As he approached he saw Jess sitting behind her desk, her face betraying nothing other than curious expectancy. Next to her, West looked as pissed-off as it was possible to be. Knowing what was coming, Carver shut the door behind him. As he did so, he noticed the way the main office had fallen temporarily silent. Conscious he needed to snatch the initiative, Carver started speaking before he turned round.

'I'm not bothered that you blew me out to Nigel Broom, Terry. And I don't give a toss if you think I'm working against you in some way.' As he faced front, West was making ready to say something so he continued. 'The bottom line is I know where the Danelian family is and we need to move, fast. We can either spend the next half-hour trying to score points off each other, or we can get on with it, which is it to be?'

West ran his tongue over his lips, threw a glance at Jess – her eyebrows had formed into two graceful arches - then swallowed. For long seconds the pair stood facing each other, neither speaking.

'Oh, for Pete's sake,' Jess said. It had the desired effect. Both men looked at her. 'Let's just do it shall we? Jamie, Terry will be happy to listen to whatever you've got, won't you Terry? Jamie, please don't wind Terry up.'

There was another brief silence before West nodded his agreement. 'Go.'

Carver described how he had traced Lucy and his meeting with her. He produced the paper on which she'd written her address. For a moment, West forgot their supposed truce.

'You let her go?'

'Had to. Otherwise we'd have wasted more time trying to get her to come across. This way we've got something to work with.' He told them of the surveillance he'd arranged through Neil Booth.

West showed surprise. 'You've checked-out the address already?'

Carver shot a glance at Jess. 'Not yet.'

'So how do you know it's right?'

Carver bit his lip. West had a lot to learn about trust. 'I watched her write it down. Believe me, it's right.'

Seeing West about to say something, Jess stepped in again. 'Don't, Terry. Just take it as read.'

West stared at Carver a moment longer, as if trying to decide whether he needed more convincing. Carver held his breath.

But when West looked up, it was to say, 'Okay. Where do we go from here?'

CHAPTER 42

The 'bong' of a doorbell roused Mikayel Kahramanyan from his slumber and he opened his eyes. But as the lead cabin-crew member's voice echoed through the plane, he remembered where he was.

'Ladies and Gentlemen, we shall shortly be landing at Yerevan. Please ensure your seatbelts are fastened, your tables are stowed and your seats are in the upright position.'

Mikayel stretched himself as far as Economy allowed and bent down to gather the papers that had fallen from his lap as he slept. The itinerary the Ministry had emailed before he left was ridiculously ambitious. Nevertheless it reflected the urgent need to identity the several 'suspect inmates' being held at various locations and return them to whatever place of detention best suited their particular propensities. With secure places at a premium, the Ministry was desperate to know which needed escape-proof locks and bars, and which might, for the time being at least, make do with hospital care. And Mikayel knew from bitter experience how difficult it could be to tell the difference.

Thankfully, the photographs contained within the enclosures had helped. Despite the poor quality of many of the images and the filthy, bedraggled appearances of the subjects - most of the pictures looked like they had been taken soon after they had been taken back into custody - Mikayel had managed to positively identify at least a third of the thirty or so faces, and put names and question marks against another half-dozen. Once he got around them all and saw them in the flesh, he was confident he would be able to complete the task without too much delay.

Only one thing bothered him. There were still nearly a dozen inmates unaccounted for, among them one or two he worried to think might still be at large. Vahrig Danelian hadn't been the only killer housed within the asylum, though thankfully, only a couple had come anywhere near to equalling his level of depravity - and violence.

Nevertheless, for that same reason he was looking forward to getting back and instigating a more coordinated search for those still missing. He couldn't escape the feeling that during his absence the efforts the authorities had invested in tracking them down had not been as strenuous as they could have been.

As he slid the papers back into his briefcase, Mikayel's eyes lit on the sleek contours of the snazzy leaving-gift Jess had given him. He was still amazed that such a breadth of capability could be housed within such a tiny device. Removing it from his case he cradled it in his palm, recalling the crash course she had given him on the gadget's many functions during that last, very pleasant evening he spent alone in her company. It had been a highly enjoyable fifteen minutes, snuggling up as close as he dared, watching her fingers dance over the icons, smelling her perfume, feeling her arm brushing against his. With her smiling face before him, Mikayel sat back in his seat and for a few last minutes, managed to forget the wretched individuals with whom he was about to reacquaint himself.

It was growing dark outside and the low-wattage bulb in the room's only lamp was fighting a losing battle against the descending gloom. A stale smell of cigarettes hung in the air, though thankfully the middle-aged woman sitting across from Carver was yet to light up. The room itself was cheaply furnished. The best a woman like Alice Halfpenny, living alone with her memories, could manage, Carver thought. He wondered when she had last bought anything new, and stifled a shudder as the thought came that he could be witnessing the future of another, someone he cared deeply about. Forcing the idea away he focused on what he was there to do.

As he looked up at the worn-out features many men had once found desirable, Carver prepared himself. She was glaring at him now, defying him to prove there was any useful purpose to be served by speaking to her. It had taken all of his powers of persuasion just to get through the high-rise flat's door and in truth, he would rather have left it to another time, particularly in view of what was happening across the city. But the ball had started rolling and he needed to be certain it wasn't going to come to a stop before making his next move. He leaned forward in his chair, as he had done once already that day, and hoped things would go better than on that occasion.

'I know I said I wanted to speak to you about your brother, Alice.'

'Hmmph.'

'That wasn't entirely correct.'

'I knew it. You lot can't tell the truth to save your life.'

He ignored her cynicism. Though her bitterness was plain to see, he also knew only part of it could be laid at the door of people like him.

'Do you ever see Brendan?'

'Phah.' Flecks of spittle crossed the divide and landed on his cheek. He ignored them. 'I've not seen him since he went down.'

'I thought you were close.'

'Used to be. But not since….' She waved a hand. 'You know.'

'But you stood by him at the trial.'

'That was before I heard… what he did.'

Carver nodded. It is always hardest for those who stay loyal, but then come to realise the truth when they eventually hear all the evidence.

'Well as I said, it's not Brendan I actually want to speak about.'

'What then? Get on with it. Eastenders is on in a minute.'

Great. He took a deep breath. *No going back.* 'I believe you used to know a detective….'

CHAPTER 43

The next day, Carver spent most of his time to-ing and fro-ing between his office and the Operation Aslan control set up in the office behind Jess's. He and West had agreed that, for now at least, West would look after the Maleeva Murder Room, while Carver would concentrate on the surveillance on Lucy Donovan and her family.

It seemed a reasonable compromise, but Carver was in little doubt that once it was all over, and The Duke was back in harness, West would be after him to do something about Carver. And though he and The Duke were close, he also knew The Duke would have to show support for his deputy. He didn't dwell on it. After his phone call to Nigel Broom that morning – 'I need to tell you what I'm doing, and why' - his boss would already have put the machinery in progress that would eventually spit out a new posting for him. Somewhere remote, he suspected, and in a black suit. No matter, right now the only thing he was interested in was ensuring that whenever Vahrig Danelian made his move on Lucy and her family, someone was there to stop him. In that regard the updates from Neil Booth's surveillance team - now coming through hourly - were bare to say the least. So far no one had left the house, though early on Lucy had been glimpsed taking in milk off the doorstep. When she hadn't appeared by nine, Jess made a bogus call to her work and spoke with her blonde colleague. Lucy had rung in sick, but had given no indication how long she might be off. Later on, an older woman - Lucy's mother they assumed - was seen in the back garden, taking in washing. There had been no sightings since.

Mid morning, the SMIU DI from Yorkshire came in with the results of her enquires with the local council, DWP - Department of Work and Pensions - and the utility companies. As well as Lucine, there were two other 'Donovans' living in the house, Tamara and Giragos, presumably her parents. Tamara and Giragos were in receipt of a surprisingly comprehensive package of benefits, including Income Support and a range of invalidity/incapacity benefits. Earlier, a NCA Immigration Desk colleague of Carver's had confirmed none of the family had ever applied for residency or citizen status. Carver wondered at the extent of the late Radi Maleeva's 'fixing operations' and made a mental note to include in his submission to Nigel Broom's strategy Document – if he ever got to finish it – something about plugging the communication gaps between DWP and the Immigration Service.

Towards lunchtime he returned to his office, closed the door, and phoned Rosanna. She was on her way back from having dropped Sarah and the kids off at home. Carver felt another pang of guilt - the latest in a long line - over the fact that the Portmeirion trip had never materialised. He made a promise to himself he would make up for it the first chance he got.

'How is it going?' Rosanna said.

The night before he had filled her in on the day's developments, as well as the operation he and Terry West had finally agreed he was now very much part of. 'No more secrets, hedging, or excuses,' he told her before he started. Which explained his 'honesty' call to Broom that morning.

'If you can't manage what I'm doing then tell me and we'll talk about it,' he told her.

Although she had agreed, he couldn't help feeling there was a void there somewhere. He hoped with all his heart that his decision to follow his instincts hadn't damaged them irretrievably. Time would tell, for now he couldn't be certain whether her enquiry meant she was genuinely interested, or just being polite.

'It's all quiet at the moment. I'll keep you posted.'

'I take it you'll be late?'

He closed his eyes for a second. The old question. 'Unless something happens.' Just before she hung up he said, 'I love you Ros,' but wasn't sure if she heard.

Jess came back from her visit to the MIR and filled him in. 'There's not much coming in yet, and house to house around where the Maleeva's live is a waste of time. No one sees anything in those big houses.'

By late afternoon Carver was pacing Jess's office. He couldn't stand these sit and wait ops. It was why he'd never been attracted to Crime Squad work. The hours spent hanging around in obs points and draughty vans on car parks would send him crazy.

'Haven't you got any work to catch up on?' Jess said, looking up from the papers in front of her. She was going over the Durzlan stuff again, comparing the details with the case-notes Mikayel had brought them. Carver wondered how she was managing to concentrate.

'I tried that,' Carver answered. 'Didn't work.'

'Well do something useful then,' she said distractedly, turning back to her papers. 'Make me a mint tea.'

'Right away, Mist-' He just managed to not say it as he saw her freeze, head still down.

He made her a mint tea.

Time passed.

CHAPTER 44

DC Dave Bradley reached behind the seat for his flask. A late cold snap had made for a chilly evening. With no heater in the obs van, it was destined to get a lot colder. By eleven, the end of the team's tour, he would be freezing his bollocks off. As he twisted the top off the flask, the warm smell wafted around the van.

'Whotcha got there Dave?' a voice said from behind. 'Left or right?'

Six weeks before, Dave's wife, Naomi, known amongst the team for being well-endowed, had given birth to twins. The jokes about her post-natal attributes hadn't stopped coming since the two members of the team designated to drop off the obligatory flowers had reported back their observations. It didn't help that Dave, not long back from paternity leave, had let slip about her using a pump, so he could share in feeding duties.

'Don't be a smart-arse,' Dave said. 'It's tomato soup.'

'That's clever,' another voice snickered. 'Does she do bitter as well?'

Dave looked in the mirror and gave them the finger, but all he could see was darkness. 'I *was* going to pass it around. Now you can just all fuck off.'

Muted jeers sounded in back.

In the passenger seat next to Dave, Glen Swift, the unit team leader, shifted his considerable bulk to relieve his growing soreness and sighed. 'Settle down team. We don't want the neighbours reporting us to the bizzies. It might be embarrassing.' Though still not loud enough to pass through the van's fibre-board baffling, the mickey-taking fell to a soft murmur.

'Bet the butter on his sandwiches is homemade as well.'

Dave shook his head, sadly, as he drank his soup. 'Morons. I'm surrounded by fucking morons. When we get back to Longsight, I'm going to-.'

'Cut it.'

Dave's mug stopped short of his lips as Glen sat up. Noises of backsides shifting on seats sounded behind.

'What is it Glen?' This from Malia, one of the two women on the team.

'Wait,' he said. He was watching the tall young man in the long dark coat who had appeared round the corner at the top of the street and was now coming down towards them. He was carrying some sort of holdall.

'Is it him?'

Glen grabbed the clipboard and studied the subject's photograph. The man coming towards them seemed heavier. Then again he could have put on weight. They'd been told the photograph was several years old. 'I'm not sure yet. The light's not too good. Simon?'

'I've got him,' a voice said in his ear. Glen felt the weight of the long lens settle on his shoulder and he pressed himself back in his seat. In this light and given the distance, there was little likelihood they would be made, but no sense taking chances. As he waited for

Simon's verdict, he pressed the button in his palm.

'Glen to all Narnia units. Stand-by, stand-by. One i-c-three, on foot, towards the O.P. Checking him out now.'

The come-backs - 'Tony, yes-yes', 'Anna, yes-yes' - confirmed the other teams had heard and were ready.

'Well, is it or isn't it?' Glen asked Simon. The man was now within fifty yards of the house. If Glen was going to call a strike it would have to be soon.

'I can't tell,' Simon said. 'It looks a bit like him but I'm not sure. He's certainly foreign.'

'Give it here.' Reaching over his shoulder Glen grabbed the camera, and zoomed in on the man just as he started to look around, as if he was half-expecting to see something, or someone.

Thirty yards.

'Click him, Glen,' Simon reminded. Glen depressed the shutter-release.

Click-click-click.

Twenty yards.

Shit, Glen thought. I can't tell either. Similar sort of look, but is it him?

Click-click-click.

'Glen?'

'Wait,' he snapped. His heart beginning to pound, adrenalin coursing.

Click-click-click.

'Come *on* Glen. He's nearly there.'

Looking into the houses. Reading numbers. Can't make him properly.

Anna's voice over the radio. 'Are we going?'

At the gate.

Still can't…. Turn this way, you bastard.

Click-click-click.
'Yes or no, Glen?'
Fuck.
Click-click-click.
'He's at the fucking door, Glen.'

Glen lowered the camera and looked across to where the man was raising a fist, about to knock. The noises behind told him they were ready, hyped.

'Glen?'

Glen Swift swallowed, and as he opened his mouth to speak he remembered why he always hated being 'Eyeball' on obs jobs.

CHAPTER 45

Mikayel Kahramanyan stepped out into the late evening chill, grateful for the chance to fill his lungs with clean air at last. The Dilizhan Gaol wasn't that old - only thirty years or thereabouts - but the conditions were a disgrace. It looked like it had never been cleaned or painted since it opened. Torn bags of refuse lay everywhere and a stale, rotting smell hung over the whole facility. He understood better when he paid a courtesy visit to the Governor to introduce himself and explain his mission. The man was obese, his office a pigsty. Anyone willing to work in such conditions was fit only to be labelled accordingly, Mikayel thought.

The point was rammed home when he was shown into the detention block housing those he had come to see. God alone knew when they had last been allowed to bathe or clean themselves. Some were incapable of doing so without assistance. Slops of what passed for food in the place pasted the floor, along with other things. Mikayel was minded to make an official complaint but knew it would do no good. This far from the capital, who would take notice? But at least he had been able to put ticks against another five on his list. *Only seven more to go.*

As he turned to his driver, he felt his exhaustion

more acutely than ever. They hadn't stopped since leaving the airport fourteen hours earlier and he desperately needed a shower and a proper bed. One of the more amenable guards had given him the name of a hotel up in the Old Town he claimed was better than the average.

'Is that it for today?' Mikayel said, hopefully.

The ministry official consulted his list in the way little men with clipboards sometimes do. Mikayel had already concluded that from the way his appointed guide was trying to cram as much into the day as possible, he was missing his comfortable Yerevan office badly.

'Ijevan is only forty kilometres away. We could do that one, then find a hotel,' the official said.

Mikayel was wary. 'Are there any decent hotels in Ijevan?'

'The Hotel Dilijan is very comfortable. I stayed there once.'

Mikayel checked his watch. It was getting late, but they could be there in less than an hour. Another hour to do the necessary, and there would still be time for a decent night's sleep.

'Alright,' Mikayel nodded, grumpily. 'But this is the last one, agreed?'

'Of course, Doctor.' The official all but sneered.

Mikayel suspected the man would be thinking that provincials such as himself had no idea what they were missing, living so far from the capital. As they reached the car, a thought occurred to him. He turned to his guide.

'I didn't know there is a prison at Ijevan.'

'Oh, didn't I tell you?'

The way he said it, Mikayel could tell he was enjoying the advantage that comes with foreknowledge. Since setting off from the airport, Mikayel had wondered, several times, if the man was keeping back snippets of information, revelling in the feeling of power it gave him.

'This one's not a prison,' the official continued. 'We are going to the morgue.'

Lucy opened the door, and blinked in surprise. The events of the past twenty-four hours had caused her to forget all about her date. And in any case he was far too early. They hadn't settled Dadda yet.

'H- Hello,' she said, trying desperately to cover her surprise. What to do? She couldn't possibly go out tonight, not now. Nor any other night come to that. Certainly not until it was all over, whenever that might be. 'I… I'm sorry,' she stammered. 'I am… we are just….' She saw the amused smile, almost as if he knew something was amiss. Had it been his purpose to catch her out?

'Am I too early?' he said, dropping the smile. 'I am sorry. I can go away and come back later.' He half-turned, as if to leave.

'NO,' she yelled, then moderated her voice. 'That won't be any good.' She saw the puzzled look. 'What I mean is….' Her mind raced. She needed time to think. 'Look, you'd better come in while I…. Oh, just come in.'

She swung the door wide and he stepped inside. Her manners almost made her offer to take his coat, but she thought better of it. He wouldn't be staying. He simply *must* not. She walked him through to the kitchen, realising as she went he would want to know why she was eating, when he was supposed to be taking her out. As she led him through the door, her mother dropped her knife and fork and looked up in shocked surprise.

'Mamma, Dadda, this is Garo, the friend I told you about?'

Her father, his back to the door, tried to swing round, stiffly. Unable to put any weight on his withered legs he could only manage a half-turn. The man made things easier by stepping confidently into the middle of the room, where everyone could see him. Lucy's father's jaw fell open.

'Mr and Mrs Danelian,' the man said, smiling, broadly. 'How wonderful to find you at last.'

As Lucy heard him use their real name and saw the look of horror on her parents' faces, her stomach dropped to the floor, and she realised.

She had brought disaster upon them all.

CHAPTER 46

Jess peered at the image in the camera's view-screen, before turning to Carver.

'What do you think?'

Carver stared at it in silence. He could understand now why Glen Swift had been undecided. There was certainly some similarity. The gaunt look. The sharp features. But he was as familiar with Vahrig Danelian's photograph as any of them. And if *he* couldn't be certain, he couldn't criticise Glen for not calling the strike. He sat back on the van's bench seat.

'You can't tell.' It was a statement of fact, not opinion. Damn, he thought.

Thirty or so minutes earlier, as they'd monitored the radio transmissions, he'd convinced himself this was it, that they were about to lift Vahrig Danelian. But when the strike call didn't come, and there followed a jumbled mish-mash of calls; 'Why the fuck not?' 'What's happening?' 'Did we go?' he could not contain his frustration. Dashing out of Op Control, Jess on his heels, he'd leaped into his car, raced to the designated rendezvous point – a community centre car park round the corner from where Lucy lived - and joined Glen and his team in the back of the van. Carver's annoyance was plain to see, but fair-dos to Glen, he'd stuck to his guns.

'It wasn't on Boss,' he said, bringing up the man's image. 'I didn't feel positive enough to call it. My decision. If I was wrong, I'll hold my hands up.'

Now, having seen it, Carver shook his head.

'You were right Glen. It was the right call.'

There were no sighs of relief or expressions of self-satisfaction from the team, certainly not from Glen. An experienced Squad man, he knew the score. They had a problem on their hands. A big one.

For several minutes no one spoke. They were all waiting for Carver. It was his decision. Eventually he looked across at Glen, sitting opposite.

'You say you think she knew him?'

Glen nodded. 'She looked gob-smacked to begin with, but then opened the door and let him in.'

'No arguments? No pushing or shoving?'

'None at all.'

'Definitely not, Boss,' Simon joined in.

Carver turned to him, nodded. Simon had been eager to back his Team Leader up from the start. Typical squad, Carver thought. But it didn't help matters. He racked his brain to remember his conversations with Mikayel. They'd talked a lot about whether his family would recognise him after so many years. Mikayel thought they would – even his younger sister, who would have been in her teens when she last saw him. Carver ran through the impressions he had formed of her from their meeting. Surely she wouldn't have let him into the house willingly if she knew it was him? Then he thought on what he'd learned over the years about the fallibility of witness memory. It had caught him out before.

'What's the latest?' he said to Glen.

The team's leader made his way to the front of the van and they heard him speaking softly over the radio. Before coming away to rendezvous with Carver he had put one of the rear cover team in closer. He was now standing outside the Danelian's back gate. Within a minute Glen returned.

'Still nothing. He thinks he can hear voices, but it could be the TV.'

'Well, no screaming is good,' Jess said. Those of the team who weren't already enjoying gawping at her turned in her direction. Seeing their faces, she said, 'I wasn't trying to be funny.'

The wry grins vanished.

Eventually Carver turned to her.

'I don't think we've any choice.'

She signed. 'Neither do I.'

For the second time that evening, Lucy Danelian stood on the doorstep, blinking in surprise. *Him*. But why was he here? She hadn't rung him. She wasn't ready yet.

She saw a glance pass between him and the younger woman next to him who didn't quite fit with her expectations of a female police officer. The look seemed to show relief and made her wonder if he thought the address she had given him might have been false.

'I'm sorry Lucy,' he said before she could say anything. 'I know this is unexpected, but I need to speak with you about something urgent. Can we come in?' He put a foot across the threshold, trying to make the decision for her.

'I, I'm not.... Th, this isn't....' Her anxiety was making her tongue tied.

'It'll only take a moment.'

Noises emanated from behind her, then her mother's voice, full of apprehension. 'Lucine?'

He gave her a sharp look, then he was in and striding down the hall towards the kitchen. Before Lucy could even react, the woman stepped in after him, taking Lucy's hand from the door and closing it behind her. As Lucy turned to her, alarmed, the woman smiled at her.

'It's alright Lucy. Trust him.'

Despite sensing that the woman was trying to reassure her, Lucy's alarm grew rapidly. Whatever was happening, it was too soon. She turned and went after the policeman.

He had stopped just inside the kitchen and she had to squeeze round him to get past. As she turned to look at him, she saw the shocked look on his face. He was staring at the table and the three people sitting around it, each in various stages of working their way through the steaming bowls of goulash before them.

For several seconds nobody said anything as they all looked at each other, apart from her father that is. Still with his back to the door, he hadn't tried to turn, but was staring blankly across the table at his wife; Too much all at once, Lucy guessed.

But the policeman seemed to be paying particular attention to Garo. Running his eyes over him, head to toe almost, and back again. Surely he couldn't think-'

'Who are you?'

It was Mamma who had spoken, her face twisted again in fear as when Lucy's first visitor had arrived.

'Mamma, this is the man I told you about,' Lucy said, sending her a warning glare. 'The one I met yesterday.'

Confusion flooded the old woman's features. 'The

policeman? But I don't understand. I thought-.'

Ignoring the curious look that had suddenly come into Garo's face, Lucy cut across her mother to speak to the man whose name she now remembered as Carver.

'What do you want, Mr Carver? My parents are easily upset. I said I would ring you when I was ready.'

'What is happening Lucy?' her mother said, voice rising. 'I don't understand all this.'

Lucy saw Carver starting to turn towards her. She couldn't let him start asking his questions.

'Well?' Lucy demanded, grabbing his attention once more.

His eyes flicked towards the table. 'Your parents?'

'Of course.'

'And this is?' He turned to the man sitting next to her mother. Garo was staring at the policeman with a look Lucy thought bordered on amusement.

'This is Garo. He is a friend of mine.'

She fully expected more to follow. Instead, what the policeman did next surprised her as much as when he charged past her. He glanced once at his partner and nodded to her, as if to acknowledge some communication Lucy had missed. Then he turned on his heel, and walked out, the woman following. Caught unaware by his unexpected departure, Lucy looked to see what Garo was making of it. But he was now watching the officers' exit with a strange look on his face. Shaking her head, Lucy made her way to the front door, where the policeman was already holding it open, waiting for her.

'I'm sorry, Lucy,' he said. 'It was a misunderstanding. I will explain later. But please, ring me tomorrow, when you are alone. We must talk.' Not waiting for her response, he left her on the step.

As they walked away, she closed the door behind them.

Coming back into the kitchen, she almost bumped into Garo, standing just inside the door. The look on his face was one she had never seen before and his dark eyes followed her as she sat down at the table. The room was silent, her mother looking scared, her father confused. She doubted he even knew what was going on. Garo waited a few moments before coming round and taking his seat between her and her mother. As she reached across for the ladle resting in the pot, he reached out and took hold of her wrist. She looked at him, surprised.

'Why does he want you to ring him?' he said.

On their way back to the van, Jess was struggling to keep up.

'Slow down a minute will you?' she said to Carver's back. 'I'm wearing Louboutin, not bloody Reeboks.'

None the wiser, he slowed enough to let her draw alongside, before taking her arm and giving her a helping hand. The van was only a hundred yards away round the corner, but he was eager to get there as soon as possible. Jess squirmed in his grasp.

'You're hurting,' she said. When he was on a mission he could be annoyingly single-minded.

Suddenly aware he was holding her the way he would a prisoner, he threw her an apologetic look. 'Sorry. We need to get back on plot. He could still turn up.'

'I'm aware of that but if you don't mind, I'd rather

do it with two good ankles.' She pulled her arm away, testily. He got the message and eased up a little.

'Sorry,' he said again.

As she fell into step beside him, silent now, he returned to the thoughts whirring through his brain.

Carver had known as soon as he saw him he was not their quarry. Nevertheless the similarities – the gaunt features, the dark, haunted look about the eyes – had aroused his interest. He was about to start tossing questions around, just to clarify a few things, when the mother's reaction warned him he was in danger of unlocking a Pandora's box. She was clearly on the edge and he sensed that if he had continued, she might have lost it altogether. The last thing he could afford right now was for it all to blow up in his face; not with Vahrig still likely to put in an appearance any moment. Besides, not knowing who Lucy's friend was – Garo, did she say? - he had no way of knowing how much he could reveal without causing her even more problems; he was certain she had more than enough to be going on with. He was clearly a countryman of theirs – perhaps even another illegal – and Carver hadn't dared say too much in case it got spread around. So, for the time being he was happier to keep things as tight as possible, at least until he knew more about the whole set-up: which is why he decided to cut things short and get out, and why he needed to talk with Lucy, soon. He had already decided that if nothing happened in the next twelve hours, he was going back in and, regardless of who was there, he would get Lucy to tell him everything. But right now he needed to get things back on line.

As they reached the van doors, they swung open. He helped her step up and in and when Jess's shapely bottom suddenly loomed in front of his face it didn't even register.

'So who is he, Boss?' Glen said as Carver finished giving his account.

'A friend of the family by the look of it,' Carver said. 'Right now it doesn't matter. I need you to get back on plot while I catch up with what's happening in the MIR.' Carver was conscious that, as with all murder enquiries, the first twelve to twenty-four hours were the most critical. It is often during that period that the crucial pieces of information come in which, if not recognised and acted on early, can lead to an investigation becoming a long, drawn out affair. He had seen it many times, especially during reviews of long-running investigations. It was his one concern about West looking after the room, but now that the alarm over this Garo's arrival was over, he felt the urge to make sure nothing was being missed. Ready to go, he turned to Jess. While he'd been briefing Glen Swift, she had been fiddling with the observation team's camera, a cable and her mobile phone, her thumb dancing across buttons.

'What are you doing?' he said.

She continued pressing. 'I promised Mikayel we'd let him know when we found the Danelians. I'm sending him a picture of Lucy.'

He waited.

A moment later she said, 'Done. Let's go.'

CHAPTER 47

The tee-shirted night attendant with the paper-thin cigarette glued to his bottom lip slammed the metal drawer shut. Before the bang finished echoing around the cold bare walls he was already flipping through his papers, searching for the next one. Mikayel Kahramanyan shook his head, disgusted at the way the man wasn't even trying to make any show of respect for the drawers' occupants.

As he waited, Mikayel wished again that he had stuck with it when he tried to insist to his guide that they leave it until morning. Rested, fed and hopefully, warmed up a bit, he would have felt more up to the task of identifying cadavers. As it was, he was just grateful there was nothing in his stomach. Had there been, he was certain he would have seen it again by now.

Hard though it was to believe, the Ijevan Town Mortuary was in an even worse state than the Dilizhan Gaol. Now Mikayel was desperate to just get it over with and get out. He didn't care what the hotel was like, he had had enough. On the way there, his all-knowing driver-guide had managed to take a wrong turn, meaning it was late evening when they finally limped into the small provincial town, forty kilometres south of where the Institute had once stood. Ignoring Mikayel's plea to show some common sense, the ministry official had insisted there was still time. How the man had managed to keep from looking guilty as they hung around for another half-hour while the town hospital's night porter rounded up the semi-inebriated mortuary attendant, Mikayel hadn't a clue.

'How many more?' Mikayel said.

The words were aimed at the man in the tee-shirt, but as he spoke he glared at the official standing against the wall, behind him. The man was hanging well back so he would not to have to witness what he had brought Mikayel to see. Mikayel couldn't really blame him, but that didn't stop him wishing he could entice the man close enough to share in the distasteful task. Most of the bodies – not all from the Institute - were not just suffering from having lain around in the sun for several weeks. Many were also mutilated. The Azerbaijanis had made sure that tales of their incursion would linger long in the memories of the border region's inhabitants.

'Two. I think,' the attendant said in answer to Mikayel's question. As he spoke he set the dolly in front of another drawer, grabbed the handle and walked the drawer and its contents into the room. As with the others, there was no covering sheet – no need for niceties in a place like this – and a groan sounded from the direction of the ministry official as a blue-black arm, pitted and torn, slipped off the tray and dangled there. The attendant ignored it.

Mikayel stepped forward and looked down, and had to make a conscious effort to control his stomach. He breathed through his mouth rather than his nose, so as to keep the worst of the smell from registering He examined the body for several minutes, walking its length, using only his eyes to gauge and measure, trying to imagine what he would have looked like alive. Several times during his inspection he referred to the list on his clip-board.

Eventually he turned to the attendant. 'You are sure he is one of ours?'

Making no attempt to hide his boredom, the man shrugged his bony shoulders. He was interested only in returning to his bottle of Arax and the state-sponsored game show he had been watching when the porter came to tell him two madmen from the ministry wanted to view his flock - at this time of night.

'I am told the others have all been identified,' the attendant said through his yawn. 'If he is not yours, then who's?'

Mikayel stared down at the body. The three he had seen so far had been the older ones, those who would not have been capable of outrunning or evading those who would kill them for the sheer fun of it. In each case, as he ticked off their names, he experienced the same stabs of guilt that nightly haunted his dreams. The knowledge that, had he not set them free the outcome would have been the same, was of no comfort and never would be. But if the body before him was one of the inmates, then he had to be one of the younger ones, that much at least could still be discerned through the swelling and discolouration. But which one? Most of the younger ones had already been accounted and of the few still missing this did not look like any he could remem….

He stopped. A glimmer of something had registered in the back of his brain, but now it was gone again. What was it? It couldn't be recognition, he thought. He was all but certain the body was not any of those whose names he had been hoping to be able to tick off. He shuddered. For some reason a strange, conflicted feeling had suddenly come over him, but he wasn't sure why. He bent closer, bringing his face within inches of the mass of flesh and bone – you could barely call it a man – on the tray. Behind him the official gagged into his handkerchief and turned to the sand-filled fire bucket he had placed beside him, for safety.

Suddenly Mikayel gave out a loud gasp and he stood up sharply, arms falling to his sides. A single word escaped him. 'NO.'

For a split second, the watching ministry official, who spent more of his spare time than he cared to admit watching poorly-made counterfeit DVDs of American horror movies, imagined something awful. Such was the looseness that came into his bowels, he actually clenched his buttocks, tight.

'What is it Doctor?'

For seconds there was only silence as everyone stared. The psychiatrist at the body. The surprised attendant and nervous official at Kahramanyan. But before anyone could speak, another sound, one totally alien in such an environment, made the official jump a second time. A jangling music, unlike anything he had ever heard before, blared out.

The psychiatrist span round, looking at his astonished guide, back to the mystified attendant then around the room. Why would a mortuary – particularly one this old – be equipped with the sort of piped-muzak system you find in shopping malls? Then he remembered.

'What is happening?' the worried official cried,

looking around him as if the walls were about to start closing in on them. This was not at all what he had imagined when he volunteered for what he thought was a relatively easy assignment. But instead of answering him, the psychiatrist was whirling around like some mad dervish, hands flying over and through the layers of anorak, jacket and fleece he had worn since disembarking from the plane.

Suddenly he stopped, looking at something he had taken from inside his jacket. The music, louder now, bounced off the walls, echoing around the chamber. The official caught a glimpse of the device in the psychiatrist's hand.

For several moments Mikayel Kahramanyan was off-balance. He had to work hard to juggle the several strands of thought that were fighting for supremacy in his brain. As he stared again at the throbbing object in his hand he struggled to recall what she had told him, part of his brain still grappling with the crazy thought that had come to him just before the noise started. He remembered thinking at the time that when you looked at the buttons it was ridiculously obvious, but right now-. He interrupted his train of thought to return his gaze to the body. *But if he-*

Boom-boom-twang. The jarring music made it difficult to think. *Why would-?*

Boom-boom-twang. Which button to press to shut it off?

He pressed one at random. The sound stopped.

Thank God.

He stared at the screen. A small envelope-icon flashed at him, beneath it, "Jess has sent you a message."

'Is everything alright, Doctor?' the official said, unnerved but also interested to see what Mikayel was looking at. He had read recently that there were now more cell-phones in Armenia than there were people, but the one in the psychiatrist's hand looked more advanced than any he was familiar with, certainly far more than his own, Ministry-issue Huawei. Perhaps the psychiatrist was not so old-fashioned after all.

'Yes,' Mikayel said. 'Just give me a moment.'

Conflicted as to what to do first, Mikayel did what at that moment was easiest. He pressed on the icon.

Despite the grimness of his surroundings and the shock still running through him, a smile came to Mikayel's lips as he read Jess's message. A ray of sunshine in the darkness. And what her message said about them finding the Danelians was of great interest.

But what did it all mean? If the thought that had come to him proved to be correct-. The screen changed suddenly. He must have pressed something. Jess's words disappeared and in their place was a photograph. The message had said something about a photograph of Vahrig's sister. This must be her.

The image showed a dark-haired young woman at the front door of a house, talking to a man in a long coat whose back was to the camera. Mikayel wondered how it had come to be taken. But the picture was not very clear. It looked like it had been taken in failing light. Nonetheless it was good enough that he could make out her features, see what an attractive woman she had grown into, free from the shame and horror. As he looked at her pretty face, allowing himself a moment's whimsy, he suddenly remembered the puzzle his friends back in England still had to unravel. He needed to-

Wait.

As he'd thought on what to do next, half his attention was still on the picture, but as he stared at it, something caught his eye, and he re-focused. He hadn't really taken it all in the first time, interested only in getting his first look at the Monster of Yerevan's sister. With Jess's message not referring to the man he assumed he was of no significance. But now, looking at it again…. The face was only in quarter profile, little more than an impression, a corner of the mouth, the nose…. But something….

Mikayel snapped his head around, looking at the body on the tray, then back to the picture.

'Great God in heaven, say it isn't so.'

The mortuary attendant had supervised enough viewings to recognise shock when it hit, to know when someone was so affected by their experience, they were no longer capable of rational speech. Now, seeing the pained look that came into this doctor's face, he knew it was one of those occasions. Strange really, he thought. Up to that moment the man had been holding up remarkably well. He turned to the official, shrugged up his shoulders and spread his hands close to his body in the universally recognised gesture of, *What gives?*

The ministry man saw the look and reciprocated. *I have no idea*. But having recovered a little from his sudden fright, he decided it was time he should impose himself. If the psychiatrist lost it now, it could delay things. And if that happened he may not be able to complete his assignment a day-and-a-half earlier than the Ministry-imposed schedule. The chance of that rarest of things, a day and a night with Ludmilla to himself, without having to manufacture elaborate excuses to satisfy his suspicious wife, would evaporate. Ludmilla would not be pleased.

'What is wrong, Doctor. DOCTOR?'

But it was too late, Mikayel Kahramanyan wasn't listening. He was running for the door as fast as his legs would take him.

CHAPTER 48

The silence between them was unusual. Most often when Carver and Jess drove somewhere together, she usually took the opportunity to talk about incidents or scenarios that, according to her, amply demonstrated the fallibility of the male species. He would invariably respond with some throw-away comment which she was never sure evidenced the deep-rooted sexism she still saw in many male detectives, or was simply aimed at winding her up. But after a day as full, hectic and nerve-wearing as he could remember, Carver assumed that Jess was as grateful as him for the opportunity to order her thoughts and simply take stock.

Not least among his own mental meanderings was what they were doing with Lucy and her family, the subject about which he was still in two minds. If their short-term safety was the main concern, they would now be in a safe house somewhere. By now he would be on his way to knowing exactly where he stood - as far as they were concerned at least. He may even have gleaned something that might help ensnare Vahrig Danelian. But was it the main concern? At some stage he would have to release them, even if only while any appeal to the Immigration Authorities was settled. And if Vahrig Danelian hadn't been located by then…. He preferred not to think about it. At least this way, if Vahrig was intending to take a pot at them on the heels of what he had done to the Maleevas, they stood a better than even chance he would be arrested as soon as he showed his face. It was just a shame the man who showed up that evening was not him. They could all now be looking forward to a night's sleep without having to worry about what the morning might bring. He was still curious to find out what the man's status was. Pound to a penny he was an illegal, like them. But right now, he was well down on Carver's list of priorities. He hoped to God that when he made contact with the MIR, there may be something there that would revive his hope they weren't all looking in the wrong direction.

'It's one of those where you're damned if you do, *and* if you don't,' Jess said.

'What?' he said, waking up and turning to her. She hadn't said more than a couple of words since leaving Lucy's. But the way she was looking at him now, she had obviously sensed his frustrations. He acknowledged her unerring assessment with a nod.

'I know,' he said. 'I just hope we get the right result in the end.'

'Don't we all,' she said. She turned in her seat to face him. It meant she was about to put something to him.

'Go on,' he said.

'I was just thinking.' He waited. 'We could pull Lucy and her family out and put some ringers in. I'm about the same age as her, and with a wig I could-.'

'I know what you're going to say and I've already thought about it. The problem is it would do for twenty four hours or so, but after that we'd have to be thinking about-.' The jangling music that suddenly erupted cut him off. 'What's that?'

'My new mobile' she said, reaching into her bag. 'I need to sort out the ring-tone.'

'You can say that again.'

She glanced at the screen. 'It's Mikayel.' She put it to her ear. 'Hi Mikayel, good to hear from you. How was your-.' The sudden end to her greeting made Carver glance across. 'Whoa. Slow down. And stop shouting, I can hear you.' She raised her eyes to Carver in a light hearted way, but it vanished almost immediately. 'What? What do you mean him? Him who…? I'm sorry Mikayel I don't understand what you're saying. The photograph? Yes…. No it wasn't Vahrig. We spoke to him. He's a- What? …WHAT?'

Her sudden outburst drew another glance from Carver and he saw the concern that was suddenly flooding into her face. She put a hand over the phone - 'Stop the car.' - then went back to her call. 'Carry on Mikayel.' Carver pulled over.

For long seconds, Carver watched as she nodded, uh-huhed, and yessed down the phone. The longer it went on, the paler she became. As she listened she stared, starkly at Carver. He felt something stirring within him, something he had felt many times before, a cold feeling of dread. Eventually she said the words Carver knew meant it was even worse than he was already imagining.

'Oh. My. God.'

CHAPTER 49

Waiting on Lucy's front door step, Carver was acutely conscious it was taking her a lot longer to come to the door than last time. He looked across at Jess. She shook her head. *It's taking too long.* He started to raise his palm to his mouth, making ready to give the word. At that moment a noise sounded through the door. *At last.*

But this time the hall light didn't come on as it had done last time. Carver held his breath as the door swung open. Lucy stood there. She seemed okay, thank God. Or was she? As she looked down on them, he sensed, rather than saw there was something different about her. He couldn't put his finger on what it was, but as soon as she spoke, he knew.

'What do you want now?'

There was a dreamy quality to the way she said it, as if she wasn't quite there. It was similar to how she had been that afternoon, a lifetime ago it seemed, when she denied everything.

'I'm sorry, Lucy. There're a couple of things we need to speak to you about after all. May we come in?' He put a foot in the door as he had done earlier. But this time she didn't move aside.

'I am sorry. My parents were very upset after your last visit. Please just leave us alone. I said I would ring you tomorrow.'

Carver's eyes narrowed as he took in her words. There was no sense in him that she was lying, he hadn't asked a direct question yet. Nevertheless….

'It will only take a moment.' He stepped up, intending to bluster his way in. But when she didn't move and he came up against her chest, he had to fall back. This time she was determined.

He thought about taking hold of her and moving her aside, but wasn't sure how she would react. If she kicked off, it could still all turn to rat-shit. But right now there weren't many choices. He took a deep breath.

'Lucy,' Jess said, gently. Lucy turned to her. Jess's face was sympathetic, but determined. 'We *are* coming in,' she continued, fixing her eyes on Lucy's. 'We aren't going to hurt you.' Her arm reached out and she pushed Lucy, gently, to one side. A conflicted look came into Lucy's face but she didn't resist. Jess stepped past her into the hall. Carver followed.

The house was silent, no murmurs of conversation emanating from down the hall. Apart from the slivers of light showing round the door into the kitchen, everything was in darkness.

'Where is everyone?' Carver said, softly.

'Mamma and Dadda have gone to bed. I told you, they were upset.'

'And your friend?'

For a second she seemed to come back, but then went away again. 'He went home.'

Carver and Jess exchanged nods, then turned towards the kitchen.

'Wh-Where are you going?' Lucy called. 'You cannot go in there.'

Carver pushed the door open, held back a second, then walked in, Jess right behind.

'You must not,' Lucy's plaintive cry echoed. 'Please.'

The room was empty. Lucy followed them in.

'What are you doing? Why won't you leave us alone? I told you. There is no one here.'

Carver tried the back door. It was locked. Another door led into a small utility room. He checked it. Nothing.

'We know your friend is still here, Lucy. Where is he?'

Lucy froze, as though in shock. Then, after a few seconds, a change started to come over her. The puzzled look in her face began to give way, turning through concern, to alarm, before finally settling into a tortured expression in which her mouth opened, her lips moved, but no sounds came out. She began to shiver.

Jess approached her. 'Where are your parents, Lucy?'

Her eyes began to glaze over, the shivering became a shake.

'She's fitting,' Jess said, coming forward and grabbing her arms. Lucy's head went back and for the first time they saw the livid red marks to her throat and the deep scratch from which a thin line of blood seeped.

'Oh Christ,' Jess said.

Carver's first instinct was to call it, but he needed to know where he was first. And the parents. Minimise the variables. Leaving Jess to Lucy, he went back into the hall.

There were two doors on his left. Long familiar with these types of houses, Carver knew they would lead into the front and rear sitting-rooms. He tried the nearest first, the back one. Turning the handle he pushed it open. The room was in complete darkness but he thought he could hear something. A murmur. Sounds of movement. He reached for the light switch, tried it. The room stayed dark.

'Hurry Jamie,' Jess called. 'She's going.'

There was a light switch on the hall wall, next to his shoulder. It would give him enough light to see by. He tried it. Nothing again.

He's removed the light bulbs.

The muffled whining from inside the room increased in pitch. A plea for help. He stepped into the darkness, groping his way. At the same time he fished in a pocket for his mobile. It would provide some light. In front of him he could just make out the shape of a sofa. But behind it he could see movement. There was a figure on the floor. The sounds - mewing noises he now realised - were coming from it. He brought up his phone, pressed the side button. The screen lit up, enough for him to see what he was looking at, The figure was Lucy's mother, lying on her side. Across the room was another sofa, behind it another figure. Carver glanced back over his shoulder. In the spilling light from the kitchen he saw Jess and Lucy's shadows, dancing on the hall wall.

'They're here Jess. Heads up.'

'Hurry Jamie.'

He bent to check on the mother, bringing his mobile closer. He was not surprised to see she was bound with rope, gagged with something he had stuffed in her mouth. The other one had to be the father. No one else. Time to call it. He lifted his hand, depressed the button and was about to speak when everything happened at once.

Somewhere in the hallway, a door wrenched open.

Jess shouted, 'HE'S HERE, JAMIE.'

A flash of movement over his shoulder as he spun around and leapt towards the door.

A scream, followed at once by sounds of scuffling.

As he burst out of the room and back into the kitchen, Carver knew.

He had chosen the wrong door.

CHAPTER 50

As Carver came through into the kitchen, Jess was picking herself up from the floor. The man, Garo, had one hand round Lucy's throat. She was barely conscious. In the other hand was a vicious-looking hunting knife, the sort with a serrated edge. As Carver skidded to halt, Garo brought it to Lucy's throat. Carver remembered at once the marks he had seen on the throat of Radi Maleeva's young daughter.

'Stop or I will kill her.' Gone now was any pretence of sanity. His eyes were crazed, the grin manic.

'Take it easy,' Carver said, stepping forward. 'You aren't going anywhere. Put the knife down.'

The man tightened his grip on Lucy and, as she groaned, pressed the blade to her throat.

In that moment, a vision of something similar, another time, another place, came to Carver. A deranged killer, a knife, a miscalculation that left someone exposed.

Please God it's not going to happen this time.

The thought came that he should just stop everything and let the man go, just turn and walk out even, anything that would mean he would not have to endure the nightmares all over again. But then sanity returned, and he knew they were not options. Not if what Mikayel had said was true.

'Move aside,' the man said, waving the knife to motion Carver and Jess round the table, clearing the way to the door. 'Or I will kill her right here.'

Carver stood his ground. 'You aren't going to kill anyone, and you aren't leaving this house. You are under arrest.'

The man's eyes widened and he scoffed. 'Do not be ridiculous. The Monster of Yerevan cannot be stopped by the likes of you. He must keep the promise he made.' He came forward, the knife still up, over Lucy's jugular. She was beginning to come round, becoming aware of her predicament. Her eyes widened in fear.

As the man neared, Carver said, 'Maybe so. But you are not the Monster of Yerevan.'

The man's brow furrowed. 'Of course I am. No man does what I do.'

Carver shook his head. 'One man does.'

The man wavered. 'What do you mean? Who?'

'The man who was put away for doing what he read about other killers and perverts doing. The man who so envied the Monster of Yerevan's notoriety he promised him he would complete his work if he ever escaped the Asylum.'

'LIAR,' the man screamed. 'I am Vahrig Danelian, the Monster of Yerevan. The Butcher of Armenia. My work is famous. Now, I will finish it.'

'No,' Carver said. 'Vahrig Danelian is dead. Doctor Kahramanyan is with his body right now, in a mortuary back in Armenia.' Lucy's eyes widened, some of his words registering. Carver continued. 'He died soon after escaping from the asylum. Caught by the Azerbaijanis and killed.' The man's eyes flashed. 'And you saw it all happen, didn't you, Antranig Koloyan?'

The man tipped his head back and let out a cry of anguish that made Carver's blood run cold. Sensing half a chance, Carver prepared to move, but Koloyan - the only inmate ever to have got close enough to the Monster to talk with him, Kahramanyan had said; the man the media had christened the Copycat-Killer - was too quick. He pressed the knife harder against Lucy's throat, ready.

'It does not matter that you know my name,' he snarled. 'I gave him my promise that if he did not escape, I would avenge him against the family that left him to rot in that place. And I intend to keep that promise.'

'No,' Carver said, but had to step back further as the man came forward, at the doorway now. 'There has been enough killing. There will be no more.'

Whether it was the determination in Carver's voice or being confronted with his real identity, Carver wasn't certain, but for the first time a look of uncertainty flitted into Antranig Koloyan's black eyes. He glanced into the back room, where his intended victims still lay bound. Then his gaze shifted down the hall to the front door - his only escape route - before coming back to Carver. He made his choice. He began backing down the hallway, dragging Lucy with him. Carver followed, Jess at his shoulder.

'Put the knife down, Antranig.' Carver said, putting a hand out in front of him, palm open. 'You cannot escape. We know who you are. There is nowhere to go.'

Koloyan reached the door. Holding Lucy with his knife-hand he reached behind with the other and released the lock. 'I *AM* the Monster of Yerevan,' he spat. 'You cannot stop me.' He flicked the door open with his foot and stepped backwards out the door.

The light from several blinding suns burst upon the house. Carver threw an arm across his face.

Antranig Koloyan spun round, shocked, to face those waiting for him. Lucy screamed as the Dragon-lamps bathed her and her attacker in the bright, white light that picked them out and made them look, just for a moment, like religious icons.

'ARMED POLICE,' a tinny voice echoed around the street. 'Put down the knife. Let the woman go and step away. We are Armed Police Officers. I repeat. We are ARMED POLICE.'

Despite all that was happening, Carver still managed to register the fact that Superintendent Della Garside, the designated Firearms Incident Commander, clearly wasn't going to leave herself open to an accusation that she did not give full and proper warning.

Antranig Koloyan's response was to scream into the lights.

'BASTARDS.'

Behind him, Carver saw the hesitation, sensed Koloyan trying to work out his options. He was behind Lucy now, using her as a shield, the knife still up to her throat. Mikayel had said he was capable of anything. All it needed was a slight movement of the wrist.

Carver took his chance.

He hurled himself onto Koloyan's back, grabbing Koloyan's wrist and forcing the knife away, at the same time wrapping his other arm around the killer's neck, pulling him back off Lucy. Shouts mixed with screams and yelled commands rent the night air as the two men struggled. Suddenly free, Lucy fell to the floor. Running shadows passed before the bright lights. But even as help came, Carver realised that the wiry Armenian was far stronger than he looked. With a scream of rage, Koloyan wrenched himself from Carver's grasp, flinging the detective backwards. Carver hit the brick wall behind him with such force the breath was knocked from him. As he fell, gasping, he saw the killer framed against the night sky. And what Antranig Koloyan did next, everyone would later swear made the hairs on the backs of their necks stand up, and their blood turn to ice.

Spreading his arms in some sort of primeval victory salute, he turned his face to the sky and let out a howl which, had they not known its origin, people would have sworn came from a mountain wolf.

It was enough to stop everyone in their tracks and for a second they all stood and stared. And it was enough time for Antranig Koloyan. The knife was still in his hand. On the ground, only feet away, was Lucy, dazed and gasping, trying to crawl away. What little reason was in him must have told him there was still time to keep some of his promise to Vahrig Danelian. No one was close enough to stop him. Raising the knife, he flung himself at her.

She screamed.

Later, when Carver came to write up his statement, he would know that his memory was playing tricks on him. Logic told him what the sequence of events must have been, nevertheless he wrote it as he remembered it.

As Antranig closed on Lucy, about to strike, he seemed to stop in mid-flight. He turned towards the lights, staggered back a step, then spun on his heels and went down, in one officer's words, 'like a sack of spuds.' Only then did Carver remember hearing the staccato of the several discharges from the Armed Response Team's weapons, echoing back and forth between the houses on opposite sides of the street. For a second no one moved, then all hell broke loose.

Carver had a ringside seat.

Shouted commands flew in all directions. Figures ran forward. Jess went to Lucy. A posse of flack-jacketed officers with the words 'POLICE' stencilled across their backs surrounded Antranig Koloyan, pointing their Heckler-Kochs and Glocks at him as if he might suddenly raise himself and threaten them once more. Carver already knew that, leaving aside any religious allusions, there was not a cat in Hell's chance that would happen.

Many weeks later, the Independent Office For Police Conduct-supervised, Post Incident Enquiry Report would show - to the Chief Constable's and, especially, the Firearm Team's embarrassment – that of the ten rounds discharged that night from four different weapons, only two hit Koloyan. The first was from a Glock-17 self-loading pistol fired by the newest member of the team, a woman officer called Becky Handsworth. It hit Koloyan in the lower abdomen, inches above the groin, stopping his charge. The second, from a Heckler and Koch G3K short-barreled rifle took Koloyan right between the eyes. He died instantly. The shot was fired by Gerry Scott, the team's most accomplished marksman. The first thing Gerry would do four months later when he resumed work following his obligatory suspension, would be to surrender his authority and withdraw from firearms duties.

As the team's designated 'paramedic' checked

Koloyan for signs of life, Glen Swift was the first to Carver's side and helped him to his feet. 'Bloody Hell, Boss,' he said. 'That was a fucking stupid thing to do. You could have got yourself killed.'

'Thanks-. Huh-. Glen-. Huh.' Carver said, still trying to gulp air into his lungs. As he stood up, Swift let out a gasp.

'Bugger me.'

He pulled Carver's jacket round so he could see it. There was a neat round hole in the material below the pocket, slightly burned around the edges. Only then did Carver realise how lucky he had been. The fact that the Firearm Team's Senior Tactical Advisor later told him it was, 'Only a ricochet,' and therefore had only a 'Sixty-percent chance of being fatal,' didn't help the memory of what might have been fade any quicker.

Jess had the sobbing Lucy up and on her feet. A woman officer came out of the house and approached her. 'Your Mum and Dad are okay love. In a bit of a state, but okay.'

Reminded of her parents' horrific ordeal, Lucy pulled herself together and made to go back in the house. In the doorway she saw Carver and stopped. He just about had his breath back.

'Are… are you alright?'

'I will be,' he said.

'Thank you,' she said. She even tried a smile behind the tears. He nodded. There would be time enough to talk later.

She turned to look back at Antranig Koloyan's body, the hordes of police and paramedics still scurrying round.

'What… what will happen to us?'

Right then Carver saw, more clearly than he had done thus far, the fear that Lucy had learned to live with. She had spent the best part of her life looking after her parents, trying to shield them from the past. But for a forgotten military conflict thousands of miles away, she would have succeeded. And in that moment he resolved that he would do whatever was in his power to protect this brave young woman from further anguish.

'I'm not sure yet,' Carver said, honestly. 'But whatever happens, rest assured, the worst is over.'

He was never more wrong.

CHAPTER 51

'He's ready for you now, Jamie.'

Carver stood up, approached the door Mavis was holding open. The sign showing above the door read, 'Assistant Chief Constable - Operations'. As he passed the woman who'd been a fixture within the ACPO secretariat as long as Carver could remember, she whispered in his ear.

'Good luck.'

The door closed behind him and he made his way to the single chair in front of the wide desk. The man behind it didn't look up but continued to scribble.

'With you in just a minute.'

Over by the window was a low table, some easy chairs. Not having been steered in that direction, Carver assumed they weren't going to come into play. It was going to be *that* sort of interview.

As he waited, he checked the long, dressing mirror on the wall behind and to the ACC's left. Reflected in it, was the clock on the wall behind him. Carver practised his spatial awareness and saw it was about right, just after eleven.

The heavily built man with the florid face stopped writing, screwed the top back on his fountain pen and threw whatever document he had been pretending was so urgent into the tray marked 'Out.' His mouth widened into what, but for his eyes, could have been taken for a smile.

'How are you after your little bit of excitement Mr Carver?'

'So-so, sir.'

The niceties over, the ACC pulled an orange Personnel file from the stack to his left. Its vibrant colour denoted CID. Carver recognised it. The ACC flipped it open, pretended to read.

'I take it you know why you are here?'

'Yes, sir.'

'Your Director seems to think that your period of recuperation on NCA has run its course.'

Carver said nothing. He and Broom had spoken frankly. He didn't have a problem with it.

'I get the impression he's not terribly impressed with your recent performance?'

Carver leaned forward. He recognised the letter in the ACC's hand. Broom had shown it to him before he sent it.

'I don't believe he actually says that, sir.'

A muscle twitched in the ACC's face, barely noticeable.

'Not in so many words perhaps. But the inference is clear.'

'Mr Broom and I spoke at length about my position. I don't believe this is a performance issue.'

The ACC's face hardened. 'Believe me Mr Carver. When the Chief Constable receives a letter from the Director of the National Crime Agency suggesting The Chief may wish to consider taking back one of his officers before the due date for that officer's period of secondment, it's a performance issue.'

Carver said nothing.

The ACC leant back in his chair. 'People say you have an attitude problem, Mr Carver. That you think you have a right to be treated differently from other officers.'

'I don't think that at-.'

'And that because of your involvement in some high-profile cases, you have the right to pick and choose your postings.' Carver kept his mouth shut. The man had a speech to deliver. 'Well I'm sorry to break your bubble Mr Carver, but I'm here to tell you that is not the case. I am the deciding authority in this force over people's careers and postings, no one else. Do you understand?'

'Yes, sir.'

'And if, after taking account of an officer's recent performance and other factors, I believe that his or her career would benefit from a change of direction, then that is what will happen.'

As if realising he was in danger of going too over the top too soon, the ACC took a moment while he calmed down. He would want to make sure the end result looked like it was a natural and considered outcome to their discussion.

Carver checked the mirror again.

The ACC went back to his file. 'I see that some of your cases have resulted in you suffering from severe stress.'

'I'm not aware anyone ever described it as 'severe'. And it was one case, not some.'

'But according to your recent Performance Review reports, it appears there are still some issues that remain unresolved in your mind.'

Carver waited until there was eye contact. 'Someone I was close to died. Someone else nearly died.'

He pursed his lips. 'I have every sympathy for what you went through. Nevertheless, in your own interests I have to consider whether it might not be better….'

Carver let him waffle on. He knew the drill. He'd had to go through it with a couple of his own staff from time to time. The difficult ones. But he liked to think that at such times he was at least honest enough to tell the person concerned *exactly* why they were being reposted. None of this, 'in your own interests' bullshit. But then the man was a Chief Officer. Some of them are like that. He was coming towards the end.

'Is there anything you would like to say? Any further representations you would like to make?'

As he realised the ACC had finished, Carver checked the mirror again.

'No, sir.'

'Very well then. I am going to record on this review form that you were given the opportunity to make representations, but you chose not to do so. Then I will ask you to sign it. Do you understand?'

'Yes, sir.'

The ACC took out his pen again. This time Carver could make out it was a Mont Blanc, something inscribed down the side. He watched as the man behind the desk wrote. He took his time, as if to let Carver know that his future was being decided by the elegant instrument that was now filling the 'Chief Officer's Decision' box at the bottom of the Career Review Document with a neat, flowing script.

When he was finished, the ACC swivelled the document one hundred and eighty degrees and pushed it towards Carver.

Carver checked the mirror, then reached down and picked up the buff folder he had brought with him. He placed it, deliberately, on top of the file.

The ACC looked at it, then back at Carver.

'What's this?'

'Have a look.'

'If this is something to argue your case, you should have presented it when I gave you the opportunity.'

'It's nothing to do with my case.'

Clearly annoyed that his carefully-choreographed ceremony was being disrupted, the ACC opened the folder. The forms had changed over the years and Carver could see that after years spent climbing the ladder, the ACC's memory was cloudy. He looked up at Carver, mystified.

'Read it. Sir.'

Even more annoyed now, it seemed, the ACC started going through the file. To begin with he didn't read, just leafed through the forms. But when the moment arrived and memory stirred, it was obvious. A red tide began to creep upwards from his neck. Carver saw his adam's-apple do a little jig. Nevertheless, he regained his composure, quickly. He hadn't got to ACC by being chicken. He did the only thing he could do. He blanked it.

'I've no idea what this is about Mr Carver, but I seriously doubt it has any bearing on-.'

'It's the Investigating Officer's Report into a series of rapes around the Stretford and Salford areas in the late nineties. They were never cleared up, and they remain undetected.' Carver paused but this time there were no interruptions. He continued. 'The closing report says, 'No suspect identified, which is a bit strange. Because apparently there was one.'

The ACC eased himself back into the safety of his high leather chair, eyeing the papers before him, warily.

'It seems that a SOCO managed to lift a print, in blood, off one of the victim's legs. An excellent piece of soco-ing for the time, given that back then some still thought you couldn't lift prints off skin. Even got a match. A bloke called Brendan Halfpenny. He's doing time now for rape and attempted murder. But he was already known back then. Indecent exposure, Indecent assault, some other bits and pieces.

'The SOCO gave his name to the DI running the enquiry. Halfpenny was brought in, questioned but never charged. When the SOCO asked why, he was told that someone in the Fingerprint Bureau had cocked up the ID. Halfpenny was alibied to the hilt apparently, and by a solicitor of all people, so it couldn't have been him. And DNA was still fairly new back then.'

'Where the fuck's this going, Carver? If you think-.'

'The SOCO knew it stank of course. But when he started asking questions the DI told him to drop it. Trouble was, the SOCO was one of the old school. Not above making the evidence fit the offender now and then. Just on those occasions when justice needed a helping hand of course. We've all done it, haven't we, Sir?'

There was no affirming nod. Just cold blue eyes, staring across the desk. Carver continued.

'The SOCO knew that if he said anything, someone would do the same to him, and that would be his pension up the spout. So he kept his mouth shut. Of course he didn't know the whole story then; the SOCO

I mean. He only found out some time after. The DI who was Officer-In-Case, and the solicitor? They were both servicing Halfpenny's sister. She was on the game but wasn't averse to giving it free to coppers and people she thought might look after her, financially that is. But there was nothing the SOCO could do see?'

The ACC opened his mouth but Carver kept going.

'Then the force opened up this nice new archive we've got down that salt-mine and everyone spent months running round, finding exhibits and packaging everything up so it could go into storage. The SOCO was due to retire round that time but he remembered coming in one night and finding the DI, he'd moved up in the world and was a Chief Super by then, going through his neatly-labelled boxes. The SOCO knew what he was looking for. But even if the Chief Super hadn't been disturbed, he wouldn't have found them. DNA was getting a lot of press and the SOCO had never forgotten. He knew that if someone got rid of the exhibits, clothing, that sort of thing, the truth would disappear for ever. So he took it. Kept it at home in his loft all these years. Until one day someone asked him about it.' Carver stopped. He looked in the mirror.

For long seconds the ACC regarded Carver the way he might a piece of dog turd on his shoe. Eventually he let out a long breath and sat forward. He drummed his fingers on the table as if he were considering. Carver knew the man didn't have any choice. The ACC nodded.

'Very good. I must admit I never thought you would go this far. But then again, someone told me I shouldn't underestimate you.'

Carver let him talk. The ACC gave a begrudging

smile.

'I have to say, credit where it's due, it's not a bad card to play, at this stage of the game. I can see now why you are so keen to stay on CID. You've a gift for it.'

He moved the folder aside that Carver had put in front of him, picked up the Career Review form and ripped it in half. He dropped it in the bin beside him, then sat back, job done. The two men looked at each other. Carver's eyes flitted to the mirror.

Eventually the ACC spoke. 'Okay, let's cut this short. I'm very busy. Where do you want? But let's not be stupid. If it looks too good, people will want to know the fucking reason why.'

Carver didn't move.

A puzzled frown came into the ACC's face. 'What? That's what this is all about isn't it? Staying on CID? Well okay then. You've got it. Now bugger off.'

Carver reached into his inside pocket and took out the four photographs. He dealt them, one at a time, so they landed in front of the ACC. Teenagers. Attractive. Happy. Smiling. As innocent as they could be for their age. The ACC looked down on them.

'It was over twenty fucking years ago. What do you want me to say?'

Carver looked in the mirror.

Eleven-fifteen, precisely.

Time.

He stood up, shook his head, and came forward. The ACC pressed himself back into his chair. Carver leaned forward and put his finger on the fourth picture he had dealt.

'She's my *SISTER*, you, CUNT.'

Two things happened.

The blood drained from the ACC's face as he realised how wrong he had been. There was a knock on the door.

'And you're FUCKED,' Carver finished.

The door opened and two men, smartly dressed in dark pinstripe suits came in. Assistant Chief Constable Paul Murphy, ex-CID DI, and one-time Investigating Officer, recognised them at once. A look of fear came into his face.

Carver stepped back. The taller, and older, of the pair turned to him.

'Finished?'

Carver nodded. 'The solicitor?'

The man checked his watch. 'Ten minutes ago.'

'You bastard,' Murphy breathed.

Derek Robinson, Deputy Chief Constable of Derbyshire Police took a step towards Murphy. What he was about to do would give him no pleasure, but he knew how important it was to get it right.

'Paul Murphy. I have been appointed by your Chief Constable to investigate a complaint made against you by a retired police officer, Mr Ronald Gover. I am now arresting you for an offence of conspiring to pervert the course of justice. You do not have to say anything, but if you fail to mention when questioned, anything….'

As Robinson gave out the statutory caution, Murphy and Carver stared at each other. Murphy wasn't listening to the man about to initiate the chain of events that would end his career prematurely, but not because he knew the caution and didn't need to hear it. He was concentrating on conveying his hatred - and contempt - for the man who, only minutes before, was going to have been his step onto the final rung on the ladder.

Murphy had known for a long time that the only thing holding him back from a Chief's job was the absence of the tick in the box marked, 'Decision Making' on the lists of prospective candidates kept in the Home Office. By doing Carver, the man whose investigative exploits had been brought to public notice so prominently, it would signal that when it came to taking the difficult decisions, he could be relied upon not to shirk from acting in the 'best interests of the service.' In the months to come, Murphy would try to convince himself he was simply the victim of a man desperate to save his CID career. But deep inside he knew. Carver's career had nothing to do with it.

And though Carver was staring towards Murphy, he was not seeing him. He had done his bit. As far as he was concerned the man was history. Instead, he was in a Manchester Arndale Centre shoe-shop, watching, embarrassed as hell, as a young girl on the cusp of womanhood, twirled before him the way, many years before that, Bruce Forsyth used to make Anthea Redfearn do every Saturday night on the Generation Game, showing her younger brother the new shoes she was thinking of buying and asking, 'Well bruv, what do you think?'

CHAPTER 52

Disturbing though it was, Jess's call couldn't have come at a better time for Carver. It was the excuse he needed to postpone trying to make Nigel Broom's clearly speculative assessments fit within the NCA Crime Intelligence Strategy Framework Document he had promised he would finish before his move across the other side of the corridor. Now, with two weeks still to go before his new posting came into effect, he was wishing he hadn't. Following The Duke's return to work, Carver's former boss had wasted no time orchestrating the transfer he kept telling everyone made 'perfect sense' and was, 'long overdue'. And having seen and felt the clamour that followed in the wake of Antranig Koloyan's shooting, Nigel Broom had, finally, seen the light and given in, gracefully.

Closing the file of papers he'd been pouring over, he lobbed it into 'pending', and rose to head over to Jess's office. *It's all bullshit anyway*, he thought as he left his office.

In truth, Carver had been working on the document for less than an hour. Most of the morning had been swallowed up by a series of meetings, urgent emails, and phone calls.

First off was an early morning meeting with Broom

himself - a preamble he guessed to his final 'farewell.' After wishing Carver well in his new post and thanking him for his efforts, Carver was surprised when Broom started mumbling something about occasions when he should, perhaps have, 'listened a little more closely' to what Carver was saying, and shown a, 'little more support' for his efforts. Carver batted it off as not necessary, but took it as the nearest thing to an apology he was ever likely to get.

From there, he went straight into another meeting, this one with The Duke himself. Supposedly, it was to go over some 'housekeeping' prior to his move. But Carver wasn't the least surprised when, as he was leaving, his old boss nodded at the several boxes of case files on the table by the door. 'If you fancy taking an early look at a couple, feel free.' Carver declined, citing, 'too much to finish up'. Outside The Duke's office, he shook his head. Since his return, The Duke had been throwing himself into his work. Everyone recognised it as the coping mechanism it was. After forty years with someone, it's not easy getting used to being on your own. Just the week before, Jess had told how The Duke couldn't wait for his former deputy SIO to start. Carver wasn't expecting to be granted any 'settling in' period.

The early meet with Broom had been arranged during a late phone call the night before. It meant Carver having to postpone his catch-up/drop-in at Sarah's on his way in to work. By the time he rang her - the moment he got back from seeing The Duke - the kids had left for school. It turned out a good thing as it gave them the chance to talk without distractions. He came away with a real sense that she may, at last, be turning the corner. She had sounded more positive about what the future may hold for them all than she had in a long time. Her new job was, he was sure, a big part if it. Which reminded him. He needed to sort flowers, or something, for the lady in Tesco's Human Resources. At the time, she had made it sound that in giving Sarah her old job back, she was simply following Company policy by recognising, Service To The Community, which fitted with Sarah's helping to identify Lucy. In reality, Carver knew she was doing him a favour. But on top of the job, Carer knew that for some, closure can be life-changing. He hoped to God it would prove so in Sarah's case.

After Sarah, he rang Kayleigh Lee to wish her luck with her exams. He had tried the night before, but his call went unanswered. He went to bed wondering if it was normal for eighteen-year old girls to not answer their phones the night before exams. In his imagination, possible scenarios as to why she might not be answering battered to be let out, but he refused to give them air. And whilst he could have settled for sending a message, he didn't relish getting one back berating him for not caring enough to speak in person. He had intended the call would be brief. But Koloyan's shooting and the police hunt for 'The Monster' had been all over the media. Having not spoken for weeks, it took close to half-an-hour to escape from under her persistent grilling.

'I thought you've got exams?' he said at one point.

'First one's not until eleven.'

After the call the thought came that, God forbid someone may one day ask him to explain his relationship with the young girl - woman - to whom he owed his life. He had tried to get a handle on it many times. He was still to do so.

The emails were responses to the replies to his own, twenty-fours previous. Of the twenty-plus invitations he had sent out, eighteen were confirming their attendance at the inaugural meeting of the Inter-European Cross Border Crime Liaison Group at the College of Policing in Ryton-on-Dunsmore in two weeks' time. Many were asking about accommodation options - something he needed to start looking at. And he was glad that his good friend, Reme Crozier, had agreed to 'chair'. The Paris Police detective was as politically astute as any policeman Carver knew. It would also forestall any attempt by Nicholas Whitely to even old scores by dropping disparaging remarks about egos and suspect motivations.

Jess was at her desk as he walked in, Alec at her shoulder. It was the first time Carver had seen Alec since his return from his Armenian jaunts. He still looked jet-lagged, and showed not a trace of having seen any sun. The Duke was in the chair against the wall, reading. He still looked gaunt. Jess had said she thought he was still a long way from being the man he once was. After Kathy's funeral they had all tried talking him into taking a break. He would have none of it, but it was early days yet.

They barely acknowledged Carver as he entered. He tried the obvious.

'It must be a mistake. Have you spoken to the lab?'

Jess looked up at him. Her face said, *Gosh, thanks. I would never have thought of that.*

He shrugged. 'And?'

'They've checked. There's no mistake.'

He looked at each of them in turn. Their faces told him they were out of ideas. 'Let me see.'

Jess pushed the lab-results across the desk and he picked them up.

The Duke tossed the report summary he'd been reading onto the desk with a gruff, 'Hmphh. If you can make sense of it, you're a better man than me Gunga Din.'

Carver spent a few minutes reading it all. Then he read it again. And again. *It couldn't be right*. He held the two reports, one in each hand, comparing them.

'You can look at them any way you like,' The Duke said. 'The result's the same. Vahrig Danelian isn't our man for the Durzlan's.'

Carver shook his head. 'This is crazy. He must be.'

'And that's not all,' Jess said. As Carver looked up, she put her feet up on the desk and folded her hands in her lap. 'Look at this.' She kicked at another report with the heel of her shoe. He picked it up. 'It's the analysis on the samples Alec brought back. From the last family Vahrig is supposed to have killed.'

Carver picked it up, remembering what she had told him about Alec's week-long tour. Apparently he'd almost pulled out what little hair he had left trying to track down the samples from the various murder scenes. Whereas those from Cyprus had been spot on, Armenian crime-scene procedures were, it seemed, still playing catch up. Nevertheless he finally managed to find a SOCO equivalent who took his job seriously and with his help finally located what he was looking for. The specimens had been stuffed into cardboard boxes and 'put away for safe keeping' in the local police station's found-property store. No one objected when he asked about taking some of them back to the UK.

As he read, Carver blinked, several times. Despite the caveats alluding to the 'regrettable' way the samples had been stored and the consequent possibility of contamination, the message was clear.

There was incredulity in his voice when he said, 'The offender's DNA doesn't match him either? How can that be?'

'Maybe Doctor Kahra-what's-his-name took samples from the wrong body,' Alec said. 'Or he was mistaken, and the body in the mortuary wasn't Vahrig Danelian's in the first place.'

Carver felt something start to creep up his spine. Surely they couldn't be that wrong, could they? He turned to Jess.

'Where's the Durzlan case-file?'

'Over there.' She pointed to the table behind the door. It was stacked with box-files and piles of folders.

'And the stuff Mikayel brought us on Vahrig?'

She leafed through the stack of folders on her desk. 'Here.'

Taking it, he spread the documents out, running his eyes over them.

Cobbled together from various sources after the originals were destroyed along with the Institute, they summarised Vahrig's extraordinary case history; summaries of his crimes, arrest and trial, ending with the date of his transfer to the asylum. Everyone gathered round. Alec spoke up.

'What're yeh thinking, boss?'

Carver didn't reply. He went to the table and returned with the box-file marked, 'DURZLAN.'

Taking out the first sheet of paper, the case summary, he laid it on top of Vahrig's notes.

After staring at it for almost a minute, The Duke turned to Carver. 'Are you after anything in particular, or just trying to look the part?'

Carver, shook his head, eyes riveted on the papers. He covered his mouth with a hand. 'Uuumm….'

Jess recognised the reaction. 'Jamie?'

His other hand came up. *Wait*. More silence.

'Ugh.' Carver flinched like he'd been punched in the gut.

'What?' they all said.

'FUCK.'

With his left hand he pointed at one of Vahrig's case notes, the one containing details of his arrest. His right did the same with the Durzlan case summary sheet. At the same time his eyes scanned another sheet from Vahrig's file, this one written in a different hand to the first. It summarised his various appearances before courts and medical assessment tribunals. They all looked. No one saw it.

'What?' Jess said. She hated it when he did this.

He checked each of them out, his excitement obvious. 'What are we looking at?'

'His arrest sheet,' The Duke said.

'And?'

'The Durzlan Case Report.'

'Look at them again.'

They did.

'What do they tell us?'

They ummed and scratched their heads. The Duke's impatience grew. 'That the Durzlans were killed some months before Vahrig was arrested.'

Carver nodded his head, vigorously.

'Wrong.'

They looked at him as if he was speaking Mandarin.

Jess checked again. 'The Durzlans were found on the twelfth August.' She referred to the arrest sheet. 'Vahrig was arrested on the fifth of December. We're assuming the family must have visited over here at the time of the Durzlan killings, or at the very least, Vahrig did. Then he returned home and was later arrested. Apart from the damned lab result, what's wrong with that?' Her annoyance was obvious now.

'Everything.'

'I've had enough of this,' The Duke said. 'Just tell us what you are saying.'

Carver grabbed the three sheets of paper and held them up next to each other. They all leaned forward, straining to see his point. Their faces remained blank.

'I'm saying, The Monster Of Yerevan is still out there.'

CHAPTER 53

Lucy Donovan set the mugs down on the kitchen table, then took her seat on the stool. Carver gave her a reassuring smile as he reached for his, before glancing across at Jess. He could see she was tense, but ready.

Carver had seen Lucy twice since that night, though each time only briefly. He had wanted to spend more time with her, to try to understand some things, but other matters kept getting in the way, not least his attempts to tie up loose ends, his own included. In the end he'd left it to Jess, which was probably best. Lucy had come to trust Jess and was now happy to talk with her at length, about herself, her parents, their history. She even remembered accompanying her parents the time they went to see Radi Maleeva. She was devastated when she heard what had befallen him and his family.

As far as Carver knew, the only thing Jess hadn't yet managed to resolve, were the details of her father's accident that left his legs all but useless. Apparently Lucy seemed sketchy about it, and the hospital couldn't find any record. Apart from that, seeing Lucy now, he got the impression she was more at peace with herself than before, though somewhat sadder. He felt the weight of their task more than ever.

'How are you coping?' he said to her.

She gave a wan smile and heaved a sigh. 'Alright, I think.' The attractive eyes that now seemed always full of sorrow turned on Jess. 'You have been very kind to us. Both of you. I must thank you.'

A knife pierced Carver's heart and he exchanged another glance with Jess. Her pained expression told him she felt the same. He turned his mug round on the table. The painted figure of a rearing stallion came into view.

'This is very hard for us, Lucy. I am sorry.'

As the words registered she froze, just for a moment, then relaxed again. She nodded. He waited until she met his stare.

'We know,' he said.

It was as if in that single instant, everything she had suffered since coming to England came back to her. The pain, the fear, the sorrow. She came upright in her chair, staring straight ahead. Her eyes widened and her features became taut as she fought to prevent herself breaking down. But after a few moments, the control she had practised for so long reasserted itself. She let it all out in a long, slow breath and turned back to him.

'I am glad.'

She didn't ask how he knew, or even why it had taken so long. She just accepted it.

On the way there, Carver had wondered whether there would be a need to explain things, not least why it had taken all this time for them to realise. And if she asked him now he would tell her, gladly. Even if it did make the police, the Institute, them all, look like idiots. But she didn't ask.

He squirmed inside as his thoughts turned again to

their ridiculous blunder. Okay, no one was actually calling it that, not even Terry West. But Carver couldn't help feeling it was one of those things that, when they heard of it, most would claim they would have picked up on. He also suspected that in 99.9% of cases, they would be kidding themselves. He had tried it out on several people - colleagues, CPS solicitors, even West himself - shown them the various documents, explained their origin, then challenged them to spot it. So far no one had. People just like to think they are cleverer, that's all.

He looked at her again, sitting quietly, waiting. He wondered how much of what was going to happen she had foreseen. So far she hadn't shown any great surprise.

'You know what we have to do, Lucy?'

Her head dropped and she nodded. After a few moments she rose, slowly. 'This way.'

As he witnessed her calm acceptance, Carver felt again the guilt-pangs he had felt on their way there. Jess kept saying it wasn't his fault - no way. After all, officially, he hadn't even been on the case. Nevertheless, he knew in his heart he had cocked up. He had been the first one to go over the documents. If it was ever going to be spotted, it should have been then. But he'd missed it.

Lucy led them out of the kitchen and into the hallway.

It wasn't as if he hadn't travelled for God's sake. Most of Europe, Russia, once, America three times – especially America - The Balkans, Egypt, Thailand. It was something he had known for a long time. Something he had consciously had to think about during some of his travels. Not this time.

She opened the door to the front room. The one *He* had been hiding in that night. It was dark.

The trouble was they had all taken it as read. The Durzlan's were murdered on the twelfth of August, no question. It was there on the case summary sheet, clear for everyone to see; 12.08.97

They approached the bed.

'Dadda.'

Carver could hardly see. *Why didn't she pull back the curtains?*

And the papers Mikayel brought with him showed the date Vahrig Danelian was arrested, several months later; 05.12.97. Also clear as a bell.

Not.

'Someone to see you, Dadda.'

Is that someone lying next to him?

He would ask Mikayel about it, when next he spoke with him. Ask who he had tasked to research Vahrig's case history and compile a duplicate dossier he could bring with him to England. He had his suspicions. He remembered Mikayel speaking one time about a young assistant who'd worked at the institute. Someone who was half-Armenian but born to a local family, a family that for some reason had come to adopt its own conventions on such things; though how they had managed to emulate the most powerful country on earth in this regard for so long without anyone saying anything was something that remained to be explained. Carver had since checked and now knew that the rest of Armenia followed Europe in the matter, which, presumably, is why Mikayel never picked up on it either.

There *is* someone next to him.

Lucy stepped away from the bed to let him in. Her head was bowed. Carver looked at the sleeping man, then back at her. Why hadn't she woken him?

'Lucy…?'

Dates.

Simple enough to write. Or get wrong. If you were brought up using the American convention of month/day/year, rather than day/month/year, as they do in most other places.

He looked across at Jess. Through the gloom he could just see her face. Realisation dawning.

'Oh, no,' she said.

Carver glanced back over his shoulder. Lucy was standing with her back to the wall, head bowed, respectfully. Jess pulled the curtains back. Light flooded the room.

Giragos Danelian's sunken eyes stared up at the ceiling, mouth gaping, the soft cushion between him and his wife still damp with his spittle. It was then Carver realised. Lucy *had* foreseen it all after all. Almost to the hour.

At first glance her mother also appeared to be asleep. Only people don't usually take their bottle of pills to bed with them. Not unless… Jess reached over and pressed two fingers to her carotid artery. She turned to Carver, shook her head.

He turned to Lucy. She was crying now, softly.

'How long have you known?' he said.

She sniffed. 'Soon after we arrived in England. I read about it in the paper.'

'You mean the Durzlans?'

'Yes. Apparently they knew us back home, though I

never met them. They would have realised. Gone to the police.'

He looked back at the bed. 'Your mother?'

'She always knew about him.' He nodded.

It wasn't that hard to understand. Lucy's mother was a simple woman. Despite her British blood she had been brought up in the traditional Armenian way. Women such as her don't expose their shame for the world to see, they hide it. Especially when the source of that shame has corrupted your only son into his same, vile ways.

Carver pulled back the coverlet. Giragos Danelain's pyjamas barely covered his withered legs. What he could see of them were covered in vivid scars, the flesh so thin in places you could see the bone right through.

'This?'

Lucy gave a nod. 'He was a mechanic. Used to repair the neighbours' cars. When I realised the truth, that they…. Him and my brother… That they had *both* been involved…. And that he was going to carry on here…. Mamma said we could not tell the police because he would go to prison and we would be sent back. It would have killed her.'

'So you made sure it wouldn't happen again?'

She nodded.

What she must have gone through….

'I waited until I found him working under a car. It was jacked up. I had to make sure he would either never walk again, or…. I knocked the jack away.'

Carver shook his head and turned to look down on the dead face of the original Monster of Yerevan.

Perhaps it was best this way. Even if he had spotted the date thing, realised that the Durzlans had been slaughtered several months *after* Vahrig Danelian's arrest, not before - why *does* America always have to be different? - he still wasn't sure they would have put it together. And if they had, so what? A horrendous trial. Her father put away, somewhere like Parkside. Lucy and her mother sent home maybe? Certainly they would be condemned to live the rest of their lives in shame and despair until one or both had had enough. At least this way Lucy would know she had saved her mother from more years of anguish.

Lucy's body racked and the long-held back sobs started to come. To Carver's surprise, she stepped into him, and buried her face in his chest, the sobbing growing in intensity.

At first he was unsure what to do. But eventually he gave in, and started rubbing his hand over her back, through the long, black hair.

'It's alright Lucy. Everything'll be okay.'

He knew it was stupid, but he couldn't think of anything else to say. Looking up, he saw the horrified expression on Jess's face and knew what he had to do, though he wished he didn't. He nodded to her.

'Call it in,' he said.

The End

Addendum - Follows…

Addendum

It was the envelope's unusual shape and size that first drew Carver's eye. Smaller and more squarely-proportioned than most of those that landed in his in-tray, it marked it as something different to the rest of the dross. When he glimpsed its original addressing - handwritten and in block-capitals - *"Detective James Carver, c/o Warrington Police Station, England, The United Kingdom,"* - he pulled it from the pile. No mention of his rank, a police force or a post code pointed to someone unused to mailing UK police organisations, maybe even a foreign source. Similarly, the, "James" and out-of-date work location hinted at the sender being not close to him, personally. The original address had been crossed through and someone - he imagined the likes of Darren or Laoni in the Warrington Station mail room - had added the redirecting address that had brought it to him.

Curiosity piqued, he turned it in his hands. The envelope's gum seal was reinforced by several strips of clear tape. The sender had gone to some trouble to ensure it remained unopened until it reached its intended recipient. Grabbing scissors from the pot on his desk, he slit through the top, looked inside, then reached in and drew out the contents - a single colour photograph. Placing it on the desk, he stared down at it.

The photograph showed two men and two women sitting around a table in a garden type setting. On first inspection there was nothing to yield any clue as to whereabouts in the world the picture had been taken. The waning sunlight and shadows hinted towards evening time. Almost immediately, thoughts about what enhancement may show up began to cross Carver's mind.

None of the party were looking to camera, suggesting the photograph may have been taken without their knowledge. One man had his back to the picture-taker, all-but screening the man opposite, apart from his left shoulder and arm. Likewise, the blond woman on the left of the shot was leaning forward over the table, so her face was also hidden. The woman to the right, however, was fully visible. Someone had drawn a ring around her in red ink, as if to make sure she wasn't missed. It wasn't needed.

She was sitting back in her chair, smiling, as if at something the man to her left had said. She was holding aloft a glass of wine, about to take a sip. She was dressed elegantly - long black dress, sparkly-black heels, simple gold chain about her neck. Large sunglasses shielded a good part of her face. Her hair was styled in a shoulder length bob. It was dark, very dark. Carver thought it might even be black.

He honed in on her smile.

His heart skipped a beat, then several more.

He turned the photograph over. On the back, in the same red ink as used to draw the circle, were the words, *IT'S HER*.

It took Carver only a few short seconds to digest the several and diverse implications contained within the photograph and the brief message. As he did so, he felt his stomach dropping away, as if he had just crested the highest point on some fairground roller coaster and was heading down. At the same time, a shaking began in his hands and began radiating out through his limbs and into the rest of his body.

Coming Spring 2019, the next in the DCI Jamie Carver Series, ***Death In Mind***.
OR, out now - ***Midnight's Door;*** A Gripping Nightclub Thriller, (in which Jamie Carver features, but not as the central character.) Click the image for full details.

Read on for a preview, or click the orange button to buy

Out now - Midnight's Door - Preview

Midnight's. The biggest, most happening club around. Danny Norton runs the door. Scared of no one, his mission is to keep people safe from those who would harm them. Right now they include the sadistic killer taking clubbers off the streets, and the drug-dealing Russian gangster who wants to use the club to grow his operation but needs to first get rid of Danny and replace him with someone more 'amenable'.

With the killer stalking ever closer and the Russian's scheming looking set to bear fruit, Danny has no choice but to fight back using methods he knows could risk all he has built up - his business, his team, his reputation. Worse, it could ruin his chances with Vicki, the club's beautiful VIP hostess. Way out of his league but right now in sore need of someone she can depend on, Danny would love it to be him, if only he was brave enough to suggest it.

A gripping tale of murder, club-door rivalry, deceit - and love, Midnight's Door delves into a world Saturday-night clubbers never get to see, and should never want to see. Read on for a preview, or click the button to buy now.

GET IT HERE

Midnight's Door - Prologue

The girl stands in the full glare of the car's headlights, like a stage performer under spotlights. She is crying constantly now, and the rough ground attacking her bare feet makes it ever harder to meet her tormentor's demands. All around is darkness. The nearest houses are those they passed just before he turned off the main road, a good half mile away. And though she can hear, clearly, the music coming from the car, she knows it is not so loud as will carry that far. Even if it were, the residents are probably used to their peace being shattered by those who make use of long, lonely lanes at night. Couples. Adulterers. Doggers.

Cold now in the flimsy black dress that is fine for clubbing but not the open-air in late-autumn, she winces as something sharp digs into the sole of her foot, the left one this time. Again she wishes she had kept her shoes on instead of discarding them for fear of breaking an ankle. Even if she could, she does not need to look to know that her soles are cut and bleeding. But despite the pain, she does not break from her task. She dare not. Since she began, she has stopped, twice, to try to plead with him. Each time her reward was a stinging blow, first to her buttocks, then the back of her thighs. And though she cannot see what he wields in his hand, the bite as it lands and the swishing noise it makes as it flies through the air tells her it must be long, and thin. Both times she felt it she let out a scream, which itself was painful. He must have crushed something, bone or cartilage, when he first turned on her, gripping her throat like a vice as he finally revealed why he had brought her here. As well as the strikes to her backside, the interruptions bring on further tirades, renewed demands that she do as he tells her, '-And stop that snivelling.'

By now, black rivulets of mascara on her cheeks and chest mark the flow of her tears. They are driven not just by pain. It has taken a while, but she now realises the full horror of her predicament. And for all that she is hurting in several places, she knows now they are just the beginning. Barring a miracle, worse is to come. Far worse.

Like all her friends, she has been party to the debates concerning what, exactly, the so-called Club-Killer does to his victims. Speculation has ranged between brutal rape followed by strangulation, to bloody imaginings involving the sorts of methods favoured by the type the media revel in labelling a 'Ripper.' No one knows for certain of course. So far the police have been selective in the details they have released. The result is that in the safety of the clubs, or at home, at work, there are some who delight in dreaming up and giving voice to tortures of the most appalling kind imaginable. Right now the girl wishes she had never listened to any of them, and does her best to focus on the one means through which she hopes she may still avoid the fate she dare not even think about.

At the beginning, he said that if she does well, he may spare her. The part of her that is still capable of rational thought knows this is a lie. Having revealed himself, he will not, could not let her live - whatever promises she makes about not going to the police. But right now, most of her brain is not operating rationally.

Right now it is ready to latch onto anything that holds out hope, however slim, she may come out of this alive.

The trouble is that, while the particular piece of music coming from the car is one of her favourites, she is finding it impossible to respond the way he is demanding. Sure, on a club night, on the dance-floor, she only needs to hear the piece's distinctive opening riffs and she is into it. Within seconds, the sensuous gyrations and provocative thrusts she practises at home in front of the mirror are in perfect syncopation with the music's seductive rhythms, its intoxicating, driving beat. When she is in that place, others stop to watch.

But right now, pain and the fear that is threatening to turn her legs to jelly make it impossible to reproduce the fluidity of movement that, on a club night, draws admiring comments. Instead, her movements are jerky, uncoordinated. The rushing noise in her ears is making it difficult to even hear, never mind pick up on, the music's rhythms.

Lifting a hand to shield her eyes from the headlights' glare, she tries pleading with him once more.

'I, I can't,' she whimpers. 'It- It *hurts*. My feet-'

'Yes, you, CAN.'

His snarling response is accompanied by yet another strike - to her lower back this time. Again she screams as pain she can only liken to being branded with a red-hot iron ripples through her. Desperate to avoid further punishment, she draws a gasping breath, and renews her efforts to keep up with the music. But she is aware that the longer the torture goes on, the harder it is becoming to control her movements, making it ever more unlikely she will meet his demands. In which case, what?

As if reading her thoughts, he snaps at her. 'Come

on. You can do better than that. I've seen it, remember? You do it for THEM don't you? Well now you can do it for ME. Come on. DO IT.'

Head spinning, the girl flexes her arms and gyrates in a way she hopes is a passable imitation of her usual performance. She does not need what happens next to tell her it is not.

She feels his hand, balling in her long hair. Without warning he pulls her head back, exposing her throat to the stars. In the dark she had not even seen him slip round behind her. Crying out in agony, she staggers back, going with the pull. Fearing what may be coming next, her instincts are to remain on her feet, whatever happens. On the ground she will be helpless, even more at his mercy.

'PLEASE,' she cries. 'DON'T.'

Then she feels him, right next to her, pushing in close. His rasping breath is on her cheek, bristly stubble rubbing against the smoothness of her skin. She is aware of a musky-sweet smell. It comes from his aftershave. She has smelled it before.

In a voice that is quieter, almost a whisper now, he says, 'You're just a fucking whore, aren't you? What are you?'

Her first instinct - survival - is to agree with him. 'I-I'm a fucking whore.'

'That's right. I bet you get off thinking about men's cocks, growing as they watch you. That's what does it for you, isn't it? Thinking about men's cocks. Growing. I'm right, aren't I? TELL ME I'M RIGHT.'

'OWW.' She cries again as his grip on her hair tightens. But some vestige of pride still remains. 'NO. I'm not like that. I just like to dance.'

'Yeah, I know. Especially when you know you're surrounded by cocks. You like cock don't you? Well here, like THIS.'

Grabbing her flailing wrist with his free hand, he yanks it back and down. She gasps as she feels him, right next to her.

'TAKE IT, BITCH,' he yells in her ear. 'You know you want to.'

Trembling with fear, fighting against the gag reflex that just the thought of touching him brings on, she dare not resist as he guides her hand to him.

'That's it. Harder. SQUEEZE it.'

Sobbing now, close to collapse, she does as instructed as his hand wraps itself round her wrist and forces her to engage with him in the way he craves. There is a flurry of movement as his body writhes in her grasp. As he pulls even harder on her hair, she feels the warm spillage on her fingers, the back of her hand. At the same time he lets out a groan.

'Uunngghh.'

But in that moment, his reflex response causes his grip on her hair to loosen. Just for a second, he lets go altogether. In that second she sees her chance, the only one she may have. She takes it. Springing forward, she tries to force her aching legs, her torn feet, to carry her away somewhere, anywhere, into the surrounding dark.

She manages only a few short metres before something soft - a scarf? - loops round her neck and yanks her backwards, pulling her off her feet. She lands, hard, on her back in the dirt, the force of it spilling the air from her lungs. Before she can replenish it he is on top of her, crossing his hands in front of her face and pulling the two ends of the garotte in opposite directions, constricting her arteries and windpipe. Her mouth opens and closes repeatedly, but in vain. Astride her, and with the car's headlights behind, he is silhouetted against the night sky. Black spots begin to flash across her vision. Some memory tells her they are the first signs of oxygen starvation.

But even as she feels her strength draining away, his grip on her changes. Clamping the ends of the scarf in one hand he lifts up the other so she can see what is there. A knife, like ones she has seen in films and on television but never in real life, flashes before her eyes. She tries to scream but the constriction round her throat renders it silent.

With his full weight on top of her, she can only watch, helpless, as he swaps his grip on the knife's handle so it now points down, rather than up. At the same time he winds the garotte round his wrist, twisting the material so it tightens further round her throat.

As her eyes began to flutter and the blade plunges downward, her last thought is how she now knows the answer to the debates about what he does.

They were *all* right.

Chapter One

Saturday. Late Evening

In the four years I've been running the door at Midnight's, I've only ever been late for work once. Sod's law, it was the night all the stuff that had been brewing for months kicked off.

By 'stuff' I mean the problems with the Russians, the attacks on the girls, the thing with Vicki. Especially the thing with Vicki. And by 'late', I mean really late. It was close to half-eleven when I finally pulled onto the car park at the back that used to belong to a carpet warehouse but since they went bust is now up for grabs.

I've gone over what happened that night many times since, and still can't say if my being late made any difference. But I can't help thinking that if I had been there from the start then maybe, just maybe, things may have turned out differently. At the very least I'd know who to blame for what happened after - me.

The reason I was late was because I'd stayed too long visiting my Dad at Stoke and got stuck coming back up the M6 Northbound when a lorry-fire turned it into a car park. And I only stayed at Dad's because he was in a bad state when I got there and it took longer than I expected to settle him before I could get away. At one stage I was thinking I might have to stay, but he eventually calmed down enough that I was happy to leave him.

I only mention all this because it was while I was sitting in the fast lane going nowhere that I got the call from Thailand. And while it wasn't directly relevant to what happened that night, it would play its part later.

The call came from Stevie B, and if I said it came out of the blue, it would be an understatement. Two-and-a-half years to return a phone call has to be something of a record.

It started with a voice I recognised saying, 'Is that you Danny?'

'Who's this?' I learned long ago never to let on until I know who it is. But I was already placing the heavy scouse accent.

'It's Stevie, Danny, Stevie B.'

'I thought you were in Thailand?'

'I am. That's where I'm ringing from. How you doin'? How's the team?'

I didn't answer straight away because I was trying to remember whether the tariff I was on included free calls from abroad, or if the call was costing me. Eventually I said, 'I hope you're ringing to tell me you've got that hundred you owe me?'

'Better than that, Danny. Guess what I'm looking at. Right now.'

Stuck on the M6, with Eric, my number two, ringing me every quarter hour to update me on the Agnes situation, I wasn't in the best of moods for guessing games.

'A beautiful sunset? A lady-boy? A wok? Stevie, you're six thousand miles away and I haven't seen you or your dumb-nuts mate, Shane, since you both buggered off to Thailand with my hundred quid. How the hell do I know what you're looking at?'

'It's Ged Reilly, Danny.'

Right then it was as well I wasn't going anywhere

because I locked up. I gripped the wheel so hard my wrists hurt. A thousand thoughts invaded my not-so-large brain. All I could say was, 'Ged Reilly?'

'Honest to God, Danny. He's right here in front of us, trussed up like a turkey ready for the oven. What do you want us to do with him? You want us to-'

'WHOA STEVIE, you-' For a second I couldn't get the words out. I'm like that sometimes. I get tongue-tied when I'm flustered. Not like my Uncle Kevin. I never saw Uncle Kevin lost for words. Not even the night my Aunty Betty stuck a knife in his ribs. 'You bloody bitch,' Uncle Kevin said. 'That was a new shirt. And it was from Next.' Then he fell down and we didn't see him again for two months, or Aunty Betty for six.

One of the things that's different about my line of work is that to do it properly you have to make people believe that you're not just hard, but sufficiently borderline-psycho that punters won't want to mess with you. The trouble is, people you think would know better actually fall for it. People like Stevie B and his mate, Shane, who if he ever took up acting, would be a shoo-in for Lennie in that great Steinbeck novel, Of Mice and Men.

Eventually I said, 'You're on a mobile, Stevie. Keep your mouth shut while I think.'

Only I couldn't. Not in the time available. What do you say to someone you wouldn't trust to wire a three-pin plug, who's six thousand miles away but tells you he's found the bastard that for the last seven years you've been telling everyone you'll put six feet under if you ever get your hands on him? When I think of Stevie B, the word 'initiative' isn't the first that springs to mind. Nor Shane.

'What's he-' I started again. 'How'd you find him?'

'He was in this bar in the middle of Phuket. The Golden Dragon it was called. Me and Shane was looking for some good quality-'

'STEVIE.'

'Oh, yeah, right. Well, he was just sitting at the bar with this right-fit Thai girl.' Stevie paused. 'Least, I *think* it was a girl. Anyways, I recognised the fat bastard soon as I saw him. We just walked up to him and I says, "Aye-up Ged. Fancy seeing you here." Then Shane bottled him from behind, just in case he had a shiv on him. Which he did. Down the back of his pants. You should have seen the look on his face, Danny, when he saw me. It was like, 'Aw, fuck.' So we just carried him out and brought him back here.'

I sucked air. 'Where's 'here'?'

'Our place. We've got a room next to a nice little knocking shop right on the beach. You can see the sea and every-'

'Your place?' Not sure I'd heard right.

'We needed to take him somewhere. Where else could we take him?'

I shook my head. *What a pair of screw-ups.* 'Stevie?'

'Yeah Danny?'

'I'm going to hang up now. Don't call me back. If anyone ever asks, you rang to tell me you're sending me the hundred quid, right?'

'Oh, okay. But what do you want us to do with-'

''Bye Stevie.' I rang off.

We still weren't moving. I stared ahead. Somewhere amongst all the brake-lights I caught glimpses of blue flashes. I thought about Ged Reilly. More to the point, I thought about Ricky Mason.

Last I heard, Ricky was taxiing. This was about three years ago and at that time Sharon, Ricky's child-bride, was well on with their fourth. I knew things weren't going too well with them so I bunged him a couple of ton via a mutual friend, just to help cover some of the bills. I remember how sad it made me feel. Me and Ricky grew up at the same boxing gym, Joe Ryan's in Bewsey. Ricky was always a better boxer than me. A lot better. After Joe took me aside one day and had a quiet word in my ear, I moved on to other things. But Ricky stayed with it under Joe's management. He was setting himself up nicely and was hitting all the right notes, until an old 'friend' of Joe by the name of Ged Reilly decided Ricky was just the sort of investment opportunity some of his Liverpool 'business acquaintances' were looking for. Unfortunately I was in Germany at the time doing personal protection for a poncy finance guy who I later learned was taking the bungs for some Euro-MP. I like to think that if I hadn't been, I'd have seen it all coming and warned Ricky off. I'm still not sure why Joe didn't. Joe was like a father to us. I don't like to think about that too much. For a while it looked like everything was going great. Ricky thought he was being groomed for the big fights and was doing alright for himself. He met Sharon and when she turned seventeen they got married. They had their first two. He was still improving. The future looked rosy.

It was the night before his first tilt at a national title he found out the truth. Months later, Ricky told me about it. The call came from Ged Reilly.

'You go down in the third and stay down.'

'You can fuck right off,' was Ricky's response.

'Listen to what I'm saying,' Ged said, and repeated

the instruction.

Ricky told him where to go again. He went on to win on points. I don't think Ricky ever appreciated how lucky he was to get away with it - sort of. By all accounts there was hell to pay. Ged nearly copped for it himself, but somehow managed to convince his 'investors' it was all a mistake, that Ricky was young and had 'misunderstood things.' Whatever, they decided to give Ricky a second chance. When the same thing happened and he won again, the writing was on the wall.

They came for Ricky when he was celebrating with his mates at Havana-Fiesta's on Bridge Street. There were over a dozen of them, all imports from Liverpool brought in specially. They met, weirdly enough, at what was then Mr Smith's but is of course now Midnight's, and hazed their way up the main street to Havana's. They were all in black and wearing balaclavas. By the time Ricky saw them coming it was too late. Four grabbed him and held him down while two did the business and the others formed a circle, warding Ricky's mates off with baseball bats and blades. The one with the Stanley knife did his back, legs and the tendons behind his knees. In all, he needed three hundred and twenty-four stitches. What the other guy did was worse. He lump-hammered Ricky's hands. A doctor at the General was heard to say that when he picked one up, it rattled like a maraca. Back then Jamie Carver was only a Detective Sergeant, but I know the police did their best. They got the names of the crew no trouble, ran an early-morning swoop and pulled them all in. But no one said a word and they all had witnesses prepared to swear that on the night in question, they were all at a rugby-do at the Royal Oak in Wavertree that lasted into the early hours.

By the time I heard what had happened and got back from Germany it was too late. The CPS had already dropped the case and despite me turning up three hostesses from the club willing to testify they saw the crew meet there, it cut no ice. And whilst I managed to get all their names – me and Jamie Carver were at school together– Ricky found out and begged me not to do anything. By then he knew his boxing days were over, and that if I got involved it would end with someone dead and someone else – me most likely - doing life. He wasn't bothered for himself, but by then Sharon was expecting her third. She had already had to put up with the phone calls. And their cat nailed to the back gate.

But I did turn up something no one else had. Ged Reilly was in Warrington the night they got Ricky. Around the time the crew-leader at Mr Smith's took the call telling him where Ricky was, Ged was seen leaving Havana's, on his mobile. I went looking for Ged but by a pure fluke - for him - missed him. Next thing, Ged's done a vanishing act any magician would have been proud of. As far as I knew, no one had seen or heard of him since - until I got the call from Stevie B.

Some good did come out of what happened back then I suppose. But for me, not poor old Ricky. To this day, the word around Warrington is that when I went looking for Ged, I found him.

I thought about what to do.

I thought about ringing Stevie B back.

I was still thinking about it when the traffic started to move.

We moved a mile. Two miles. Speed picked up. The blue lights had gone.

I rang Eric.

'Twenty minutes,' I said.

Chapter Two

As I pulled onto the car park I pressed re-dial. Eric answered at once.

'Back door,' I said.

'Winston's on his way,' Eric said, then hung up. Things were obviously happening. By then it was over forty minutes since I'd rung to say I'd be there in twenty. After a couple of miles the motorway had bunched up again and we'd crawled a while more.

I spotted an empty disabled bay close to the back door. I floored the pedal and roared up to it then hit the brakes and yanked the wheel right so the truck skidded the last few yards and came to rest with the nearside wheels up against the kerb. I was pleased. The last time I'd tried it, the back end had ended up in the flower bed.

Jumping out, I grabbed my jacket off the back seat, then jogged over to the rear fire-exit, shrugging into it as I went. The door opened just as I got there. Light spilled out, but not much. Winston Ajero is six-four and built like the proverbial brick s***house. All I could see was a dark silhouette. But then all of Winston is dark, and his uniform - suit, shirt, tie - is black. The way his rasta-braids stood out against the light behind, reminded me of the last holiday I took with Caroline in Majorca. Palm trees against the sunset.

As he stepped aside to let me pass, he handed me a clip-on tie.

'Thanks Win,' I said.

'S'okay boss.' As always, 'boss' came out, 'baaaz.' When he's working, Winston likes to play up his Jamaican roots. Off-duty, you wouldn't tell him from any other Manc.

As I headed inside I called back, 'How're we doing?' Behind me I heard Winston rattling the fire-exit's push-bar, making sure it was locked.

'They're in the office, baaz,' he drawled. Winston has a habit of answering some other question to the one you've asked. Then he added, 'An' dat guy Charnley's been in again. Sniffin' roun'.'

'Right.' I filed it away for later. Dave Charnley and I used to work together. Now he runs his own door company. But not the one that has the contract for Midnight's. That's mine.

The corridor curved to the right, following the contour of the outer wall. Built in the sixties, Midnight's was originally a cinema. As I hurried along I could feel as much as hear the music coming through the wall on my right. By now the floor would be bouncing. At the front door, the corridor joins with the lobby, but I peeled off before, heading for the office. I could check the door later. Besides, I already knew what I would find. The previous week we'd agreed with the Police they would make their appeal and hand out flyers tonight. One-by-one they were getting round all the clubs. But I needed to sort the Agnes thing out before I got involved in anything else.

In the office, I found Eric, Vicki and Mr Midnight himself, Frank Johnson, crowded around the CCTV. Behind them, arms folded and looking serious, was Tony Chapman. Tony manages the place on Frank's behalf. Least, that's what he's supposed to do. As I came in they all looked round.

'About time,' Frank said.

To say he looked stressed, would be another

understatement. Midnight's owner, I always thought Frank looked like he would be more at home running a carpet warehouse, than a nightclub. Thinning grey hair, wire-rimmed glasses, business suit that would stand a good press. Crumpled-incompetence I call it. That said, I've no reason to believe carpet warehouse managers are particularly incompetent. And to be fair, Frank owned three night clubs around the Northwest all of which were doing okay thank you very much, despite the recession. As is her way, Vicki didn't acknowledge me but went straight back to the monitor. Tony stayed with his arms folded, looking stoic. I think he practises it. Only Eric moved, stepping aside to let me in.

Eric Pritchard and me go way back. His dad and my dad were best mates. He's been my number two ever since we started up. A hard-bitten scouser, he taught me everything I know about door-work, having learned the trade first in the city, then later in the pubs around Huyton and Kirkby during the time the Wallaces and Rathbones were at each others' throats. He was on the door of The Laughing Cavalier in Huyton the night Jimmy Wallace got his legs blown off. He once told me that when the car pulled up, he recognised Deggsy Rathbone just before he pulled his balaclava down. But he never said a word to any one. 'Not my business,' he said.

Taking Eric's spot, I found myself next to Vicki. She was wearing her usual perfume. At this distance, its scent was pretty intoxicating. I tried to play it casual, making out I was focused, like a Security Guy should be.

I said, 'What've we got?' But the only thing in my mind at that moment was that I'd never been so close to

Vicki as I was right then. The screen was angled slightly away from me. The way the strip light overhead was reflecting, I didn't have the best view, or so I told myself. I went, 'Tch,' and leaned to my right so my arm pressed up against hers. She didn't move and her gaze stayed rooted on the screen. I had no idea what that meant, but my imagination ran riot. I'm a real dick when it comes to women like Vicki.

Vicki Lamont is Midnight's resident, VIP Hostess. Young Miranda helps her out now and again, but she's not a patch on Vicki. Vicki is amazing. She has this gorgeous mid-brown hair that falls in waves across her face in a way that gets men going and always reminds me of Kim Basinger in LA Confidential, one of my favourite films. Thin around the waist and with a face that wouldn't be out of place on the front of one of those women's glossy magazines, she still has a girly look about her, though she won't see thirty again. A club like Midnight's needs a VIP Hostess who's classy and has certain qualities. Vicki ticks all the boxes and more besides. She takes her job seriously and is good at it. Say what you like about Frank Johnson, he has some excellent contacts and manages to book some good VIP Guests. Most of the time they're soap stars or one of those celebs who've appeared on some singing/dancing reality programme, but now and again he gets a real Pop Singer. Rick Astley is a regular, naturally, though he's getting on a bit now. Most of them are okay. They know their star will only shine so long, so they don't want to fuck it up. Others are real arseholes, out to boost their ego by showing they can still get people to run around after them while they act like spoiled kids. That's when Vicki comes into her own. I've seen her use humour, diplomacy, patience, and anger to get them to perform the way they're being paid to. I've seen her play coy, daft, flirty and downright seductive which, naturally, upsets me. But at the end of the day she sticks to her job description and doesn't do add-ons – 'favours' - like some hostesses I've known. Some of the team call her, 'Ronseal' - *Does exactly what it says on the tin.* Seeing as she comes from Widnes and her dad was a rugby prop-forward, she's pretty remarkable. I've only ever seen her struggling once. It was a Saturday night and I was walking past the Green Room when I heard a commotion inside. I won't say who the guest was but suffice to say that back then his name was 'household'. He'd had one Number One and has had a couple more since. The noise I heard was something between a scream and an angry shout. I stopped dead. It was followed by what sounded like some sort of scuffle and then I heard Vicki, giving a very clear, 'Get *OFF.*' Other than escorting them to and from the dias in the main dance floor, we're not supposed to have anything to do with the guests. I knocked on the door.

'Vicki?' I said. 'Can you spare a minute?'

There was more scuffling, then urgent whispers which I couldn't make out despite trying. A moment later Vicki opened the door, just a few inches. She sometimes wears a blouse and skirt, which can look professional while still being sexy as hell. On this occasion her blouse had come undone so she was showing more cleavage than when I'd seen her earlier. A stray lock of hair was hanging across her face. She was breathing heavily.

'What is it, Danny?'

'I need a word, if you don't mind?'

She gave me a long look. It was the first time I ever noticed how green her eyes were. I wasn't sure if what I saw in them at that moment was relief, annoyance or shame.

'Just a moment.' She shut the door.

There were more whispers. What sounded like another brief scuffle, followed by a sharp slap. I'd had enough and was about to go in when the door opened again and she came out. She closed it, firmly, behind her. Her face was red. She looked close to tears. She took a deep breath, composing herself.

'Everything alright in there?' I was desperate not to embarrass her.

She seemed to think about it. She didn't ask what I'd called her out to speak about but simply said, 'Would you mind the door a minute?' I like to remember there was a pleading look in her face, but I've probably imagined that bit.

'No problem.'

She disappeared down the corridor towards the Ladies. I thought about nipping in and having a quiet word with me-laddo, but opted not to. The embarrassment factor again. Hers mainly, but the club's also.

When she returned, five minutes later, you'd never have known. She was all together, hair put right, relaxed. And her usual distant self.

'Thank you, Danny.' She said it the way a school teacher might thank one of her kids for a small courtesy.

She opened the door, wide enough this time for me to see inside. The wanker was reclining on one of the cream leather sofas, drinking from a prissy martini glass. As he turned to look round, butter wouldn't have melted. Vicki made sure to hold the door open long enough so he could see me.

'That's not a problem, Danny. Thanks for letting me know. We'll be along in a few minutes.'

'Okay. I'll wait here until you're ready.'

She shut the door.

I remember to this day the feeling I had standing in the corridor that night, looking out for her. Firstly the buzz from the little play-act she'd involved me in. Secondly the thought that I was now her White Knight and she would be forever suitably grateful.

Five minutes later she came out with him in tow. They were laughing and joking. There wasn't a sign anything had happened. He avoided looking at me and she only did to say, 'Lead the way, Danny.' As I went in front, he was making stupid jokes like he actually thought he was being funny. She even laughed at them. It was all I could do to stop myself turning round and giving him the slap he deserved. Later that evening, when it was all over and we were closing up, I saw her chatting to Frank outside the office. As I passed them by he said, 'No problems tonight, Danny?'

'Very quiet,' I said. I tried to catch her eye but she blanked me, as always. I hung around longer than usual that night, waiting to see if she would seek me out, say anything. She didn't. I was there with Eric when she left through the front door. 'G'night guys,' was all she said. The following night she didn't mention the incident. Neither did I.

Eric brought me back to reality.

Sidling round to Frank's other side, he started playing with screen icons. I gave him my attention.

'Not long after we opened, young Nick on the Dusktil-Dawn Bar saw two of Yashin's goons talking to Agnes and Bernadette. Ten minutes later they weren't there. That Adagio For Strings thing was playing but he couldn't see them on the dance floor. Nick thought it strange so he told me.' I nodded. It was a good call. Everyone knows Agnes loves The Adagio. Eric continued. 'I checked the CCTV and we got this. I've pulled out all the relevant bits and streamed them together.' He clicked 'play' and stood back.

The sequence started with a view from camera twelve which covers the lower dance floor and the left-hand side of the bar. It was busy as always, but there was no mistaking Agnes and Bernadette, perched on high stools sipping non-alcoholic strawberry daiquiris through straws. I knew this because it's all they ever drink. A few yards to their left, in the shadows, two dark figures were leaning into each other. It was obvious they were stalking them. After a few seconds they moved in. As they came through to where there was more light I recognised the taller one as Bergin, Yashin's main man when it comes to pulling girls. I didn't know the other's name, but he was Yashin's as well.

According to the CCTV log, the encounter at the bar lasted just short of ten minutes. Eric fast-forwarded through most of it but the body language read like it was from a Pulling For Dummies Manual. Bergin and his mate were hunting, Agnes and Bernadette their prey. There was no sound, but I had no problem imagining the guys' conversation running the gamut from jokey banter to, 'Buy you another drink?' through leery cajoling to, 'Come with us, you'll be okay.' And while Agnes and Bernadette's first response was the frozen silence I'd have expected, it wasn't long before the men's practised technique began to work.

As I watched it all unfold, I became more and more angry.

The Russians had been coming to the club for months by then. Bergin, at least, had to know about Agnes. Even if he didn't, a minute spent talking to her would be enough for him to realise.

Agnes is in her mid-twenties. She's a regular at the club from Thursday through to Saturday and has been for a couple of years. Pretty, with long, dark hair and a model figure she's one of the best movers I've ever seen. Whether it's something to do with her condition or just a natural gift, Agnes's mind and body have a relationship with music that has to be unique. Someone once told me it's to do with her being on the autistic spectrum. Certainly, she has none of the social skills most girls who frequent nightclubs have. She just comes for the music and the dance. Once the disco starts and she gets into it, she goes into a sort of trance that I've seen last right through a night on occasions, only coming out of it when the DJ shouts, 'Goodnight!' The moves she pulls are amazing. If she ever went on a talent show, her story and what she does would win it, hands down. I've always assumed that the dancing is some sort of therapy. Bernadette is her regular companion and 'minder', though she seems to share some of Agnes's traits which makes the 'minding' part a bit thin. In a place like Midnight's, Agnes and Bernadette would normally be vulnerable. But everyone knows them and keeps an eye out, which I've always thought is nice. It was why young Nick called up so quickly. The last part of the video's first segment showed Agnes and Bernadette finishing their drinks then going off with Bergin and his mate. The video cut to the camera in the lobby behind the main entrance. The two girls appeared from the bottom of the screen, being shepherded by the Russians. Bergin opened the door that gives onto the stairs leading up to what used to be the stalls and now houses the private rooms and suites. In the background, I could see Winston and another of my team, Eve, out in front of the lobby, but they were busy managing the queues and didn't notice what was happening behind. The camera changed again to the one in the corridor at the top of the stairs. Having got the girls away, the men's manner changed suddenly, hurrying them down the corridor to the Ten-to-Midnight Suite. The big bugger, Alexei, was in his usual position at the door. He saw them coming and wasted no time opening it to let them in. As Bergin ushered the girls inside, he took a last look around – there was no doubting he knew exactly what he was doing – then followed.

'That's it,' Eric said.

'How long ago?' I said, preferring to ask rather than try to work it out from the time stamp on the screen.

'An hour and twenty. Apart from Bergin coming out ten minutes later and then returning with more Champagne no one's come in or out.'

I turned to Frank. The look on his face, I could tell he was waiting for it. He knew my views about him letting the Russian take a long-lease on the Ten to Midnight Suite. We'd talked about it several times. But at the end of the day, how Frank runs his club is nothing to do with me. My job is simply to advise on how to make sure everything runs smoothly. Besides, what he was getting off Yashin for exclusive use of the suite every night equated almost to a full night's takings. And Frank isn't so moral as he would pass up on a return like that. I could see he was waiting for the, 'Told you so's.' He would get them. But not yet.

I turned to find Vicki, ready and waiting. She looked beautiful. Worried, but beautiful. 'Are you up for going in with me?'

She didn't hesitate. 'Yes.'

I could have kissed her.

But Frank was uneasy. He turned to Vicki. 'What about Jack? Shouldn't you be seeing to him?'

He meant Jack Carpenter, the night's VIP Guest DJ. The only thing I knew about him was that since joining the cast of some teenage-college soap set somewhere south of the River Mersey, the viewing figures had rocketed.

Vicki waved Frank's concern away. 'Miranda's with him so he's happy. This is more important.'

Good for you, I thought. Up to then I'd always imagined Vicki doing exactly as Frank wanted. But I could tell he still wasn't happy.

'What are you going to do?'

I couldn't help noticing that Tony-the-Manager was staying out of it, saying nothing and just watching what was going on. I often wonder what he gets paid for

'Exactly what Eric was going to do an hour ago,' I said. 'Before you stopped him and told him to wait for me. Get Agnes and Bernadette out of there.'

'But you know the agreement, Danny. It's a private party. I'm not sure-'

I rounded on him. 'Whatever your agreement with that Russian prick is, it doesn't extend to kidnap, or anything between assault and rape.' I was a fair bit sharper with him than I'd intended, but it had the desired effect.

His face paled and he threw a wary glance at Tony. 'Come on, Danny. That's a bit-'

'Don't tell me I'm being dramatic. If you don't believe me, the police are in the lobby. Go and ask that DCI Carver. Those are two vulnerable girls up there. Ask him about the law on consent. And while I've got the contract for the door, I'm in charge of safety and security. That includes the clientele.' I pinned him with a look. 'Have I got the contract, Frank?' He stared back at me. He knew what I was getting at. That I knew that Charnley had been in. Something else for another time.

After a couple of seconds he looked away. 'Yes,' he said.

I turned to Eric. He was already wired for sound, the mic button showing on his shirt. 'Tell Eve to meet us in the lobby.' He nodded, and turned away. As he spoke into his shirt, I went back to Frank. 'Maybe you'd like to go upstairs and have a coffee? It might be more relaxing than watching?' I nodded at the screen.

He hesitated then started to rise. 'Right.' He didn't look too well.

Ready to go, I turned to find Vicki staring at me. It was a look I'd never seen before. 'You okay?' I said.

She gave a little nod. And I swear to God, there was almost a smile there when she said, 'Definitely.'

Chapter Three

Eve was waiting when we reached the lobby. The look on her face, I could tell Eric had already told her what we were about.

Eve Mai-Ling is A-Team as well. She's tall for a Vietnamese, about five-eight. Dark and willowy, she wears her jet-black hair short. She lives with a red-haired Irish girl called Colleen, who I've met. I once heard someone describe Colleen as, 'Junoesque.' I'm not sure what that means exactly, but it somehow seems to fit. I don't know what their interests are and I don't care, but Eve is into martial arts and I've always suspected she quite enjoys the rough stuff. That's not to say she isn't professional. I've never seen her come even close to losing control. Just the opposite. I once saw her deal with two lads from Wigan who were kicking off in the queue and weren't for doing what she was telling them. They were both beefy and I was ready to lend a hand any time she needed me. She didn't.

I took a few seconds to fill Eve in, then we all trooped up the stairs. As we turned the corner into the top corridor, Alexei saw us coming. His hand went to his mouth and he talked into it. Then he squared round to face us in classic doorman stance, legs apart, hands clasped across his front .

'Good evening, Mr Norton. How are you?' His accent was a bit like the bloke in the old, 'Wadivar Wodka, from Varrington' advert a few years back.

'Not bad Alexei. We're just going to have a word with your boss.' As I made to step round him, his hand came up to press against my chest. I could have reacted, but I didn't.

'I am sorry, Mr Norton. This is a private function. I must first speak with Mr Yashin.'

I looked down at his hand, then lifted my gaze so our eyes met. After a couple of seconds he looked past me, checking out the others behind. He must have seen sense because the next thing, he took his hand away and stepped aside. I took out my pass key, unlocked the door and went in. The others followed.

As we came in, music was playing. The first thing I saw was Bergin and his mate coming at me in a way I would describe as 'purposeful.' They had obviously got Alexei's message. Their shirts were open to the waist and Bergin's pupils were dilated in the way I've seen many times. At the extremes of my vision, I was conscious of several men and women dotted around the room, all in various states of excitement. But whatever they'd been doing just before we came in, they weren't doing it now. Alexei's message had seen to that. I decided not to waste time pissing about but to send a message of my own. I took a step forward to meet Bergin head-on and pipped him, just the once, in the middle of his face. There was a nice-sounding crunch, his nose exploded and he went down like a sack of potatoes. Eric was about to do the same with his mate, but he had the sense to do a quick reverse. Everyone froze. The music stopped.

Down the far end of the room, near the dance floor, Yashin was on one of the sofas. Sasha, the blonder of his two floosies. next to him. His shirt was fastened but not his belt or the top button of his trousers. A glass coffee table in the middle of the room was suspiciously empty. Rainbow smears of wet showed under the lights. Someone had recently run a damp cloth over it. Next to it was a guy carrying a bar towel in one hand, various bits and pieces in the other. I thought about what a forensic examination of the towel would show.

I didn't have to look for Agnes and Bernadette. They were on the dance floor, in their knickers and bras. I couldn't tell if their confused looks were due to the music having stopped or something else. Floosie Number 2, Misha, the darker one, was between them. She was holding up their dresses like she'd been about to help them back into them. Vicki and Eve went straight over, snatched them out of Misha's hands and started helping the girls dress. At this point Yashin stood up. There wasn't a trace of any embarrassment and he kept his eyes square on me as he did up his button and fastened his belt. Then he wandered down to meet me and Eric. Behind me, a couple of his men were helping Bergin to his feet. He was groaning and slurring Russian. The only word I could make out was, 'bastard.'

Yashin played it straight. 'What is going on, Mr Norton? Why are you here? Where is Mr Johnson?' Nothing about what I'd done to Bergin.

I decided that if I said any of the things that I wanted to say right then, it would cause more problems for others than myself. So all I said was, 'These young ladies shouldn't be here. We're taking them back downstairs.'

For a second Yashin looked like he was thinking about arguing. His first thought was probably around why, considering how much he was paying for the room, couldn't he do as he pleased? Deep down I was hoping he would, when I would have happily put him right about a few things. But he must have realised which way the wind was blowing as all he said was, 'I'm sorry, I did not know that. I understood they were two of your dancers.' As he turned back to the dance floor, Vicki straightened up from dressing Agnes and gave him a look that I swear, if she'd given it me, I'd have dropped dead.

He clicked fingers at his women. 'Sasha. Misha. Do not just stand there. Help Miss Lamont.'

The two women jumped to it, but Vicki made a 'stop' sign. 'We can manage, thank you.'

Along with Eve, she guided Agnes and Bernadette off the floor and to the door. As she passed by me she whispered. 'Thanks.' It was all I needed. I closed on Yashin until we were nose to nose. It helps sometimes when you want to make a point.

'This was a mistake,' I said. He didn't flinch. I didn't expect him to. But I saw the ice form in his eyes as he stared me out. Right then I knew that from now on and until things were resolved, I would have to watch my back. I turned to the door. The women were gone. Eric was eyeing one the Russians like he was daring him to have a go. 'Eric,' I said. After several seconds he nodded, then backed off into the corridor. I followed him, closed the door.

Outside, we faced each other. There wasn't a trace of humour in Eric's face as he sang the words, 'There's going to be trouble.' I twitched an eyebrow. Only then did he let out a wide grin. 'But it was fun. Can we do it again sometime?'

I caught up with the women down in the store room that also doubles as a first aid suite. Vicki and Eve were talking to the girls who were responding in the semi-robotic way that, for them, is normal. I nodded Vicki to step outside.

'How are they?'

'They seem okay. They say they were just dancing. Neither of them is saying anything about anyone interfering with them in any way.'

'So how did they end up half-naked?'

'They said everyone was talking about how hot it was, then someone told them they could take their clothes off if they wanted to.'

'Really?'

Vicki gave a shrug. 'That's their story. To be honest, knowing how they both are, it could be right.'

I shook my head. The Russians weren't daft. 'Any sign that they were given anything?'

'Not that I can tell and they say not. I think we got there just in time. The way everyone was when we first went in, I suspect things were about to go a stage further.'

'My impression also.' I gave her a sideways grimace. 'Police?'

She batted it straight back. 'You're in charge of security.' But then she eased a little and added, 'If it makes you feel any better, I can't see there's anything to be gained. The girls are okay and they aren't making any complaints.'

I nodded, glad I didn't have to worry about her thinking I was after brushing anything under the carpet. 'Can I leave them with you? Something else I've got to do.'

'No problem. I'll arrange a taxi and see them home. What's next?'

'The police appeal.'

Her mouth made an exaggerated, 'O' shape. I fought against the obvious image until it went away.

About to leave, I stopped at the door. 'What happened upstairs. Will that cause you problems?' I was conscious that while Yashin wasn't a 'guest' as such, he was still classed as VIP

She barely thought about it. 'Don't worry about me. I can handle him.'

Heading to the lobby, I worked myself into a muddle trying to work out if she'd simply meant to reassure me there was no need for me to worry, or whether she didn't like the idea of me worrying about her.

Sheesh.

FREE DOWNLOAD

Get the inside story on what started it all...

amazon   nook   kobo   iBooks
android   Windows   BlackBerry

Get a free copy of, *THE CARVER PAPERS,* - The inside story of the hunt for a Serial Killer, - as featured in LAST GASP

Click on the link below to find out more and get started

http://robertfbarker.co.uk/

Robert F Barker was born in Liverpool, England. During a thirty-year police career, he worked in and around some of the North West's grittiest towns and cities. As a senior detective, he led investigations into all kinds of major crime including, murder, armed robbery, serious sex crime and people/drug trafficking. Whilst commanding firearms and disorder incidents, he learned what it means to have to make life-and-death decisions in the heat of live operations. His stories are grounded in the reality of police work, but remain exciting, suspenseful, and with the sort of twists and turns crime-fiction readers love.

For updates about new releases, as well as information about promotions and special offers, visit the author's website and sign up for the VIP Mailing List at:-

http://robertfbarker.co.uk/

Printed in Great Britain
by Amazon